Jane Bell knew quite ....an
worrying about her f... all
day at the behest of h.. Life
seemed a puzzle. As Jane proceeded down................................. d to
another she wondered more and more why anyone married and had
children and the troubles of a home; for, really, though Mrs Raven was
well off, her life seemed one long worry. All morning Jane thought of
Fred and her evening out; and yet, if anything ever came of her evenings out with Fred (or Ernest), she supposed it would be marriage with
Fred (or Ernest) and children and troubles.

Life seemed so different from the pictures. There were no stair-rods
on the pictures, or stopped-up sinks, and if there was anything of that
sort, it was made funny, which it very seldom was at the Ravens'.
Her own life certainly was very humdrum, yet Jane did have one big
thrill on her birthday: Mr Bryan, who was an artist, and yet a real
gentleman too, paused on his way down the stairs and kissed her 'for
her birthday'.

That one poor little kiss did it. Kind Mr Bryan had given Jane's
romantic dreams a face and a reality which they had not possessed
before, and from now on it was Mr Bryan she thought of when she
went out with her nice steady boatman, Fred, or bitter, socialist Ernest,
and from now on her dreams made her life go disastrously wrong.
But whatever her troubles, Jane had one constant, stable source of
happiness – the river running wide through Hammersmith, through
London, and out to the sea: for Jane belonged to the water and loved
the water even more than she loved the pictures.

A. P. Herbert

THE WATER GIPSIES

PENGUIN BOOKS

Penguin Books Ltd, Harmondsworth, Middlesex, England
Penguin Books, 625 Madison Avenue, New York, New York 10022, U.S.A.
Penguin Books Australia Ltd, Ringwood, Victoria, Australia
Penguin Books Canada Ltd, 2801 John Street, Markham, Ontario, Canada L3R 1B4
Penguin Books (N.Z.) Ltd, 182–190 Wairau Road, Auckland 10, New Zealand

—

First published by Methuen 1930
Published in Penguin Books 1960
Published in Peacock Books 1973
Reprinted 1979

—

Made and printed in Great Britain
by Hazell Watson & Viney Ltd
Aylesbury, Bucks
Set in Monotype Fournier

To my Wife, with Love

CONTENTS

I

JANE

JANE BELL did not have a very happy birthday, and it was like nothing that she had seen on the pictures. Her birthday began about one o'clock in the morning, when Mrs Raven's Margaret woke up and complained of pains; Margaret's complaints woke up Tom, who fidgeted till three o'clock. Jane slept from three till six, when the alarm-clock under the bed woke all three of them. She jumped up quickly, afraid of over-sleeping, sponged her face with cold water, and dressed. She peeped through the blind, but did not pull it up, for there was a hope that the children might sleep a little more. It was a fine summer's morning, with a low mist on the river, and the tide was rising, rippling over the mud. She wished she had slept at home on the barge, where someone would have wished her many happy returns, but Nurse was away on a holiday and Jane was helping with the children. She went downstairs quietly, glad to escape from them, for, though they were little dears, they were a worry, and not in her line; but she was always glad to oblige Mrs Raven, who was so fussed with her family and household cares. She lit the gas-ring, put on the kettle, and prepared one tray for the Ravens' tea and another for Mr Bryan's.

Florry was not up yet, and Jane reflected, as she often did, that really she did the whole work of this house. But while she waited for the milk she thought about Fred, for it was Friday and in the evening she would be going out with Fred, if neither of the children had fits (there was generally some disaster on her evening out). But she would go out tonight, fits or no fits, for, after all, she was twenty today, and something ought to happen on such a day; and she did not see Fred so often. Not that much was likely to happen with Fred, if a girl saw him every night for a twelvemonth. Still, an evening out ahead brightened up the morning, and for a moment she thought of taking up a cup of tea to Florry, in her bed. But she thought better of it, for Florry had too much of her own way, and was always getting round people with her persuasive tongue and her fits of temper. So Jane was not going to encourage her, and she sat and drank a cup of tea herself, thinking about Fred, and about Ernest, her other young man, and wondering why neither of them was quite satisfactory. Then she made a cup of tea for Florry after all, and took it up to her. Florry said that she was just that moment getting up, and that Jane was a good girl; then she drank her tea and turned over and went to sleep again.

Jane took up the Ravens' tea and drew the curtains. Mr and Mrs Raven lay in their bed like two dead bodies, as usual, and Jane felt superior, as usual, as people do who have left their beds earlier than others; and she wondered, as usual, what it was like to sleep all night in the same bed with a man; and she concluded, as usual, that there was not much to be said for it, for Mr Raven had pushed his wife over to one edge of the bed and pulled the bedclothes over to his own side. Mrs Raven opened her eyes and closed them again; but Mr Raven showed no sign of life at all. Jane went on to Mr Bryan, the artist, who had the top floor. There were no curtains to draw here, and Mr Bryan lay wide-awake in the sunny room, staring at the open windows. She liked this visit better, for here was somebody who knew that she existed and said 'Good morning' and smiled at her. This morning he said 'How are you?' as well, and to her surprise she said, 'Quite well, thank you, Mr Bryan. It's my birthday.' He said, 'Eighteen?' and she said, 'No, twenty, Mr Bryan.' He said, 'Well, God bless you. I must draw you one day,' and she said, 'Thank you, Mr Bryan,' and went out, blushing.

Once or twice before Mr Bryan had said he would draw her, and she did not know whether to be pleased or not, for she had often studied his pictures of ladies while she did his room, and as a rule his ladies wore no clothes and had triangular legs; and wherever a lady was round, so far as she knew, Mr Bryan put straight lines and sharp corners. Florry said she did not think these pictures were drawn by Mr Bryan at all, but were the work of his godchild, or a niece, perhaps, only she seemed to get no better at her drawing. But Jane liked Mr Bryan's blue eyes and cheerful smile and healthy brown face; and he gave very little trouble in the house, though he might not know much about the shape of a lady's legs. So she went downstairs more cheerful, dressed the children, and tried not to be sharp with Tom, who made a fuss about wearing his new combinations. Then there was the long business of the children's breakfast, with which Florry was late, as usual, and the business of after-breakfast, which was even more trying. When that was done there was the grown-ups' breakfast and trouble was always likely to come of that. This morning Mr Raven saw something in *The Times* about the state of the country which upset him, so he complained about the toast and the tea, and about the cleaning of his boots; for Mr Raven was a Civil Servant, and the state of the country very often upset him, especially in the morning. At dinner-time he was stronger and enjoyed all the calamities in the evening papers. Mr Bryan did not bother about the state of the country, but looked at the pictures in the *Daily Mirror* and ate what was given him.

Then Florry and Jane had their own breakfasts, and in the middle of it Mrs Raven came in and made plans for everybody for the day. And in the middle of that Mr Raven went off in a hurry and came back in a hurry and shouted down the basement stairs to inquire who had hidden his umbrella. So Jane ran up and showed him where she had put it in the coat-cupboard, because Tom would play with it. Mr Raven said it was an extraordinary thing that he couldn't leave an umbrella in his own hall, and went off angrily to govern the country.

Jane did the bedrooms and emptied the slops, and began to do the stairs; and then the bell began to ring as the tradesmen called. Florry very often turned deaf or discovered some engrossing task about bell-ringing time, for she disliked answering the door, except to her friend the man from Harrods, who called much later. This morning she had found it necessary to beat a rug in the garden, so Jane ran up and down from her stair-rods to the door, and took in the milk and the potatoes, and the fish and the bread. All the young men said it was a nice morning, and gave her a special smile, for she was a favourite, and the milkman would have stayed talking; but Jane was no more than polite, for she was thinking of Fred today, and, besides, she had too much to do. Nothing seemed to go right this morning. Something was wrong with the geyser, the sink in the scullery was stopped up, Mrs Raven telephoned and fussed up and down, poor thing, and in the middle the man came to measure the dining-room chairs, and Tom, who was always falling down,

fell on to a broken flower-pot and cut his knee. Jane was sorry for
Mrs Raven, and always did her best to help, because Mrs Raven
met her troubles bravely, though she did fuss. But it was a good
thing when she went out to shop and people could get on with their
work in peace. As Jane proceeded downwards from one stair-rod to
another she wondered more and more why anyone married and
had children and the troubles of a home; for, really, though Mrs
Raven was well-off, her life seemed one long worry. All the morning, however, she thought of Fred and her evening out; and yet, if
anything ever came of her evenings out with Fred (or Ernest), she
supposed it would be marriage with Fred (or Ernest) and children
and troubles; so life seemed a puzzle.

Life seemed so different from the pictures. There were no stair-
rods on the pictures, or stopped-up sinks, and if there was anything
of that sort, it was funny, which it very seldom was at the Ravens'.
Jane's father played the cello at a cinema, and sometimes the cornet,
so that what she and her sister did not know about the pictures was
not worth knowing. And she believed that the exciting life of the
pictures was real life and this business of stair-rods and washing-up
was a mistake. Either it was a mistake (which she sometimes feared
would last for a lifetime), or else it was only the first reel of a
drama, from which, if one managed properly, one would emerge
to happiness and wealth and a long kiss in public.

Jane saw Life in capital letters. She saw it in terse dramatic
phrases like the titles of the pictures and the bits of writing which
from time to time explained them. When Florry was unkind to her,
she thought of herself as an 'Orphan of the Storm', or 'One of the
World's Waifs'. But her favourite was the 'Pawn Who Became a
Queen', which was the theme of 'Mated'; and often she saw herself
hopping, skipping, and steadily advancing over the squares of Life
to the ultimate square of Queenery and Joy. Anyhow, she knew
quite well that she was born for better things than stair-rods.

She stood up to ease her back by the window which looked out
over the river. There was a soft breeze from the south-west, and the
breeze ruffling the tide made a million sparkles in the sun. Down
by the barge which was her home she saw Lily sailing about in their
crazy little boat. She saw that Lily had set the sail badly, and she
wished she was on the water with Lily; for she belonged to the

water and loved the water even more than the pictures; and she had a feeling that if ever she lived like the pictures it would be on the water. Perhaps that was why she liked Fred, with all his faults; for Fred belonged to the water too, and worked a canal-boat, which was now unloading in the creek at Hammersmith.

Mr Bryan, coming downstairs and seeing the light on Jane's brown hair and the serious considering expression on her face, which he liked, thought also that Jane had been born for better things. Her hair was bobbed now, like the young ladies', though not so clean. She had very large brown eyes, a small straight nose, and a small round face. He did not know if she could be called intelligent (he did not insist upon great intelligence in women, though he might pretend that he did among the intelligent). But it was a brave little face, attractive to the eye and to the sympathies. Mr Bryan thought she must have a secret worry and secret impossible dreams. She had something in her and was worth drawing. She looked up as he came down, the stair-rod in her hand, and he said, 'Busy?' She looked out of the window and said, 'It's a very high tide, Mr Bryan,' for everyone speaks about the tide at Hammersmith, where this great wonder happens twice a day.

'It's a shame to be indoors,' he said, not meaning it much, but she said, 'Yes, Mr Bryan,' with such a wistful tone that he knew she did mean it, and it touched him. He took one of her hands, stooped down, for she was small, and kissed her lightly, saying, 'That's for your birthday.' She did not giggle, or simper, or cry out, 'Oh, Mr Bryan!' but she said, 'Thank you,' and looked after him solemnly as he went on down the stairs. Afterwards she told Lily that this was the first real thrill of her life, though of course there was nothing in it. It was the first time anything happened which was at all like the pictures; and though by all the rules she knew that she had been 'insulted', she felt proud. She passed on to the next stair-rod, and sang to herself a song called 'Always'.

When the stairs were done she took the children to the Recreation Ground – Tom in the pram and Margaret walking. There was trouble because Margaret wanted to take her elephant, and Mrs Raven had said not. Tom was let loose in the Recreation Ground, and Jane sat on one of the public seats and talked to a very fat nurse with a very young baby in a very large pram. Jane mentioned that it was her evening out and she was going out with her friend, and the nurse said:

'Thinking of marriage?'

'He's never spoken yet,' said Jane.

'Some of them never will,' said the nurse, 'without they're galvanized'; and she brooded darkly over some old memory. 'It's different today,' she went on at last. 'If I'd had the opportunities of the young girls of today I should have been married forty years ago. We had to wait till a gentleman spoke. Nowadays, if he don't speak, the young woman speaks for him, from all that I hear.'

'Do you wish you was married?' asked Jane curiously.

'I've been forty years,' said the nurse, 'looking after other people's babies.'

'That's more than I'll do,' said Jane.

'Well, don't be too ladylike, that's all,' said the nurse. 'That was my trouble. Specially with the shy ones. My friend was too shy to express his feelings, and I was too refined to show mine. All he wanted was a little encouragement – that I do know. But could I give it to him? No. So we drifted apart.'

There was silence for some time after this, while Jane wondered whether Fred needed galvanizing; and then Tom fell down and cut his knee again. The old nurse rose and slowly went away, murmuring endearments to the other people's baby under the hood of the pram.

On her way home Jane passed by a row of little houses where three wives stood at their doors and discussed the drawbacks of that married state for which the fat nurse had hankered in vain. Mrs Rogers said, 'I said to him, I said, "If you strike me again, it's the end," I said'; and Mrs Parrish said, 'Just what I said to Parrish many a time.' Jane decided again that life was a puzzle and she had been born for better things.

All day she seemed to be at it. After lunch Mrs Raven took the children out and she did out the dining-room. After that she did get a moment to herself, slipped upstairs and had a bath and washed her head, for Fred's benefit. It was the one great blessing of her life with the Ravens, the bath, for there was no bath on the barge except a round, yellow, flat thing in which she and Lily would stand and scrub each other on Friday evenings if it were not too cold. While she lay in her bath she heard Mr Bryan singing in the next room. She wondered suddenly if he would like to draw her in her bath, and blushed; and she noticed for the first time that when she blushed, she blushed down her arms, which seemed a strange thing to do. She dried her hair over the gas-stove in the kitchen, till Florry came down and told her how a young girl at Woolwich had done that, and, falling asleep, had burst into flames; for Florry was a romancer, and had a story about everything.

She put on her cap and apron, in which she looked still less like a housemaid, and more like a very young actress playing a house-maid, with her shining eyes and hair fluffed out after the bath. She took up Mrs Raven's tea, and gave the children their tea, and washed up the tea-things. Then the washing came back in a huge basket, left by a hunchback who admired her; and while Mrs Raven had the children in the drawing-room she sorted out the linen, counted the handkerchiefs and the pillow-slips and the stiff-starched shirts, carried armfuls of the heavy sheets upstairs to the linen-cupboard and put everything away. Then it was time to bath the children. They sat at opposite ends of the bath and sailed boats and splashed her. She laughed and seemed as much amused as they were, but all the time she was thinking, 'What a long day; but I shall see Fred tonight.'

No sooner were the children safely tucked in bed and eating their bread and milk than it was time to lay for dinner. Naturally, because it was her evening out, Mr Raven came home later than usual. This was because someone had asked a question in Parliament about the Supply of Young Women for Domestic Service. Mr Raven knew more about that than anyone else at the Ministry, though he did not know much about Jane, not even her surname or the colour of her eyes. Still, he knew the statistics, and could tell you the number of women on the register for the last five years without looking at the *Board of Trade Gazette*. The result of this question in Parliament was that the Ravens were still dining at a quarter past eight, and she was to meet Fred at half past. So when she had taken in the savoury and carried down the meat-course back to the kitchen, she said, 'Well, I'm out of this – Fred's waiting, and it makes him wild,' though this was not quite true, for Fred was never wild, and, being a waterman, was used to waiting. But Jane was tired of this day, and it was her birthday, and really Florry did less and less for her money. She felt rebellious, and was not going to make her hands hot and red with washing-up just before she met Fred. By rights her day out should have begun long ago, after lunch, but she had a bad habit of lingering on while there was any work to do. Florry knew of this habit, and thought it good, so she looked at Jane in sorrow. It was the custom between them that Florry did the drying while Jane stood over the greasy basin in the sink, fished out the knives, and scoured the butter off the plates. It was a very rare thing in these days for Florry to do both the washing and the drying, so she opened her mouth to say sharply that some people were in a great hurry to run away from a little work. But then she remembered that Jane had brought her a cup of tea in bed that morning, and she hoped this would happen again; also she was romantic, and it pleased her to think of Jane in the arms of Fred. So she said kindly, 'Cut along then; only don't get into trouble – that's all.'

'No danger of that,' said Jane. 'My friend and the Salvation Army are brothers.'

Still, Florry's warning gave her a little excitement as she took off quickly her cap and apron and put on her dark red coat, her 'nude' silk stockings, and her little red hat, which she fancied was perhaps on the wicked side. Certainly she had no wish to get into trouble, for she was a good girl, or thought she was, though nothing had ever happened to put the matter to the test. But tonight, after this long day of trouble and fuss, she did feel the need of something with a flavour to it – something worthy of a girl who was twenty today and born to be a queen. And she did hope that Fred would be a little less like a brother to the Salvation Army tonight.

2

FRED

On the pictures, or in books, when a young man is expecting a young lady who is late, he behaves in an excited manner which is complimentary to the young lady. He peers in this direction and in that through the shadows, biting his lips. His face becomes very pale and drawn and his hair disordered, and he stands under a street-lamp with his mouth twitching. Other couples pass by him who have succeeded in meeting at the appointed time, and when he sees these he suffers torments of envy. His eyes roll and he staggers like a drunken man. In quick succession he registers many emotions, and there is not the smallest doubt about the state of his mind.

But Fred was not like this. Jane arrived twenty minutes late, having stopped at the barge to kiss her sister and peep at her birthday presents. The meeting-place was the fifth elm from the public-house, the Black Swan. She had begged Fred to be there in good time, so as to secure the fifth elm before any other couple, for these elms were favourites with lovers, and especially the fifth, which was the last in the row and farthest from the street-lamp. So Fred, who was faithful if he was nothing else, had probably been waiting there for forty minutes. But he was not peering along the street or pacing up and down like a tiger, or tearing his hair, or rolling his eyes. Fred was leaning against the elm, with his foot on the low river wall, a cigarette in the corner of his mouth, and his cap on the back of his head, which rested against the tree-trunk; and he was staring at the river as if nothing important was in his mind. He should have been distracted, but he looked contented.

Jane tripped up to him, her little feet pattering, her breath coming and going, and she said, ''Evening, Fred.'

Fred turned and took the cigarette out of his mouth and said, ''Evening, Jenny.'

Fred was the only person who called her Jenny, and she liked it.

She put up her face, and Fred kissed her, putting his hands, like two bags of lead, on her shoulders. Jane remembered that another man had kissed her that day, and she remembered that kiss, so light and quick, and yet electric, making her tingle. Fred's kiss was like a lump of dough, clumsy and heavy and, truth to tell, damp. She did not tingle at all; she felt disappointed and a little guilty, but more disappointed than guilty. Fred put his arms awkwardly round her, his great hands grasping her shoulder-blades. He was very strong, he smelt of tar and wood-smoke, and Jane thought that if he would use all his strength on her and hug her heartily, as she had seen the 'Man of Passion' do at the Blue Halls, she might perhaps be thrilled after all. But Fred did not do this – not because he did not worship her, but because he was shy and thought she would object.

So they stood by the fifth elm, she like a nymph in the embrace of a timid bear. The street-lamp made five deep pools of shadow between the elms and the river wall, and in each of these pools there was a couple, standing like stone figures against their tree or sitting on the wall. But the top of the wall was a sharp edge, not flat, and many lovers had complained about it.

'I'm late, Fred,' said Jane. 'Was you wild?'

'No, Jenny,' said Fred in his soft deep growl of a voice. 'I knew you'd come.'

Jane supposed that this was a compliment, but she could not help wishing that Fred had been just a little wild. 'Do you still like me, Fred?' she said.

'Yes, Jenny.'

She pulled him a little aside, so that he was in the lamplight, and searched his tanned, good-looking face for some evidence of that passion. He met her gaze gravely; but he did not knit his brows or bite his lips, as she knew that true lovers did, nor could she see Smouldering Fires in his honest grey eyes.

'Well, you don't register much, do you?' she said.

'Register?'

'Well, no one could call you a Valentino, not for emotion, could they?'

Fred felt that something was expected of him, so he came back into the shadow and kissed her again, clumsily, on the nose, because Jane moved at the critical moment. If a kiss was not light and electric, like Mr Bryan's, it should be endless and clinging, as it was on the pictures. She did not enjoy these uncomfortable dollops of affection.

But she looked at the river and knew that she wanted something. The river and the night were beautiful, and beauty made her want something, though she could not tell what, and she could not talk about it. The tide was rising again, and one of the first tugs came through Hammersmith Bridge, moving very slowly, for she was before her time. For a moment or two she was end-on to the lovers, both port and starboard lights staring at them together. Then as she turned the bend the red eye grew smaller and vanished, and the green eye swelled and came on alone. Her silent tail of barges swung round after her into the lake of light above the bridge, where the flowing tide ran like a stream of silver. A man called a greeting from the tug to a watchman at the boat-houses, a brilliant motor-bus swam swaying over the bridge, and above the bus, though Jane did not know it, hung Orion and his belt. But she followed, fascinated, the green eye of the tug, for she knew all about tugs. 'The *Margaret*,' she said, and 'That's right,' said Fred. The tug went lazily past them, with a lazy chunk-chunk of the engine and a lazy swish at the bows, till at last the green eye narrowed too and was gone; and then there was nothing left but the little white stern-light of the last barge of all dwindling into the darkness beyond the island. Jane followed it with her eyes till it was gone, for although maybe the barge was bound no farther than Brentford, it was bound by water for the Great Unknown; and Jane felt that she was a Slave to the Wanderlust, which was a caption out of the 'Knight Errant'.

She remembered that Fred had once said that he would like to take her for a trip up the canal with his father and mother, and she wondered if he had meant it. But Fred was so unsatisfactory — what did he mean?

She sighed and said, 'It's ever so nice tonight.'

'Yes,' said Fred.

'It's my birthday, Fred.'

'Go on?'

'Yes, it is,' said Jane a little impatiently, for it was one of Fred's trying ways to answer 'Go on?' incredulously to the most simple statement.

'Well, I wish I'd known,' said Fred heavily.

'What would you have done if you'd known?'

'Well, I dunno,' said Fred.

'Then what's the good of wishing?' said Jane.

Fred made no answer to this, but sat down suddenly on the wall, still encircling her mildly with his terrific arms; but now her knees were fixed painfully against his, and the rest of her was leaning uncomfortably over him, and they were still as remote as two people on the Underground Railway. But Jane knew that Love is chiefly Suffering, so she did not complain; and this sudden sitting down of Fred was the nearest thing to an amorous gesture that Fred had ever done.

'You haven't wished me many happy returns,' she said.

'Well I do, Jenny,' said Fred.

He laid his head upon her breast and was silent. She was stirred a little, and remembered something she had read about the Maternal Instinct, but this did not console her much; her knees hurt, and she felt that they were in a very foolish position. She looked along to the other elms, and saw that the other couples were locked each in a close embrace, and lost to the world. No tug, no passer-by, no star distracted them.

From the nearest elm she heard shy laughter, and a girl's voice said, 'You mustn't, George!' She guessed that George was messing about, and it was something to be sure that, anyhow, Fred would never do that. But would he ever do anything?

Fred, meanwhile, was longing to stand up suddenly and crush her against his blue jersey in a mighty embrace. But he did not dare, he did not know. He had heard how girls of the best sort would slap a man's face when clasped in that manner. They would bite and scream and summon the police; and from these situations arose those ugly charges of assault and so on. It was not to be supposed that a girl so lovely and excellent as Jenny Bell would want to be hugged by him, whatever nonsense she had talked about registering; indeed, he could not understand how she had endured the daring approaches he had made already. And he respected her so much that to risk her contempt was not to be thought of.

Besides, there was his father, and he could not ignore the wise, stern warning of his father against a boatman marrying a girl 'off the shore'. Fred was worried.

'If you don't mind,' said Jane, 'I'll sit down too, Fred. I've the cramp all over.'

He loosed his iron grip, and she sat down on the sharp edge of the wall. She remembered what the nurse had said about galvanizing, and she slipped her arm about him. He put his arm round her, and they sat with their heads together, staring at the elm, and said nothing at all for a quarter of an hour.

Then the two Misses Anstruther, who had been having a little music with the Wilsons, passed homewards along the pavement on the other side of the road. And Jane heard the older Miss Anstruther say it was disgusting, all these couples in the dark. The younger Miss Anstruther answered, 'Yes, isn't it?' and something about the police. Jane wondered if they would have found it disgusting to sit with Fred on the sharp edge of a wall, and suddenly she threw up her head and laughed aloud. The couples under the elms did not even turn their heads, but the Misses Anstruther quickened their tiny steps, and the policeman under the lamp-post looked suspiciously at the fifth elm.

'What's the matter?' said Fred.

'I was thinking.'

'Go on?'

'It's funny, isn't it,' said Jane. 'They say love is the greatest thing in life, and yet when a person's in love there's nowhere to go – not for you and me.'

'That's right,' said Fred, not knowing what she meant; for to Fred it seemed natural and proper that the poor should have to make love in holes and corners.

But Jane had a roving imagination, and she saw thousands of couples under the London stars, huddled behind trees, leaning against walls, sitting on hard benches, if they were lucky, on wet nights, on cold nights, in Lovers' Lanes and passages, on pieces of waste ground, frowned upon by the Misses Anstruther and sometimes moved on by the police.

Yet this love was the great and noble adventure of life, with which all the books and pictures and comic songs were concerned, the one thing common to the rich and the poor; and it did seem strange that when the poor were in love the most private place they could find was the corner of a public street. And this evening that she was spending with Fred was the most exciting thing in the week, and that was funny too. She wondered if among all the couples of London there was a single girl who had such a dear old sheep as Fred for a lover. And she wondered if even those luckier girls under the other elms had found out the real truth about Love's Bliss? Anyhow, there must be something more in it than had come her way, and she meant to find out what it was. But probably she would never have much help from Fred.

Fred shifted his position on the wall and said, 'What are you thinking, Jenny?'

'This wall's no cushion,' she said.

'You're right,' said Fred.

After this exchange the lovers sat silent again, while Fred nerved himself for an audacious stroke. At last his arm tightened about her and he said, 'Jenny?'

'Yes, Fred?'

'You know what I said about taking you a trip up the "Cut" one day?'

(The Cut is the irreverent name of the boatmen for the Grand Union Canal.)

'Yes, Fred,' said Jane.

'Well, I can't do it, Jenny – not yet.'

'Oh!'

'It's father, you see.'

'Yes, Fred,' said Jane. 'Let's stand up, shall we? I'm sore.'

They stood up, and Fred leaned against the tree, holding her hands.

'Father's particular, you see, about taking a girl off the shore.'

'I live on the water,' said Jane.

'But you were born on the shore, you see. That's what he says.'

'Well, don't worry, Fred. It don't signify.'

'Well, what I thought,' said Fred, for the first time stumbling in his speech as he unfolded his tremendous scheme, 'the next time we come down, you take the dinghy out and show him what you can do, you see, and then he'll see, you see.'

Jane saw, but she was not sure that she wished to be chosen in marriage for her methods of handling a boat. So she said, 'Well, I don't know that it matters all that amount, Fred.'

'But it does,' said Fred. 'Say you will, Jenny.' And he spoke with an urgency and fondness so out of the common with him that she could not bear to be unkind, and she said:

'All right, Fred. When'll you be back?'

'Three weeks. Perhaps four.' Fred stepped to the wall and looked down at the river. The mud, the reeds, had disappeared, and the water was lapping against the wall. There were two green eyes passing now, and all down the river the tugs were hooting to warn the wharves at which they were to call. The busy hour of the river was beginning. 'I've got to go now, Jenny,' said Fred. 'We'll push out and anchor as soon as we float.'

'All right,' said Jane. 'Kiss me, Fred.'

Fred kissed her more boldly than before, for now that his plan for the persuasion of his father was afoot the future seemed easier. They they walked along to the creek where Fred's father's boats were lying against Mulberry Wharf. There were two of them, the *Prudence* and the *Adventure*, long, narrow vessels built for the canal, and painted gaily in the ancient style of the canal with Castles and Hearts and Roses. They were worked along the canal to Birmingham and back by Fred Green and his father and his mother and his young brother Arthur, and a brown horse called Beauty, of which Jane had heard many fine stories. And now they were to be picked up by a tug and towed up the tideway to Brentford, where Beauty was waiting.

The boats were just afloat, and old Tom Green called impatiently to his son, as he stepped into the beam of light which came from the cabin of the *Prudence*. Tom Green stood forward on the *Adventure* with a long pole, and at the tiller of the *Prudence* stood an old woman with wild grey hair, a sharp face, a shiny black dress, and a leather belt. Her voice was permanently husky from some old affection of the throat, so that every syllable seemed dragged from her in pain, and her kindliest utterance had the malevolence of a hiss. When she said, 'Come along, son,' it sounded like an imprecation, and Jane drew back frightened into the shadows.

'This is my friend, mother,' said Fred. 'Dad, this is Jenny.'

''Evening, miss,' cried the old man kindly; 'but we've got to leave you.'

Mrs Green said nothing, but her sharp eyes seemed to pierce the shadows as she peered at her son's young woman.

'Good night, Jenny,' said Fred, and shook her hand and dropped on to the *Prudence*. Fred on a boat was a different person, she saw—neat and quick, as he cast off the mooring ropes and ran along the narrow plank amidships and picked up his pole, and with long, strong thrusts drove the vessels under the little bridge and out into the tideway. 'Good night,' said Fred again, and 'Good night,' hissed Mrs Green, as if it were a malediction. They were just in time, for as the tide caught them the tug *Richmond* hooted from the bridge, a thrilling, pleasant sound which Jane had loved all her life.

She walked back to the elm and watched the *Richmond* sweep up and round, putting her nose to the tide. The three fat coal-barges she had in tow swung round astern of her; there was the hollow clang of iron barges meeting, Fred's voice calling in the darkness, a tinkle from the engine-room bell, more calling and clanging, the creak of the tow-ropes as they took the strain, the red eye swung out of sight and gave place presently to the green, and the *Richmond* steamed swiftly away towards Chiswick and the west.

Jane thought that she had seen a wonderful thing, though she had seen it often before; for this was Fred and the *Prudence* bound on a voyage of Mystery and Adventure, though the beginning was only Hammersmith and the end was only Birmingham. She was fired by the drama of that departure, and she wished she was in the *Prudence*, beginning the four-days' voyage to Birmingham, and travelling through the night with Fred. Or better still, perhaps, with Mr Bryan.

3

THE *BLACKBIRD*

WHILE Jane admired the disappearing *Prudence*, Fred sat in the tiny cabin of that vessel and described to his father the great qualities and beauty of Jane. Tom Green said what he had said before:

'It's no good taking a girl off the shore, my lad. It never was and never will be. You've got to be born to the life to stick it, my lad. Look at Bill Baker that took a girl out of a shop. Willing as you like – and she left him in six months.'

'Jane isn't a girl in a shop,' said Fred. 'She lives on a barge.'

'But was she born to it?' said Tom. 'You was born on this boat, and I was born on this boat, and my mother before me was born on this boat. But was *she* born to it, lad?'

'I dunno that she was,' said Fred; 'but she belongs to the water. She can sail a boat.'

'She can't sail a boat on the Cut,' said his father. 'If she's not born to it, she won't stick it. You know that. D'you think she'll stick it yourself, Fred? Honest?'

'I think she would,' said Fred stubbornly.

A husky, sibilant voice spoke out of the darkness, where Mrs Green stood at the tiller: 'She's neither one thing nor the other.'

Fred was silent, as he often was when his mother made a remark.

Jane was not born to a barge, but almost as long as she could remember she had lived on a barge with Lily and her father. Her mother had died when Lily was born, and after that her father had come down in the world and lost his money and come to London and bought the *Blackbird*, because he was born at Liverpool, and was fond of the water; and because the *Blackbird* was cheaper than any house that he could find; and also because, without his wife's guidance, he had always done the most extraordinary things.

The *Blackbird* was an old London River sailing-barge, though now she had neither mast nor rigging, but lay, a sheer hulk, against Valentine Wharf, a little below the Black Swan inn. Mr

Bell had chosen this place for the *Blackbird* because of the Black Swan, which seemed to him an omen, for he was that kind of man. Now he earned a little money by playing the cello (or the cornet) in a cinema, and lost most of this money by betting on racehorses. But while his wife lived he had been the business manager of a repertory theatre in the north; his wife had sung at concerts, and managed the theatre.

Mr Bell paid six shillings a week for his moorings to the owner of the wharf, Mrs Higgins, who was also proprietress of the Black Swan. But he had neither rent nor rates nor taxes to pay, and could devote almost everything to his racehorses. They lived on the barge in spacious squalor; she was eighty feet long and twelve feet wide, and dirty all over. Mr Bell had no strong sense of class or caste, and was a natural picnicker. His life had become more and more of a picnic. Lily was like him, and when Jane was busy at the Ravens' they washed up every third day.

They lived in what had been the cargo space of the barge, decked over. There was one living-room, which was the size of many a rich man's drawing-room; but it had nothing in it but one table, two chairs and a stool, two cats and an anchor, a low bench against the port side, three old tarpaulins hanging on hooks, a coil of rope in one corner, Mr Bell's cello in another (when he was playing the cornet), and in a third a crystal set which they were tired of. The floor was of bare boards, which Jane swept twice a day, and down the centre ran the great square beam which was the keelson and foundation of the barge. As he stepped over this the stranger bumped his head against the roof. On the table, which had a green baize cloth with holes in it, there were to be seen at any hour of the day a dirty plate or two, a teapot, and a pot of jam, half empty, and the wreck of a loaf of bread. The Bell daughters lived chiefly on bread and tea and jam, on sardines and sausages, and potatoes and apples. And they looked very well on it.

Forward of the living-room was the principal state-room, where Mr Bell slept; and beyond that a smaller cabin, which was Jane's; and beyond that a great waste space which was full of lumber, rotting ropes, old gum-boots, cans of dried paint, and a few rusty tools and another anchor. Properly used and reconstructed the *Blackbird* could have housed three families. But under Mr Bell's government she seemed too small for three persons. Lily slept aft in a tiny cubbyhole, a mere hole in the wall in what had been the cabin when the barge was in commission and the hold was full of cargo. This hole was always an untidy tumble of bedclothes from the moment when Lily got up to the moment when she went to bed. There was very little light in the living-room. Mr Bell had fitted one small skylight, and by degrees was adding tiny windows at the side; but this was a great feat of carpentry, and, what with his cello and his horses and losing his tools, a window took a long time, and a window a year was about all he could do. However, he was always on the point of beginning another window. By night they had an 'Aladdin' lamp, which had been a wonderful bargain at a sale in King Street. It combined all the advantages of paraffin and gas, and really, Mr Bell would say, was as good as electric light, though it only illuminated a small round patch at the table end of the room. The *Blackbird* was perhaps in many ways a deplorable residence; but still, outside was the open water and the wide sky. Looking westward up the river the eye could travel a mile or more, and the south-west wind which beat upon her flanks had come two miles without touching a house, which was more than many a rich Londoner could say of his residence. If down below the Bells lived in a slum, they were countrymen and sailors and children of the sun when they came on deck.

Various authorities had suspected that the Bells were not existing according to the best ideas of modern civilization, and had done their best to interfere with them. Once an Education man had nosed them out delightedly, but discovered only that the girls had been punctually attending a council school for many years; and Lily had stayed on with a trade scholarship for two years beyond the usual age. An inspector of the Port of London Authority called once or twice in his motor-boat, because he felt sure that the home of such a family must be either insanitary or unhealthy or unseaworthy. But there popped up the ladder through the narrow hatch two girls with cheeks so glowing, eyes so bright, and arms so chubby that even a public official could not condemn them as unhealthy; and if their hair was tousled and perhaps they did not wash so often as the inspector, he could not think of any regulation which was concerned with that. As for 'insanitary', Mr Bell proudly

27

showed him that they had every convenience on the wharf; and it was no business of the Port of London Authority what time Lily made her bed. As for 'unseaworthy', the barge was solid as the hills, and might last as long. The river-police shook their heads at the girls because they would sail their crazy dinghy in all weathers, and took particular pains to go out in the hard south-westerly gales which make Hammersmith almost as dangerous as the Horn. But the girls always laughed at them and seemed quite at their ease; and the more the spray soaked them, the more the boat heeled, and the more water she took on board, the more they laughed. The river-police had no authority to rescue suicides till they entered the water, so they did not know what to do. Besides, they did not really understand sailing, and did not know what was dangerous and what was not, though they were quite sure that something ought to be done about those girls. So they shook their heads again, and went on, remarking that, anyhow, they were well-plucked ones.

By land, the Metropolitan Police had no jurisdiction over the barge. But they used to peep through the rickety fence that bounded the narrow wharf, and feel in their bones that there must be something irregular which could be taken notice of. Some of them did not approve of the way the girls bathed in the summer, diving from the barge and standing drying in the sun, and laughing and enjoying themselves. For small boys used to peer through the holes and say 'Coo!', which the policemen thought was against public decency, so they moved the boys on. But they could not move the girls on, for anyone may bathe from a vessel or boat, and they wore neat, dark costumes well within the law, though it is true they were tight, and here and there had little holes in them.

So the Metropolitan Police, like the other authorities, shook their heads and passed on, feeling obscurely that no one should be able to live in this strange free manner in the County of London in the twentieth century, half-way 'twixt land and water, as it were. 'No better than gipsies,' as Constable Boot expressed it. And if there was nothing unlawful in that, well, there ought to be.

Authority might shake its head over the barbaric upbringing of these two girls, but they were healthy and alive; and as for the mind, apart from education, they were not without the refining influences of modern civilization, if authority had only known. They had the pictures constantly, for it was always a clause in Mr Bell's contracts that his girls should be on the free list; and even when bread was short they could feed the mind on Hollywood. Mondays and Thursdays they saw the new programme, and were again encouraged by the success of virtue and the eventual discomfiture of wickedness. On these occasions, whatever the family misfortunes, they slipped up through the hatchway and across the muddy wharf, miraculously arrayed in silk stockings and fur collars, and the inspector of the Port of London Authority would not have known them.

Then they had the wireless, which they turned on often for the 'jazz' bands, and sometimes for good music, if Mr Bell insisted. While the dog Toby lived they sometimes turned the wireless on for a talk on 'Carburettors' or 'The Care of Bees', for Toby had barking fits, and, as Lily had discovered, could very often be quieted by an educational Talk. But Toby was dead, they were tired of the wireless, and got more satisfaction from the *Sunday Gazette*.

Mr Bell had the *Sunday Gazette* every week. It was the only paper he read, and he read it all Sunday. The girls read it all the rest of the week, while Mr Bell was out. Not that Mr Bell kept it from them, but if they read the police-court cases out loud he generally said something. And they preferred to read the cases out loud. They would start on page one and go steadily through the paper, column by column, but missing out the sport and politics. Since this was the only paper they read, they formed a very poor opinion of human character, especially the character of men. From it they learned that the majority of men come sooner or later to murder or larceny, abduction and rape, bigamy, assault, embezzlement, or arson, and various other crimes which they did not understand. At the end of each case there was generally a little argument about the meaning of terms. Lily had an inquiring mind, and was not to be put off with phrases like 'proposals of a certain character'; she wanted to know exactly what was proposed; she wanted to know the precise distinction between 'intimacy' and 'misconduct'; she was always asking 'Why?' and 'How?' and as often as not Jane could not tell her. Sometimes, when she did know, she would remember that she was an elder sister and refuse to say; and then they would quarrel. Lily would complain that she always told Jane everything she knew, which was true enough; and she knew a lot, for Lily was the giddy one, and went out with wild boys.

As for the position of women in the world, that was made plain in this paper: they were defenceless creatures and had an adventurous time. They were carried into woods and throttled by bank-clerks. They were attacked in railway trains, they were enticed into motor-cars and whirled away to lonely parts of the shore. The governess on her innocent bicycle was set upon by masked men and gagged in a ditch; the young girl tripping home across the common was stopped by a well-spoken ruffian on a motor-bicycle, who asked her the way, dragged her into the gorse, kissed her, knocked her on the head with stones, and turned out to be a schoolmaster. It was a very strange world presented weekly by this paper to the inquiring girls. No one was safe in it, and men were capable of anything. And among all these perils the female victim seemed altogether helpless; by no act of negligence of her own did she ever affect the event; or, if she did, it never came out in these cases. Woman was an insect at the mercy of a monster; she was betrayed, deceived, seduced, wronged, ruined, assaulted, violated, or raped – and she had nothing whatever to do with it.

They had a happy evening with the *Sunday Gazette* on the Monday after Fred's departure.

'It seems to me,' said Lily at the end of the Murray Case, 'the more good you are the more trouble you get into. So why worry?'

'Don't talk like that,' said Jane. 'If a girl gets into trouble it's as much her fault as the man's.'

'Then why don't they say so in the papers?' asked Lily.

Jane did not know. Perhaps the message of the paper was much the same as the message of the pictures – that wickedness was wrong and unsuccessful. And this, no doubt, was the intention of its good proprietors, two of whom were noblemen. But this was not exactly the message which it brought to the two daughters of the *Blackbird*. Even on the pictures they preferred those moments when the innocent girl was in danger of losing her honour to the dark gentleman to the happy moments at the end when she was reunited to the fair one. And the weekly misfortunes of their sex in the *Sunday Gazette* did not excite in them horror and loathing, but curiosity and, truth to tell, a certain envy.

'I'd like something terrible to happen to me,' Lily murmured, closing her blue eyes dreamily like some Victorian miss yearning for the affections of a clergyman.

'Don't be silly, Lily,' said Jane sternly, for they had just been reading the sad tale of five young women who had been shamefully persuaded by some sailors to embark as stowaways in a merchant-ship, and had been carried unwilling all the way to South America, supposing in their innocence that it was all a lark, and that after a day or two the captain would turn the ship round and bring them back to Bristol. She thought that Lily must have this dreadful narrative in her mind, and she was shocked. But she confessed to herself that she too had had secret imaginations of that kind, in which she had been violently carried off in a ship or motor-car, or even on horseback, as maidens were in history or on the pictures or in the *Sunday Gazette*, to be ruthlessly subdued by some strong though abominable male. These awful thoughts she had always put from her most firmly after a short time, and it was disturbing to have to suspect them in the fair and fluffy head of her sister Lily.

The next remark that Lily made was even more shocking. 'Ruined,' she murmured, lying on the *Blackbird*'s deck with her feet waving behind her and her eyes on page sixteen. 'I think it must be rather fun.'

'Lily!'

'Come off it, Jane,' said Lily. 'Well, I dunno. You know all that stuff in the stories about the young man saving her from worse than death. Worse than death!' said Lily contemptuously. 'Well, I don't believe it is.'

Jane said nothing, but she decided, like the river-police, that something ought to be done about Lily.

There were other civilizing influences in these girls' lives. When they had done the 'cases' in the *Gazette* they did the 'cross-word puzzle'. They did it every week in the hope of a prize, and Mr Bell had bought them a dictionary; and in the dictionary they looked up the words which baffled them in the 'puzzle', and some of the words which had baffled them in the paper.

Their other link with the great world was Mr Bell's connexion with horse-racing. Mr Bell had never seen a horse-race. In his youth he had once or twice had personal dealings with horses, always unhappy. As a boy he had been sent by his father to a riding-school for a treat. At the second lesson he had had the misfortune to be mounted on a horse which was called Conqueror and had been trained with the yeomanry to lie down and act as cover while his rider fired over him. While the horses were walking round the school and the instructor was explaining to the pupils the method of making a horse walk sideways, and how to open a gate in the hunting-field, the young Albert Bell fell into one of those dreams of future happiness which all his life betrayed him, and let the reins hang loose. The horse Conqueror, perhaps reviving old memories, perhaps sensitive to neglect, lay down quietly, but without warning, on its side, and deposited Albert on the tan, but did not break his leg. With the experience gained in six lessons of this kind, Albert was later persuaded to attempt a number of gentle animals at an uncle's farm. None of them shook his conviction that the horse was a capricious, cunning, and evil-minded animal, and that he himself had no special genius for its control. On the contrary, he found himself positively a corrupting influence; for however gentle and well-behaved they had been before, no sooner was Albert on their backs than some imp of mischief seemed to possess them, and animals called 'ladies' horses', with a reputation for temperance enjoyed for years, were guilty of acts of violence and folly which astonished the ladies, accustomed to ride them. His aunt's white mare, irreverently named by the family the 'Palfrey', was not known to have a weakness, unless it could be called a weakness to halt by the roadside from time to time to eat grass. His aunt had never discouraged this little habit, but Albert conceived it to be humiliating, and endeavoured to correct it by hauling up the Palfrey's head. The Palfrey retaliated, to the general surprise, by walking backwards very quickly, snorting unpleasantly, until it was allowed to eat again. At an annual rally of the Boy Scouts at which he found himself (by accident) on horseback, Albert thought it undignified that his mount should stand with her head in the grass while the band was playing the National Anthem; and, ignoring the warnings of experience, he tried to persuade her into a more erect and military position. The Palfrey immediately walked backwards in an uncontrollable manner into the heart of the Scouts' band, where she put one hind foot through the big drum and brought the National Anthem to a premature conclusion. Albert's aunt was convinced that the strange conduct of the Palfrey was due to some peculiar defect in Albert's management, and Albert did not know what to think. But from that moment he determined to have no more to do with the incalculable creatures.

All this is important because of the strange faith in horses which he acquired in later life; and not only in horses, but in the ability of mankind to predict their future actions by reference to their past. In the *Sunday Gazette* were the advertisements of several gentlemen who had this power, and were anxious to use it for the enrichment of others. Among these was one named Steve Merry, who had Mr Bell's particular confidence and custom. Steve sent secretly to his clients the names of the horses which would be successful in selected races, and the order in which they would finish the course; and he published each week a list of cases in which these forecasts had proved accurate. 'I will make your fortune,' he said frankly, and Mr Bell took a kindly view of anyone who was prepared to make his fortune. In order to demonstrate his good faith, Steve undertook to send a parcel of forecasts free of charge to gentlemen dealing with him for the first time; and it was this generous act which had won the custom of Mr Bell. He accepted the offer, and one out of the six horses named by Steve was, in fact, successful in a race, though Mr Bell did not, unfortunately, back it, because in that case he thought that he knew better. Still, he was impressed, and now nearly every week a small postal order would go to Steve; and Steve would send him 'Splendid Doubles' and 'Infallible Naps'. But meanwhile Mr Bell had himself become a student of 'form', and, forgetful of his youth, believed that it was possible for an ordinary man, by examining closely what a horse had done under such-and-such conditions, to foretell what it would do under different conditions. So he pored most carefully over the column by 'The Seer' in the *Sunday Gazette* in which 'The Seer', after a scientific comparison of the pedigree, history, handicap, jockey, physique, and private idiosyncrasies of the son of Sarpedon with those of the daughter of Cyllene, would definitely decide that if anything should beat the Manton filly it would be Lord Loofah's gelding; while, for his part, he would not be surprised if Lord Crosstree's nomination flattered his supporters, and very likely the horse which led this to the post would win. It was hard work sometimes to discover from these careful pieces of prose what horse, if any, 'The Seer' himself would back; but Mr Bell gave his whole mind to it, and was now able to distinguish with ease the Manton filly from the daughter of Cyllene. Moreover, he had soon begun to form conclusions of his own, which differed sometimes both from those of 'The Seer' and those of Steve Merry. And sometimes, unfortunately, he would trust his own judgement when Steve's turned out to be right; while often and often, as he would explain to Jane, he had faithfully followed Steve when if he had only stood by his own opinions he would have won a large sum of money.

It was a disheartening business. Mr Bell made three or four bets a week, and backed a winner about once a month. But a series of small losses, as he would explain to Lily, was to be expected, and must be cheerfully set off against the chance of heavy gains. For example, there had been Eurydice, the glorious horse (or filly?) Eurydice, which, backed by Mr Bell for ten shillings in a reckless moment, had come home a winner at thirty to one. Fifteen pounds odd! This had happened, it is true, some three years earlier, but Mr Bell still spoke of it as if it had been the day before yesterday. And indeed there still lingered traces of Eurydice to gladden the heart. Lily still wore her Eurydice bangle, and Jane's pearl necklace was Eurydice's too. And every horse which carried Mr Bell's half-crown was to be another Eurydice.

But that same imp which had possessed the horses of his youth pursued, it seemed, his animals today. The hottest favourite of the market, the most 'Infallible Naps' of Steve, when backed by Mr Bell, would mysteriously lose their powers and belie their 'form', or meet with some misfortune which none could have foreseen. They developed coughs at the last minute, or inexplicable swellings at the knees; they crossed their legs or refused to run downhill, or revealed some idiosyncrasy never before suspected. And if they themselves were blameless, a dog ran through their legs, there was dirty work at the corners, or they were 'interfered with' by other horses at the start.

The girls looked on at their father's operations with charity, and even with sympathy. For one thing, they seemed to have some sort of kinship with the pictures. The racecourse, like the pictures, was a world in which, at any moment, the poor and lowly might suddenly be blessed by fortune. Indeed, Jane had often a secret thought that if ever she was to live like the pictures she would owe it, as like as not, to some staggering speculation of her father's; for she could not think of any other agency which was likely to bring it about. None the less, she knew very well how many half-crowns were carried away on the backs of racehorses, which might well have been spent upon the *Blackbird*, on food and clothing and a blanket or two, to say nothing of windows. And she was careful to be up when Mr Bell came home on Friday nights, in order to extract for the housekeeping as much of the weekly wage as it was kind to take from him.

Sometimes, after a month of losses, she would protest, but very mildly. Mr Bell, who knew his daughter's weakness, would confess his own, but add that what he did, he did very largely for his daughters' sake; for, things being what they were and the world a hard place, in no other way could he hope to provide them with those luxuries which they deserved. And Jane, who loved her father, would assure him she knew that very well – that, really, she was not complaining, but she did hope that he would have some winners soon. Mr Bell would reply that he conducted his business with the utmost economy – that, for example, he seldom wasted money on buying an evening paper to ascertain the result of a race, but would hang about till he could get the news by word of mouth from a newsboy at the Broadway; that she must never forget the case of Eurydice; and that he had a red-hot tip for the three-thirty on Tuesday. Jane would say, 'It's quite all right, father,' and kiss him warmly; and, nerved to greater efforts by this encouragement, Mr Bell would put five shillings on the three-thirty instead of half a crown.

Besides, there was the general romance of the distant racecourse, which, though they had never seen, the girls had often imagined – the lords, the crowds, the gaily-coloured jockeys, the motor-cars, the jolly bookmakers, the towering grandstands, and, heart and centre of it all, the gallant horse which carried their father's fortunes, and, with everything against it, beset by enemies, might still win home and make him happy in the evening. He kept nothing from them. 'What horse are you on, Dad?' was Lily's morning greeting, and till afternoon there ran a little current of hope about the *Blackbird*. The Manton filly galloped in their thoughts, Lord Loofah's gelding gave colour to the day, and for an hour or two they were partners with the rich.

Each of them had read a book or two. Mr Bell had a little row of books saved from the wreckage of his life – some old *Ruff*'s *Guides to the Turf*, *Bends and Hitches*, the *Arabian Nights*, a nautical almanac, *Black Beauty*, *Smallboat Sailing*, *Stories of the Stage*, and a few old detective tales in which wicked murders were committed on the first page and punctually punished on the last through the acumen of an amateur cruelly handicapped by the antiquated methods of Scotland Yard. The girls liked these best, and would sometimes borrow stories of this kind from the Penny Library at Mr Peacock's tobacco shop, for kind Mr Peacock let them off the pennies. They had read large parts of the *Arabian Nights*, but thought them less meaty than the *Sunday Gazette* and not so well written. They expected literature to be as spasmodic as the pictures, as pithy as the *Gazette*, and served in lozenges like the learning on the wireless. They enjoyed long words, but could not endure long sentences. So they did not waste money on books. But lately Lily had joined a syndicate of girl friends which bought and circulated selected volumes in the Paper Library of Passion Tales, and these were well worth the twopence.

Mr Bell took them to church on Christmas Day, when there was no Sunday paper to read. The vicar called from time to time, but never found Mr Bell at home. The girls received him very politely, demurely, and silently, and answered 'Yes' and 'No' in turn. When he hoped that they would be seen at Matins next Sunday, they said that there was much to do on the barge, and they could not tell till their father came home, but they would mention the matter to him, and probably they would come.

Such were the forces of modern civilization which worked upon the daughters of the *Blackbird*. And perhaps it was not surprising if Jane, as Mrs Green had said, was neither one thing nor the other. But, considering what happened to Lily and Jane and how many authorities had wished to interfere with them, it may be thought odd that no one tried to protect them from the pictures, or the *Sunday Gazette*, or the speculative dealings of Mr Bell.

4

THE BLACK SWAN

LILY said that her father was making up to Mrs Higgins of the Black Swan. Jane did not know about that, though she thought it might be likely, after the surprising publication which she had found in her father's cabin. But she said nothing about that.

On the Thursday her father took her to the Black Swan, and she began to think that Lily might be right. He had an hour or two to himself between the afternoon and evening performances at the cinema, and he asked her to slip out from the Ravens' and meet him if she could, about six o'clock, for he wished to talk to her, but not before Lily. Nurse was back, so she slipped away successfully. She found her father sitting in the garden by the quoits ground, a mild and bitter and a ginger-beer before him, his pipe in his mouth. He looked melancholy but contented. He had a melancholy, feckless face, with weak blue eyes and a wispy moustache, which was a nuisance with beer. He looked a man of sorrows, and people pitied him in buses. But, as Mrs Higgins said, he was never one to complain, and everybody liked him at the Black Swan. In the right company he spoke with a stately verbiage, but when at the Black Swan he talked like the Black Swan. They knew that he had come down in the world, and no doubt he knew it, but they could not have told it from his manner. He had no superior ways. So all the quoits-players looked up and said cheerily, 'Good evening, Mr Bell,' and he felt himself among friends.

The garden of the Black Swan on a summer evening was a friendly and a peaceful place, though every man there was as likely as not to be out of work within a week, or in some way at grips with misfortune. The centre of it was the quoits ground, about the length of a cricket-pitch, on which the Black Swan team was now doing battle with the Lord Nelson visiting-team from Putney. An ancient, heroic, dignified game, like something in the *Iliad* or an English *Aeneid*. The quoits were massive pieces of iron, weighing, in the best matches, some sixteen pounds. At either end of the

ground were square pits of clay, and in the centre of them a small
buried peg. The matches were a series of single combats; each man
had two quoits, and the game was twenty points. The full match
might last for hours. Old Ned, the waterman, was pitted now
against a huge constable from Putney – massive men both, with the
judgement of philosophers and the backs and muscles of Titans.
No chickens could play this game. Each man had at the target end
a sort of second, or adviser, who with slips of paper would mark the
position of the peg or the strategic spot where they would have the
quoit fall. These had strange technical cries and whimsical fashions
of encouragement. 'Come on, lad,' cried Boulter from the water-
works to the veteran Ned. 'Don't be afraid, boy. This is where I
want you.' And stooping, he pegged with a forefinger a white slip
of paper in the narrow inch of clay between the two quoits which
lay by the peg already. 'You've nothing to fear, lad. Let her go!'

One foot forward, Old Ned balanced his huge frame, his wide,
wise forehead glistening in the sun with sweat. He swung his arm
back – everything was in the balance and the swing – took one
step forward, and with an elephantine grace flung the great quoit
in the air – a thing, thought Mr Bell, to split the skull of any man
that stood beneath it. But Boulter still crouched confident over the
mark, knowing his man. And the quoit fell between his knees,
plumb on the mark, splitting and burying the slip of paper and
dividing the two other quoits.

'That's my beauty!' said Boulter to the unshaven old hero, and
a murmur of praise ran along the loyal watchers of the Black Swan.
Then came the policeman's second, with his slip of paper and his
own strange language. The policeman's throw was not so true, but
when he walked to the other end with Ned – two Hectors, two
Robin Hoods – they found the four quoits overlapping in a narrow,
miraculous ring.

Along each side ran a low wooden rail and benches, and on the
rail was a shelf for the elbow and the beer. Here sat a score or more
of the neighbours with their harmless glasses, sunning themselves
after the day's work, watermen talking of tides and the selling of
boats, one or two of those artists watching the game, wives discussing with relish the trials of life, while their dogs and children
ran loose about the garden. Mr Bell surveyed the scene with con-

tentment, for he was a companionable man and lonely and it brought company to his soul. He thought how strangely like a village was this corner of London, where there were true neighbours still, and simple sports in the open air. And he thought how strange were those Temperance folk who could see in all this nothing but 'alcohol', for whom this ancient meeting-place of the poor was no more than a drinking-den. He had heard from Mrs Higgins that she was worried about her licence; for she had heard that these same folk were working up for another 'assault' on 'redundant' licences in the neighbourhood; and if the licences were reduced it would be the small houses that went, for there was more profit to the brewers in the gaudy gin-palaces in King Street, and it did not matter if the little house was fifteenth century, and had quoits in the garden – to those folks it was 'alcohol', and one of these days the Black Swan would go as the Waterman had gone.

Then, as Lily had suspected, he thought very kindly of Mrs Higgins. And he thought of himself, very pleasantly, as master of the Black Swan. It would be no mean thing to preside over this respectable house, which caused so much pleasure and so little harm, to be a sort of leader among these friendly people who knew him, close to the river and the *Blackbird* (which he had always said was an omen). And though he knew he could not manage a theatre or a family, he was sure that with Mrs Higgins's help he could manage a pub.

Besides, he was lonely. Once or twice, lately, when Jane had sat on his bed in her nightgown, to talk about housekeeping and kiss him good night, he had thought what a fine, pretty girl she had grown; she might marry any day, and then there would be no one to keep Lily in order. In the end even Lily would go, and then he would be all alone. He had thought once or twice of Mrs Higgins, but he had no money, and who was he to propose marriage to the Black Swan? Then he had played with the plan of advertising for a 'Widow Without Encumbrances', as shy men did, he knew. He bought a paper called the *Marriage Mart* and found five pages full of 'Energetic Spinsters' and 'Refined Widows' anxious to meet with a view to matrimony, genuine, sincere, respectable, domesticated, fond of music, and all the rest of it. The paper fascinated him, and indeed its system had a certain kinship with the hobby of his life; one by one he read through the long columns of descriptions with the same attention which he gave to a list of race-horses or 'The Seer's' estimate of form, though he did not forget that in this case the estimates had been prepared by the competitors themselves. There were two or three entries which took his fancy, but none which provoked him to invest in a reply. Instead, he composed a modest description of his own character and circumstances and sent it to the editor.

The *Marriage Mart* came out on Thursday, and he had the paper in his pocket now; and while he was waiting he could not resist taking it from his pocket and reading his contribution again, with a gambler's interest and an author's pride.

Jane slipped into the seat beside him without a word, and drank her ginger-beer at a gulp. Then, 'What's that, father?' she said, looking over his shoulder. But she saw at once what it was, and with Lily's suggestion in her mind, her own fantastic suspicion returned. Mr Bell flushed guiltily.

'Father!' said Jane, 'you're not — you're not *advertising*!'

Mr Bell was too fond of his daughter to lie to her, so he pointed uncomfortably to his composition. Jane read it, horrified. 'Poor father,' she said. 'Advertising! Whatever is the matter with you?'

'You talk as if it was a disease,' said Mr Bell, a little annoyed. 'It's for your sakes, Jane, you and Lily. You need a mother.'

'You do, father,' said Jane kindly, 'but we're all right.'

'You're all right, Jane; but Lily's going wild.'

'I know,' said Jane, thinking of Lily's recent remarks. It was Early Closing day, and Heaven knew who Lily was with, and what she was doing.

'She ought to go to work.'

'I know,' said Jane again. 'But Lily don't like work.'

'I've been wondering,' said Mr Bell. 'We might sell the barge and go to Liverpool. Your aunt could look after you, and I could get work.'

'I'd rather have a mother, thanks. I don't want to leave the barge, father. I love the old barge.'

'The Mersey's a fine river,' said Mr Bell feebly.

'Should we live on a barge, father?'

'No. Your aunt wouldn't live on a barge.'

'Well, I won't go to Liverpool. I don't know about Lily.'

Lily did not love the barge as well as Jane, for there was always something to be done which Lily ought to have done, and had not.

'Well, it's one thing or the other,' said Mr Bell with an attempt at firmness.

'Well, if we must have a mother,' said Jane, 'I won't have one out of an advertisement. So there !'

'All right, Jane,' said Mr Bell sadly, and he put the incriminating paper in his pocket. 'It was foolishness, and I didn't really mean it. It was for your sake. I'm worried, Jane. I've been unlucky this week.'

It was many weeks, Jane knew, since Mr Bell had had a lucky week.

'Why don't you give it up, father?' she said gently.

'It's all an investment, Jane. At any moment I may strike it lucky. Remember Eurydice?'

'Yes, father,' said Jane, who knew she should be angry, but, as usual, was only sorry.

'I've a first-class tip for the Derby,' said Mr Bell, and was silent, watching the door of the kitchen, for at this hour, sometimes, Mrs Higgins took the air.

'I wish you had a mother, Jane,' he said at last.

Jane was more sorry for him still, and although she had no wish for a mother, she said, 'Well, father, isn't there anyone you like? What about – well, what about Mrs Higgins, or someone?'

Mr Bell flushed again, but with pleasure, and Jane felt the satisfaction of a mother who has given her child a successful treat.

'I can't, Jane – not without money. But I've got a plan,' said Mr Bell dreamily. 'I've got a plan. You're a good girl, Jane,' and he squeezed her hand.

Jane was touched by his emotion, but she wondered what new insanity was in his mind, and she was about to ask particulars of the plan, when Mrs Higgins appeared at the kitchen doorway.

'Well, I must get back,' said Jane, 'and lay the dinner. See you tonight, father. Be good.' She kissed him and added, against her better judgement, 'Best of luck !' And, with romantic imaginations, she departed. 'Weak,' she thought, 'we're all weak.'

'What will you have, Mrs Higgins?' said Mr Bell, rising gallantly.

'Thank you, Mr Bell. Mine's a port and lemonade.'

She sat down beside him, and, queen-like, surveyed her domain, bowing to the quoits players and beaming at the wives, while Mr Bell ordered her strange refreshment.

Emily Higgins was a comely widow of forty, and, truth to tell, a little too youthful and gentle in appearance to be the convincing mistress of a public-house. Sometimes, even with Harold's assistance, she had difficulty in clearing the bar at closing-time so promptly as the law requires. And at these times, though not at many others, she felt the loss of Higgins.

Like Mr Bell she had had her troubles. For many years she had served behind the bar at a West London theatre, till Higgins won her heart during a play which was too deep for him. Together they made the Black Swan prosper, but Mr Higgins had Mr Bell's disease, and gambled, more grandly still, on the Stock Exchange. He died in debt, a strong Conservative, who hated all newfangled nonsense and was killed in a one-way street.

'Well, here's all you wish yourself, Mr Bell!' she said. 'That girl of yours is a pretty thing. She and Ernest are quite thick, I believe.'

'I'm glad,' said Mr Bell. A double wedding, he reflected. He and Mrs Higgins, Ernest and Jane. 'Those girls need a mother,' he went on, gazing at his glass.

Mrs Higgins eyed him sideways, but made no reply. Like Jane, against her better judgement, she had a weakness for Mr Bell, and found in his fecklessness and modesty a pitiful charm. But, as Mr Bell had guessed, she needed money more sorely than a man.

'How are your troubles?' said Mr Bell at last, using a formula which was common at the Black Swan.

'Mustn't grumble,' she said; and this was commoner still. 'Ernest is a worry. Last Sunday he spoke in Hyde Park. But he's a good lad,' she concluded with a sigh.

Ernest, to the horror of his parents, had turned into a Socialist, and belonged to the League of Red Youth.

She went on to speak of the Temperance folk, who were prowling and prowling around, like the hosts of Midian, and now she was haunted by a fear that they would pounce and destroy the Black Swan before she had put anything by.

'Mind you, it isn't everyone I say that to, Mr Bell, but I know very well it won't go no further.'

'Thank you,' said Mr Bell, 'I'm proud of the confidence.'

Old Ned was still performing prodigies of valour. Mr Peacock from the tobacco shop had come in in his white collar and neat clothes. Mr Bryan, the artist, much less tidy, was next to him, and they were both arguing about the qualities of a boat which was for sale with Andrew the ferryman. Beyond them was a Civil Servant who had come in to buy ginger-beer and had stayed to watch the game. The sun had tipped the roofs to the west, and the garden wore a golden glow.

'I wish,' said Mrs Higgins, eyeing her kingdom with a gentle bitterness, 'these Mr Busies would spend an evening in this garden, or even in the bar, and then turn round and tell me I'm a haunt of wickedness. Do you ever see a man go off these premises the worse for his glass, Mr Bell? Did you ever see Old Ned reeling home in his cups?'

'I can't say that I did.'

'Not once in a month of Sundays. It isn't for the beer they come here, I always say, Mr Bell – well, they come for that, of course, I won't tell no lies, but it's the company and the conversation that draws them just as much. As I said to Mr Peacock yesterday, this house is the poor man's Carlton, I said, and the Carlton has no trouble about licences, that I will swear. And I can prove my words,' said Mrs Higgins, now generously warmed by her convictions. 'You see that family over there, Mr Bell – the Palmers, I mean, three brothers, father, and mother? They used to live along the road at River Villas, Mr Bell. The boys was born there, and now they're scattered over the length and breadth of London and two of them married. They come here every Thursday of their lives for a little family reunion, and white collars, too, all of them. There's many another I could mention too that come here regular for the conversation, though they've left the neighbourhood and it costs them a penny tram ride; well, it can't be the beer that brings them, because if it was only that they could get it at every corner, but wild horses wouldn't drag some of them into that gin-palace in King Street. And there's old Andrew, can't hardly walk, but here he is three nights a week, though he passes three houses on the way. Well, do you mean to tell me, Mr Bell, that it's the beer that brings him?'

'It isn't the beer,' said Mr Bell gravely, 'so much as the bonhomy.'

'You've hit it,' said Mrs Higgins with approval. 'And, if you ask me, there's more harm done by betting on horses than what there is done by the drink.'

'I dare say you're right,' said Mr Bell guardedly, for by a sure instinct he had never spoken of his racing investments to Mrs Higgins, and he did not know how much she knew.

'Yet one they call the sport of kings,' she continued, 'and the other's the poor man's wickedness. Sauce for the goose, sauce for the gander, I say. It's the old story. One law for the rich and another for the poor. If it was this golf they played in the garden instead of quoits, it would be a different pair of shoes, believe me. There's many a rich man behaving himself this living minute a lot worse than you'll see in my bar, Mr Bell, and no bother about licences, or hours neither. Good evening, Mrs Paddock. And how's the world using you?'

'We mustn't grumble, Mrs Higgins. Paddock's legs bad again, can't go to work; and they've took Ethel to the infirmary. Scarlet fever.'

'Go on?'

'Come on sudden Saturday evening.'

'Poor little mite! Going on all right?'

'Nicely, thank you. Well, it might have been worse, I say.'

'Just what I was saying to Mr Bell here. You never know when you're lucky, do you?'

'That's right. Well, I must get back to Paddock with his medicine.'

'A drop of what he fancies? Well, there's nothing better. Anything I can do, Mrs Paddock, you know you've only got to ask?'

'I know that, Mrs Higgins, and thank you kindly. Good evening. Good evening, Mr Bell.'

The woman shambled off with her jug, leaving Mr Bell with the warm inward glow which was often kindled in him by the courage and kindness of his neighbours in trouble. Mrs Higgins, he knew, lent money to many of them, and seldom at interest.

'It's a hard world, Mr Bell,' said Mrs Higgins, and they mused in silence about that.

'You and me have a good deal in common, Mrs Higgins,' said Mr Bell cautiously at last.

'We've both had our ups and downs, Mr Bell, if that's what you mean.'

'More downs than ups in my case,' said Mr Bell. 'But I'm hoping for better things. I've got a plan,' he said mysteriously.

'Go on?' said Mrs Higgins, mystified.

'I'm expecting,' said Mr Bell, weighing his words, 'a windfall – a very considerable windfall.'

'Well, I hope you may get it, Mr Bell.'

Mr Bell waited a moment, and then said, 'Did you ever think of marrying again?'

Mrs Higgins faced him full and examined him, so that he blushed.

'Not without it did good to the business,' she said deliberately. 'Well, what I mean, not without he brought a little capital, Mr Bell. It wouldn't be right.'

'Just what I thought,' said Mr Bell, and nodded sagely and returned to his glass. He had done all that in the circumstances a man could do. And Mrs Higgins's next remark showed, he thought, that his intentions had an interest for her.

'How soon would you be expecting your windfall, Mr Bell?'

'Two or three weeks,' said Mr Bell airily.

'Well, I wish you luck. And now I must take the bar and let Harold have his supper. Good evening, Mr Bell.'

And Mr Bell was left with his mild and bitter, brooding over his plan.

5

ERNEST

THE next day, being Friday, Jane went out with Ernest Higgins. Ernest was lean and lanky, good-looking but sharp-looking, with small, quick, birdlike eyes. Ernest was in the service of the Underground Railways, and at present was employed at Down Street Station, sometimes on the platform, and sometimes working the lifts. He was a stern, unbending Socialist, and on and under the lapels of his coat were the buttons and badges of various leagues which were sworn to fraternity and bloodshed. He was Organizing Secretary to the Hammersmith Branch of the League of Red Youth. Jane had met him first at Baron's Court Station, when for a short time she took the Ravens' children to kindergarten. Baron's Court is a draughty station, and had helped to embitter Ernest. He put in for a transfer, and was moved to Down Street. Down Street had done him no good, for at Down Street there was too little to do, and he saw too many of the rich. Few people used the station except the residents of Mayfair and persons on their way to the Piccadilly clubs, where, Ernest suspected, they would eat too much.

A peculiar type of military officer was frequent in his lift, and after inquiry Ernest found to his horror that he was daily assisting to and from their food the less opulent members of the Cavalry Club. The station was lonely and had yellow tiles, and every second train flashing through made it look lonelier and yellower. He served no passenger whom he regarded as a worker, and very few who were fit to live; while the trains full of clerks and typists which passed him gave him small comfort, for they were all part of the capitalist system, and the capitalist was an open sore in his tender soul. There were long periods when no one wanted the lift at all; the lift had a little desk for the issue of tickets, and he would sit at this and gloomily read translations of continental works concerned with the iniquity and abolition of the capitalist system.

Down Street confirmed his faith. But what had first set him

against capitalism was a youthful experience of mass-production, which had also been his first experience of work. He had been employed in a toffee factory. For seven hours a day he stood beside a moving band which carried past him an endless chain of toffee-tins upside down. It was Ernest's duty to pick up each tin, reverse it, and replace it the right way up. After some months he decided, very rightly, that this was not a good way of spending the day. He did not know what he had done when he had done it, and whatever it was, he did not feel that that was what he was for. Whenever Ernest talked about this experience Jane felt that he was talking sense, for it sounded like stair-rods and washing-up. But of the rest of his talk there was very little that sounded sense.

Fred said too little when he took a girl out; Ernest said too much. His talk was a strange mixture of Nationalization and Love, neither quite convincing. Yet Jane was ready to be convinced and anxious to be carried away. He had a dream, she could see, however vague, and having a vague dream herself, she liked him for that. And she did her best to picture the misty 'Commonwealth' he spoke of, in which, she gathered, there was to be no more washing-up, or, if there were, it would be done by herself and Mrs Raven alternately; and Florry would love her and she would love Florry, and Florry would enjoy answering the door, because she would be working for the State and not for a brutal private employer. She liked the long words Ernest used, and when he told her she was an 'economic thrall' or a 'woman of the proletariat', she felt important. But she did not know what he meant, and whenever they came down to what he meant, which could not always be avoided, she was baffled. Then she would argue, and this annoyed him.

Tonight she was a little late again, and Ernest was a little wild, as Fred had not been; but it was rather temper than passion, she thought. He was waiting at the corner of the passage by the water-works, under the oak-tree. Ernest preferred this place to the elm, because it was darker; there was a fence on both sides. But it had rained that afternoon, the trees dripped on Ernest, and there was a puddle in the corner. Ernest wore a bowler hat and a dark blue tie with white spots.

'Sorry I'm late, Ernest,' said Jane. 'I was kept.'

'Who by?' said Ernest suspiciously.

'Mrs Raven had company.'

'What right has she got – ' growled Ernest. 'Well, it serves you right. I've told you before you ought to chuck it. A domestic servant's no better than a bond-slave.' If there was one piece of capitalism which angered Ernest more than another, it was the spectacle of a domestic servant.

'I thought you was all for service?' said Jane, dimly recalling some slogan of that kind.

'All for service, and none for profit, I said.'

'Well, that's me,' said Jane. 'God knows I don't get much profit out of it.'

'The service of the many, not of the few,' snapped Ernest.

'Well, I dunno, I'd sooner serve a few people I know than a lot of people I don't.'

'You've got a *bourgeois* psychology, Jane. That's what's the matter with you.'

'You're standing in a puddle,' said Jane.

They moved away from the puddle and Jane said, 'What's that, Ernest?'

'What's what?'

'What you said I'd got. The *borjwaw* thing.'

'You don't think proletarian. You think like the bosses. You ought to say to yourself, night and morning, "Boss is boss, and class is class, and proletariat is proletariat. And I'm proletariat." But you don't. They've got you, body and soul.'

'Who's got me, Ernest?' said Jane, knitting her brows.

'The bosses. Body and soul.'

'I don't see that, Ernest. I like Mrs Raven,' she added irrelevantly.

'There you go again. There's no liking between class and class. That's how they dope you. You've got to be class-conscious, Jane.'

'What's that, Ernest?'

'Class is class,' said Ernest, 'and ever more shall be so. Your boss is one class and you're another. And her class is against your class. We're out to down Capitalism, and the *bourgeois* is the parasite of the capitalist state, and he that is not for us is against us. See?'

'That don't sound sense,' said Jane. 'You might as well say that he that is not against us is for us.'

'So he is,' said Ernest incautiously.

'Well, I don't see that,' said Jane. 'You might as well say that a man who wasn't knocking you down was in love with you.'

'You don't know what you're talking about,' said Ernest shortly.

'That's why I'm asking you,' said Jane, knitting her brows. 'Are my bosses *borjwaw*?'

'That's right. Parasites.'

'Well, Mr Raven works for the Government. I thought you wanted everyone to work for the Government.'

'A Workers' Government. He don't produce nothing.'

'Well, they've produced three children, and that's more than many can say.'

'Capitalist spawn,' said Ernest.

'Come to that, Ernest, what do *you* produce?'

Ernest was silent. It was difficult to say exactly what he produced at Down Street tube station. A little weary of argument, he remembered suddenly that he was by way of courting Jane, and that, in the heat of Socialism, he had forgotten to kiss her. He put his arms round her and kissed her violently and long, more violently than ever before – perhaps because she had teased him and provoked him with her arguments, and this was a way of showing her what was what.

And it has to be admitted that, high-minded as he was politically and moved by the noblest aspirations for the betterment of man, Ernest had not, where women were concerned, that purity of thought which might have been expected.

Jane yielded herself to this hot embrace, but, hanging passive in his arms, was not quite sure what she thought of it. This indeed, was how she had hoped that Fred would hug her, and it was certainly more like the pictures, but she wondered if it was Love's Bliss and decided that it was not. After a little she withdrew her lips, breathless, and when he pursued them still turned her face from side to side, innocently trying to escape him. But this, she found, inflamed him more; she struggled, his bowler hat fell off, but at last he held her closer than before. She was afraid now that she liked it, but felt that she should not.

A heavy drop from the oak-tree fell on the back of Ernest's neck, and he released her.

'You ought not to kiss me like that,' said Jane seriously.

'Why not?'

'It isn't right'; and suddenly she laughed.

'What are you laughing at?'

'Would you say an artist was a *borjwaw* – a painter, I mean?'

'Artists are *bourgeois* if they have a capitalist mentality,' said Ernest, 'but there'll be room for them in the Workers' State.'

Jane chuckled again. She was thinking of Mr Bryan and wondering what Ernest would say if he knew that she had been kissed by a *borjwaw*.

He divined that she was laughing at him, and took a crushing hold of her again. And so they stood, locked together in the muddy corner.

The tree dripped softly upon them, and soon there began a gentle patter in the leaves, for the rain had returned. Ernest, not content with his conquests, began to paw about. Then Jane whispered an angry word, and thrust him away, for it was only yesterday that she had spoken to Lily about letting boys paw her about.

'Leave me alone,' she said, setting her hat straight. 'Let's go to the pictures.'

'I don't want to go to the pictures.'

'Well, if you can't behave yourself – Besides, it's raining.'

The rain was gathering force, and Ernest unwillingly consented, being indeed on fire. But he picked up his bowler hat and walked decorously beside her to the picture-house, explaining on the way the general arguments for the Nationalization of the Means of Production, Distribution, and Exchange. Jane said nothing, for she was wishing secretly that they had stayed under the tree, and she was shocked at herself for wishing it. She felt naughty and weak and trembly, and she took Ernest's arm. Ernest pressed it to his side and said, 'What I want you to get into your head, little Jane, is this idea of the Socialist Commonwealth. Sort of big brotherhood, you see.'

Jane wondered what would be the position of the little sisters.

The picture-house was a brand-new structure of great magnificence, the kind of building which one imagines that Dido built for a temple at Carthage. It had a Palladian façade in shiny green stone, lit with electric torches in black. Far down the main road it glared like a fire. The entrance-hall had a tessellated floor, a Moorish roof in gold, and innumerable flunkeys in silver and dark blue. Jane grandly presented her pass, they were given two one-and-threepennies, and passed up a long staircase carpeted in lush red velvet. Ernest kissed her at the corner, but this was a gentle, Socialist kiss, and quite nice, Jane thought. But she said firmly, 'Now, that's enough.'

The auditorium, if such it could be called, was like a cathedral, a cathedral designed by a drunken architect after reading the *Arabian Nights*. Far up in either wall was a towering green arch, as if the drunkard had intended to build a transept, but, forgetting the transept, had filled in the arch with black marble. And down both sides ran massive columns in the same green stone, supporting with smaller arches an imaginary clerestory. The roof was a vault of blue mosaic, and in it, when the lights were up, shone a million stars. The vast proscenium arch, flanked by two alabaster pillars, had three sets of velvet curtains which rolled aside in succession to reveal the name of the film, the censor's licence, and the names of the principal performers. On the north side was a great organ; there was an orchestra of thirty-two, with two grand pianos.

In this temple of the 'Shadow Drama' sat two or three thousand humble people, inhaling romance and American culture, sucking sweets, holding hands, and thoroughly happy. For their one-and-threepence the two young things had slip-up fauteuils in plush, more comfortable than the most expensive stalls in the richest theatre. The principal drama of the evening had just begun, and they followed to their seats an invisible handmaid with an electric eye which led them miraculously through the darkness like the pillar of fire.

Ernest was impressed and silent. He despised the pictures, not because they were bad art but because they were capitalist art. True, they made the workers happy, but even this annoyed him faintly, for it was only one more subtle device of the capitalist for the drugging of the proletariat.

A woman behind them, who had seen the picture before, explained to her friend both what was happening and what was about to happen, so they were able to follow the drama with ease. Ernest saw on the screen a young blonde woman in capitalist dress who seemed to be the heroine. 'All this,' thought Ernest, 'will have to go.' The young woman was moping over her childhood's toys, which she took out of an old chest. She was kneeling on the floor and now and then rolled down her cheeks a hot tear of glycerine for the toys reminded her of Richard Lee, the young Britisher who had been her nursery playmate. But most she wept over a doll in sailor's dress, for it looked like Richard. But Richard was in England, and Nancy was at a whaling-station in Alaska, and her father wanted her to marry a dark man named Samuel Siggs, who held a mortgage on the house. Her father was a retired whaler, and a Quaker, and now he was old and ill, so Nancy wished to please him. But suddenly the sailor-doll seemed to speak, and it said:

'*I am coming to you , Nancy.*'

The doll swelled and grew to life-size, till it filled the whole screen, and the woman behind Ernest said that really you could have sworn it was speaking. Then the doll grew more and more like the photograph of Richard which Nancy had in a locket round her neck, and Jane said wasn't it wonderful the way they did these things. But Ernest was wondering whether he should hold Jane's hand and how he should do it, for she was sitting remotely in the far corner of her seat. The girl in front of him had her head on her friend's shoulder, and he wished that Jane would put her head on his shoulder; but Jane appeared to have views about behaviour, and he was afraid that he had gone too far in the passage. So Nancy decided that she would not marry Siggs, whatever happened; her father was angry, and went to bed very ill, but she was adamant, and thought of Richard. Ernest put out his hand cautiously, but could not find Jane's hand, so he laid his hand on Jane's knee; Jane moved her knee and the hand fell off. Nancy's father sent for Siggs, and gave him his daughter's hand in marriage. Jane nudged Ernest and said, 'There's father.' Ernest said, 'I know'; but Jane said, 'My father, I mean.' And, looking over to the right, Ernest saw dimly Mr Bell in the orchestra, playing the cello. He was playing the 'Preislied' from the Meistersinger, though Jane did not know that; but she knew that it was the love-tune, because Nancy was thinking of Richard again. And when she nudged Ernest he had caught hold of her hand which now he was holding tightly under the arm of the seat between them. Jane's hand was cool and small, but Ernest's was hot and damp. Two days later Richard sailed into the harbour, and asked for Nancy's hand in marriage. Her father said, 'Thee hast not harpooned a whale, lad,' for the man who married his daughter must have harpooned a whale, or he was not a man. Ernest liked this part, because it showed up the *bourgeois* Richard who had never harpooned a whale, and was not a worker.

But Richard said he would harpoon a whale, and go with the expedition. Then the old man said, 'But thee is not a Quaker, lad.' But Richard was ready for anything, and said he would be a Quaker. Ernest's hand grew hotter and hotter, Jane's was clammy, and her wrist was sore against the metal arm of the seat. She tried to draw her hand away, but Ernest held on, so she drew his hand gently on to her knee, which was more comfortable, though Ernest took this as a mark of affection. Then Siggs followed Nancy into a wood, and said if she would not be his he would do something about the mortgage, and that would upset her poor sick father. Nancy bit her lips, but she said she would not be his. And all the time Richard was creeping up closer, behind trees, because an old retainer had followed Siggs into the wood, and then run off and told Richard. But Siggs did not know this, so he said that if Nancy would not be his she would lose her honour, so she might as well be his and save trouble. And Nancy said she would not lose her honour for anyone, but she looked worried, and bit her lips again. And Ernest moved his knee an inch or two, and put his knee against Jane's knee.

Jane thought she would move her knee away, and then she thought, 'Well, what does it matter?' and left her knee where it was. So at the last minute Richard came up and knocked Siggs down. Siggs was discomfited, and Richard kissed Nancy and made faces, and Ernest's knee grew still more affectionate; but the next night Siggs and a gang knocked Richard on the head and hid him in the hold in irons, and the next morning the ship sailed for the whaleries. Then there was an interval and the lights went up.

During the interval Ernest bought a shilling box of chocolates, and they both looked round to see if there was anyone they knew in the seats behind them. Jane tried to catch her father's eye, and thought that he was looking more melancholy than usual.

When the lights went out again it was the whaling expedition, Jane's father played whale music, and Ernest made no bones about it. He put his arm through Jane's and held her hand, and his knee against her knee, and his foot against her foot; and so they sat in the darkness, knee to knee and toe to toe, but Ernest's hand was very hot, and Jane's was a little sticky from the chocolates. Siggs, who was the mate, kept Richard hidden in a small cabin in the hold and fed him every other day on little bits of bread. Richard grew very wan and constantly bit his lips. But he kept thinking of Nancy, and Jane's father played the Preislied. Then there was a mutiny against Siggs, Richard was let out, and Siggs was put in the hold instead; but Richard saw that he had the best of everything. Jane said, 'Change hands, I've got the cramp,' and took another chocolate. They sighted whales and Richard harpooned a whale at the first attempt. Ernest sniffed at this, because Richard was a blackleg and did not know his job. But he did not feel strongly about it, for he was thinking of Jane. He leaned his head towards Jane and touched her hair. Jane was sleepy from the smoky air, and she thought she might as well be friendly as not, so she leaned her head against Ernest's head. It was very uncomfortable, and Ernest had pins and needles in the leg, but he would not move. The whale was pursued and killed and cut up, and Jane's father's forehead was shiny from the energy of the music, but Jane did not take in this part of the story, for she was thinking. She thought that this knee business was a strange way of love-making, but still it was a new experience, though it did not thrill her, like Mr Bryan's kiss. She remembered that Ernest did not know anything about Fred, and that Fred knew nothing about Ernest, and she thought that perhaps she was on the way to trouble. She let her head fall on to Ernest's shoulder, because that was more comfortable; but Ernest thought it was passion, and gripped her hand. She wondered again if this was Love's Bliss, but thought not; she was afraid of Ernest, and drawn by Ernest, and he made her feel naughty, but perhaps that was all.

On the way back to the whaling-station there was a great storm and Richard saved the ship. But during the storm Siggs escaped from the hold and swam ashore. He rode home on horseback and told Nancy that Richard was dead. Nancy's father was now at the point of death, and to ease his last moments she said she would marry Siggs. Ernest whispered, 'Do you like me, Jane?' and Jane said, 'Yes,' but she added, 'a little bit.' When Richard had saved the ship he found out that Siggs had escaped. He guessed that the man's intentions were not honourable, and galloped through the rain to the meeting-house. Just at the same time Nancy was driving through the rain to her wedding, and so much rain music made Mr Bell hotter than ever. But Richard had farther to go, and the Quaker wedding was begun without him. Jane was very sleepy, her head ached from the whale music, and she closed her eyes. But just as Nancy was biting her lips in an agony because the time had come for her to say the fatal words which would make her Mrs Siggs, Richard was seen staggering through the tempest up the drive, for his horse had been tripped up by an accomplice of Siggs. Nancy threw a glance of hatred at her bridegroom, and a tree was blown down just in front of Richard. Ernest had no sympathy with the *bourgeois* Richard, so he closed his eyes too, and Jane fell asleep. Richard spurned the tree and went on; Nancy opened her mouth to say the first fatal word, and then Richard's face was seen at the window. Nancy began to shut her mouth, but just in time Richard smashed the window and entered the meeting-house. He told the congregation about Siggs, everyone was indignant, Siggs made faces, and it was arranged that Richard should marry Nancy there and then. When Nancy's father heard that Richard had harpooned a whale and married his daughter he became a new man, and left his bed at once, for he had never really liked Siggs. Richard said he would pay off the mortgage with his share of the whale, and their lips met in a long kiss. Mr Bell played the love-tune, the great organ joined in, and Ernest opened his eyes. He nudged Jane, Jane woke up, and they looked at the long kiss together. The organ played Mendelssohn's Wedding March, and Ernest looked at Jane and said, 'You and me, eh?'

The lights were up, and Jane looked at Ernest, considering. He was good-looking, certainly, though he had small eyes and a greedy mouth, and his hands were damp. She thought this must be her first proposal of marriage, and felt kindly towards Ernest. But the strange thing was that at that moment she thought of Mr Bryan. She said, 'Well, I dunno, Ernest.'

A voice behind Jane said nastily, 'May I pass, please?' They stood up hurriedly, very stiff, and Ernest rubbed his leg where the pins and needles were. Ernest wanted to walk home by the river, but that would have taken them through the passage, so Jane chose King Street and River Road, though that was longer. Ernest was annoyed and said nothing at all till they came to the little gate in the fence beside the wharf which was Jane's front door. Then he cheered up; the rain had stopped, no one was about, and he prepared to kiss her. Jane was just wondering whether she would let him kiss her again, and thinking that perhaps she would not, for she was enjoying a new sensation of power, when they heard in the still night strange sounds of music.

'The love-tune!' whispered Ernest, who found this miraculous.

'The cornet!' whispered Jane, astonished.

She slipped through the little gate and on to the moonlit wharf, Ernest behind her, and softly they picked their way through the litter of packing-cases, barbed wire, corrugated iron, and the wreckage of old boats, and stood looking down on the *Blackbird*.

On the main-hatch of the *Blackbird* facing the river, sat Mr Bell, with his cornet, trying to play the 'Preislied' to the Hammersmith stars, baying the young moon with Wagner. He played in a muffled way, as soft as a cornet can play. The sound was weird and melancholy, and to Jane the whole scene was frightening, for she had never seen her father do such a thing before. Was this an indiscreet tribute to Mrs Higgins? Was it madness, or was it what?

'Well, father?' she said with an anxious air.

Mr Bell stopped playing, turned his head an inch or two, and said over his shoulder:

'I've lost my job, Jane.'

Then he put the cornet to his lips again, and took up the tune exactly where he had left it.

Jane put her finger to her lips, and waved Ernest away. And Ernest went away quietly without his kiss. He knew the meaning of those terrible words.

6

THE PLAN

Mr Bell had several excellent reasons for believing that he knew which horse would win the Derby, and on the Sunday following his dismissal he put them to a convincing test.

As to that dismissal, he had shown, it appeared, a British dignity and independence. It was a long, rambling story about the Musicians' Union and a failure to pay subscriptions, a friend of the manager's who played the cello, something about a B Flat, smartness of appearance, Mr Bell's enemy the oboe-player, what the musical director said, and the management making a fuss about the girls' free seats.

'A trumped-up job,' Mr Bell thought, and he was not going to stand it. He had a week's notice, but he scorned it, and the week's wages too. He would not even go back and play on the Saturday.

'I took my instruments,' he said, 'and left the building.'

The girls applauded his nobility and firmness, but Jane urged him to go back on the Saturday and finish his engagement. Not for the money, she said, but for fear he should get a bad name for desertion.

Jane was feeling a little guilty because she had taken Ernest in on her free pass, which was intended only for herself and Lily. She had known it was wrong, but it gave her such an importance. And perhaps, she thought, it had been the last straw. She confessed her fault.

'Very likely,' said Mr Bell airily. 'They're capable of anything. *Cassus belli*, I dare say, but they had it in for me, you see. Don't you worry, Jane. I told you it was trumped-up.'

Jane was relieved. But Mr Bell, like other weak men, could be a mule when he wished. He would not go back.

'They'll be sorry for this,' he said. 'Besides,' he added grandly, 'I've other things to do.'

And indeed he was busy maturing his Plan.

On this Sunday afternoon they had the first swim of the year.

Mr Bell rowed them upstream in the leaky boat, decently draped in towels, and Lily trailing her feet over the stern. They talked compassionately of the plight of the picture house, bereft of Mr Bell over the week-end; and soon it seemed that Mr Bell was teaching the whole cinema industry a lesson. Jane had a vision of that manager crawling on to the barge and imploring Mr Bell to bring back his cello. Salary, what he would.

They reached the Eyot about slack water, and Mr Bell rested, waiting for the ebb. The river was busy with holiday traffic, loaded pleasure-steamers ploughing up to Kew, sailing-dinghies, eights and single-scullers, hired skiffs for lovers and noisy bands of youths, rich, rapid launches trailing large red ensigns and bound for Hampton Court, and fat, full motor-boats at one-and-six a journey, which the girls despised because they did not know the rules of the road, and blew their horns at sailing-boats. The Sailing Club were holding a race, but without guns because it was Sunday, and Mr Bale's big *Violet*, the first back from the mark-boat at Barnes, came running softly home before a light breeze from the west, close under the Surrey bank.

'Silly mutt,' said Lily. 'He'd get more wind in the middle.'

'He gets the stream with him there before the tide turns,' said Jane. 'I wish we could sail in the races, father.'

'Not in this old bundle of leaks, thank you,' said Lily.

'One day, my dears,' said Mr Bell dreamily, 'perhaps you'll have a better boat – as fine a boat as there is in these waters.' And he fixed his eyes on the fleecy skies as if it were from there that the desirable vessel might be expected to approach.

The *Violet* came abreast of them, a whispering ripple at her bows, and Jane, try how she would, began to blush; for Mr Bale had a man with him, and he looked like Mr Bryan. Mr Bryan saw her, nodded, and smiled with his eyes.

'Look at Jane blushing!' said Lily wickedly. 'Who's your fancy-boy, Poppy? That why you want to go yachting?'

'Quiet, Lily,' said Mr Bell, for whatever he might be about the morals of his daughters, he was stern upon matters of taste.

Jane said nothing, as angry with herself as with Lily. If forty Freds and forty Ernests came sailing by together, she told herself, they would not make her blush. She did not blush when she called

Mr Bryan in his bed; then why should she make a scarlet fool of herself when she saw him in public across a river? Since that birthday morning Mr Bryan had scarcely spoken to her, and once more she determined not to think of Mr Bryan.

Stealthily and almost imperceptibly the ebb had begun to run, and they drifted down along the island, where swans nested, herons fished, and moorhens crept in and out among the reeds. Now Jane caught her father's arm and pointed excitedly. A bright bird shot from the clay bank under the willows, sped low above the water, and disappeared, a flash of blue among the osiers.

'What's that?' said Mr Bell.

'Kingfisher,' said Jane, her eyes shining, her blushes forgotten.

'Kingfisher – so it was,' said Mr Bell. 'Well, I never! In London!'

'I've seen him twice,' said Jane.

Lily did not see the kingfisher at all, being occupied with a boatful of rude boys, who were waiting, as she knew, to see her remove the towel.

Jane looked about her proudly, at the sunny river, which belonged to her and had a kingfisher, at the far white sail where Mr Bryan was. 'We won't go to Liverpool, father,' she said.

Since the job was lost there had again been vague talk of Liverpool and finding work there.

'It may not be necessary,' said Mr Bell mysteriously, and again regarding the sky. 'If a certain proposition turns out as I expect it won't be necessary. Well, in with you, girls.'

Jane slipped off her towel, took one step to the stern, and was in the water. The watching boys saw as much of her pretty form as she had seen of the kingfisher's. But Lily was kinder, and made a great business of it, poising and balancing and shaking her golden head in the sun, then dipping her toes in the water, embracing herself and exclaiming against the cold, and in no way seeking to conceal from the public that her figure was rounded and young. She was an inch or two taller than Jane, but not quite so slim; and Jane said that she would be fat at forty. The rude boys shouted, but Lily did not seem to know they were there. Then Jane, unrefined in revenge, cried, 'Come on, Lily, and less of the cold meat show!' The boys tittered, Mr Bell said 'Go on, Lily, you're making an

exhibition of yourself,' and Lily, disconcerted, fell flat on the
water, and stung her stomach and legs. The fickle boys, who had
thought her an angel, now thought she was silly, and rowed away,
jeering.

The girls were strong swimmers, and swam down easily three
hundred yards to the barge. They climbed up the ladder and once
or twice dived in again, Lily with less of a fuss than before. Mr
Bell watched proudly from the boat, and 'Swim like fishes,' he
said to himself. 'Fine girls!' Mr Bryan, walking home from the
Sailing Club, found a row of small boys peeping through holes
in the fence, and took a peep himself. And the nymph with the
graceful shoulders and the curving sides and slender wet limbs, he
recognized with surprise as the servant who gave him his tea in the
morning. For, very properly, no doubt, we do not think of domestic servants as persons with figures. Jane dived and disappeared,
Mr Bryan waited a moment, then remembered he was a gentleman
and walked on.

When they had dressed and were drying their hair in the sun on
deck Mr Bell came up through the hatch with a long cutting from a
newspaper and sat down importantly between them. He wore an
old blue reefer coat and grey flannel trousers with a hole in the
seat.

'Now, girls,' he said, 'pay attention. I have here a list of the
entries for the Derby. Some of the horses will, of course, be
scratched. But I want you to go carefully down the list, pick your
own winners for me, and write them down separately. Don't say a
word. Here's a pencil.'

Jane said, 'We don't know nothing about them, father.'

'Don't matter. Go by the names. It's what all the fine ladies do,
I believe. But do it very carefully. It's important.'

Lily said, 'Rot, Dad!' and laughed.

But Mr Bell said, 'It's no laughing matter, Lily. I may say I rely
a good deal on your judgement. And you don't know how much
may depend on it – for all of us.'

His voice trembled as he said this and Jane thought he was
going to cry. Even Lily was sobered. They put their wet heads
together, and gravely, wonderingly, read down the long list.

Lily was first. 'I've got it!' she cried, but Mr Bell put his finger on his lips; she wrote down her winner, and waited for Jane. Jane was as slow in choosing a winner as Lily had been in taking the plunge. She felt herself the mother of great events and hovered uncertainly between this attractive animal and that; between Mulberry and Bull's Eye, West Wind, Brian Boru, and Prudence. So many of the creatures had names which seemed of good omen to her or her family. Then far down in the list she saw a name which she had hurried past before, and knew at once that this must be her father's winner, if not perhaps her own.

With shaking fingers Mr Bell unfolded the slips of paper.

Jane had written 'Black Prince'.

Lily had written 'The Black Prince'.

Lily crowed, but Jane was silent, watching her father's face, which was transfigured with ecstasy and awe, as if in the presence of some religious portent.

'That settles it,' he said, grasping their hands. 'Thank you my dears. This is a miracle.'

They both felt proud of themselves for having taken part in a miracle, but Lily said 'What's the big idea, Dad?'

Then, solemnly, slowly, with many interruptions from Lily, Mr Bell expounded the big idea.

For a long time now, it appeared, the fingers of Fate, all eight of them, had been pointing to the Black Prince. Many weeks before, when Mr Bell was playing the cello, the Double Bass, in return for some small kindness, had whispered during the interval that the Black Prince was a good thing for the Derby. The strange appropriateness of this horse to one who lived in the *Blackbird* and coveted the Black Swan, had attracted him at once. On inquiry he learned that the Black Prince belonged to a man named Bell, who lived in Liverpool. Two weeks later, in conversation with old Andrew, the ferryman, who had a married sister who had inside information, he heard that the Black Prince was considered by the knowing to be a dark horse.

But he was not the man, as he hastily explained, to be led by mere gossip and favourable omens. He had looked up the history of the horse, and got some valuable information from, among others, the Second Violin, who knew, perhaps, more about horses than any other member of the orchestra. (The Strings had always been the racing set.) It appeared that the Black Prince had never actually won a race, and had only once been placed, after the leading horse had been disqualified. But in every case there had been some peculiar circumstances which had prevented the Prince from showing his true form, and accounted for his failure without doing him discredit. He had not had the right weights or the right weather, the right jockey or the right distance. The horse was believed to be a stayer, but his owner had foolishly, or perhaps cunningly, entered him for short races only. He was by Edward out of Cleopatra, and his sire came of good staying stock, while his dam had had a fine turn of speed in her day. The horse stood unnoticed, with many others, at a hundred to one, but Mr Bell, for all his experience, was still inclined to put more faith in long-priced outsiders than in favourites.

Then, like a voice from Heaven, Steve Merry had spoken. Steve had sent him, not as his 'Nap', but as a 'Gentleman's Long-Price Gamble', the name of the Black Prince. This was the judgement of reason and experience at one with the hinting of the stars. And now, to crown all, had come the tremendous double omen of Lily and Jane. It no longer seemed possible to Mr Bell that the Black Prince should not win the blue riband of the turf. He had the same certainty of conviction, he said, which had inspired him long ago to invest in Eurydice. It was unmistakable.

'In spite of everything, girls,' he said, 'I believe I've got a star.'

'Of course you have, Dad,' said Lily fondly, stroking his hand.

But Jane wondered secretly if perhaps her father was a little mad.

And now came the big idea. This gift of the gods, this crown of all Mr Bell's labours on the turf, was not to be wasted. He was tired, he said, of pottering about with half-crowns. He proposed to risk all upon a single throw. 'What all?' – thought Jane, and 'We haven't got much to risk,' said Lily.

'Well, I happen to have at my disposal,' said Mr Bell, 'the sum of a hundred pounds.'

The girls gasped, Lily crowed and exploded with questions. A hundred pounds! Wherever from? But Mr Bell held up his hand for silence, and continued with the big idea, as if a hundred pounds could be picked up anywhere. The big idea was, simply, to stake the whole of the hundred pounds upon the Black Prince.

'All or nothing,' said Mr Bell grandly. 'I'm tired of pottering.' It was a fortnight to the Derby, and in a week, he was sure, there would be thousands after the Black Prince. So the thing must be done at once, before the odds came down. He would do it to-morrow. The odds were still a hundred to one, and a hundred pounds invested in this manner would bring in ten thousand pounds.

Lily gave a whoop: 'No work for me then!' But Jane was silent, anxiously considering this stupendous lunacy. She knew very well that she ought to disapprove, the one sane member of the family, and yet the sheer grandeur of the plan impressed and appealed to her. It would have been bold enough before Friday, but now, with her father out of work, and no money in sight but her own little earnings, it was heroic, staggering. That Friday night, sitting on her father's bed, she had talked over plans of a very different kind with him. Lily must go to work. She was eighteen now. The kind Government would have placed her at a milliner's at the end of her trade scholarship, but Lily was lazy and had backed out. Well, now, if it was not too late, she must go, or find something else. As for Jane, she had hoped to escape from the Ravens, come home, and look after the barge, which Lily would never do properly. But now she would have to stick it. Mr Bell must look for work, apply for the dole, and between-times do the housekeeping. At the worst, there would be Liverpool and the well-off aunt.

And all the time, thought Jane, a little hurt, the sly old man must have had in his head this Plan, and perhaps in his pocket this mysterious sum of money. She could not imagine where that had come from, and at present she was afraid to ask.

But Lily and her father were deep in the future, and busily spending the ten thousand pounds. To begin with, they would all go to the Derby and see the horse win. Then Lily would learn dancing and run a school of dancing, which did not sound like work but would mean many young men. They would buy this boat that Mr Bell had spoken of, but also a long white launch with a noiseless engine and a huge red ensign. The *Blackbird* would be done up and used for week-ends. Perhaps Lily could turn it into one of these night-clubs. Mr Bell confessed that he might marry again, and perhaps buy a public-house. He looked sideways at Jane, and so did Lily. Jane, thought Lily, would marry her fancy-fellow in Mr Bale's boat, and have several babies. But not she, Lily – no fear.

'What else shall we do?' said Lily at last, and really they could not think what to do with their money.

Jane, listening to them, found that she too was deep in her own little dream, and, pinching herself, decided that it was time that she was a mother to these children.

'Where does the hundred pounds come from, father?'

'Never you mind, my dear,' said Mr Bell darkly. 'Call it a nest-egg.'

'Well, ought you to put it all in one basket, father? It don't seem sense. Why don't you keep some of it back, just in case – '

'No hedging!' said Lily gallantly, and her father smiled his approval.

'I wouldn't say anything if you were in work, father. But you know what it is – '

'After the Derby I shan't want work,' said Mr Bell. 'No, Jane, Lily's right. It's all or nothing this time. All or nothing. Look at it this way,' he went on reasonably. 'Say I keep ten pounds back – that's ninety pounds. Ten pounds at the odds is a thousand. So you've lost a thousand pounds for the sake of ten. Well, what's ten pounds? That's the way I look at it. It's spoiling the ship for a ha'porth of tar.'

Jane could think of no answer to this. But she wondered again if her father was queer. She studied him fondly, but he did not look ill. Indeed, he sat up straight and proud, with a new kind of dignity upon him.

'Jane's got cold feet,' said Lily.

'I'm sorry if you don't like my plan,' said Mr Bell, becoming suddenly pathetic again. 'I thought you'd like it, Jane. I'm doing it for you.'

'But I do, I *do*!' cried Jane, and flung her arms about him, and kissed his stubbly chin. And from that moment she was lost. After all, it was a very wonderful plan. For a poor man, out of work, with two grown daughters, to risk his nest-egg on a single gamble, had a touch of greatness which could be respected. It was the kind of thing which was done on the pictures, and done successfully.

If Charlie Chaplin backed the Black Prince it would certainly win. Comforting phrases in capital letters came back to her: her father was *Dicing With Destiny, Putting All To The Hazard, Challenging Fate*; and she felt better. Perhaps he was right, he had a star; perhaps she had a star; perhaps even Lily had a star. And it was this Black Prince which was ordained to carry them from Pawnery to Queenery. Certainly, she was sick and tired of stair-rods and the scullery, and longed to be free – free to look after her own home properly, shop when she liked and sail when she liked, go out with Ernest or up the canal with Fred. And now she began to feel herself ungrateful to her father, and looked with a sort of awe at the heroic little man who had conceived this marvel, and sat like Napoleon with his arms across his heart, gazing at the sunset with prophetic eyes.

The sun had gone behind the waterworks, the *Blackbird* was in shadow, but all the western sky wore a lovely flush, and the clouds over Richmond swam like coral in the water. Silent, the Bell family admired the most wonderful of moving pictures, and across that rosy screen they saw the Black Prince galloping to victory.

That night, because of their great wealth, they opened the tin of sardines which Jane had been keeping for a rainy day, and in thick tea they drank the health of their horse. The next day Mr Bell had a fat letter from Liverpool. He went out in the morning, and was away all day, and in the evening announced that all was in order. All the week they grew richer and richer. There was no more talk of looking for work, and Lily and Mr Bell became so opulent in their habits of life while Jane was working at the Ravens' that her careful housekeeping collapsed. Rather than shatter the great illusion in this anxious fortnight she went secretly to Mrs Higgins and borrowed money. Meanwhile the future expanded daily. Lily talked now of a theatrical career, and, as for Mr Bell, Jane thought that if it were not for Mrs Higgins he would buy not the Black Swan but the Savoy Hotel. However, he found time to varnish the dinghy, and spoke now and then of making a new window.

Jane asked Lily, and Lily thought that their father was all there. She thought it was the most sensible thing he had ever done.

On the Thursday or Friday a terrible thought came to Jane.

'What happens, father,' she said, 'if the Black Prince is scratched?'

'He won't be,' said Napoleon confidently.

'Yes, I know. But supposing he was?'

'He wouldn't run.'

'And what would happen to the money then?'

'I should lose it,' said Mr Bell slowly. 'I hadn't thought of that.' He touched his worried brow impatiently. 'But it will be all right, Jane. You'll see.'

7

THE BLACK PRINCE

THE rain depressed everybody except Mr Bell, who said that the Black Prince would be favoured by the heavy going.

Almost any Englishman can steal a day off for the Derby, if he gives his mind to it, and here they all were in the rickety taxi, Jane and Lily and Mr Bell, Fred (unloading at Hammersmith again) and Mrs Higgins, and even Ernest, riding to Epsom in the pouring rain.

It was a shame, the rain, for none of them had seen the Derby before, and, for parties like this, the going there is three parts of the fun. Mrs Higgins had been so pleased by Mr Bell's invitation that she had offered to pay for the transport. So they had hired Mr Ewer and his taxi for the day. Mr Ewer lived just round the corner, and it was like Mrs Higgins to do a neighbour a good turn; but Ernest thought they would never reach Epsom, and said so. Mr Ewer was another of these unfortunates, whom Ernest despised, in spite of his love for the oppressed worker, an inefficient, querulous little man who could do nothing right and had more grievances than he had teeth. Mr Ewer's taxi was like Mr Ewer, and seemed always about to fall to pieces. The roof leaked, the windows rattled, there was a constant smell of petrol, and from below came horrid grindings and thumpings, as if the bowels of the old machine were complaining. With the heavy load and the frequent stopping the engine became very hot. Steam spouted and hot water spat from the radiator. Then Mr Ewer would stop, to the fury of the traffic, put in his head and say, 'I never knew such a thing to happen before,' and go off to borrow cold water from a cottage, while a crowd would collect to watch the geyser.

The race-goers sat uncomfortable and stiff in the stuffy cab, listening to the ceaseless patter of the rain on the roof, and dodging the drips. Mrs Higgins sat in one corner, Jane in the other, and Lily between them. Mr Bell and Ernest sat bolt upright on the small seats opposite, and Fred was outside beside the driver. Mr Bell and

Jane wore tarpaulin coats, and the smell of these at least made a contrast to the petrol.

Ernest had been a wet blanket from the first. He could never enjoy a human entertainment in a human way, but must always look at it with what he called the 'proletarian eye', or 'from the workers' viewpoint'. Almost everything he saw through the cab windows reminded him of the need for the Nationalization of the Means of Production, Distribution, and Exchange. And he distrusted the whole institution of racing for a number of reasons. It brought the 'classes' together, it made for 'irregularity of income', it was 'capitalist', it encouraged the workers 'to approve of capital and to desire it', and by giving them pleasure 'doped and deluded' them, so that they forgot about their 'wrongs' and the 'Socialist Commonwealth'. So he had joined the party as a favour, and sat with his nose very high in the air. Nevertheless, Jane's knees were between his, and he pressed them endearingly and firmly, till Lily said suddenly, 'Ernest's playing "footie".'

Ernest glared at her, and relaxed the pressure of the knee which was next to her. Jane gave Lily a reproving dig with her elbow, but Lily felt better. She was still a little sore because no friend of hers was of the party. She had been afraid that most of her young loves would not mix well with it, and her one staid admirer could not get the day off. So at the last moment Fred had been invited. Lily did not like Ernest, and from what she had seen of Fred in his oilskins she thought he was a 'pudding'.

Jane was not too comfortable because this was the first time that Fred and Ernest had seen or heard of each other. Fred sat silent outside on the floor, thinking about Jane and hoping that the stuck-up fellow in the cab belonged to Lily.

Mrs Higgins was hot and puzzled. From certain dark remarks of Mr Bell she had gathered that this expedition was in some way connected with herself and his intentions. But she could not understand how Mr Bell could hope to get from the Derby a windfall which would be worth her while.

Only Mr Bell was perfectly content, serene and confident, the torch of a great faith shining in his eyes. Jane thought she had never seen him look so happy. He spoke now in deliberate, kingly tones. He looked at his party benignly, pleased with the pleasure he was giving them, and not to be ruffled by the rain or Ernest or the boiling motor-cab. He wore an old bowler hat perched jauntily on one side of his head; somewhere in the *Blackbird*'s litter he had found an old pair of field-glasses with one eye-piece broken, and these were slung about the tarpaulin with a double length of tarred string. From time to time he consulted one of his bundle of newspapers, chuckling over those which in their forecasts had made no mention whatever of the Black Prince (it was just as well that everyone had not discovered his secret), but delighted, nevertheless, by 'Tydeus' of the *Glass*, who said that he would not be surprised if the son of Cleopatra proved a happy speculation for a place. The faithful 'Seer' had said on Sunday that if the going was heavy the Oxbridge colt might easily reverse the unfavourable impression which his defeats at Newmarket, Doncaster, Sandown, and Kempton Park had aroused. The *West London Gazette* selected him for third place. No one went so far as to suggest that the Black Prince would win. But Mr Bell did not care. No one had expected Eurydice to win.

A long, rich limousine swept up beside the cab and halted in the crowd. A lordly chauffeur lay at the wheel, and behind him they saw a nest of gay young faces, white skins, and flashing teeth, military moustaches, pearl necklaces, cigars. The sight gave pleasure to Mrs Higgins, who loved all mankind (except the Temperance folk), and to the Bell family, who had no envy and expected in a short time to be rich themselves. The girls stared and tried to pick up an idea or two for clothes.

But Ernest, his lip curling, said, 'See them toads?'

'Toads?' said Mrs Higgins, as if she did not understand. She was fond of Ernest, but wished he would keep his politics to himself.

'That girl's furs,' said Ernest, 'would keep me alive for a year.'

'Perhaps they're doing more good where they are,' said Lily.

'Well, I'm as good as they are, aren't I?'

'You may be as good,' said Lily, 'but I wish you was as pretty.'

Ernest scowled and his mother made an effort for peace.

'What's the matter with you, Ernest? They're happy and we're happy, and that's all that matters on Durby Day, isn't it?'

'Yes, that's the dope,' said scornful Ernest, quoting from a recent speech. 'Peace and good-will among the classes! The flesh-pots for them, and the crust of bread for you and me. And all happy together!'

Ernest glowered at the car-full of parasites, all unconscious of his gaze; and Lily said:

'Why don't you get out and tell them what you think of them? I dare say they don't know.'

'I wouldn't waste my breath on them.'

'That's right,' said Lily. 'You keep it for Parliament. And if I were you, I shouldn't waste any more of it on us.'

After these words Lily put her head on Jane's shoulder and closed her eyes, with the irritating suggestion that she had triumphantly concluded the argument and was now about to sleep.

Mrs Higgins, who was annoyed by her son's exhibition, said, 'They're human beings, aren't they, the same as yourself, Ernest? I thought you was all for brotherhood.'

Ernest made no reply, but glared at a female parasite with flaxen hair and lovely eyes, who, her lips desirably parted, was watching Mr Ewer pouring water into his radiator out of a milk-jug.

'Seems to me, Ernest,' continued Mrs Higgins, who knew all her son's arguments by heart, 'that this brotherhood of yours don't go very far. Anyone that agrees with you is a brother, and the rest is toads. All these Croatians and foreign fish are your brothers' (Mrs Higgins was here referring to the 'Hands off Croatia Movement', which Ernest strongly supported), 'but a nice-looking English girl is a parasite. It isn't sense. If you ask me, any Englishman that treats me civil is my brother, and I don't care if he goes to the Durby in a Rolls-Royce or a wheelbarrow.'

'It's no good, mother,' said Ernest patiently, not turning his head; 'class is class – and you can't get away from it.'

Here Lily opened her eyes, and followed Ernest's to the lovely blonde.

'If you ask me,' she said naughtily, 'Ernie's got a crush on the straw-headed fairy'; and she laughed her tinkling, mischievous laugh.

'Lily, Lily!' protested Mr Bell mildly.

They all looked in the same direction, and Ernest flushed angrily, for, truth to tell, his gaze was political no longer, but desirous.

'I wouldn't be in that car,' he said hotly, 'for a hundred pounds.'

'Well, we'd let you go for ten bob,' said Lily.

'Lily, Lily!'

Fortunately, at this point, Mr Ewer opened the door and said miserably, 'I never knew such a thing to happen before. But we'll be all right now.'

The block melted, the limousine slid out of sight, and the cab jolted on. Ernest's affectionate knee increased its pressure, as if to show Jane that he did not really love the blonde parasite. Jane eyed him sadly; she had not supported him in the argument, and thought he had made a fool of himself, but she was sorry for him, and so far as it was possible she expressed all this with her knee.

Jane was very silent. She alone of the Bells had not absolute faith in the Black Prince, though she had not dared to whisper it, and she was afraid.

They crawled through the outskirts of Epsom, and marvelled at the multitude of motor-cars, the limousines like battleships, the two-seaters like roller-skates, the private omnibuses, packed with aristocrats, the beer-parties in the charabancs, the pearly costers halted by the roadside, dripping but cheerful, and the children who ran beside them or climbed upon the footboard, chanting, 'Throw out your coppers! Throw out your mouldy coppers! Mrs Higgins drew forth a sixpence from an ancient purse, Mr Bell in his grand new style flung out handfuls of pennies, and bowed like Royalty from the window. A tiny, impish, irresistible face invaded Jane's window and she cried, 'Oh, Ernest, give me a penny for him!'

'Against my principles,' said Ernest grimly. 'Begging's got no right to be in a civilized State.'

'Come off it, Ernest!' said Lily rudely.

Ernest grew fierce. 'D'you think I'm going to prop up capitalism by doling out charity to the starvelings of the workers? Leave that to Baldwin, thank you!'

'Three cheers for Baldwin!' said Lily, who had begun the journey with no politics but was now a raging Tory.

'Where does your father work?' said Ernest to the boy.

'Out of work,' lied the child.

'Then tell him from me to go the Guardians!'

72

'Chuck it, Lord Salisbury!' said the urchin, supposing now that he had to deal with a member of the Carlton Club, and disappeared.

'Well, thank God, I've got no principles!' said Lily. No one else spoke, and a chill fell on the party. They felt that Ernest was right, and themselves weak, sentimental beings. That was the worst of Ernest. He was so terribly right.

Half-way up the hill to the course the radiator boiled over again, and they waited till it cooled, for there were no milk-jugs in range. They had set out at nine o'clock to make sure of a position close to the course, but now it was noon, and when at last they reached the top they could find no place for the cab from which there was even a distant view of the course. Frightened by the police, harassed by touts, and now and then sticking in the mud, Mr Ewer at last guided his shaking cab to a remote corner of the Down on the wrong side of the hill behind the Grand Stand and Mr Bell readily paid ten shillings to an evil-looking person who had annexed that corner for the day. Then they got out, stretched their legs, remarked that it was raining still harder, and opened the cardboard boxes of provisions and took out the basket of bottles.

'That is the Grand Stand,' said Mr Bell with a proprietary air.

'Anyone would think he had shares in it,' muttered Ernest to his mother.

It was now that for the first time Fred and Ernest exchanged words. Jane watched them, fascinated, out of the corner of her eye. Fred the peaceful, in oilskins, looked bluff and belligerent. Ernest the implacable, in his bowler hat and old black great-coat, looked feeble and mild. Each guessed that the other was after Jane. Like two dogs sniffing, they hated each other, and growled in their bellies.

'Coming down, isn't it?' said Ernest, turning up his collar.

'You're right,' said Fred.

But these soft words were like the fierce challenge of two stags preparing for battle in the glen.

They ate and drank hurriedly, impatient for the course. One of the girls asked Mr Ewer what was his fancy. Mr Ewer said he would have something on Deborah, and all agreed that Deborah was a horse to be avoided, for it was not conceivable that this misery's selection could be successful.

At last Mr Bell marshalled his party and led them off to see his Epsom, which he had never seen himself. But so often had he conned over the little maps in the newspapers that indeed the picture of Epsom in his mind was as clear and detailed as the inside of the barge.

They pushed in a huddle through the crowd, dodging umbrellas and squelching in the mud. Mr Bell led the way, looking round anxiously to be sure of the safety of his flock, one hand holding aloft an umbrella, which was always just not over the head of Mrs Higgins, the other closed tight on his field-glasses, for, as he well knew, it was the custom to steal these valuable instruments. 'They cut 'em off you,' he explained; 'cut 'em off your back before you can turn round.'

A gipsy woman with a baby sidled up to him and whimpered fluently, 'Something for the lucky baby, kind gentleman. Hold up, Lucky Mary, and show the gentleman your face. She'll bring you luck, sir; you'll never regret it. King George gave her a sixpence, sir, the day he won the Two Thousand Guineas. You've got a lucky face, sir; you'll have good fortune, sir – it's in your face. You'll have beautiful children, gentleman, and travel abroad. The lady's a lucky face too, sir. You'll be very happy. God bless you, sir. Say "Thank you," Lucky Mary.'

Mr Bell beamed happily when he heard that he had a lucky face, and gave Lucky Mary sixpence. His pockets were nearly empty, but his heart overflowed with the benevolence of a millionaire.

Photographers, tipsters, fortune-tellers, and ice-cream merchants clamoured for their custom. There was no time for photographs or fortunes. But when a man in a purple bowler hat came up to Mr Bell and said simply, 'Will you give me a shilling, sir?' without offering any services in return, Mr Bell could not refuse him. The man took off his hat and presented Mrs Higgins with a picture-postcard of the Duchess of York, and everyone was happy.

At last they faced the great roaring amphitheatre across the course, all misty in the driving rain.

'That is Tattenham Corner,' said Mr Bell, as if he had haunted Epsom for thirty years. 'The start is over there. There is the winning-post. The Paddock is beyond.'

They gazed in silence at the historic scene, the classic lunacy of the English race. The bookmakers snarled like animals in the rain; the caped policemen stood glistening in the rain, like rows of wet seals; the merry-go-rounds swung round merrily in the rain, and from across the dip came the blare of their wild, pathetic music; the wizards sat in the rain with their thimbles and peas, their cunning cards and tricky necklaces; the tipsters ranted in the rain; the gipsy mothers fed their babies in the rain; the rich walked mincingly about their enclosures in the rain, and the poor stood eating oranges in the rain, drinking fizzy lemonade in the rain, shying balls at cokernuts in the rain, dancing in the rain and kissing in the rain, or crushed each other in patient, sodden, chattering rows against the railings of the course. And Mr Bell looked royally across the Downs – his Downs – for was not all this noise and bustle, this defiant revel of a multitude in the rain, directed only to one end, the triumph of the Black Prince, and the enrichment of Mr Bell?

They walked across the course just before it was cleared for the second race, and dug their heels curiously into the fateful turf. Ernest, joining battle early, held Jane firmly by the arm, and Fred, brooding and patient, came behind with Lily. Lily talked without ceasing and Fred said nothing at all; but their dislike of Ernest was a bond between them.

They walked along the line of yelling bookmakers, the girls pointing and exclaiming as if the worthy gentlemen had been so many monsters in the Zoo. And soon Fred had his little victory. Jane, with that secret fear in her heart, had planned with Lily a little flutter of their own, so that they might perhaps have some consolation for their father, just in case the Black Prince ... They had ten shillings between them, saved out of the money Jane had borrowed from Mrs Higgins. And Jane was all impatience to invest it at once. But Jane was shy of the explosive bookies, and Ernest, as usual, had views.

Suddenly she turned back to Fred.

'Fred, come and help me. Ernest's broken out with principles again.' Jane was cross now, and spoke as if they were spots. 'Ernest, trot on and tell father to wait for us.' And Ernest walked on in a sulk.

'Now, choose a nice one, Fred. Ernest says they batten on the something of the proletariat, but I can't help that.'

The happy Fred chose Bill Oates, of Wandsworth, a fatherly gentleman in a pink top-hat. He had white whiskers, a pale blue sash, a scarlet banner, and a smile which spelt goodness and loving-kindness, and in hoarse tones he constantly repeated that he was the 'Old Firm' and must not be deserted. Jane felt that it was a good action to bet with this frail and deserving old man.

'Come along, lady! Bless your pretty eyes! What's your fancy, lady? Lemonora? Thirty-three to one, Lemonora. Five shillings each way, Lemonora, thank you, lady. The Old Firm, the Old Firm, don't desert the Old Firm!'

Tremblingly, important and proud, Jane put away her betting-card, which bore the saintly likeness of Mr William Oates. Her father, with a fond smile, was watching her, as some bishop might see his child preach his first sermon. 'Hedging, eh?' he said tolerantly. 'Well, well!'

They walked on towards the winning-post, studying the bookies' slates, and were surprised to see that the odds generally offered about Lemonora were far higher than those of the venerable Oates – forty, fifty, and even sixty. They were inclined to blame Fred until Ernest said, 'What did I tell you?' and then they defended Fred and were reconciled to William Oates.

There was a roar, for the second race was off. They pressed up behind the mass of people who stood seven deep against the rail. They were facing uphill, and could not see one inch of the course: they could see only hats and umbrellas and the backs of necks; they did not know the name of the race nor the names of any of the horses; not one of them had sixpence on the race. But there they stood painfully on tiptoe, craning their necks, patiently waiting for they knew not what. The wave of shouting rolled up to them, there was the thunder of hoofs, and between two heads Jane saw the flash of a jockey's cap and a stooping silk shoulder. The straining crowd relaxed, and Jane's first horse-race was over. But in the excitement the watchful Ernest had recaptured her arm, so he at least was satisfied.

Lily said then that she would like to see the Black Prince, and they all set out for the Paddock. It was hard work moving through the crowd; they lost their way behind the Grand Stand, and a policeman told them it cost money to enter the Paddock. It seemed a shame that they should not be able to look upon the Black Prince for nothing, when they thought what a link there was between them. But the girls were tired, Mrs Higgins was flustered by the crowd, and Mr Bell was afraid that if they went on they would never be back in time to see the race. They had decided to make for Tattenham Corner, and it seemed ten miles to Tattenham Corner, such thrusting and dodging, and their feet so wet. Mrs Higgins said several times that she would fall down dead if she walked another step. Jane began to be irritated by Ernest's arm, which was rather a caress than a support. But Fred was a help to Lily, shielding her from the crowd, and she warmed towards him. Lily, of course, had come in her best coat instead of her tarpaulin, and she was wet through. Fred had decided that he was nothing to Jane. The rain seemed to grow worse. But on trudged the dauntless pleasure-party, determined at all costs to see the Derby.

They neared Tattenham Corner, just as the police were clearing the course. There seemed no corner anywhere; the crowd was many deep along the rails. Bewildered, like sheep with the dog at their heels, they retreated aimlessly before the mounted men, who frightened Mrs Higgins. And suddenly they found themselves miraculously in the front row of a mob of people stretched across the course at the Corner, and looking up the straight to the finish.

'No better place anywhere,' said Mr Bell proudly, as if he had designed it all. But, 'Fortune favours the brave', said Mrs Higgins. The rain had stopped, so Fred took off his oilskin and laid it upon the ground for Mrs Higgins to sit upon. But a mounted policeman posted himself before her. Everyone assured her that a policeman's horse could do no wrong, but Mrs Higgins said that there was no horse born that she would trust to that extent. The crowd swayed and strained, stealthily fighting for places, and Lily and Fred were squeezed into the second row. Mr Bell took out his race-card and they studied the colours of the Black Prince and Lemonora, and tried to commit them to memory. The Black Prince was 'black cap, cerise sleeves, white, orange hoops'. Lemonora was 'pink and white cap, green sleeves, chocolate, white hoops'.

'Black cap, white sleeves, chocolate hoops,' repeated Jane madly, while Mrs Higgins had the card.

'What's cerise?' said Mrs Higgins.

'It means cherry,' said Mr Bell.

'Well, can't they speak English at Epsom?' said Mrs Higgins.

'Ernest's colour,' said Lily. 'Pale Socialist.'

'Thank God that horse has gone!' said Mrs Higgins. 'Stand firm Mr Bell, this woman's pushing. If you want to stand in front, madam, say so, and I'll call the police, but if not, perhaps you'll take your elbow out of my appendix.'

Lily, suddenly sobered, whispered secretly to Jane, 'Jane, I've got cold feet too.'

Jane shivered; she was in a fever, terrified, miserable, thrilled. 'Black cap, cerise sleeves, white, orange hoops. . . . Pink and white cap, green sleeves, chocolate' . . . No, that was Lemonora. It was funny that she was thinking more of Lemonora now than of the Black Prince. Was that because of her own bet, or because she did not really believe in the Black Prince – never had? 'Black cap, cerise sleeves, white, orange hoops' . . . But the Black Prince *must* win. . . . If he did not win, what was to happen? How was she to pay Mrs Higgins? To say nothing of the hundred pounds. . . . And all their dreams. . . . The Black Swan, the sailing-boat, Lily's dancing lessons, Mrs Higgins, the motor-launch. . . . Black cap, cerise sleeves. . . . And her father? Would he go really mad? Jane glanced at him. He was still in his imperial mood on the surface, and he said to Mrs Higgins, 'You will see the field come round that corner. But before that we may get a glimpse of them on the hill.' But Jane saw that his lips twitched, he closed his eyes, and, though Jane did not know it, he whispered to himself, as he had whispered last night beside his bed, 'Oh, God, make the Black Prince win! Oh, God, make the Black Prince win, and I will be a better man.' Black cap, cerise sleeves. . . .

'There they come,' said Mr Bell. 'The parade.' The first of the horses were prancing and showing off far away before the Grand Stand. Mr Bell lifted his crazy glasses to the limit of the tarred string and gazed expertly into the distance. 'Ah, yes, the favourite. . . . What number is the Black Prince, Jane? . . . Seventeen? . . . Yes. What colours again? . . . Black cap, cerise sleeves, white, orange hoops. . . . Of course. . . . Yes. . . . Black cap. . . . I see a dark horse, but the hoops? . . . What colour hoops, Jane? Orange? Yes. . . . Those are pale blue. . . . Ah, now. . . . Black cap, cerise sleeves. . . . Yes, there is the colt. . . . I see him now. . . . Looks in fine fettle too. Well, there they go. . . .'

The last horse cantered away to the start, and Jane looked fondly at her father again, certain in her own mind that he had seen no more of the Black Prince than she had. And she too prayed, 'Oh, God, make the Black Prince win. . . . Oh, God, make father happy. . . .'

Then came a terrible time. A hush fell upon the waiting people. The rain fell again, and Jane could hear nothing but the patter of the rain and the beating of her heart. There was a sudden swirl and heave in the crowd behind, but Ernest's arm was round her and held her in her place. She was surprised and pleased, and suddenly she craved his sympathy. 'Ernest,' she whispered, looking up into his eyes, 'wish for the Black Prince, will you?' And she looked so sweet and appealing under her funny little sou'wester hat, with her eyes shining and her face wet with the rain, that Ernest for once forgot his principles; he became human, he was caught in the lunatic drama of this race, and he said, 'I do, Jane, I do.' Jane pressed his hand gratefully and he was rewarded.

Would they never start? Black cap, cerise sleeves, white, orange hoops. . . . Pink and white cap, green sleeves, chocolate hoops. . . . Lily began to learn the colours of the favourite, Cherry Ripe, as well: 'Pink cap, orange sleeves, purple . . .' And this muddled every one.

Mr Bell, with his glasses raised, was pretending that he could see what was happening at the start, but nobody believed that he could see anything. 'Two of them seem fresh,' he murmured. 'The favourite, I think, is giving trouble.'

'Where's the Black Prince, father?'

'I cannot distinguish.'

'Well, would you believe it,' sighed Mrs Higgins; 'he's brought that horse back again to the very identical spot! Officer, either that horse goes, or I go. *That's* my little gentleman! Don't lose your place, Mr Bell.'

Jane looked up in her father's face, and whispered, 'It will be all right, father, I know it will.'

But in Mr Bell's mind there was nothing but the image of a black horse which he had never seen, and the roar of the multitude, 'The Black Prince wins!'

'They're off!' Jane trembled and clutched her father's arm, she felt her flesh wither as if she had suddenly turned yellow. Black cap, cerise sleeves. . . . Along the top of the hill they saw through gaps a string of flying dots.

'There they go,' said Mr Bell. 'I can't see . . .' The crowd surged forward, and suddenly the most important thing seemed to be to keep her father in his place. He *must* see the Black Prince win! . . . He was holding up his glasses, feebly turning the screw, and looking this way and that. 'What colour sleeves, did you say, Jane?' 'Don't push, don't *push*!' she cried in an agony, and braced her back and dug her heels into the ground. But it was no good; the burly fellow had squeezed in front of them. . . . 'Beg pardon, miss; they're pushing behind.' . . . Another heave and they were back in the third row, all four of them. Jane could have cried for her father's sake. The field came in sight up the hill, the crowd yelled and struggled, she could remember nothing of the colours except 'black cap, cerise sleeves . . . pink and white cap. . . .' The horses thundered down to the Corner; she had to stand tiptoe to see them, and then she could see only a flying muddle of colour. They went too fast, she could fix her eyes on nothing. Yes, there was a dark horse among the first few. The Black Prince! No, the cap was not black. The cap was pink and white. . . . Lemonora! They were crying, 'The favourite wins! Deborah wins! Hermit! Merrylegs!' The Black Prince was on no one's lips. Yes, there was one. . . . Ernest – *Ernest!* – was crying like a madman, 'The Black Prince! The Black Prince!' But what had happened? Where was the hope of the Bell family? The first horses were away round the corner. And then among the last few stragglers she saw a black horse go by; she saw unmistakably the black cap, cerise sleeves, the white jacket, the orange hoops. It was the Black Prince – last but three. Jane felt suddenly weak. She glanced at her father, but he had not seen. He was gazing through his one-eyed glasses up the straight, still blissfully trying to follow the black horse which he too had perceived among the leaders – the dark horse Lemonora.

'It's all right,' he said, lowering the glasses; 'he has the race well in hand. Going very strong.'

Jane choked a sob in her throat. The race was over, the crowd surged forward over the course; already the news had flashed uncannily back to them. 'Deborah,' said everybody. 'Deborah! Mr Ewer's fancy!' Deborah, Brighteyes, and Lemonora. Lemonora – the consolation! Jane could not face her father; she slipped away from him and found Fred.

'Fred, I believe we've won something on Lemonora. Look after father, Lily; we'll meet you at the taxi.' And she scampered up the course with Fred.

As they ran, dodging in and out among the people, they worked out breathlessly their winnings on Lemonora. Thirty-three to one, a stake of five shillings, and a quarter of the odds for a place. That was eight. Eight times five was forty, forty shillings – two pounds. Forty shillings, after all their hopes; forty shillings was their miserable harvest. Yet even this was something; it would help to pay Mrs Higgins, and Jane felt somehow that she must run to make sure of it, her humble consolation. It would please her father, perhaps, that she had won something on her first bet. But why had they not put fifty pounds on Lemonora? That would have been – what? Eight times fifty: eight noughts are nought – four hundred pounds. Four hundred pounds! Not ten thousand, perhaps, but what wealth! Compared with forty shillings. Jane again wanted to cry when she thought of it. She blamed, not her father, but herself. Now it seemed that it must have been obvious from the first that Lemonora would be third and the Black Prince low down among the 'also rans'. Always in her heart she had known that the Black Prince was a fraud. She had never believed in him; her father was mad, but the fault was her own. She should have been wise, she should have been strong.

'Just about here was his berth,' said Fred, looking round.

They halted. On every side were bookmakers cheerfully disgorging money, but they could not see Mr William Oates.

'There!' cried Jane, 'he's next to that man!' And she pointed ahead to Mr Gus Morris of Finsbury, whose pale-blue bowler she remembered. But beyond Mr Morris was a gap in the line. They stood and stared at this gap. In it were two old boxes and a broken umbrella, and a few torn betting tickets, but no William Oates. No red banner, no pink top-hat, but a few poor people staring sadly like themselves. Mr William Oates had departed.

'Slipped his moorings,' said Fred uncomfortably.

'Do you mean he's a welsher?' cried Jane, still refusing to believe.

'Looks like it, Jenny.'

'Oh, Fred, it's too much!' And now at last poor Jane laid her head upon Fred's oilskin chest and cried and cried before the noisy crowd, mourning her forty shillings.

Fred was puzzled, for he did not know the full tale of the Bells' misfortunes, and embarrassed because people looked at him, and remorseful because he had selected William Oates. But still he liked to have Jane crying on his chest; and he thought, 'What about it, Ernest, my lad?'

It was soon over. 'We won't tell them, Fred,' said Jane bravely, drying her eyes. 'Pretend we got the money, won't you? I knew this would happen, Fred. That's why I ran.'

With this poor consolation they tramped back to the taxi. Everywhere were bookmakers paying out money, and it seemed hard that out of so many their William only should have turned deceiver; everywhere were laughing people, heartlessly gay, and Jane felt that they should all be told of the Bell family's misfortunes. They passed four men chanting a hymn and holding aloft a red and white banner –

THE WICKED SHALL BE TURNED INTO HELL

'That's something, anyway,' said Fred, thinking of Mr Oates. And Jane was a little comforted.

A wretched little company waited at the taxi, finishing the beer. Mr Bell sat in a corner, his eyes closed, not saying a word. He would not even look out to see the King's car go away. Mrs Higgins had had a pound on Cherry Ripe and lost it. The forty shillings cheered everybody (except Ernest). The journey had not been for nothing. Mr Bell opened his eyes, said, 'Well done, Jane,' and closed them again. The unlucky Mr Ewer had backed Deborah and won ten shillings. And with this poor freight the little cab crawled homewards.

They were all exhausted and only Ernest seemed to remain master of his fate. It was raining hard, and Jane insisted that Fred should come inside. But Ernest did not suggest that he should go outside. It was awkward for the three men dividing the two small seats between them; so Ernest suggested that he should sit on the back seat with Jane on his knee. And, since no one had the spirit to oppose it, this was arranged. Mrs Higgins and Lily fell asleep at once; Mr Bell did not sleep, but his sad head rolled like a dead man's from side to side when the cab jolted. Fred ate a banana and gazed broodingly at Jane across the cab. Jane did not like to sleep on Ernest's lap under the eye of Fred, but sat perched on those bony knees, wearily awake. No one spoke.

It must be said to the credit of Ernest that he respected the mood of the party and did not once point out the need for the 'Nationalization of the Means of Production, Distribution, and Exchange'. Nor did he draw any moral from the misfortunes of the day, but sat nursing his principles in silence. He was sorry that Jane had won money by a bet, and he faintly regretted that human moment in which he had forgotten principle and shouted wildly for the horse Black Prince. He turned over in his mind many sound reflections upon the economic evils of gambling, and its influence upon the poor. And he felt, very rightly, superior to these poor mortals in the cab.

But meanwhile, Fred's head nodded at last, and in the dark corner Ernest's superior fancy turned lightly from economics to thoughts of love, and Ernest's hand crept round Jane's weary form, and fondly clasped her stomach. And so by slow degrees he drew her to rest upon his superior breast, and Jane, too tired to object to anything, fell asleep upon the superior shoulder.

So they travelled for many miles, and only the vigilant Ernest was conscious of his surroundings. Then the cab stopped suddenly, Mrs Higgins woke up and looked at her watch, Fred woke up and saw Jane in the arms of Ernest, asleep, Mrs Higgins looked out and saw a public-house, Lily woke up and said she was cold, Mrs Higgins said why should they not stop and have something to keep out the cold, Mr Bell said, 'We've no money,' and closed his eyes again, but Lily said, 'What about our forty shillings?' She woke up Jane and said, 'Where's our forty shillings?' and Jane had to confess the whole truth about William Oates. Mr Bell said, 'My God!' without opening his eyes, and everyone felt this was the last straw, except Ernest, who was glad. The cab rattled on, a little world of gloom. No one slept any more. But the shameless, superior, triumphant Ernest enjoyed himself still.

At Kew Bridge fell the final blow. There was a grinding, rending, clattering sound beneath them, and the greater part of Mr Ewer's engine fell in little bits upon the road. Mr Ewer got down slowly, went back and stared curiously at the odd pieces of metal strewn upon the highway, returned to the cab, opened the door, and said, 'I never knew such a thing to happen before.' Mrs Higgins had sevenpence, so they came back from the Derby in a tram.

8

MR BRYAN

It turned out next day that only an uncanny combination of misfortunes had prevented the Black Prince from winning the Derby. At the start he had been 'interfered with', at the first corner he had been badly 'cut into', and shortly after there was some sad bumping and boring. A general conspiracy of the other horses and jockeys engaged had blasted the Bells' hopes. This news seemed somehow consoling to Mr Bell, for it showed that fundamentally his judgement had been sound. It was better to be blasted by misfortune than by folly.

'I knew,' he said at the family *post mortem* in the evening. 'I knew the colt had the legs of the field, if he only had the luck. But the best judgement in the world can't cope with accidents. Never mind, girls,' he said bravely, 'the luck will change one day.'

'No, it won't, father; this has got to stop.' Words tumbled in confusion from Jane's trembling lips, for it was time to be a tyrant, and last night she had lain awake rehearsing the part. If she weakened now, the next minute, she knew, they would all be picking winners for the Gold Cup. 'Your horse wouldn't win, father, if all the other horses lay down. You'll never back a winner if you live to be a hundred.'

'Eurydice . . .' murmured Mr Bell, gazing in surprise at Jane's excited face, pale with the effort to be tyrannical and firm.

'Every man has one stroke of luck in his life,' said Jane, 'and that was yours. But you won't have another; and, what's more, you're not going to try. I'm putting my foot down.'

Jane, as she said this, made a delicate stamp, like a young hind pawing the ground, and since she had a teapot in one hand and a pile of dirty plates in the other, it was funny, and Lily laughed. Jane put the pot and plates on the floor, sat down beside Lily, and pinched her thigh fiercely to secure her support.

'It's no good, father. Lily and me have made up our minds.

Either you promise to give up the betting or we walk off and leave you – don't we, Lily?'

This being the first that Lily had heard of this resolution, she opened her pretty lips to say, 'I dunno'; but, receiving a second, and more violent pinch, said, 'That's right, Dad,' instead.

'The luck will turn, Jane,' said Mr Bell feebly.

'So will the worm,' said Jane, astonished at herself. 'I'm the only one of us that's bringing in a halfpenny, and I'm not going on slaving in that house if it's all going on horses. So you see.'

Jane pinched herself now, to be sure that it was really herself who was saying all these extraordinary things. Never in her life had she thought of herself as 'slaving'; it was an expression of Florry's, and of course Ernest's. And here she was throwing it at her poor father, of all people!

Still, she must keep it up. 'Is it a promise, father?'

'Very well, Jane,' said Mr Bell meekly. 'I've told you all along that I only did it for you.'

And he looked so miserable that Jane longed to reprieve him, to give him a good tip, and send him off to Epsom. But instead she said, 'I owe Mrs Higgins five pounds. How much do you, father?'

'A hundred,' said Mr Bell with an attempt at ease.

'*A hundred pounds!* To Mrs Higgins?'

'No, Jane – to your aunt.'

Jane gasped. 'Was that the hundred you said you had by you?'

'Yes, Jane,' said Mr Bell, and hung his head.

'My God!' said Lily.

Jane could make no comment on this piece of news. She said, 'Well, that settles it. You'll have to go to work, Lily.'

'I won't go into service, not for anyone.'

'Well, you can go to that Education place tomorrow and see if they'll have you still for the millinery. You'll take her, father. And you'll make your bed before you go, Lily – see? We're going to have an alteration here. And now you can wash up, because I'm going across to see Mrs Higgins.'

Lily, sobered by the situation, and taken aback by this new Jane, piled the plates in silence.

Jane kissed her father, and he said, 'You're a hard girl, Jane, but you're right, I suppose.'

'It will be all right, father,' the hard girl said, and going up on to the wharf cried quietly against the fence. But it entered her mind that she was a case of '*Out of the Mouths of Babes and Sucklings*', which was a striking caption out of The Baby Queen, and she went on comforted to borrow some more money. For what she earned from the Ravens was eighteen shillings a week.

The next morning, when she took up the tea, Mr Bryan said, 'Well, Jane, you'll be rid of me soon.'

'Rid of you, Mr Bryan?' said Jane blankly, tray in hand.

'I'm leaving here.'

'Leaving us, Mr Bryan?' Jane thought, 'Oh, Lord, another smack in the face!' and she was afraid that her voice sounded the same note. It did.

'But I'm not going very far. I've taken a studio. Not far from you, I believe.'

'Not that one on the wharf, Mr Bryan?' said Jane, trying to keep perfectly calm.

'That's the one. And when I'm settled in, you're going to come and sit for me, aren't you?'

'Sit for you, Mr Bryan?'

'I mean, I want to do a picture of you.'

'Very well, Mr Bryan.'

'When can you come?'

'Friday's my day out, Mr Bryan. I could come in the afternoon.'

'Next Friday?'

'Yes, Mr Bryan.'

'Half past two?'

'Yes, Mr Bryan.'

'All right, then. Half past two.'

'Thank you, Mr Bryan. I've turned on the bath.'

Jane went out with her tray, thinking, '*Lured to the Haunts of Bohemia. Estelle Falls in with Bad Company*.' She was excited, she was thrilled. And all she had said was, 'I've turned on the bath.'

*

The Honourable George Gordon Bryan was born with a silver spoon in his mouth, and had as soon as possible ejected it. He was a rebel, or so he thought, against his own class. He could not prevent his parents from sending him to Eton, but after four years he nearly succeeded in being removed for a tiresome habit of travelling up to London and visiting the music-halls, while his unseemly caricatures of the tutorial staff had never endeared him to the authorities. Among the boys he was considered strange because of his attitude to games. In his last year he would without doubt have played for the XI if he had consented to devote himself to cricket, but he preferred to go fishing, or to wander about the country-side observing the behaviour of small birds. This shameful act of renunciation had no precedent in the history of the school, but for his caricatures and his cricket he was, nevertheless, elected to 'Pop'. The young bloods of athletics, however, were never his favourite companions, and his best friend was a bookish, spectacled boy called Raven, who was generally bowled by a half-volley, fielded short leg, and wrote better Latin prose than Cicero himself. Bryan had no liking for Latin prose, though he had a passion for the poet Homer; but Raven knew all about birds, they both hated running and liked long walks, and these, so far as any one could see, were the only foundations of the friendship.

Gordon's father, the seventh baron, had intended him for Cambridge and the House of Commons, but Gordon, again shaking off the laurels, insisted on going to Australia instead. His brother, the heir, was a Member of Parliament, and his father punctually attended the House of Lords whenever the Liquor Laws, the Divorce Laws, or horse-racing were the subject of debate; and Gordon said that three members of the same family in public life was more than any country deserved. He did not regard himself as a heaven-born painter, so at least his father had no tiresome arguments about Art to put up with. He shrugged his shoulders and slightly reduced the boy's allowance. So Gordon travelled to Australia in a small cargo-steamer instead of by the Peninsular and Oriental Steam Navigation Company. On the way out he assisted from time to time in the stokehold, but did not pretend, as the common cant is, that this is a noble or an interesting occupation, and soon gave it up. He then spent the days drawing the most extraordinary unlikenesses of the crew, which were his first attempts at serious work. In his last term at Eton he had come under the influence of the Neo-Post-Impressionists, whose

Exhibition he shamefully attended when he should have been watching the Eton and Harrow match.

This school, of course (not Harrow, but the Neo-Post gentlemen) has set its face against all naturalistic forms of expression in art, and particularly against the sterile reproduction of the human form as we know it. Their pictures, for the most part, are essays in abstract design and are seldom concerned with anything more solid than a parallelogram or an equilateral triangle, though, try how they may, such concrete objects as stove-pipes, bowler hats, wood-blocks, factory-chimneys, and odd parts of women's faces will wander into their compositions. The more conservative members still audaciously persist in representing the human form, but preserve their consciences and their membership by expressing it in terms of parallelograms, equilateral triangles, wood-blocks, stove-pipes, and bowler hats. It was in this kind of way that Gordon Bryan painted the simple sailors of the *Sea Horse*, giving full value to the ventilators, the derricks, life-belts, funnels, and any other geometrical shapes which happened to attract him. Here, for the first time, he suffered the social disadvantages of modernism in art; for the honest seamen argued, with some reason, that these strange portraits must be either imbecile or insulting. Liking the man personally, they charitably plumped for imbecility, a view which was supported by his voluntary labours in the stokehold. He left the ship at Sydney, firm friends with every one.

He liked the Australians at once for their friendliness and gaiety and happy innocence of aristocracy. In the great bar of the Australia Hotel a merry young man invited him to a sheep-station five hundred miles away, and repeated the invitation, sober, in the morning. On the sheep-station, far out on the borders of the back-blocks, for no particular reason Bryan spent two years, first as a 'Jackeroo' or apprentice, and then as a recognized human being. Here he drafted sheep, and talked sheep, and even sheared sheep, and fell mildly in love with a lady who lived one hundred and fifty miles away and rode over for a week-end once a year. The next two years he passed on a cattle-station farther north, where he dipped cattle, mustered cattle, rounded-up cattle, drafted cattle, talked cattle, and fell mildly in love with a lady who lived three hundred miles away and motored over for tennis once every six months.

Once he went down to Sydney for a week and fell mildly in love with a lady who was leaving for Ceylon the next day. He liked the life, the sun, the gum trees, the picnics, and the people, grew brown and lusty and acquainted with horses, and such painting as he did had a disgraceful taint of the naturalistic. But after four years he grew tired of ignoring the invitations of his family to go home, and went.

At Colombo, unfortunately, he met Miss Sybil Colebatch, the eldest daughter of the Governor of Ceylon. Still more unfortunate, she travelled home with Lady Colebatch, in the S.S. *Pindi*.

After three years at Government House, Miss Sybil was poised uncomfortably between two worlds. She was accustomed to say, 'Do this,' and somebody did it; she had clapped her hands and grave men like Rajahs appeared bowing from four corners, and in all this she delighted. But in the things of the mind she felt herself starved; she detested the barren, the non-existent culture of the colony. At home she had always read the latest book as soon as it was heard of, but now it was out of date long before she heard of it. In Chelsea she had hovered on the fringes of the highbrows; in Ceylon, she felt, there were no brows at all. She never saw a new play or a new picture; she pined for the Leicester Galleries, the Russian Ballet, and the audacious performances of the Sunday night societies. But she missed Government House the moment she set foot in the *Pindi*. She wanted the gorgeous East and the West End all in one.

George Gordon Bryan was the nearest approach to that combination in the *Pindi*. She liked the looks of him; she saw him sketching a radiator and judged that he was Modern. Gordon had not seen any one like Sybil since he was a schoolboy, and, because of her blue eyes, her pearly skin, and her fair, proud head, was willing for a while to be the conquered East. It was a change to meet a woman who talked neither of sheep nor cattle nor horses, and yet was acquainted with the simple life of the British Empire. So he shifted her deck-chair from the shade into the sun, and from the sun into the shade, stopped reading when she wished to walk and stopped walking when she wished to read, collected the books, bags, and brooches which she left about the ship, persuaded her to take a Benedictine after dinner, permitted her to dress him for the fancy-dress dance, taught her to play shuffle-board, partnered her in the treasure-hunt, gazed deep into her peerless eyes and listened attentively to her opinions about art, life, literature, the passengers, and Ceylon. But these opinions she kept simple and broad, though refined, and suitable to a gentleman who, however aristocratic, had spent four years in Australia.

Long before Port Said the passengers said things; and they were true. For to Sybil Colebatch George Gordon fell a victim at last. In the Red Sea they became secretly engaged, on the boat-deck. And had Sybil steered the same wise course as before they might even have been married. But Sybil, as is usual in the flush of success, forgot her wisdom. As they travelled northwards from hot to cold, from white drill to woollen jerseys, she threw off the barbarous languor of the tropics, and became more and more artistic, intellectual, and refined. As the temperature descended Sybil's brow seemed to rise. She flung Italian painters about like so many quoits; she dug out of her trunks the writings of a man called Proust, who could devote a whole book, it seemed, to the flicker of an eyelid. Her conversation became very subtle and oblique, and, on the noisy ship, very difficult to follow, like Mr Henry James read aloud on the Underground Railway.

The sight of her fellow-passengers, none of whom, she felt, had even heard of the man Proust, grew painful to her. She spoke of them, not by their names, which she never remembered, but by the names of various painters of whom they reminded her. This young woman was 'The Gauguin', and that 'The Van Gogh', while the men were ranged from 'The Hogarth' to 'The Picasso'. She had a habit of making confidential remarks on their appearance and dress in flute-like but penetrating tones, after which she would laugh adorably (but loudly) and flash at Gordon her captivating eyes. Gordon found this embarrassing, having by nature the opposite habit of friendly toleration, which Australia had fortified. Also he discovered that he was not enough interested in art and literature to discuss them with satisfaction all day. And more and more he retired from his beloved into the smoking-room and talked to the Australians about sheep.

Sybil passed easily from talking to lecturing. On the second day out from Port Said she asked to see all his drawings. She turned them over almost in silence, murmuring from time to time, 'Interesting', 'How virile!', and 'Fascinating pattern'. But that evening she announced that what he was cut out for was public life. She was honest about it. 'You have talent,' she said, 'but I don't think you're a good enough painter to give your life to it.' Which was a brave thing to say, and, for all he knew, true. So for the rest of the voyage, while he arranged her cushions, she arranged his career. By Malta he was in the House of Commons, off Stromboli he rose to an Under-Secretaryship, and before Marseilles he was Chief Whip. Gordon hated plans and had travelled fifteen thousand miles to avoid Parliament. Moreover, these excursions into public life discovered multitudes of mutual friends; and Gordon was reminded of the Decies, the Anstruthers, the Foljambes, and many other families who painfully recalled tea-time every second Thursday at No. 7 Belgrave Square.

Sybil was a puzzle. She shared, at first sight, so many of his leanings, but she seemed to have a genius for exaggeration, and spoiled everything by overdoing it. He had revolted against regimented cricket, but liked honest exercise. Sybil thought it an outrage that any British boy should be asked to move a muscle when he might be reading the Restoration Drama, and she could not herself be persuaded into anything more active than the game called shuffle-board, in which the player stands almost immobile and with a long pole propels a flat wooden disc a few yards along the deck. George Gordon liked sausages, but did not dare to mention this; for he felt that either Sybil would cut sausages out of his life or they would have sausages at every meal. He landed at Marseilles still loyal and engaged, but lacking the fine free rapture of the Red Sea. Sybil, by the way, thought kissing rather vulgar.

The family welcomed the couple with delight, and a communication was made at once to the Central Office of the Conservative Party. Meanwhile, Sybil began his education proper. She took him to matinées on sunny days, she took him to the Film Society on Sunday afternoons; she took him on Sunday nights to peculiar plays by Czechoslovakians; she took him to the 'Ring', to the Wallace Collection, the Tate Gallery, the Poets' Corner, to the Russian Ballet, the Negro Dancers, and the Hampstead Theatre, and to show him that she was no highbrow she took him

to the Coronet Club, the Eton and Harrow match, and to Ascot on
Gold Cup day.

And, strangely enough, the Coronet Club, Lord's, and Ascot
were perhaps the three last intolerable straws; for these showed
him finally that he could not endure the society of Society, whether
they talked about Proust or about polo. The general scene of Ascot
delighted him: the moving masses of colour, the thin green river
of the course, the sun and the shouting, the rolling downs and dim
blue hills, and the stately advent of the Royal party. There was no
'Socialist nonsense' in his head; he approved in theory of this
parade of nobility and leisure, provided that he was not part of the
show; and he regarded himself as a 'good Conservative'. No, this
strange youth found Society *socially* wanting – a dull class, unreal
and unattractive. And of all the works of man he abominated most
the top-hat, the tail-coat, and the lavender spat. Other men might
wear them if they would, but on his own person they made him
feel foolish and unhappy.

(No attempt is being made here to defend these preposterous
opinions; they are merely recorded for what, if anything, they are
worth.)

He disliked his hat, he disliked his trousers; he disliked the label
which hung upon his breast – 'Royal Enclosure. The Hon. Gordon
Bryan'; and, irritated by these things, he began to dislike the people.
Strolling in the Paddock with Sybil, who was like a lily just opened,
and as free from care, he sourly studied the faces. Many of the men
were fine-looking, bronzed, handsome, healthy, though cast all in
the same monotonous mould. Many of the younger ones were
vacuous and feeble, and moustaches grew over a suspicious number of the mouths. All, like the racehorses circling in the middle,
had labels on them, which revealed their pedigree and importance.
But no one, after all, goes to Ascot to look at the men. The women
too wore labels, and needed them grievously, Mr Bryan thought.
The women were the great surprise and disappointment. Many
times his eye was caught by a dazzling frock, a dainty hat, or a provoking glimpse, a promise of beauty; and then the lady would turn
to show a face empty, expressionless, fatigued, and plain.

'My God, how ugly they are!' he exploded at last.

'Who, dear?' said Sybil.

'These women. I've not set eyes on a single winner. Except you.'

'Don't be so Australian, dear,' said Sybil, by no means flattered, but rather resenting the aspersion on her caste. 'I've seen some very charming girls.'

'Well, I've seen one or two. But what is two among the whole of *Who's Who*? Think of the time they have, the money they spend, the trouble they take! They ought *all* to be beautiful! It's all they've got to do. And if they can't be beautiful there's nothing to be said for them.'

'Are you going Bolshie, dear?'

'No, dear. But all I can say is this,' said Mr Bryan, worked up, 'if you took the first fifty typists you met in the City, and the first fifty girls out of any big store, and fifty chorus-girls and fifty manicure-girls and fifty parlour-maids, and washed them and scented them and dressed them up in these clothes, and hung labels on them, and set them to walk up and down in the Paddock, you would see a show that's worthy of this country. ... My God, there'd be so much beauty that no one would look at the races!'

'Oh, well, if you prefer typists – ' said Sybil. 'We'd better go back, or we shall miss the next race.'

During the three-thirty they both reflected on this ridiculous conversation, and Gordon reflected that it was a strange reason for the first real coolness between a plighted couple, the gentleman's complaint that he could see no other attractive women.

That night, at the Coronet Club, he had another prolonged view of Society, and thought them a poor lot. Few of them were young, and none, he thought, attractive. There was not one arresting or creative face, nor one that spoke of a simple soul: only a dull uniform of birth and breeding, wealth and white ties, fine linen and fatigue. No man in that room would have dared to enter it in a dinner-jacket. No man had an opinion of his own. And even the few stray authors and actors there had loyally left their souls in Bond Street, and were submerged and indistinguishable among the noble herd.

And Mr Bryan, with prophetic eye, saw himself sucked into that herd. Month after month, and Season after Season, and year after year, he would go to the same parties and see the same people, wear the same clothes, and eat the same food as the rest of the herd; go to the same fashionable plays, and say the same fashionable things about them; learn the latest step when he was told to, and give it up when it became taboo; go to the same Academy, same Ascot and Lord's, same Goodwood and Cowes; shoot the same birds on the same day; and flee to Monte Carlo by the same express. Never again would he do anything unusual, or anything that was not in the book of rules, or a fashionable 'stunt'. Nothing real or simple would happen again, or if it did it would be kept very dark. He would be as much master of his fate as a member of a trade union in a general strike. He would constantly wear a top-hat.

And, ten to one, this girl of his would have him into Parliament; and that would be a second set of rules and regulations, pretences and restraints, piled one on top of the other. Committee meetings, lunches, constituents, questions, at homes, dinners, debates, receptions, divisions – he knew what a life his brother led. And constantly the white tie, constantly the stiff, starched, abominable shirt.

Poor Sybil unfortunately chose this moment to discuss his political career. The band was playing 'O Baby!' and the nobility were performing the newest dance, which was based upon the actions of American negro women when waddling through a swamp with babies on their heads. To this foundation the dancing-schools had added a step resembling the movements of a crab which has had one claw crushed and is uncertain of its destination, a sort of sideways dithering, with much wriggling of the hips. The dancers throughout gazed fixedly at their feet, and looked desperately unhappy. Sybil pointed out young Lord Waters who had done so well in the House. He excited in Gordon neither envy nor ambition. He had a fluffy soft moustache and an air of over-breeding, like a King Charles spaniel or a blue carnation. 'A horrible fellow,' thought Gordon. But, to do him justice, he looked bored. Sybil pointed out that Gordon would be able to practise his art in his spare time. Mr Winston Churchill, for example, found time for painting and writing as well. And if a man had a definite business in life he enjoyed 'that sort of thing' so much more when he could get away to it. Gordon perceived that Sybil thought less and less of his art. It was a harmless hobby; he would be allowed to paint in the holidays, as a child is allowed to have the paint-box out on Sunday. She might be right; he only knew that he liked doing it, and wanted to do it more and more.

Lord Waters was dancing with a very fat woman and looked very ridiculous. Sybil said she was Lady Marvell, who had so much influence with the Party. A few more weeks, thought Gordon, and I shall be hung like a pendant on that ample bosom. He took Sybil out to dance. The floor was crowded now, for a common fox-trot was the tune, and they stood wedged among the couples, scarce moving geographically, but jigging busily with the feet and shoulders. Everybody talked, and at the end of a sentence moved on an inch or two, bumped gently into the next couple, and the gentleman said, 'I beg your pardon.' The gentleman bumped turned his head with a smile of ineffable forgiveness, which was almost a thanksgiving. So they moved on, like animated statues planted on a glacier. 'Typical,' thought Gordon. 'Society can only dance in a place so fashionable that no one can dance in it. Why try?' Sybil talked all the time in his ear about a Czechoslovakian play which proved that Man was lower than the animals. She thought it was stimulating. Gordon bumped Lord Waters and was bumped by Lord Marvell, and apologized, and grinned, and grinned again. He felt somehow guilty because he was not enjoying himself, for, after all, they were his own breed, these people. 'It's hot,' sighed Sybil. 'It's a hot-house,' said Gordon, and suddenly felt better, for he had remembered the great tent full of orchids at that dreadful flower show to which Sybil had taken him, top-hat and all. And these were orchids, he saw now, these noble, expressionless faces about him, forced artificial blooms without fragrance or simplicity.

In the tent, he had thought, they were reaching out for him, those peers of the floral kingdom, those waxen monsters with their spotted tongues and aristocratic, unnatural shapes. Lord Waters was an orchid; even Lady Marvell, in an elephantine fashion, was an orchid, an *odontoglossum*. And they were trying to catch him and keep him in the hot-house, keep him and cultivate him until he grew complicated and proud and unreal as themselves, till it was natural to be unnatural. 'I won't be an orchid,' he said, suddenly determined. 'All the same,' Sybil was saying, 'there is a sort of *rhythm* in the Expressionist plays.' 'Let's sit down,' said

Gordon, feeling himself dangerous with unexploded irritation. But about what? Was it Lord Waters or the crowd, the dance, the heat, the governing classes or public life; was it something to do with his painting, with top-hats, with highbrows, Czechoslovakia, tail-coats, or the absence of beauty at Ascot? Perhaps it was all of these things; perhaps, to be honest, he reflected gloomily, it was only one thing, that he had made a mistake about Sybil.

But, whether or not, he would not be an orchid. And after that flashing resolution the end was certain. He would *not* be badgered into the House of Commons, he would not be part of Society, he would not do the Season and wear a top-hat and be crushed and flattened at these parties nightly. He would go on with his painting, however poor, because he believed in it; he would consort with simple people, the modest primrose or the graceful daffodil, but not, if he could help it, with the *Orchidaceae*.

Slowly and painfully he broke these heretical resolutions to Sybil.

'My dear,' said her mother, 'it sounds like the Savage Club. He must be one of these Bohemians. Lost caste. It's terrible. But you know, his grandmother ... A throw-back, I suppose. Well, one thing's certain, dear, you can't marry a Bohemian. Your father would resign.'

Sybil, too, saw the end approaching, threw off a lecture or two, tried tears and entreaties, and at last, preferring to be mistress of her fate, released him gracefully, before he had dared to think of such a thing.

He then went to Iceland, painted glaciers and whalers and grew a beard. He came back after eight months, removed the beard, and settled down as a paying-guest in the Ravens' home. He liked the river, he liked the stolid Raven, and, for a time, he liked Mrs Raven too, though Sybil had planted in him an unfortunate prejudice against educated women; and Mrs Raven was very highly edu-cated.

For a year he lived there happily, working very hard; and during this time he became acquainted with most of the modern young artists. A painter with money was a portent among them, and a pleasant one; and they argued that a young man who drew such very triangular legs must have something in him. Many of his pictures seemed to have so little meaning that it was suspected that their meaning was profound. And, being modern and fluid and likely, as they knew, to overflow into some wild new phase themselves at any moment, they took a generous view of other men's triangles, lest the next day they should burst into rhomboids or polygons. Besides, he was jolly company at a studio party, and mixed well with everybody, whether it was Russians or Bloomsbury, or the Campden Hill crowd, or theatre people; danced well, drank well, could eat kippers in the early morning, and never rammed his triangles down other people's throats. He went to the play now and then, but not to those which he would have seen with Sybil, because everybody else had seen them, and never to 'first nights'. He kept a boat at the bottom of the garden, and with the Thames to play with had no need for golf-clubs or any other elaborate exercise. He was now bronzed and muscular and tall, and with his little moustache had a fresh-air, military appearance strangely out of tune with his extraordinary pictures, which, one would have said, had grown up unhealthily, like mustard and cress in a cellar. He liked pretty women, but did not run after them; often they ran after him; but he had learned wariness and was never seriously entangled. Indeed, in the studio world there seemed to be few serious entanglements, which was a great part of its charm. All that absurd ritual and tradition of the orchid world and the stage, where a kiss must mean a marriage or else a divorce, and there is nothing between friendship and passion, had no existence. These gay, free people had too little time and money to be thinking always of marriage, and too good hearts for the Sybilline traditions. They met and liked each other and kissed sometimes in corners, and went on with their work without making a drama of it. Yet the sacred institution of monogamy was perhaps as sacred and certainly as safe in the abandoned studios as it was under more respectable roofs.

It was only Mrs Raven who drove Gordon from the Ravens'. For Mrs Raven would make a drama of it.

Mrs Raven, like Sybil, was intellectually starved; and Mr Bryan thought it hard that he should be loved by two women in that condition. Unlike Sybil, Mrs Raven admired his paintings. She had been a wrangler at Cambridge, so perhaps had a tendency to triangles. Honest John Raven worked hard and late at the office, and sometimes brought home papers with him, or if not he talked 'housing' or threw off little anecdotes about 'National Insurance'. The advent of Mr Bryan had brightened Mrs Raven's life, though she did not see enough of him. She was busy with house and family all day, and many evenings he was out. They were upon terms of easy companionship, or so he thought; she was young and attractive in a soft and velvety style; and she had always seemed sensible except on the rare occasions when she entered his painting-room or talked about his work. She spoke then in such terms of extravagant praise that he thought she must be mad. Fothergill, Anstey, Backhouse, the names of all the best modern artists tripped discredited from her lips. Mr Bryan's triangles were better than any of them. He was the Michelangelo of triangles, a wonder, a genius. Mrs Raven's praise of his pictures gave him an uncomfortable feeling that they were no good. So for a long time he had not invited her to see them.

She had hinted once or twice that she was ready, even anxious, to sit for him. He could not imagine why; for he had no illusions about his style of painting, and he knew very well that John Raven would hate to see his soft, round wife turned into triangles with a stove-pipe in the background. Besides, he had not the least impulse to paint her; she suggested nothing to him. So her sitting had been as politely as possible postponed or discouraged.

And then one day, poor creature, she had blurted without warning into drama. They were sitting after tea in the cool drawing-room which looked out on the river. He was filling his pipe and she was turning over the pages of a recent volume of free verse which she had bought at a charity bazaar. She was trying to like it because it gave her the same sensations as Gordon's triangular pictures, so she supposed it must be good. There seemed to be no particular reason why any line had begun or ended where it did rather than somewhere else. Many of them consisted of a single monosyllable, such as the word 'what'; and these made the nearest approach to a definite metre or rhythm. Many of the words and phrases were pleasant-sounding in themselves, but could they have been shaken in a sack and written down again in the order in which they fell out the poems would have seemed the same.

Strange things happened in this verse. Flowers were noisy and rain was green, tables had rhythm and carpets sang; while bisons, parrots, and elephants were common objects, whether the poem was about passion or the Piccadilly Railway. And for the words bison, parrot, or elephant, the words lobster, parasol, or inkstand, or any other words, could almost anywhere have been substituted without injuring the sense. But the parrots had as much reason to be there as Mr Bryan's stove-pipes, so Mrs Raven did not know what to think.

'What do you think of that?' she said, and handed him the book, open at a poem called 'Passion'.

He read through the poem, giving his mind to it, so that his pipe went out. The words made no impression on his mind at all. They might have been a price-list or a catalogue of bulbs. But he too saw that this work had a sort of kinship to triangular legs, and with the cautious generosity of one modern to another he said:

'Alive, isn't it? Got something in her.'

'Yes.'

He lit another match and puffed at his pipe. She watched him. It was a pipe which she had given him for Christmas, a hygienic pipe with an aluminium tube in it. The pipe did not draw. The pipe, instead of allowing the smoker to absorb the poison by degrees, stored it up in the tube and at intervals expelled it into the mouth in one concentrated dose.

'I wish,' he said, puffing, 'that someone would sell an ordinary, Christian, unhealthy pipe. These hygienic things are enough to make a man give up smoking.' He had forgotten who had given him the pipe. And whether because of this or because of the poem called 'Passion', Mrs Raven suddenly clenched her hands, went very white, and said:

'Why are you so cruel to me?'

He looked at her, astonished. Her face was changed, hard and suffering as he had never seen it.

'Of course, it's your pipe,' he said. 'I'm sorry. I forgot.'

'Why have you come here and ruined my life?' she said stubbornly, not looking at him but at the fireplace.

'What do you mean?' he said.

'I love you. Didn't you know?'

Alarming information! He stood up and knocked out the full pipe in the fireplace.

'Why did you do that?' she said.

He stared stupidly at the smouldering dottle in the clean grate.

'I can't think!' he said. What a question!

She stood up and came to him and took hold of his coat and looked up hungrily into his face.

'And you don't like me at all,' she said. 'Not a bit.'

'Yes, I do.'

'No, you don't.'

'But of course I do!'

'Do you really? Very much?'

'Of course,' he said again. Absurd conversation!

'Say it! Say "I like you very much!"'

'I like you very much,' he said stiffly, appalled by her eagerness.

'Say you love me! Say it!'

'Good God, Margaret, what's the matter with you?' He did not seem to know this wild young matron who was clinging to him. She was possessed – a different creature. He could hear her children yelling in the garden. He was horrified – not because she had said so much, but because he could say so little. What a bore Love could be!

'I love you,' she whispered. 'I'd do anything for you – run away with you, leave everything. I'm sick of it. You've done this, Gordon, don't you know? But you're so blind. I've bottled it up all these months, but now I don't care. You've ruined everything, Gordon, and you must give me something.'

She gripped his coat and again looked up at him with that terrible appeal in her eyes. He was stirred by compassion and humility and pride, as any man must be to whom such things are said. And he put his arms round her and held her close and kissed her, not as he felt, but as he thought she wanted. Even as he embraced her it crossed his mind that he should be feeling guilty in this, the classic situation of wrongdoing, but instead he had a horrid sensation that he was doing a good action. She was a young, soft, clinging creature in his arms, and he liked her; but that was all. It was embarrassing. But pretty women, after all, had to suffer this sort of embarrassment all the days of their lives. The great thing was to be kind.

He put her gently away. She gave a deep sigh of content. And then, insatiable, she whispered again, 'Say you love me, Gordon.'

But he would not say that.

'It isn't much,' she insisted. 'Say you love me a little.'

He began, 'But I –' But he could not finish that either. He thought that perhaps it would have been kinder to be cruel from the first. He said softly, 'Don't, Margaret.'

She became suddenly sane again, and sank on to a sofa. 'Light your pipe,' she said pathetically.

He kissed her hand and took his pipe and went out.

He had given her something – all that he could – and he hoped foolishly that this would be enough. But always her eyes, her voice, told him that it was not enough. That compassionate embrace had been too kind, and whenever they were alone he knew that she was waiting for, willing him to be kind again. The part of Joseph is not one that can be played for ever by a paying-guest, and for many good reasons he had no mind to play any other. And so he set about looking for a studio.

It was a queer thing, he reflected, that the first appointment he made for the studio should be with the maidservant of Mrs Raven, who wanted so much to sit for him.

9

THE BLUSH

THE studio was beside the river too, fifty yards above the *Black-bird*, with a small bare yard running down to the river-wall. Like most studios, it looked a poor place for any kind of study. It had a piano, a bed, an anthracite stove, a divan, a sink, easels, a gas-ring, and the usual mess; and at the end, behind a partition, a small lumber-room and a bathroom. On the shelves, and on the floor, and on the walls were the works of Mr Bryan. He had never been able to display so many in one place before; he had taken some time and trouble over the arranging; and it was now possible to see in order of time the successive stages of Mr Bryan's art. There were the caricatures of Eton days, which, though deliberately setting out to distort their subjects, were much nearer to being likenesses than any of the later portraits. Then there were the early post-Eton triangles, with subjects for the most part imaginative and abstract, and titles vague, like 'Mêlée', 'Rout', 'Conflict', and 'Azimuth'; then the more virile, but still triangular, portraits of the *Sea Horse* period; and then the Australian work. Here could be detected a slight lapse into the naturalistic; partly because somehow he had not seen the sunny spaces of Australia with quite the same triangular eye, and partly, perhaps, because the brutal Australians had said things. Also, in that continent he had yielded a little to the influence of a native artist, Mr Norman Lindsay, who had discovered a new use for the firmament in art, and filled it with coveys of naked women. In Mr Lindsay's pictures it rained naked women, while in the foreground the fruitful earth erupted naked women in great numbers and in postures of infinite variety and wildness. And at this stage there began to appear in Mr Bryan's skies an occasional flock of naked women in flight, but still, of course, with breasts like gargoyles and behinds like cardboard boxes. After these there came the Iceland, whaler, and glacier pictures, and these, having followed the revolt against Sybil and the orchids, were more in the old geometrical, rebellious style. The last, or Hammersmith, period, showed a greater variety; for, to tell the truth, the artist at this time was in something of a muddle; or, as an art critic would have put it, his genius was still fluid. There were some of the old stove-pipe pictures and one or two large pictures full of cubic women in the Lindsay-Bryan style, and there were some river scenes of the Australian natural kind, and he had done one or two paintings of barges up the canal or at the wharves which really were very like barges. He liked painting a barge because it could easily be made to look like a barge and a coloured proposition of Euclid as well.

But, besides painting, he had during this period launched out into other arts as well. Sometimes, after a barren morning, it crossed his mind that what he was really intended for was a sculptor or a woodcarver. So now and then he bought clay and modelled clay in the rugged style of Mr Epstein, or so he thought; he had carved two or three walking-sticks for friends and made some experiments in etching. And the tools and the products of these various arts were no mean part of the furniture of the studio.

*

He could not tell why, but he was mildly excited by the thought of Jane's visit, and took more trouble to set things in order than he had ever done for a model before. It was a shock, somehow, to see her come in in her 'day-out' clothes – the red hat and the dark red coat and skirt. He had never seen her except in her cap and apron or her work-a-day dress, and had forgotten, as one does of policemen, that she might have other clothes.

She was not shy, nor yet forward, though she too was excited. 'You've a nice place, haven't you?' she said. 'What a lot of pictures!'

'Have a look round,' he said. 'But you've seen most of them, I suppose?'

'Some of them,' she said, making a grave inspection of the Lindsay period. 'Did you do all these, Mr Bryan?'

'Yes.'

'Oh! Florry said she thought some of them were done by a child.'

She made this statement simply, without humorous intention.

'Did she indeed?' said the artist. 'And what do you think of them?'

'I can't make them out,' she said after a pause. 'They don't seem like *you*, somehow, Mr Bryan. Oh, barges!' and she passed on eagerly to the Hammersmith period. 'Brentford, isn't that?'

'Yes.'

It was ridiculous, but the modern painter was definitely pleased because Jane Bell, who brought up his morning tea, had recognized his picture of Brentford Lock as a picture of Brentford Lock.

'But when the lock empties,' said Jane disappointedly after another examination, 'that barge will drift under the bridge.'

'Will it?' said the artist. 'Why?'

'Because she isn't tied up.'

It was quite absurd – he remembered how he had ignored the mooring lines of that barge, for the very good reason that they did not fit into the pattern of his picture but cut across it and spoiled it – it was absurd, but now he was sorry that he had left the barge defenceless and untethered so that she would charge sideways under the bridge when the lock was emptied, as he had known very well would happen.

'Quite right,' he said humbly.

'You ought to know better than that, Mr Bryan,' said Jane, encouraged.

'I do,' he said, almost conscience-stricken. 'And what about this one?'

'This one' was the portrait of a lady. She stood before a set of airy banisters which were not attached to any stair and did not reach the floor. Her face was partly dark green and partly pale green, like the parti-coloured seas of Cornwall. She had only one eye, and that was a large oval of white specks which overflowed on to the spaces usually reserved for the nose and forehead. She had two breasts, one the size of a melon and the other no larger than a plum. Her hair, unhappily, grew only on one side and hung down over her left shoulder in melancholy snakelike wisps, some black, some cream-coloured. Across her stomach she held her right forearm, which, affected with some form of elephantiasis, grew larger and larger from elbow to wrist and terminated in a monstrous talon. Beside her sat another female shape of similar appearance, but with a white face and green hair. The only other object in the picture was a table, but the table was drawn severely in the normal likeness of a table, with straight legs and a square top. It seemed strange that such a painter and such ladies should have to do with so commonplace a table. Without the table the ladies might have been taken for supernatural or fantastic creatures, griffins, gnomes, or extinct monsters; but this dull perpendicular kitchen-table made it clear that these misshapen horrors were female human beings.

Jane gazed at the standing lady, lost in wonder. She thought of her own body and of Lily's pretty body, which were the only bodies she knew: and she wondered that a nice gentleman like Mr Bryan could make something which she knew was ugly out of something which she felt was beautiful.

Mr Bryan watched her, wondering what she would say. His artistic friends looked at that picture and said, 'Best thing you've done'; his semi-artistic friends scratched their heads and murmured, 'I see what you mean ...'; Mr Raven had said, 'My God!'

Jane said at last, 'Is she a relation of yours, Mr Bryan?'

Mr Bryan said 'No.' He thought she meant that only some close family tie could excuse what he had done, and laughed; but she meant that she did not want to be rude about a sister or an aunt.

'Well, I'm sorry for the man she marries,' said Jane. 'Are you going to paint me like that, Mr Bryan?'

'I'd like to some time,' he said, 'if you wouldn't mind.'

Jane blushed, because she saw that 'like that' might mean 'with nothing on', though she had meant with one eye and a green face. But Mr Bryan's figures were so modern that it was difficult to realize that they had nothing on.

He saw the blush, and said, 'Of course, I wanted to do you washing up, in your working clothes.'

'Don't you like these?'

'Not for painting,' he said tactfully. 'But never mind. I wonder how this would suit you?' He held up a red velvet frock which had been worn by many models of about Jane's dimensions.

'Red's my colour,' said Jane, eyeing the dress with favour.

'Well, would you mind? You can change in the bathroom.'

Changing, Jane felt excited and reckless. 'I'm in one of my moods,' she thought. 'Ready for anything.' She fancied herself in the red velvet, which fitted her very fairly; the looking-glass was only a foot square, and too high for her, but by kneeling on the edge of the bath she could see enough of herself to be sure that she looked well. '*Jane Dons the Purple*' she thought. Perhaps this was the first move upon the road to queendom; and she stepped across the studio as dignified a pawn as possible. But it was a pity her hands were so pink and rough from washing-up, and her shoes went oddly with the dress.

'That's fine,' said Mr Bryan. 'Now sit down and be comfortable.'

Jane sat on the divan and stared fixedly at the easel, like a person about to be photographed or cross-examined.

'Sit anyhow,' he said, 'and talk, till I see what I want.'

'Talk Mr Bryan? What about?'

'Anything. Tell me the story of your life. Where do you live, and why do you bring me tea in the morning?'

He felt suddenly ashamed that he knew so little of this fellow-creature who had lived and slept and worked in the same house. He knew that she could sail a boat, for he had seen her. By accident he knew that she had a good figure; perhaps, all unsuspected, she had a soul or a massive intellect. She might have hopes, fears, ambitions, passions, love-affairs; men might be mad about her; she might be married; but all he knew was that she brought up the morning tea, did the stair-rods and the washing, carried in the next course, and sometimes sent his shirts to the wash with his links in them. He knew that domestic servants had private lives, because now and then they cropped up and interfered with Mrs Raven's arrangements, but they were always hidden and unconsidered, like their legs.

'Well, we live on the barge – you know that – ' began Jane.

'Yes, of course. I saw you bathing one Sunday.'

'I never saw you, Mr Bryan.'

'I looked through the fence,' said Mr Bryan. 'Very rude of me.'

'A lot of people do,' said Jane, matter-of-fact. 'It's Lily. She will show off. Lily's my sister. Father's stopped up the holes now,' she added.

'Is Lily the fair one?'

'Yes. One of Nature's butterflies, we tell her.'

'Well, she's got a lovely figure,' said the artist, busily drawing. 'So have you.'

'*The Shackles of Convention Fall Away*,' thought Jane. 'My figure!' In two years neither Fred nor Ernest had detected her figure. But now she did not blush. Indeed, the human picture of Mr Bryan peeping through the fence at Lily bathing was a bond between them, and she felt easier. This was what had always drawn her to Mr Bryan, that he seemed to know that a person was a human being. '*Acquaintance Ripens Into Friendship*,' she thought, and she put her hands behind her and leaned back, because that was more comfortable, and they *were* so pink.

'That's fine,' he said. 'Stay like that. How much do you earn?'

'Eighteen shillings a week.'

'Good God!' he said.

'Well, I'm getting more now, since the Derby, because five nights a week I help at the Black Swan. That's another nine shillings, you see.'

'Behind the bar?'

'Yes.'

'After working all day at the house?'

'Yes, Mr Bryan. It's a lot of standing. But I can do it.'

'Good God!' he said again, and drew in silence for a little.

'You could get more for sitting,' he said at last.

'Sitting, Mr Bryan?'

'Sitting for painters. Like this. It's half a crown an hour, you know. You've earned one and threepence already,' he added, jocular.

'Oh, but I didn't come for *that*!' cried Jane, aghast. 'I only came to oblige you, Mr Bryan.'

'Oh, but you must –'

'I wouldn't think of it!' '*Where Money Passes, Love Must Halt*', she knew.

'Oh, well, never mind that,' he said, respecting and astonished by her distress. 'But you could get a lot of work. I'll introduce you to some friends of mine. Would you like it?'

'I couldn't say, Mr Bryan.'

The idea that anyone would pay her half a crown an hour for sitting in a chair was difficult to grasp.

'Sitting's better than standing, you know. Better than washing-up.'

Better than washing-up – the everlasting washing-up: the grease, the steam, the plates with butter on them, the water too hot for the hands or too cold for the grease, the scouring of pans, the hunting for knives in the foul basin, the heat and smell, the sink stopped up, the tea-leaves glued into the teapot, the mustard and the bits of food, the corners of the milk-jug, the drying and piling, the carting of the plates and hanging up of cups, and then a new pile of dirty things discovered somewhere; the rough, pink hands! No more washing-up – what a dream! No more rough hands.

'Is it really half a crown an hour?' she asked.

'Some models get more. But it's hard work, you know. You have to sit very still.'

She made a swift calculation. If she did this strange sitting-still for six hours a day, which was surely easy, she would earn fifteen shillings in a day – nearly a week's wages!

'Well, I'd like to try,' she said. 'Of course, I wouldn't worry if it hadn't been for the Derby and Dad losing his job.'

'How was that?'

Feeling now as easy as if she were talking to Lily, she began the long tale of the Bell misfortunes, the Black Prince, the Derby, and the load of debt, how she felt responsible for everything because of that free pass at the cinema, and how she had jumped at Mrs Higgins's kind offer of work in the evenings, and Lily's frivolity and Florry's laziness, and everything. But the tale was all courage and charity and never complaining. Mr Bryan listened, thrilled and admiring, and pleased with himself because he had been right. She *was* a brave little soul. He found himself, fantastically, comparing her with Sybil, and thought, 'She's real; she's a real person.' It was wonderful that all the time he had known this girl she had had all these excitements in the background of her life, this wild barge existence, with the lunatic cornet-player who could stake his last hundred on an outsider; and yet she had never shown a sign of it. Even, no doubt, on the morning after that Derby she had come up, as cool and quiet as usual, with the morning tea, as if there were nothing else in the world that was in her mind but his tea, and John Raven's bath, and Mrs Raven's children. Almost without noticing it he could have paid off that debt to Mr Bell's Liverpool aunt and the trifling pound or two to Mrs Higgins. But instead of that this little girl was standing for long evenings behind the bar at the Black Swan after long days of every kind of labour at the Ravens'. So far apart were their worlds, though they had slept on the same floor, they were like two stars which revolve about each other and never touch. Now he felt himself drawn towards the Bell family; he longed to present Mr Bell with a glorious winner, and Lily with suitable employment, and Jane with whatever her heart desired. But probably he would never be allowed to help; she would not even take half a crown for sitting. If Jane had not been quite good to look at he would never have heard of the Bell misfortunes; neither, he reflected honestly, would he have cared to hear about them.

She was, without doubt, good to look at. Now she was at ease and talking about Lily, her small face had thrown off its domestic livery and was alive and human as he had never seen it at the Ravens'; but often would return that expression of thoughtful gravity which had first attracted him, seeming to say that she carried a wealth of responsibility on her small shoulders. She had an unconscious trick of lowering her head and looking upward with those profound brown eyes, while she made with great solemnity a remark of no importance, as when she had said that Mr Bell had stopped up the holes in the fence. This habit pleased him, he did not know why. It was as if her mind were far away with matters of infinite moment; and indeed at these times she was generally thinking of her high Destiny or plucking some fine flowered phrase from her anthology of captions.

Her voice pleased him too. She dropped no aitches; she said 'you see' too often, and there were little phrases and inflections which Sybil would have classed as 'common'; but as the tale of the Derby flowed softly on it did not weary him as the lordly drawl or manufactured sparkle of Sybil's friends had wearied him. And how much better was the tale of the Derby to hear than anyone's opinions about the 'Expressionist drama' or 'rhythm in painting'. It was very strange that he should be thinking so much about Sybil, who had not entered his head for many weeks. And now he said suddenly, 'Is Ernest your young man?'

'He is and he isn't,' said Jane. 'So is Fred. But I'm not potty about either of them.'

He was somehow pleased that she was not potty about Ernest or Fred.

'Is Ernest potty?' he asked.

'He makes out he is, Mr Bryan. But he's a Socialist, so it may be all talk. Fred's potty, I think, but he don't say much. It's all vice versa in this life, isn't it? And that reminds me, I ought to be going, Mr Bryan.'

'Fred?'

'No, it's Ernest tonight.'

'Very well, but you must come again.'

He stood up and surveyed what he had done. And 'Good Lord!' he said. What he had done, a pencil drawing, was extraordinary. Without intending it, even without noticing it, he had drawn Jane in a new style – a style not his own; no triangles, no cubes or stove-pipes, but a simple figure with two eyes, with a nose and a mouth and two arms the same size – a figure, moreover, which was quite like Jane. He had come very near to the unforgivable in art, a resemblance, almost a 'photograph'. What did this mean?

When foolish Philistine persons disparaged his pictures of ladies because the ladies of their acquaintance were more curved than cornered, more round than oblong, and rarely had bright green faces, he was accustomed to answer that that was how he *saw* the ladies in question; he was true to his vision, and there it was. But why had he not seen Jane Bell with a green face and a rectangular nose? Could it be that her rock-like sanity had infected him? Could it be that he was so much interested in Jane Bell that he had forgotten about art and drawn her naturally, as the spirit moved him?

'It's nice,' she said behind him. 'I like it better than the others.'

'Do you? So do I,' he said, and wondered what the Neo-Post-Impressionists would think of so treasonable a statement.

'I'll give you some introductions,' he said; and while she took off the red dress he scribbled three notes, wondering with a private chuckle how the wild Potts and Latimer and Jefferson would *see* Jane Bell. It would be amusing, he thought, to arrange an exhibition, in which there should be nothing but pictures of Jane Bell by thirty modern painters. *Then* the Philistines would see how different the same object could appear to different eyes.

'Take these as soon as you can,' he said. 'Not in the morning. Well, of course, you can't. And will you come next Friday?'

'Very well, Mr Bryan.'

'But next time it's business, you understand.'

'Business, Mr Bryan?'

'Three hours. And half a crown an hour.'

'Oh, no, Mr Bryan. I couldn't do that.'

'Is it the time?'

'No, the money.' She would *not* take money from him.

'You funny child!' he said. 'Then I can't ask you to come.'

She wavered. This was terrible. She must come again.

'Well, we'll see about it, shall we?' she said at last. 'Anyhow, I'll come.'

'Very well. Good-bye.'

They shook hands, and smiled at each other like old friends, and she went out gay and delighted by she knew not what. But she knew that she meant to be a model, and, after a study of her envelopes, she took a penny bus to the studio of Mr Potts.

Ernest had fits that evening when he heard that Jane had visited four *bourgeois* artists in the same afternoon. But they were nothing to the fits which Ernest had on the following Friday evening.

Jane had a good report to make to Mr Bryan that day. Mr Potts and Mr Latimer had both booked her for six mornings, and Mr Jefferson had made vague promises. She had given Mrs Raven a week's notice from Saturday, and in two days would be a professional model.

'Fine,' said Mr Bryan. 'I'll give you some more letters.' But it crossed his mind that poor Mrs Raven would be in a fuss again, looking for another girl. And so she was.

'There's only one thing, Mr Bryan,' said Jane slowly, looking at the floor. 'Mr Potts said that he might want me to sit in the nude, you see, and, what I was wondering, would there be many like that?'

'Very likely. Do you mind?'

'I don't know,' said Jane, troubled. 'I was wondering would a girl lose caste? Because I wouldn't want to lose caste. Ernest says that a girl loses caste if she sits in her clothes; but, of course, Ernest would say anything.'

'No, you wouldn't lose caste,' said Mr Bryan gravely. 'Many models have married great men. Would Ernest rather you went on washing-up?'

'You can't tell with Ernest. He wouldn't be satisfied if everyone was the Archbishop of Canterbury. But would *you* think the worse of me, Mr Bryan?'

'Why should I? I want to paint you myself.'

'I don't think I'd mind if it was you,' she said.

'Well, would you like to try it? This afternoon?'

'Yes, Mr Bryan.'

'What about your father?'

'I shall tell him I did it for a bet,' she said. 'Then he won't mind. He doesn't count, poor dear.'

Undressing in the bathroom, Jane told herself that she must be a 'wanton', because, for all her palaver, she did not mind at all. She knew that she ought to be trembling with modesty and hot with shame. Lily had said that in such a case she would die of shame, but Jane had told Lily that no one would have guessed it from the way she went on when she was bathing; and now she thought that in this matter she and Lily were perhaps a pair, for she was glad to be undressing for Mr Bryan to see her, only she hoped that he would not give her one of those lop-sided busts like the lady with the green face. Fine feathers might make fine birds, but with nothing on she was as good as anyone, so she had often thought when she undressed at night, *Clothes do not Make the Gentleman*, as everybody knew. Once or twice she had seen photographs of Society girls bathing in France, and they looked just like Lily or herself. Mr Bryan had noticed this figure of hers when he saw her bathing; he did not like her best clothes, and now when he saw her as she really was, without cap and apron, and nothing to show that she was a woman of the proletariat, or whatever it was, perhaps he would realize that she was no ordinary girl. She peeped in the little glass and decided that no one could tell her from the Duchess of

York. She had forgotten to take off her pearl necklace, but thought that it looked well, and kept it on.

Nevertheless, she did feel pink as she sat down on the divan and held back the cloak to let it fall from her shoulders. She had a horrid fear that her arms were blushing again, and, looking down, found that it was true; and so much did she resent this that she was ready to wrap the cloak round her again.

'I blush down my arms,' she said. 'Silly, isn't it?'

He said quickly, 'That's an idea. Could you stay like that?'

None of his models had ever blushed before, and now she had given him an extraordinary idea – extraordinary, that is, for a Neo-Post-Impressionist or triangular portrait-painter – and that idea was to paint her exactly as she was, to capture the shy moment of unveiling, her hands above her shoulders holding the cloak, and the delicate flush in her face and neck. The picture would be called 'The Blush', or 'The First Sitting', and it would be sadly like an Academy picture – a picture with a story, or a coloured illustration in a Society weekly. Indeed, by the subject, the picture was doomed to be academic, for even Potts or Latimer would hardly attempt to paint a blush that was green. But such was the strange influence of this servant girl that the academic no longer revolted him. She made him *feel* academic. All the last week, since her first visit to the studio, his painting-mind had been in a muddle. He had twice sent his green-lady model away because he could not go on with her latest portrait, in which her face was pale blue. The upper part of her was almost completed in various shades of blue; but now, when he looked at her legs they appeared to be flesh-coloured; and since she could scarcely be a mixture of flesh colour and blue, it was difficult to proceed. Her breasts, which had once, without doubt, been irregular polygons, were now inexplicably round; and the saucepan in the background seemed to have lost much of its significance. So in despair he had fallen back upon some of his miscellaneous arts, had moulded two fire-dogs, and begun carving a cigarette-box.

'It will be tiring,' he said. 'Say when you're tired.' And he began work eagerly. This time there was no talking.

Not for a long time had he been so excited by a piece of work. He had painted too long to be excited by the nude as such. Very few of his sitters had moved him personally – they stirred him no more than a naked leg of mutton; indeed, some who had seemed to have a faint attraction with their clothes on had lost it the moment they took them off. To paint from the nude, so far from encouraging passion and immorality, is in most cases, for the artist, a wholesome experience; and many a non-artist might be the better for it. So it could not be the spectacle of Jane's slim young middle and small young breasts which excited him. But, whatever the cause, none of her podgy predecessors had made him feel with such absolute confidence that the picture he was making would be the greatest picture in the world. Whatever the cause, he was as much inflamed by this new adventure into academic art as he had been, he remembered, when he first began to draw noses in squares.

After twenty minutes he let her have a rest. After another twenty minutes he made her some tea. 'You sit splendidly,' he told her, and she was pleased. Jane had found out already that this sitting was not, after all, such an easy job. She grew stiff and tired very soon; she had pins and needles in the first half, and cramp in the second; and she reflected curiously that all relations with men seemed to lead in the end to cramp and pins and needles, for she had had them both with the placid Fred and the passionate Ernest. The pose was a severe one and too much for a beginner. But after tea Mr Bryan was more feverishly possessed by art than ever. He saw by the clock that twenty minutes had passed, but thought that Jane seemed happy and could stand another minute or two. Every minute taken from the picture seemed a deprivation, an outrage, a crime against humanity. Engrossed, entranced, he forgot about time, and about humanity. And Jane, it is true, was happy enough. She was blissful. She could see his eagerness, and rejoiced in it; but she hoped it was more for herself than the picture. For now she had decided that Mr Bryan was the Valentino of her life. Her arms ached, her fingers tingled, she had to pinch the cloak to be sure that it was still there; her back was stiff, her eyes drowsy, and the weight of her head upon her neck was unendurable; yet she endured it. Not for any reward would she have stopped him. She fixed her eyes upon his face, and, with the thought of him, kept herself erect and lively, thinking that by this ordeal and suffering she was giving herself to him and yet being respectable, though

Ernest, no doubt, might have something to say. The thought of Ernest and what he might have to say mysteriously revived her. For some reason she looked forward, maliciously, to telling Ernest that she had sat before Mr Bryan with nothing on; and this thought preserved her for another five minutes. But she felt suddenly cold and bloodless in the face, she felt that something was going to happen to her, she could do nothing to prevent it, there was a singing in her ears, a buzzing in her head, Mr Bryan worked on happily at her legs, and Jane fainted.

When she came to she saw Mr Bryan's face close to hers, she felt his arms supporting her, and she closed her eyes quickly, wishing that this state of things should continue. He had picked her up, and, not having much knowledge of faints, laid her upon the couch, fetched water in a cup, and sprinkled it on her forehead, for he had read that this was done. She lay so like the dead that he lifted her up and feebly held the cup before her lips, as if the expectation of this draught might restore her. Pathetic little morsel! Her hands were rough and her hair wanted a wash. And he thought of Sybil Colebatch, with her scents and skin-creams and frequent baths.

He kissed her lightly, compassionately, without excitement, as one pats the head of a dog. But to Jane this was such pleasure that she thought she might faint again indeed. She lay quiet in happy abandon, savouring her joy. She had forgotten her faintness, she had forgotten she was naked, she was alone with Mr Bryan, who had kissed her, and she was beginning to live like the pictures. She opened her eyes at last and smiled at him and showed him a face transfigured and radiant. He was astonished, but he kissed her again, lightly again, though not so lightly as before.

But Jane asked no more; an electric flame shot through her and she was sure that at last she had found Love's Bliss.

Then he stood up, a little ashamed of himself, and wrapped the cloak about her.

10

HANDS OFF CROATIA!

JANE behaved badly to Ernest that evening. For a special treat he took her to the Palais de Danse because he felt that on the previous Friday he had been a little harsh with her, perhaps, about the artists. After two dances Jane suggested that they should sit down and have a lemon-squash. She was elated and bored, she could think of nothing but Mr Bryan, and she could not be bothered to follow the laborious steps of Ernest, or suffer gladly a succession of collisions. Ernest did not want a squash, and the one attraction of a dance for him was that for long periods he might, without protest, hold Jane in his arms. If they were going to sit remotely in different chairs and suck squashes through straws, he had much better have saved his money and hugged her for nothing under the elm-tree.

But he consented with a good grace, and ordered the drinks. He complained, however, of the number of people who were there in evening-dress, and said it was time that sort of flummery was done away with, especially at a place which was intended for 'the People'. Jane said she liked to see them; it made a change. Ernest said that Labour would make a change one of these days, and Jane laughed heartily. She laughed at everything he said, sucking at her squash and teasing him with her eyes over the straws. She thought that Ernest was a poor fish tonight.

'You're a cold cod, aren't you, Ernest?' she said, pitying him.

Ernest stared at her, annoyed. She had never ventured to pity him before. 'Here, what's the game?' he said; and then, suspiciously, 'What you been doing this afternoon?'

'Nothing much,' she said casually. 'I've been sitting again.'

'Oh, you have, have you? Where?'

'In the nude.'

'Sitting in the – ' began Ernest. 'What d'you mean?'

'The nude. Nothing. I earned five shillings.' This was not quite true, for she had refused the five shillings; but she thought the five shillings might mollify Ernest's economic mind. He was every bit as indignant as she had hoped.

'Do you mean to say,' said he, 'that you've been sitting *stripped* before a man?'

'M'm,' said Jane, nodding, through her straw.

'Well, I'm – ' said Ernest, too staggered for comment. 'What's his name?'

'Bryan.'

'The same fellow? The one that was lodger at your place?'

'That's right.'

'Anybody else there?'

'No.'

'Just you and him?'

'You heard what I said.'

'Well, I'll wring his bloody neck!'

Jane's drink came to an end with a derisive gurgle.

'What'll you do that for, Ernest?' she said politely.

Ernest glared, maddened by her tone and by his own suspicions. 'Did he interfere with you?'

'Oh, yes, of course – you would think of that!'

'Well, did he?'

'No, he didn't. And if you're going to be rude I'm going.'

She turned away from him and looked at the dancers. A waltz was being played; the white lights had been turned down and the floor was illumined by coloured rays from both ends of the room. The colours changed every few seconds, and the dancers drifted round with expressions of unspeakable melancholy, now green, now heliotrope, and now bright yellow. Jane felt romantic, but not for Ernest. Still, weak as ever, she thought, she was a little ashamed of the way she had behaved. For she did not really feel bold and wanton about Mr Bryan, but rather humble. But that was the strange part of Ernest: somehow he always provoked her to do things which made her sorry afterwards.

'Well, you're a nice one!' he said at last, and she was sorry no longer. 'Feel proud of yourself, I dare say?'

'Didn't you say I ought to raise my stattus?'

'Of course I did. But if you think you've raised your stattus, I don't. You've lost caste, I should say. Respectable girls don't act that way.'

'We're very polite, aren't we? Didn't you tell me domestic service was a degrading thraldom?'

'Dare say I did.'

'Well, I've given my notice. I'm going to be a model. I've raised my stattus. I'm a professional woman, see?'

'You're not going on with it?'

'Aren't I, then? I've got engagements.'

'In the nude?'

'I dare say,' said Jane. 'I'm not particular,' as if she had been a model for twenty years.

'Well, if you're not particular, I am.'

'What's it got to do with you, Ernest?'

'Look here, my girl —'

'I'm not your girl.'

'Well, you can please yourself, but if you can't act respectable, you and me will part, that's all.'

'All right,' said Jane, 'let's part.' And she stood up, really angry now. 'You're very respectable all of a sudden, aren't you? Long may it last!'

This stroke went home, for in Ernest's confused wrath there was perhaps more envy than moral horror or solicitude for Jane. The idea that a casual *bourgeois*, no doubt as unscrupulous as all capitalists, should have received from Jane a privilege denied to her honest proletarian admirer, inflamed and scorched him; and who shall blame him for that?

'No offence, Jane,' he said, changing his tone, for he did not want to part from Jane, sit in the nude or no. 'Can't you see I'm only thinking of you? What do you know about the man? Sit down, do. You don't see what I mean.'

But Jane, finding that a firm word worked wonders, even with Ernest, was tasting power and enjoying it. It was strange and fine to have the mighty Ernest in this humble state, and it would do no harm to keep him thus. She would not sit down, and they left the hall of revelry in silence.

They walked in the road, as everybody does in King Street in the evening, and on the way Ernest developed the notion that he was only thinking of her. What he meant was, how was she to know that one of these artists would not take advantage of her? They were a queer lot, by all accounts; well, all he could say was, if one of them so much as touched her, he, Ernest, would murder him.

Jane said, 'I can take care of myself, thank you, and you can leave my friends alone.'

Ernest, with a new and more dreadful suspicion, stopped dead in the street, and said, 'You're not gone on him, are you?'

A man with a barrow halted behind him, and said, 'Now then, Romeo, hit her in the home, can't you?'

Jane walked on, and Ernest had to trot to catch her up. This was like the pictures, this was Life, Jane thought, high and mighty Ernest trotting after her like a little dog, and making faces like Novarro.

Ernest came up alongside and repeated his question.

'What if I am?' said Jane. 'Let's cross here.' And she darted across in front of a tram.

Ernest had to wait for the tram, and trotted again. 'What if you were?' said he. 'Well, you'd better forget it, that's all.'

'What d'you mean?'

'You'll come to a bad end, that's what I mean. There's only one thing his class wants out of your class, and that's something for nothing – see?'

'What's class got to do with it?'

'Class is class,' said Ernest, 'and you can't get away from it. D'you think he'll marry you, or what?'

'I haven't thought anything about it.' Which was very true.

'Well, if you don't want to be a broken blossom, you'd better not think any more, that's my advice.'

But Ernest's excellent advice had only put new and more fatal notions into her head. She was now considering this marriage idea.

'Isn't our class as good as his class, Ernest?' she said at length.

'Better,' said Ernest shortly, for he always suspected mischief when she quoted his opinions.

'Well, then, why shouldn't our class marry his class?'

'It's oil and vinegar. They don't mix.'

'Well, how are you going to get this brotherhood, if there's no mixing?'

'There's no brotherhood with the *borjwaw*.'

'Well, you said I had a *borjwaw* mentology, or something, didn't you, Ernest?'

'*Sy*-chology,' said Ernest.

'Yes. Well, if I've got a *borjwaw* what-is-it, I'd better marry a *borjwaw*, seems to me.'

'All right, try it!' said Ernest, furious, 'and join the army of the exploited! The streets of London are paved with women of the proletariat who put their trust in the master classes – '

'Don't you make speeches at me, Ernest!' said Jane.

'Well, all I know,' said Ernest, abandoning argument, 'if that bloke so much as touches you, I'll put him in the Thames.'

'You'll mind your own business. You're always talking stuff about the independence of the female proletariat, and then the first chance I get of a little independence you turn round and abuse me. That's like you, all over.'

Ernest muttered something about economic pawns and was silent. They had reached the little gate in the fence and were both angry, and Ernest, remembering bitterly that this evening was to be a special treat, cursed Mr Bryan and all his artists. Inflamed with jealousy and just rage, he seized Jane roughly in his arms.

'Let me go!' she cried, struggling; but, even as she did so, she thought '*Alone with the Adventurer Rose Repels his Dishonourable Advances*'.

He kissed her hotly, saying, 'Sauce for the goose, sauce for the gander – see?' and meaning by the goose the detested Bryan.

She wriggled in his arms and hid her head; then bit his finger and tore herself away. She stood trembling a moment, looking at him. 'You worm!' she said, and slipped through the gate.

But she had scarcely crossed the wharf before she was ashamed of herself. 'I must be a wanton!' she thought, because she had almost enjoyed that struggle. And she knew she had not treated Ernest fairly, worm though he was.

And so, on Saturday, when Ernest appeared at the Ravens' back-door to ask her out on Sunday, she felt kinder, and said, 'All right, Ernest; only no jawing, and you behave yourself – see?'

It was a great day, that Saturday, the last day of her economic thraldom, and she had to be kind. She felt so kind that she was sorry for Mrs Raven, who was losing her, and by the evening she was almost of a mind to take her notice back, because she knew the house would be upside down without her, and she did *not* believe that Mrs Raven was suited yet, though many girls had called. With Mrs Raven it was a case of many called but few chosen.

But Jane did not intend to be weak any more, for the weak fell out of the film before the first reel was over. And all Saturday, whenever she had to do anything which she much disliked doing, she did it fiercely, saying to herself, 'The last time, the last time!' When the sink was stopped up and she had to put her arm down the drain and ferret about among the tea-leaves, when the cat was sick in a corner of the drawing-room, when Nanny asked her to keep an eye on the children for three minutes and stayed away for thirty, when little Tom poked a stick in Margaret's eye and Mrs Raven came down and said there was never all this yelling when they were with her, when impatient telephoners refused to give their names, and Mr Raven said how often had he told her to get everybody's name, when Florry took the last two new potatoes, when Mr Raven walked in muddy boots across the nursery floor just after she had scrubbed it, she thought always, 'All right, but it's the last time.' Still, it would be strange to have no part in this house and all its daily troubles and excitements, and she did not know how they would manage without her.

It was her pride to be always the one who knew where everything was, whether it was candles, the corkscrew, or Mr Raven's umbrella: when he had been hunting for one of the four corkscrews for five minutes it gave her pleasure to be able to put her hand upon two of them immediately. So much so that, as Mr Raven suspected, it was a temptation to put things away in places where nobody would think of looking for them. Letters left in the dining-room would go behind the books on the first shelf; studs she hid in drawers, and razor-blades in jewel-boxes. Today she took the corkscrews from her cunning corners and laid them in an obvious drawer with the sensation that she was resigning a kingdom. She was a power in this house, after all, and now she would be a power no more.

But washing-up for the last time put an end to these regrets. Since it was the last time Florry let her do both the washing and drying as well. The Ravens had had two neighbours to supper, and there had been liver and bacon, which meant mustard and grease; and artichokes, which meant oil and vinegar; and strawberries, which, like artichokes, meant remains and mess. Jane thought she had never known such messy washing-up. A thick scum swam upon the surface of the basin, and the mingled fumes of hot oil and bacon-fat and gravy and cabbage filled the little room. One kettle of boiling water was not enough, for she had to change the water three times. She was conscientiously determined to leave a good mark behind her, gave every plate an extra rub, and spent a long time ferreting about in the corners of the milk-jug and the sauce-boat. She fished out the knives one by one instead of by handfuls, as usual, and rubbed them singly, as if they were to be exhibited in a glass-case. Florry sat on her hard Windsor chair and read the evening paper, looking up from time to time to make a pained remark, such as, 'Suppose you'll be laying in late tomorrow morning?' or 'Some people don't know when they're well off.' Jane made no reply, but thought to herself 'The last time, old sour-face!'

And on Monday she was to sit for Mr Bryan again. On Monday and Tuesday and Wednesday and Thursday and Friday – all the week, except Saturday. Unless Mr Bryan had to go away, and as to that, she was to find out on Sunday evening, when he would know. But surely he would not wish to go away; surely he would wish to stay at home and go on with her picture.

She put all the plates on the rack, and all the glasses in the cupboard, and all the knives and forks in the basket. She cleaned out the sink and took out the grating from the drain and carefully removed the tea-leaves. She rinsed and squeezed the dish-cloths and hung them on the line to dry; she got out the teapot, the cups and saucers, the sugar and the milk, and made the tray ready for the Ravens' evening tea; she filled the kettle and put it on the stove, so that now Florry had nothing to do but light the gas and carry up the tray. Then, conscious of a good work well done, she looked about her and said, 'That's the lot, I think.'

Florry threw one look at the tray and said without gratitude, 'You've forgotten the spoons.'

Jane fetched the teaspoons and in Florry's little room put on her coat and hat. She went upstairs with the idea of saying good-bye to Mrs Raven, and listened at the drawing-room door. She had somehow looked forward to this farewell: she saw Mrs Raven grasping her hand and saying, 'Thank you, *thank* you, Jane, for all you have done for this house. How we shall manage without you I *don't* know!' But she could hear Mrs Raven talking with her guests, and, as it happened, the elder Miss Anstruther was at that moment remarking that nowadays if you gave servants an inch they took an ell. Jane concluded that Mrs Raven had forgotten her, and she crept downstairs again; which was unjust, for Mrs Raven came downstairs a few minutes later to say good-bye to Jane and found that she had gone.

The farewell to Florry was disappointing too, for Florry only said, 'Well, au revore; you'll be glad to come back in a week or two, I dare say.'

It was like Florry to make her feel guilty in her moment of triumph, and when for the last time she slammed the front door behind her Jane felt more guilty than triumphant. This was the first grand turning-point in her existence; the New Life was spread before her; she had improved her 'stattus', thrown off her bond-age; and no one encouraged her – not even Ernest. And now she was wondering whether Florry would remember to do Mr Raven's tennis-shoes in the morning.

But suddenly it flashed upon her that she, Jane, would not be there in the morning; and, flinging Mr Raven and his tennis-shoes behind her, she ran as fast as she could to the beloved *Blackbird*.

The entertainment which Ernest had in store for her the following afternoon turned out to be a Monster Demonstration and Mass Rally in Hyde Park in support of the 'Hands Off Croatia' Move-ment. To do him justice, he had proposed to take her to Hampton Court and see the Maze, but on Saturday evening he had received an invitation to speak from Platform 2, and he thought that the Mass Rally would be good for Jane.

So Jane found herself marching along the Victoria Embank-ment in columns of fours. Ernest was on one side of her, and on the other an envenomed old lady with a wrinkled face, who as she marched muttered maledictions on the Conservative Government.

Not far in front of them was a banner, and not far behind them
was a brass band. On the banner was written:

> WORKERS OF BRITAIN
> STAND SOLID
> FOR YOUR
> CROATIAN BROTHERS

And Jane could see other banners, some gaily coloured, tossing
and fluttering at intervals in the long column far ahead of her. She
had never been in a procession before; she had never walked about
London in the road and had the traffic stopped for her; she had
never marched to the music of a band, and though it was a puzzle
to know how to walk in time, with one band behind and another
just in front, she enjoyed it. Also she enjoyed seeing ordinary
people clustered on the pavement and staring at her curiously as if
she were something in the Lord Mayor's Show. The banners and
the music and the marching excited her; they seemed to fit in with
the grand new independence which she had just put on, they spoke
of hope and determination and better things; she began to think
that there must be something fine in the 'Hands Off Croatia'
Movement, and she wondered where Croatia was, and who was
laying hands on Croatia, and why.

She did not like to ask Ernest, who had turned suddenly silent,
because he was getting his speech by heart. The lady on Jane's
right was busily discharging information, certainly, but it seemed
to have little to do with Croatia. Jane gathered that for the old lady
the demonstration was demonstrating not so much affection for
the unfortunate Croatians, whoever they were, but detestation for
the British Government.

The band behind them stopped playing for a space and Jane
heard her neighbour cry, 'Forgers! Blackguards!' in tones of great
bitterness. 'A nice thing!' she cried to no one in particular. 'The
Home Secretary a forger! They put my uncle in prison,' she added,
and marched on mutely with that thought for a few paces. 'Fifty
millions to persecute the Jews!' she continued, then: 'Churchill
was in it! And they talk about Parnell! *Parnell indeed!*' she
shrieked, turning her leathery old face to Jane. 'What about the
Hackney election?'

Jane did not clearly understand these observations, so she said politely, 'What exactly are they doing to Croatia?' for she felt that a person with so many grievances would be acquainted with the Croatians' troubles. But fortunately, as she spoke, the brass band behind them blared out afresh, and her shameful ignorance was drowned in the music of the 'International'.

The old lady, however, perceiving that she had been addressed, paused in her stride, nodded delightedly, and putting her hands to her mouth, shouted in Jane's ear, 'That's right! You'll do! You're the sort we want!'

Jane paused also to receive this message, the man behind her trod on her heel, and the marchers were thrown into confusion as far back as the band. Jane blushed, Ernest looked crossly at her, and she decided that she would not ask for information again.

By Trafalgar Square the novelty of the procession had worn off, and Jane began to feel tired. Her thoughts turned from the ill-treated Croatians to her dear Mr Bryan; she hoped the Mass Rally would not last too long, for Mr Bryan had said that he would be out after six, and if she could not call at the studio she would have to telephone, and the telephone was expensive and alarming.

They marched along Piccadilly, where Ernest made remarks about the gentlemen's clubs, and hinted that one day these buildings would be put to better uses. Jane had never walked so far in her life, her feet were burning and her legs ached. But as they swung into the Park between the waiting lines of motor-cars and omnibuses every band played at once, every banner was raised another inch or two, and every back was straightened; and Jane, padding painfully at last over the yellow grass, was touched again by the excitement of the march and worried no longer about the whereabouts of Croatia.

The next thing was that she was wedged in the third row in front of Platform Number 2 and smiling up at Ernest, who was smiling down at her kindly from the platform. It was hot, the supporters of Croatia were hot, they smelt strongly of humanity and smoked very strong tobacco; yet Jane was glad to stand still at last and have something to lean against, if it was only a hot Socialist.

The first speaker began, 'Comrades, you know me,' and went on to say that he had been in prison. This announcement was received with loud cheers. This speaker did not speak for long, and said nothing at all about Croatia, though he mentioned his objections to our Capitalist Government. It was his business to introduce Comrade Watkins, who had not only been in prison, but had only just come out of prison. Comrade Watkins then stood up, the envenomed old lady said, 'Bravo! Watty,' there was more applause, and Jane began to feel a little ashamed that she had never been in prison.

Comrade Watkins was a small, dark, chubby man with burning eyes and a high voice. He looked very well after prison, and much better fed than most of his audience. He had the practised orator's trick of breaking up his opening sentences into small sections, with great pauses between them, which made the audience feel that the section next to come would be of profound significance. This trick he had learned from the Earl of Derby at a meeting of the Liverpool Conservative Women's Association many years before, when Comrade Watkins was a stage-hand. He began:

'As you 'ave 'eard —
I 'ave enjoyed —
The 'ospitality —
Of 'Is Majesty's Government.   (Great laughter.)
I 'arbour no ill-will —
Against 'Is Majesty's Government —
They did me proud — (Laughter.)
They 'ave my gratitude — (Laughter.)
They 'ave my prayers — (Great laughter.)
For what are my sufferin's, comrades — ?'

No one seemed to know what his sufferings were, and indeed, he was one of the very few persons present who had already had two good meals that day. He raised his voice: '*What* are my sufferin's, after all — when weighed in the balance — against the solidarity — of the toiling masses?' (Approving sounds.) 'But let me tell you *this*, my friends.' Comrade Watkins paused again, and, turning his head from side to side, glared fiercely about Hyde Park, as if to challenge any man to prevent the speaker from telling him this. No one, however, offering any objection to his telling them this, he said: 'Let me say *this*, comrades,' and paused again.

'That my sufferin's – and my incarceration – is only one more nail – in the coffin – the *coffin* – of 'Is Majesty's Government.' (Loud and prolonged applause.)

Comrade Watkins had now warmed his audience, he had stamped his personality upon their tender minds, and he gathered speed.

'Comrades,' he said, 'I am not going to come any 'umbug over you, I am not going to use the language of chicanery and hyperbowl at this great meeting this afternoon, but I say without fear of contradiction that the behaviour of the Government in the West 'Am controversy 'as been a scandal and a dudgeon to the public life of the country.'

Here he stopped suddenly and looked about, as if expecting support, and many of the loyal comrades again made encouraging sounds; but Jane began to weary of Comrade Watkins. She did not know what a dudgeon was, and she could summon up no resentment about the incarceration of Comrade Watkins; but she found herself painfully nervous about Ernest's speech and astonishingly anxious that he should speak better than Comrade Watkins. The infectious fever of politics had caught her, and she was still hoping to hear from somebody the geographical position of the Croatians, the details of their wrongs, and the measures by which it was proposed to alleviate them.

But Comrade Watkins had other fish to fry. When he had done with the West Ham controversy he passed on to the Education scandal, and from that to the conduct of the police at Huddersfield, and from that to the barbarous character of the Home Secretary, the bungling of the expedition to the Dardanelles, the persecution of the Jews in Roumania, the rent of municipal houses, the price of beans, the aspirations of the subject races, and an outrageous observation of the Chancellor of the Exchequer on the third reading of the Finance Bill. Over the whole field of human affairs Comrade Watkins ranged easily and ferociously, never at a loss for a word; and almost the only subject on which he did not touch was the menace to Croatia. He gesticulated often, and his face glistened with sweat. When Jane looked up at him, the bright sun behind him dazzled her eyes, and when she looked down she felt rude. Also, she was much afraid that if she stood for very long in that crowd she would faint. And the thought of fainting reminded her of Mr Bryan and the importance of escaping from the Mass Rally in good time to call at the studio, and she became less and less interested in the remarks of Comrade Watkins. She peered about her among the crowd, and thought that most of those near her seemed nice, quiet, sensible men like Fred, and she wondered why they listened so attentively to the remarks of Mr Watkins, which seemed to her to have no sense at all. Then, in an eloquent aside upon the vices of the rich, the speaker said, '*I've* seen the fine ladies walking like peacocks down Rotten Row ...' and far back, upon the outskirts of the crowd, among the holiday-makers who had drifted to the scene, a voice said innocently, 'You mean pea-hens!' Many laughed, but the nice, quiet, sensible men about Jane flared up instantly, and, turning their heads, cried furiously, 'Chuck him out!' and 'Wring his bloody neck!' So angry were they that Jane's affectionate mind went with them, and she found herself resenting bitterly that flippant interruption. So excited was the orator that he took off his coat, and, gesticulating more freely, demolished in a phrase or two the capitalist law courts, and the House of Lords. He was now so hot that Jane became fascinated by the drops of sweat which trickled down his nose and trembled at the end until some passionate gesture shook them off upon the chairman or the turf below him.

With the gesture which destroyed for ever the pretensions of the League of Nations, a sort of shower descended upon the parched and possibly grateful Park. Comrade Watkins then took his collar off, and having handed his collar and studs to the chairman, began to march up and down the platform as he spoke. But after the pea-hen interruption he never had the same firm grip of his audience, and presently the chairman tugged delicately at the seat of his trousers, and Comrade Watkins sat down. When he sat down he left very few of the institutions of the British Empire standing, but Jane was no wiser about Croatia than before.

Ernest had never been in prison, so when he was called upon there was no applause. Jane's heart beat strongly for him, and she felt that if anyone interrupted she would die. But very soon she was at ease, and proud of him. She was surprised by the strange voice in which he spoke, a voice which she had never heard before.

But it was a fine, brave, confident voice, and it pleased her that he went straight to the matter of Croatia, about which they were all there to demonstrate. It seemed that the Capitalist Governments of Europe were not keeping their hands off Jane's comrades in Croatia. In fact, there was a plot against the innocent Croats, and Ernest proved this by a brief account of the conduct of the European Governments in China. Croatia was being encircled, isolated, she was a pawn in the economic machinations of Wall Street. Mr Churchill, as usual, was in the plot, and with him, on this occasion, were Mr Baldwin and the steel kings. Ernest was a good speaker; he spoke easily and quietly and sincerely. Jane felt that whatever it was that he meant, he meant it, that there was in his heart a real brotherly pain for the far-off people to whom somebody was doing these horrible things. And Jane, moved at last, tried to picture in her mind what manner of folk these Croatians were. She wondered if they were black. She saw them as a thin, black, stunted race, living in mud huts, surrounded by snow, and probably wolves. They had numerous babies which were kept in baskets like litters of puppies, and owing to the behaviour of Mr Churchill these babies were not getting quite enough milk. But Ernest had plunged into an historical argument and Jane did her best to follow him, amazed by his knowledge. The Treaty of Brest, the Brussels Agreement – Treaties fell from Ernest like ripe plums. 'What *is* the Polish Corridor?' he asked. No one knew what the Polish Corridor was, and nothing that Ernest said afterwards enlightened them; but for a long time afterwards the Polish Corridor remained in Jane's mind as a mark and example of Ernest's high qualities.

But Ernest, like the other speaker, and like all the speakers who have ever spoken, went on too long; and Jane, though she admired him still, grew less and less interested in the suffering Croatians. And as her mind wandered from Croatia, her bodily discomfort claimed her attention. From peering up at Ernest her eyes ached and her neck was stiff, she felt limp and flabby, and thought that she recognized the first approaches of the faint. She reasoned carefully with herself whether it would be more upsetting to Ernest to go away while Ernest was still speaking, or to fall flop under Ernest's nose. She decided to retire quickly, if she could, and hoped that Ernest would not notice. So when Ernest was answering a question about the Polish Corridor she turned round and pushed gently, saying, 'Let me out, please.' The men saw her pale face, and made way for her kindly. On the edge of the crowd she turned her head and glanced guiltily at Ernest. Ernest, still talking, had reproachful eyes upon her, for he did not see that her face was pale, but only that she had gone away, and by her going distracted his audience. She saw that she had done a dreadful thing, but sat down on the grass and felt better away from the stuffy crowd. One of the picnic-parties who hovered on the fringe, enjoying the fun but comparatively indifferent to the future of Croatia, gave her a drink of milk from a flask. She asked them the time and they said half past five. A small panic seized her, for now she would have to telephone to Mr Bryan, and she could not even telephone until the Mass Rally was over. For one thing, she had no pennies. From where she sat she could see Ernest still speaking, but could not hear a word he said, which was strange but restful. She thought he looked rather fine and handsome on the platform in his blue suit, with his eager expression, his curly forelock, and waving arms; and she was proud to see all those people paying attention to what he said. Perhaps after all there was more sense in what he said than she had thought. But she prayed that he would stop saying it very soon, and very soon he did.

Then Comrade Councillor Groves of Stepney moved the resolution, which was a very long resolution indeed and began: 'That this meeting, assembled under the auspices of the Joint National Council of the Anglo-Croatian Workers' Committee, and the Executive Committee of the "Hands Off Croatia" Movement, records its detestation of the policy of the Government towards the economic encirclement and industrial serfdom of Croatia, Ruthenia, Lithuania, and the sub-Baltic States, and which by sabotaging the international solidarity of the workers it is the aim of the present Capitalist Government to do, and this meeting determines to by every legitimate means resist, etc., etc., and which, etc., etc. . . .'

Councillor Groves spoke to the resolution for five minutes, and Comrade Ladder seconded it for seven. Jane was sure that by now it was ten minutes to six, and was in an agony about her telephone-call, which every minute grew more terribly important. She disliked Comrade Ladder, and did not care what injury was done to the Croatians. She wanted to telephone to Mr Bryan and to hear his voice. Ernest sat on the platform still, smiling up at Comrade Ladder and never once looking in her direction. She might be dead for all he cared. And she thought it strange that one who could be so large-hearted towards the remote Croatians (perfect strangers) could be completely selfish towards his best girl. But the whole thing was strange. All these simple Freds, these railwaymen and plumbers and out-of-works, they had their own troubles and their own girls, no doubt; and what were they all doing, wasting a fine Sunday afternoon on the Polish Corridor and the troubles of the Croatians whom they had never seen? She suspected that somewhere in it there must be something that was sensible and good, for it seemed so very unselfish. But why did not Ernest come and take her to the telephone?

The 'Red Flag' was sung and Jane stood up at the edge of the audience. She did not know the words of the song, and no one about her seemed to know them except one small boy who sang them very lustily and clearly. Jane, thinking that she owed this to Ernest, followed the boy in a confidential treble a few words behind. At about 'Chicago swells the listening throng' she saw that Ernest was standing beside her, silent and scowling, and she sang more devoutly than before.

After the last fraternal chord Ernest said, 'Well, you're a nice one! Couldn't you wait a minute?'

'I was done up, Ernest. Ready to faint. It was so hot in there. You spoke very nicely, Ernest. I wouldn't have missed it for the world.'

'Well, you distracted 'em,' said Ernest.

But seeing him a little mollified she said quickly, 'I've got to telephone, Ernest. Where do I go?'

'Telephone? Who to?'

'Business, Ernest. It's one of my engagements. And I'm late as it is.'

'Well, what's the hurry?' said Ernest, standing stock-still.

'The gentleman's going out after six, you see' – and she knew at once that she had used a fatal word.

'Gentleman, eh?' sneered Ernest. 'This Bryan, I suppose?'

'Well, it's none of your business,' said Jane, grown bold with desperation. 'I told you no jawing. And if you won't take me, I'll go by myself – see?'

But having no pennies she knew that she was in a weak position; so she took hold of his arm and led him vaguely away towards Kensington.

'Marble Arch Station,' he said sourly, and they walked in that direction, not saying a word.

When they came to the station and he had given her the pennies, she said, 'Would you like to take a walk while I telephone, Ernest?' for she saw that Ernest would be an embarrassment.

'No, thank you,' said Ernest shortly. 'I'll stay here and look after you.'

All four telephone boxes were occupied, and outside three of them were people waiting. Jane and Ernest encamped outside the fourth box, and stared through the glass into the little cabinets which had heard so many beating hearts, so many lies and loving words and sorrows. In the first box was a commercial traveller explaining to his wife at Guildford why he had missed the mid-night train and the morning train as well; in the second box a young bachelor was inviting a young actress to accompany him to Maidenhead; in the third box the daughter of wealthy parents was pouring out her heart to a young literary man of whom those parents disapproved. And in the fourth a married woman was saying good-bye to the third officer of a liner about to sail for China.

This woman had only just entered the box and seemed to have all time at her disposal. She dropped her bag once or twice and picked it up with maddening deliberation, she read the printed instructions twice, and then, after searching in her bag, came out and asked Ernest if he could change sixpence. She was given a wrong number, and suffered this with patience; and when at last she heard her officer's voice, fitted her elbow into a corner, and, leaning against the side of the cabinet, settled herself as if for sleep. Jane watched impatiently her moving lips and nodding head. From time to time she turned her sad eyes and rested them on Jane and looked right through her, lost in her own romantic sorrow.

Jane had no pity for her sorrow, nor she for Jane's anxiety, and Ernest was bitter against them both. Yet these three persons had met together that afternoon to record their brotherhood with an unknown people on the farther side of Europe.

'D'you know the number?' said Ernest suddenly.

'No,' said Jane, feeling foolish.

'What's the name?' said Ernest, picking up the book.

'Bryan,' said Jane boldly, but blushed and felt guilty, and was furious with Ernest for making her feel guilty.

Ernest found the number, and they glared again at the unfortunate woman, who was asking the officer if he really loved her. At last she put down the receiver and stared at it for a moment or two as if it were her lover's vessel disappearing round a headland. Jane tapped her foot, and Ernest said sarcastically, 'Don't hurry, my girl, there's no one waiting.' For other people's love-affairs are generally foolish. But when she came out she said she was sorry with so sweet a smile that Jane was instantly her friend. The box smelt of disinfectant, cigar-smoke, and the woman's scent. Ernest proposed to come into the box with her, but Jane said she could manage, thank you. But she had only once used the telephone before, and she read the directions very quickly twice – quickly because she could see by the clock that it was five minutes past six, and twice because she was in such a confusion of mind that the words meant nothing to her. She took off the receiver and listened, trembling; her heart beat more wildly far than it had beaten for Ernest's speech. She could not have said why, but the moment seemed tremendous; she felt fear and excitement and great expectation, but knew not what she expected, except that she would hear the voice of Mr Bryan, who had held her in his arms and kissed her, that warm companionable voice which thrilled her.

A cool voice said startlingly, 'Number, please?' and, stammering, she gave the number. Nothing happened. Eight minutes past! Perhaps he had gone out. She could not imagine a more terrible blow. She was late, she had failed him; and all through Ernest and his stupid Croatians. She peeped sidelong through the glass to her left and saw the young girl, her face mournful and tender, still whispering to her lover. She peeped sidelong through the glass to her right and saw the cold little eyes of Ernest fixed jealously upon her. She wondered if all that she felt was in her face, and wished that he had the decency to keep away. The lady who had telephoned before her opened the door and said, 'Sorry, I left my bag.' A voice said wearily, '*Two* pennies, please.' She put one penny in the slot, dropped another, picked up the lady's handbag, smiled at the lady, pulled the door to, stole a fearful glance at Ernest, slid in the other penny, and at last, breathless with agitation, heard a voice say, 'Hullo!'

Mr Bryan's voice!

She gabbled in her nervousness, 'It's me, Jane Bell, shall I come tomorrow, please, Mr Bryan?' She felt as if she had run a mile.

'Who?' he said, mystified.

'Me. Jane. Jane Bell, Mr Bryan.'

'Oh, *you*!' he said in a tone of great surprise. But was he not expecting to hear from her, then? She had imagined him, she realized now, sitting waiting for a bell to ring, looking anxiously at the clock.

'Yes,' she said. 'Shall I come tomorrow, Mr Bryan?'

'No. Look here,' said the voice, so strange and distant. 'I shall be away this week, and when I come back I'm going abroad, so I shan't be in London till the spring, I'm afraid. See you then, perhaps.'

Jane had read about hearts standing still, and she thought that hers had halted now. She put a hand to her heart. But all she could say was, 'Yes, Mr Bryan.'

'Good-bye, then,' said the voice cheerily. 'Oh, hullo! You got those introductions?'

'Yes, thank you, Mr Bryan.'

'That's good. You'll get plenty of work. Good-bye.'

There was a sort of click, and then silence. Jane kept her mouth to the transmitter, and her ear to the receiver, and at last she said timidly, humbly, without hope, and almost in a whisper, the ridiculous, the tragic, the inadequate word, 'Hullo?'

There was no answer. Slowly, unwillingly, as if there still might come from it some kindlier sound, she returned the receiver to its little bracket, and stood staring at the instrument as that other woman had done. She had forgotten Ernest, she had forgotten that others might be waiting for the box. This was the end of her expectations, the sudden grave of Love's Bliss, this horrid smelly little box of silence. She stood staring at the neat inhuman machine until Ernest rapped on the glass beside her. Then she said, 'Pull yourself together, Jane Bell,' and went out.

'Funny sort of "business", wasn't it?' said Ernest, but not unkindly, for he saw that she had 'taken a knock' and was glad of it, but did not wish to rub it in. 'Did you speak to your "gentleman"?'

'Oh, yes.'

'Anything the matter?'

'Oh, no,' said Jane coolly. 'He don't want to draw me this week, that's all.'

'Like a walk in the Park?'

'No, thank you, Ernest. I'd sooner go home.'

All the way home in the bus she said nothing at all, but went over and over in her mind those hateful seconds on the telephone. It was bad enough that Mr Bryan was going away, as it seemed to her, for ever; but that this should mean nothing to him! For it must mean nothing. Or why was his voice so cheerful and commonplace? It had made her feel like his servant again. But surely she had been more than his servant in the studio? Was this the same man who had held her in his arms and kissed her reverently, in the Fairbanks manner? Had that meant nothing? Perhaps she had spoken stupidly on the telephone, and annoyed him; she repeated endlessly every word she had said, but what had she said, after all? 'It's me, Mr Bryan. Shall I come tomorrow?' There could be nothing very wrong in that. She put the chief blame on Ernest and his Croatians, for they had prevented her from calling at the studio. Then at least she would have seen him face to face and had a proper good-bye perhaps, instead of that perplexing telephone affair. Then she would have known whether he really liked her or not. Perhaps she might call at the studio in the morning. But for what excuse? What could she say? If she did that, perhaps he might snub her properly. She felt snubbed already. No, the best thing to do was to forget about him. These artists were flighty ones, Ernest had said, and probably Ernest was right as usual.

Anyhow, she was not going to show anything. She thought:

'*Jane with the Anguish of a Woman Slighted in Her Heart Carries a Smile on Her Lips.*'

For May Merlin had done that in 'Disillusion'. And she said airily (she hoped), 'It's a nuisance, Ernest. I'll have to look for another job this week.'

But Ernest was not deceived. 'Class is class,' he said, 'and you can't get away from it.'

11

UP THE 'CUT'

ON the next morning, Monday, the *Prudence* and the *Adventure* tied up in the creek, and Fred called on the *Blackbird*. Mr Bell had taken Lily to see a Government man about the milliner's job, and Jane was alone, washing-up and thinking that it was better to wash up her own things than other people's, but wishing nevertheless that they were Mr Bryan's.

Fred said, 'There's a nice breeze, Jenny. Like to go out in the boat?'

He did not say that he wanted her to show off her nautical accomplishments before his father, but she guessed it. She was feeling sore and inferior from the day before, and the arrival of the adoring Fred comforted her. She said, 'All right, Fred,' and got out the ancient sail.

Fred did not offer to help, but watched admiringly her quick, small fingers at work with sail and halyard and cleat. The sail was grubby and had holes in it, the tack-lashing was not Manilla, but a piece of strong string doubled, the rudder was held together with nails and string, and the sheet looked like a length of blind-cord; but the sail was set as well as any mortal could have set it. Fred wished that his father could have seen Jane throw her small weight on the halyard, for this would certainly have satisfied him that she was a fit wife for a boatman on the Grand Union Canal.

The breeze blew smartly from the north-west, the tide was making up, and the sun shone warmly out of a cloudy sky. Old Mr Green sat in the garden of the Pigeons with his pipe, waiting, as he had promised Fred, to see the fine watermanship of Fred's girl. But Jane, perversely, chose to beat up-river, in the wrong direction. Chiswick Church and Chiswick Mall, behind the rich untidy green of the island, was like a country village in the hazy morning light; and Jane, after a long look, said, 'Pretty, isn't it?', meaning by that that she thought it very beautiful.

Fred was not interested in Nature at that moment, but was

thinking that his father would not be favourably impressed by a distant view of Jane and Fred disappearing up the river. So he said dishonestly, 'Let's run down a bit. Mother said she'd like to see you again' – though Mother had never so much as mentioned Jane.

Jane said, 'There's no hurry, Fred,' and to tease him sailed on for two or three tacks; and Fred, though in a fever of anxiety, did not dare to state openly that this was the day appointed for the entrance examination for the Grand Union Canal. But at the top of the island Jane put the tiller over and let the sheet slip through her hand, and they ran down swiftly against the tide, the narrow boat rolling in the gusty breeze and churning up a noisy wave at the bows. Fred peered anxiously ahead towards the Pigeons, and at last, having discovered the familiar curves of Mr Green, said in great astonishment, 'There's father at the Pigeons!'

Jane smiled gravely at him, and said, 'Well, what a surprise!' but she waved her hand to Mr Green as they foamed past the Pigeons. Mr Green took his pipe out of his mouth, and held up his tankard of old and mild. Just then, luckily for Fred, Jane saw to starboard a great quantity of driftwood bobbing westward on the tide. She cried eagerly, 'Oh, firewood!' and putting the tiller over, jibbed suddenly, so that the boom swung across and swept Fred's felt hat into the river, at which Mr Green laughed long and loudly.

But Jane, ignoring Fred's felt hat, had hauled in her sheet, and was bearing down delightedly upon a drifting plank; for many of the inhabitants of Hammersmith, and especially those humbler ones who dwelt in boats, depended very much for their fuel upon the chance flotsam of the river. For the most part this was collected laboriously, a bit here and a bit there; but sometimes the tide, and especially, it was said, for some mysterious reason, a spring tide, would send up from the docks a great cloud of wood. And then, as when the Cornish fishermen see suddenly the small fry leap in terror from the sea, and knowing that the mackerel are at hand, cry 'There she goes!', and in haste put out their boats, so did the provident and poor of Hammersmith cry 'Wood!', set out in small boats, and gather in the harvest.

Such a cloud of desirable wood was it which had attracted Jane. There were long white planks fresh from the sawmill, seasoned old fragments, the scourings of wharves, fine-shaped wedges to split them with, and innumerable sticks for kindling, baskets and bits of barrels, fragments of broken furniture, old brooms and packing-cases and branches of trees, seasoned wood, tarred wood, greasy wood, muddy wood, but all excellent for burning. Most people went 'wooding' in rowing-boats, but Jane had invented and per-fected the new sport of 'wooding' under sail, which had its own rules and observances, and was like some sort of tent-pegging by water. She flashed past the tarry plank which had first taken her fancy, and, taking the sheet and tiller in one small hand, with the other she seized and dragged aboard the prize. No mean feat for a girl, thought Fred, with the sheet pulling like a horse, and the boat travelling fast; but it was a point of honour with Jane to keep the sail full and never slacken speed, except for a piece of wood sus-pected of hidden nails. Now she went about smartly, made for Fred's hat on the other tack, and brought off a great right and left, the hat to starboard and the head of an old broom to port.

From the garden of the Pigeons Mr Green applauded this per-formance with a throaty cheer. Fred flushed with pride, and Jane, pleased herself, began to show off. There was no doubt that she could handle a boat. The battered, leaking, ill-found vessel of the Bells' became a lively, intelligent creature in her hands; she could do anything with it, and moved swiftly back and forth among the drifting harvest, turning, twisting, and swooping like a seagull ranging for fish. Fred's proud heart swelled and he glanced often towards the Pigeons to be sure that his father was missing nothing. But at last Jane tore her finger on a nail, and Fred, solicitous, said, 'That's enough, Jenny.' They took back to the *Blackbird* two winter weeks' supply of fuel, and left it on the deck to dry.

Fred went anxiously to the Pigeons and found that Jane had passed the preliminary examination with flying colours. 'She can handle a boat, cert'n'ly, lad,' said Tom Green. 'We'll take her up the "Cut".'

So Fred returned, and shyly made the official invitation; and Jane accepted it, for now that Mr Bryan did not want her this week it was comforting to find that somebody wanted her.

They started the next morning, and on Tuesday night Jane slept in a very small bed with Mrs Green, which she did not much enjoy. But the day had been thrilling, and, drugged with air, she slept well. At Brentford, opposite Kew Gardens, where they left the tideway and entered the canal, they passed into another world, peopled by another race. The narrow opening stretch between the river and the principal lock at Brentford High Street was crowded with barges lying on both sides under the warehouses, loading, unloading, or waiting for freight. The air was full of shouts and sacks of flour and the rattle of cranes, and the ribald cries of the warehousemen. The barge-folk gave them a quieter greeting. Everyone seemed to know the Greens; the men threw them a friendly word and the women as a rule said a soft 'Good morning' or nodded gravely without speaking. Jane blushed all the way to Brentford, for everyone looked curiously at her, and she felt a stranger in a strange land. There were no lewd cries or whistles from the boatmen, though she suspected, rightly, that many of the strange sounds among the warehouse workers were in the nature of comment upon her face and figure. It was the women of the barges who frightened her, the queens of these little kingdoms, dark-eyed, gipsy-looking, weatherworn creatures, with shawls over their heads and children crawling about their feet, who stood at the doors of their cabins as they have stood for generations, patiently waiting for the next move onward in their wandering existence. The smoke of their domestic hearths went up from the little chimney before their faces, their babies crawled on the deck beside the chimney, tethered with string and next door to the inevitable lark in its cage; their elder children clambered among the cargo and all about the narrow vessel which was their home and nursery and school and playground; their only neighbours were the people of the barge which happened for the time being to be tied up beside them; the tiny cabin before them, a few feet square, and not high enough to stand in, held all their wordly goods, their kitchens, their romances, their bridal-beds, their husbands and babies, their past and present and all their future. Most of them, as Jane knew, had never known a different sort of home, had never slept under a different roof; and here all their lives they would labour and love and bear their children. And there was something in their dignified, enduring eyes which seemed to say to Jane, 'Who are you to come among us, and how do you hope, weak girl, to live as we do?'

But once away from the disturbing eyes and confusion of Brentford, she felt happy. The canal plunged suddenly into the rustic solitudes to the south of Ealing. For a mile or so there were fields and green trees all about. Through the trees there was seen frequently a scurrying of District trains, but at the next lock a heron rose from the towing-path and flapped royally away. The horse Beauty marched steadily along the towing-path, his nose in his dinner, not hurrying himself; and beside him walked Mr Green, sometimes encouraging the feeding Beauty with a cry, sometimes stopping to pick an early blackberry or wild flower in the hedge, sometimes whistling, but for the most part reflecting on life, and wondering if Fred's girl would turn out a good one. And behind Beauty stole silently the two laden barges – or rather boats. For, as Fred very soon explained, these narrow canal craft are not barges, nor are their crews bargemen nor watermen, but boatmen, and watermen are those who work the wider barges of the tideway. The *Adventure* came first, the *Prudence* followed after. Their motion was as gentle as the coming of sleep; their blunt, round prows did not divide the water, but caress it; there was no sound but the ripple along the shore and the slow clip-clop of Beauty's feet, and these sounds said 'Peace', and brought peace to Jane's soul.

Mrs Green and Arthur were in the *Adventure*. Mrs Green, like most of the older boatwomen, was dressed in black – a long black dress down to her ankles, black stockings, and thick black boots like a man's. She wore at her throat a large photograph of Mr Green in a brooch, and from her ears dangled large ear-rings of green glass. Her hair was bound tightly across the top and round the back of her head in six or seven thin plaits; and this gave her from behind an air of youth and skittishness which was startlingly denied when she turned her sharp face.

Now she turned often and gazed grimly back at the *Prudence* where Jane was steering with Fred at her side. Fred wore an old cloth cap and a tie, but no collar. Steering the long craft was not so easy as it looked, and Fred, as anxious and as proud as a mother, showed her all the little tricks, and bubbled over with advice and commendation.

'You've got a lot more to say up here, Fred,' said Jane, surprised. 'Quite found your tongue, haven't you?'

'I'm on my element, you see,' said Fred. 'Swing her round now, Jenny. That's the girl'; and as they slid into the cool darkness under the railway bridge he took a quick look ahead at his father and mother, slipped his arm round her shoulders, and kissed her soft cheek.

'I'm glad you came, my little Jenny,' he whispered.

'So am I, Fred,' said Jane truthfully, pleased by this abandoned action; but she thought of Mr Bryan.

They met two power-boats, newly painted, and Fred explained about the Castles and the Roses. The canal craft, like their women-folk, were individual and different from other craft. They were long and narrow, to fit the locks, and with their gay colours and elaborate decorations they too seemed to say that they were of the gipsy breed. They were painted, every one, the ancient traditional style of the canal, handed down by generations of boatmen. 'Castles', 'hearts', and 'roses' were the three indispensable themes of the decoration – roses for beauty, hearts for romance, and castles, maybe, for worldly honour. On the flanks of every cabin was a different castle, a wild and foreign-looking castle on a hill-top, a castle out of a fairy-book; but this turned out, upon inquiry, to be a romantic study of some real English castle not far removed from the canal; and somewhere, sure enough, in a corner would be a romantic stream disappearing under a bridge, which was the artist's attempt to express the Grand Union Canal in terms as noble as the castle. Forward on the hatch-cover would be a large, red, flaming heart on a field of white, the shield and forehead of the boat. Then in the cabin, which was all panelled with grained wood, were smaller castles and smaller hearts and panels of diamonds and clusters of roses, in brilliant reds and yellows and greens; and every domestic vessel – the great water-can on the deck, the biscuit-tin on the shelf – had its roses. Just inside every door on the left-hand side, in exactly the same place, were fixed a few shining brass knobs and bosses, like the ornaments of bedsteads and cart-horses; and, highly polished, they made a brave show. Some cabins had only two or three brass knobs, and some a dozen; at holidays, when times were good, the lady of the boat would buy another brass ornament or two, and by the number of brass ornaments the knowing might know if the family were prospering steadily or not.

Old Mrs Green had seventeen brass knobs, and when the sun shone in through the door the cabin was dazzling. Beyond the brass knobs was the tiny stove, polished and speckless. On the stove stood always a vase of wild flowers, plucked from the hedges by Mr Green as he stumped along with Beauty; and on each side of the stove were hung festoons of ornamental plates – fine decorated plates with gilded edges or filigree borders, and pretty pictures of Victorian ladies or dancing shepherdesses, and in great gold lettering, 'A Present from Bombay' or 'Banbury Cross'. A glittering brass culinder was over the stove, and among the plates were hung little brass ornaments – a tiny brass anchor, a candlestick, a cannon, and a big brass spoon. Over the small hanging lamp was a burnished shield which shone like the sun. Beyond was a cupboard which had a castle on the door, and was fringed with framed photographs of Mr Green as a young man and Fred as a baby, and Mrs Green's mother on the beach at Blackpool. Opposite the stove was a low chest or locker which served as a seat; then came a curtain, draped back during the day, and hung with more photographs, and behind it the bed. The bed let down out of the wall, and nothing was to be seen of it by day but a panel and a castle, and in the bed-space were kept a small trunk and a broken gramophone. Not one inch in this Lilliputian home was wasted for service, yet every inch was a decoration. To the stranger peeping in from the lock-side it seemed no more than a kennel, a doll's house, but if he sat inside for a few minutes it seemed to expand; there was so much to see in it that the wandering eye enlarged its tiny measurements and saw it as the Green family saw it. And certainly there was many a great drawing-room or artful Chelsea bedroom which had less of the look of a comfortable home.

The tiller and the rudder were gaily painted too, and round each of them a length of thin line was twisted in that complex ornamental knot which watermen call a Turk's head. Whenever the boats came to rest for a day Mrs Green scrubbed and pipeclayed the Turks' heads, so that the strands were snow-white. From the rudder-head a plume of horsehair streamed astern. On the deck a spare rope lay religiously coiled and flat. The Greens kept no songbirds.

Everything about their boats was tidy and clean and proudly cared for. Soon Jane saw other boats which had lost their spirits; their Turks' heads were dingy, and their brass knobs lustreless, and she became a partner in the pride of the Greens, and determined that in future the *Blackbird* should be clean and bright and tidy like the *Adventure*.

Approaching the next lock Fred gave her her first lesson in the mysteries of locks. It was a precise and delicate ritual in which every member of the family had his proper part. The lock was open and ready for them. The horse Beauty strained and stumbled up the steep incline of gravel, and, halting at a shout from Mr Green, went on with his dinner. Mr Green lifted the glistening tow-rope over the rails of the lock-gate, and taking a turn with it round a fat bollard of oak, tapered down to the shape of a top by the pressure of countless ropes, checked and stopped the *Adventure* against the left-hand wall. Meanwhile Mrs Green had cast off the tow-rope of the *Prudence* and Fred steered her in alongside the *Adventure*. Just before the gate he slipped ashore at the mossy steps cut in the wall, and, running up, checked her with the stern-rope. Arthur, on the other side, was already thrusting with his back against the great beam of the gate to close it. Fred did the same on the right. Then each took from his belt the shining iron 'windlass' or handle which every boatman carries, and went quickly to the far end to raise the 'paddles' and fill the lock. Before the gates were fully closed Mr Green was at work on one of the paddles, and a great spout of silver water gushed in before the *Adventure*'s bows. Fred was a few moments later, and then there were two small roaring cataracts both soon to be buried in the rising flood which they themselves had created. Arthur relieved Mr Green and worked the second paddle on that side; the paddle at this lock was old and stiff and gave Arthur some trouble; but Fred was stronger and turned the stubborn handle round as if it had been the handle of a barrel-organ. Jane watched, delighted – the strong arms of Fred, the noisy spouts of water, the surge and gurgle under the surface, and the two boats mounting swiftly up the shining walls. At length, as the lock filled, there was a sudden quiet, the boats rode level with the lock-side, the last important drops trickled in at the corners of the gates, and Fred and Arthur stepped back to their tillers. There is something satisfying to the simple soul in the filling of a lock or in the rising of the tide; something complete and definite and powerful has been accomplished and some dim sense of this gave pleasure to the simple Jane.

The last trickle was silent, and now at last the gates would open, Mr Green had a cunning device of his own by which, with an artful hitch of the tow-rope round the rail of the farther gate, the horse Beauty was made to open both gates; and he was proud of this, for in most boats this was done laboriously by one of the crew. Beauty turned his head as if to ask if this business was ever going to be finished. 'Hey, lad!' cried Mr Green, Beauty pawed the gravel, and the gates swung slowly open. Mr Green's running hitch slipped off the gate, and the taut rope, loosening, scattered a shower of brilliant rain. The *Prudence* dropped astern, Mrs Green made fast the line at the right religious point and on the vessels went. They had worked hard for many minutes, and were a few feet higher for their pains. There are a hundred and fifty locks between Brentford and Birmingham, and this was only the third. At every lock the ritual was the same. The *Adventure* slid in along the left-hand wall and never the right. Fred worked the right-hand paddles and Arthur always the left. But to Jane it was a beautiful and marvellous procedure, and she never threw off the fascination of the locks – those primitive miracles by which man has made ships to climb over mountains.

The locks are the landmarks and milestones and strenuous obstacles of the water highway. At the locks the boatwomen draw their water, buy bread and milk; the lock-keeper comes out of his little house and, leaning over his garden fence, distributes the news of the day. On closing day the village lovers hang over the high gates and watch the boats go through, drawn by the water and the strange charm of the gipsy vessels. The old man sits above the lock and fishes. Two boats meet at a lock, and while they are waiting there are a few, bold, laughing moments between the son of one and the daughter of another. They fancy each other, but the lock is filled, the girl steams out of the lock for Birmingham, the boy moves into the lock for London, and Heaven knows when they will exchange so many words again. Sometimes beside the lock an old inn hides among the trees, and there there will be boats tied up for the night. The men stable their horses and go into the public bar for old and mild and a noisy game of dominoes; the mothers go too, or stay in the boat with their babies; all night they sleep under the lock, where there is always the music of water, whether it be a murmurous trickle or the swollen roar of a full 'pound' cascading over the gates. And at five o'clock they rise up and travel on through many locks to sleep again to the music of a lock.

At the next lock Jane was allowed to try her hand with the windlass, but, straining with a will, could only move the stiff cogs a circuit or two, and that with painful jerks. Mrs Green, with a sour smile, watched from the *Adventure*, but Fred said it was only a knack and she would soon have it. Jane, blushing and ashamed, swore that she would.

Next was Hanwell, where the canal climbs a hill beside the lunatic asylum, and there are seven locks in a quarter of a mile. They rise up in a stately perspective under the long curve of the asylum wall, a fine geometrical procession of terraces, a little askew because of the curve; and Jane thought shrewdly that it was the kind of picture which Mr Bryan would like to draw.

It was a slow passage through these locks, for there was much traffic coming down, and they must wait in every lock till the descending boat was ready to leave the lock ahead of them. Also, at each of these locks were two mysterious side-basins, and these too had 'paddles' to be wound up or dropped at the exactly right moment. Fred explained the importance of these, and how, with so many locks together, they were necessary to preserve the water in the 'pounds'; and Jane said humbly, 'Yes, Fred,' but did not understand it.

The locks seemed endless, but at last they reached 'the top' at Southall, and by that time the mysteries of locks were all revealed to her. She had learned to take a turn round a bollard with the stern-rope, and ease it a little through her hands as it took the strain. She knew how to drop a 'paddle' without catching a finger in the whirling cogs. Better still, she had lifted three paddles without the aid of man, heaving with all her small might on the stubborn handle; her arms ached and her hands were blistered, but she felt that she had proved herself, and Fred was pleased.

Then came a dull six miles past Southall and West Drayton,

tall factories, rows of mean houses and never a lock; but at last the canal crept out into the fields, and a leafy reach led up into Cowley Lock, where there was an inn beside the towing-path, and here they lay for the night.

Mr Green led Beauty away to be stabled and fed, and Mrs Green lighted a little wood-fire on the bank and boiled the kettle there, because she had just polished up the stove and it was a pity to spoil it. Jane made herself useful, got out the mugs for tea, and cut slices of bread and cheese. There was not room for every one to sup in the cabin, but Mr Green pulled down the bed from the wall, and invited Jane, the honoured guest, to sit beside him. Mrs Green sat on the locker, and Fred squatted on the step in the doorway. Arthur thought there were too many, and went off to the pub.

Mr Green, sipping his tea, said, 'Well, young lady, you're welcome to the "Cut". We'll make a boatman of you yet. And how'd you like to live in a house like this?'

Jane looked admiringly at Mrs Green's brass knobs, and said, 'It's ever so nice, Mr Green.' But she thought to herself, 'It's a bit small.'

Mrs Green said, 'Nice enough for an outing, but what about a lifetime?'

Mr Green looked proudly round his tiny home and said, 'Well, I was born in this boat, and my father was born in this boat, and his father before him, and I don't ask for nothing better. Watergipsies, that's what we are. I don't want no pictures – there's all the pictures I want,' and with his bread and cheese he pointed at the fairy castle on the cupboard door. 'Castles and hearts and roses, that's the old style, Miss Jane, and good enough for me. And, come to that, we get pictures all day, don't we, old lady, moving along?'

Mrs Green made no response to this flash of poetry, except to say, 'D'you want more tea?'

Mr Green said what he wanted was an old and mild, and, crouching carefully, he climbed over Mrs Green and Fred, and departed for the pub. Any sort of movement was difficult in the cabin; Jane felt crushed under the low roof and wanted to escape. Mrs Green said she would follow her lord when she had washed up.

Fred said, 'Coming for a walk, Jenny?' but Jane said she would stay and help Mrs Green. She thought she had Mr Green on her side, but Mrs Green, she was sure, still strongly disapproved of her, and though she had very little thought of marrying Fred, she liked to be liked, and to be a success, whoever it was.

'Go with your father, boy,' hissed Mrs Green, and Fred went, disconsolate.

Washing-up was a simple affair, for it meant dipping the mugs and plates in the canal, and wiping them with a dirty rag. Mrs Green said nothing at all. She had a habit of saying nothing at all, and this was even more frightening than her hissing, unfriendly utterances. While she was making the bed ready and tidying the cabin Jane took the stick-mop and busily swabbed all the stern part of the barge. She drew much pleasure from the sudden freshness of the paint-work, and tried to twirl the stick across her arm as she had seen the boatwomen do; but this was too much for her. However, Mrs Green came out of the cabin and looking round, said almost with approval, 'Not so bad, my lass.' Jane's instinct had been right; for Mrs Green cleanliness of the *Adventure* was next to godliness, or even higher; and Jane felt she had won a good mark at last.

In the warm public bar Arthur was playing darts and Fred and Mr Green were playing dominoes with a very noisy old boatman from the *Seven Sisters*. Jane drank lemonade and Mrs Green stout, and for a long time neither of them said a word. Fred's eye wandered continually from the dominoes to Jane, till Mrs Green told him about it.

In half an hour it was 'Time, gentlemen, please', and they all returned to the boats, stepping carefully over the narrow gate of the lock. The night was fine, the stars of Heaven swam in the lock, and Jane would have liked a little walk with Fred. But early to bed is the boatman's habit, and Fred, besides, was afraid of his mother.

Mr Green retired to the *Prudence* and slept with Fred, Arthur slept in the tiny cubbyhole forward, and Jane, in some alarm, sat on the locker in the *Adventure*, and prepared herself for a night with Mrs Green. In the *Blackbird* everyone undressed for bed, and Jane had brought her nightie in a calico bag. She began to undress, and had almost taken off the grey jersey which Mrs Raven gave her when she saw through the neck-hole that Mrs Green had already completed her preparations for the night. Mrs Green had taken off her boots. She then crawled on to the bed, breathing heavily, and turned her face to the wall. Jane thought, 'My nightie will be a knock-out', and hastily drew back the jersey over her head and pulled it down again. She then took off her shoes, and, as a small assertion of independence, her stockings as well, and lay down in her clothes beside Mrs Green.

'Good night, Mrs Green,' she said, her voice very small.

'Put out the light,' croaked Mrs Green, like one laying a curse, and Jane was so much alarmed that she took four puffs to blow out the lamp.

Mrs Green then made a great heave with her body, and thrust out her stern, so that the narrow ledge on which Jane lay was reduced by half. Mrs Green snorted, as if to say, 'I'll teach you to run after an honest boatwoman's son,' and almost instantly began to snore. She had carefully closed the door, but the sliding hatch above it was open a little, and Jane could see a square foot of sky and three bright stars. She could hear the melodious murmur of the lock-water, and sometimes the hoot of an owl. She lay listening and looking and thinking of Mr Bryan. She said to herself that it was a funny world. After all her grand expectations about Mr Bryan, to be sharing a bed with a smelly old woman who slept with her clothes on! Mrs Green might keep the boat clean, but Jane was sure that she did not wash herself as often as Jane did. This sleeping in clothes had impressed her strongly, and Jane for the first time in her life had a sense of class-superiority. If she married Fred she would be lowering herself, instead of raising herself by – yes, she had really thought of it – by marrying Mr Bryan.

But Mr Bryan, of course, was all over, and Jane thought about Fred. She wondered what it would be like to share a little bed like this with Fred. Mrs Green drew up her knees so that Jane had to clutch the side of the bed to keep her place. It would be another thing, of course, if it was Fred. She would have the inside berth, next to the wall, for one thing, and Fred would do what he was told, for another. But how about a lifetime, as Mrs Green had said? How about night after night in a bed like this? Not so bad, perhaps,

if it was Fred. The cabin, after all, was as large as her cabin in the
Blackbird though much less airy and high. She gasped in the stuffy
heat, and her limbs felt sticky under her clothes. But Mrs Green
slept well enough. Her snoring ceased suddenly, and, after a deep
sigh, began again on another and more contented note, like the
second movement of a symphony. Would Fred snore, Jane wondered? Somebody had told her one could cure a man of that.
Apart from this bed question, it was a fine life, certainly. Her
Destiny was on the water, she had always thought, and it would be
a fine thing to belong to the canal, and be a sort of sailor, as nearly
a sailor as a girl can be. She travelled in her mind again those few
exciting miles from Brentford, and thought chiefly of the brave
things she had done herself, as men go over their cricket triumphs,
or score great goals in recollection – how she had caught the rope
which Fred had flung to her, how she had worked at those back-
breaking 'paddles', how she had surprised Mr Green by her
handling of the tiller and pleased his wife by swabbing the deck.
Tomorrow she would do better still and show them that a girl
off the shore could be as good a boatman as anyone.

But in all this there was not much queenery, she thought, and
nobody at all like Mr Bryan. Probably she would come down to
sleeping in her clothes like Mrs Green. Nevertheless, she had half
a mind to marry Fred, if he asked her again. When Fred and
Arthur married, the old people would retire, Fred said, and live at
Brentford; and then she would be Queen of the two boats at
least. Her boat would be the cleanest on the canal, with more
castles than any of them, with bright white Turks' heads and innumerable brass knobs. Life was a muddle. And with this incon-
clusive reflection, lying still on her back (for she was afraid to
move), Jane fell asleep.

12

NOCTURNE

At five o'clock in the morning Mr Green fetched Beauty and they set forth again. The boatman's working-day, if he works with a horse, is from sunrise to sunset. A white mist lay low on the country, and the light was thin and bloodless; sometimes, from the stern of the *Prudence*, the horse Beauty could not be seen, and the two quiet boats seemed to glide through the mist by some ghostly power. The Green family were silent, or spoke in low tones, as if afraid to wake the sleeping world, though perhaps no ear would have heard them if they had shouted. Jane, at the tiller, whispered that she was cold, and Fred put his arm round her and said nothing, and they were happy.

The sun found them creeping northward among the woods above Uxbridge. A light breeze came up from the south and drove the last scared islands of mist along the water before them. The solemn, staring cows stood revealed in the fields, a moorhen scuttled into the reeds, colour and sound came back into the woods and warmth into the body, the mist melted away, and the long, straight reach of the canal lay like a silver ribbon ahead. No man was to be seen. Beauty quickened his pace, and Mrs Green made tea.

All day the sun shone, all day the horse Beauty clip-clopped slowly northwards, and all day Jane knew more and more the tranquil fascinations of the canal. From this point it was all fine country, with, at intervals, the fringes of a tiny town, past which the canal ran proudly, sufficient to itself. The slowest highway in England, it seemed to have sought out the quiet corners of the country and thrown over them for ever the spell of its own antiquity and slowness. No fancy modern mansions, no great hotels stood on its banks; no pleasure-parties or gramophones disturbed its silences; nothing on it nor beside it happened quickly, not even the strong steam or motor-vessels could make it modern; and though for many a mile it might run between the high road and the railway, it still remained a quiet world of its own, despising expresses and the rushing cars, and as remote from them as if they had been in the air. The passenger looks down from the flying train upon the canal, and thinks it a meagre and a murky stream, and wonders idly whither it flows. But the boatman at his tiller looks up and sees the railway tiny and the canal large, a river of adventure and hardship and toil, with a people of its own and a hundred years of custom and tradition which were old before the railway was imagined. Every boatman feels this and is proud of the 'Cut', and jealous for it. And this affection takes hold of those who live beside it or go upon it. It is in the public houses and the rows of cottages and in the children playing on its banks. Ernest, born to the town, and the owner of a motor-bicycle, might have escaped it; but Jane, grown on the water, was an easy prey. By the afternoon of this, the second day, she felt that she had travelled many miles and many days into a world which was new, but a world to which she belonged. Her father, Lily, the *Blackbird*, and Ernest seemed a hundred miles away, in the background of another life; all that mattered was the next lock, whether it would be 'ready' for them, and whether she would distinguish or disgrace herself in the working of it. And even her foolish ache for Mr Bryan was easier.

For a few miles up to Rickmansworth they seemed to have lost the railway and the road, and journeyed through a country solitude of farms and fields. Then on through the lovely park below King's Langley. Huge oaks and elm-trees climbed the green slopes, water-lilies fringed the banks, and rippling streams ran in and out of the canal, splashing merrily down the mill-race, tumbling in tiny cascades to the watercress beds, or forcing a slow path through the jungles of duckweed and vivid green forests of starwort. They crept round sudden corners into reaches cavernously dark with the shade of great trees, where no man would have guessed that this was the same grey man-made waterway which crawls past Paddington. They passed old houses hiding in the wood, and old walls hung with rock-plants or carpeted with ancient moss, and old cottage gardens which were a sudden blaze of flowers – a screen of ramblers or a regiment of sweet-peas. They seemed a thousand miles from London, though by the map they might be twenty. And the lordly swan, moving lazily from under their bows, seemed to say, 'This is no place for Trade.'

Now they began the long climb up the gentle slopes of the Chilterns. There was a lock every quarter of a mile, and sometimes a cluster of two or three. There was another pair of boats not far ahead, going the same way, so that every lock was 'against' them; that is to say, they had to empty it before they could enter, and then fill it again – a double process. Luck is a great force, even in the navigation of a canal, and some days, the boatmen say, everything goes well, and others not a lock is ready for them. Now, to save time, with so many locks together, Fred marched ahead along the tow-path to get them ready, and by the time that Beauty had plodded up to one he would be busy emptying the one above, Jane with him, while Arthur steered the *Prudence*. She enjoyed this, because now she was really a help, as Fred said, if it was only saving him a walk round the lock to shut the farther gate. Fred had given her a leather belt and a spare windlass to tuck in it, and she tried to march along the tow-path as she had seen the sturdy boat-girls do, with her arms swinging across her body in front, and the windlass swinging in the belt behind her. All the afternoon they slowly climbed the hill, and crossed the fields, a few feet up, a few hundred yards on. But Fred pointed to a hillside patched with corn and yellow mustard which had been above them, and was now below, and Jane agreed that it was a wonder.

At Berkhamsted, not far from the 'Summit', the locks came thick and fast – one at every street corner, said Fred. The banks were alive with old men and children fishing for gudgeon; the children crowded round the locks to see the boats go through, and Jane felt proud that she belonged to the canal and was a spectacle. And here began the 'dramma' of Ruth.

Another boat had just come down, so that the locks were ready for them, and Jane and Fred had returned to the *Prudence*. They passed a big timber-yard where two boats were loading. They were called *Mary* and *Martha*. From the cabin of the *Mary* a girl popped up her head, a few feet only from them. She was a comely, lusty girl, short and strong in the true breed of the canal-girls: short for the cabins and strong for the locks. She had bare, muscular arms, and these and her face were coloured a warm russet; she wore black ear-rings and her eyes were black; she had a tip-tilted nose and a startled, fierce expression; her black hair was untidy and her white blouse dirty, but Jane felt herself a feeble creature in the presence of Ruth Walker.

''Evenin', Ruth,' said Fred, with an uneasy tone, as the *Prudence* glided past.

Ruth saw Fred first. Her face was eager, but her voice was shy. ''Evenin', Fred,' she said. 'I left you – ' Then she saw Jane and stopped. She said, 'Hullo!' and stared at Jane, a hard, fierce stare. Jane felt hot.

The *Prudence* glided on. Ruth ducked her head under the cabin-top, and disappeared. Jane heard her cry 'Dad!' as one who has news to tell. Fred cried 'Ruth?' anxiously. Fred looked hot also. There was no sign from the *Mary*, and Beauty clumped inexorably on. The *Adventure* swung round the bend and was half-way through the bridge when Ruth's head appeared again, and the head and chest of a tall man with a soldierly moustache. 'That's her father,' said Fred. The two couples stared at each other over the lengthening stretch of water until the low corner of the bridge came between them.

'Case of so near and yet so far,' remarked Jane. She supposed Fred had been walking out with the girl, and she remembered now that one of the Brentford women had said something about 'Ruth'; but she did not mean to ask questions, because Fred had been very good about Ernest, and had made no unpleasantness beyond saying once that Ernest's way of talking gave him a stomach-ache. However, curiosity was too much for her, and she said, 'Friend of yours, Fred?'

'I seen her Whitsun,' said Fred, uncomfortably, and, since it was August now, Jane thought, evasively; but what he said was true. Courting on the canal is a haphazard, difficult affair, and even more the sport of chance than it is in other quarters. By chance the *Prudence* and the *Mary* were both lying up at Leighton Buzzard over the Whitsun 'stoppage', when locks are repaired and all traffic ceases. Ruth and Fred had walked out for three days, and since then had never happened to be stationary at the same place at the same time.

Their boats had travelled up and down the canal, as remote as the lovers on the Grecian urn. They met suddenly, between locks, as the *Mary* and the *Martha*, which were power-boats, purred up, tut-tutting, and overtook the *Prudence*. And as they slid past Fred would look at Ruth and say, 'Hullo, Ruth,' and perhaps she would blush, remembering old caresses. Then they would call out their plans and movements, and wave a hand and be lost to each other again. Also, they left little messages at certain locks, dictated to the lock-keeper or one of the toll officials, for neither Ruth nor Fred could read or write. Many love-affairs began thus promisingly and lingered on thus distantly, like the loves of song-birds separately caged, until through some new accident they matured or dwindled. And Jane was here the fatal accident.

Jane was pleasantly stirred by this encounter. The jealous glare of the girl, the hostile pursuit of those two pairs of eyes, the sudden meeting and instant separation, so much expressed and so little said – it was wonderfully like the pictures. She saw it clearly on the screen. '*An Old Flame*' would be the introduction, then '*Ships That Pass in the Night*', and then '*Ruth Declares War on Her Rival*'. She could see Ruth and her father kneeling on the floor, rolling their eyes.

She did not feel jealousy or pique about Fred's old flame; rather he rose in her opinion, for there must be something more in him than she suspected if he had clicked with that attractive girl. And Fred as the hero of a real 'dramma' was much more interesting than he had been before.

The sun went down, and in the warm twilight they climbed up through the last few locks. About eight o'clock they tied up for the night below the Cow Roast. The Cow Roast Inn is the first land-mark of the 'Summit'; and the next lock beyond it begins the descent of the Chilterns. Contrary to his habit, Mr Green did not at once take Beauty to the stables, but tied him to the fence. One of the Company's men from the check office said, "Evening, Fred Green. I've a letter for you.' Fred said, 'Thanks, Mr Oliver,' and held out his hand. The man seemed surprised, but glanced at Jane, smiled knowingly, and with an enormous wink gave Fred the letter, which bore no stamp. He was in the habit of reading Ruth's letters to Fred, and thought Fred to mean that this was not a con-venient occasion. But Fred was not ashamed of Ruth Walker.

He stood shamefaced a moment or two, fingering the letter, but not opening it; and Jane said at last, 'Why don't you read your letter, Fred?' and then, remembering the remark which Ruth Walker had left unfinished, 'Is it from the dark girl, Fred?'

Fred said, 'I dunno, Jenny. I dare say.'

'Well, go on, Fred. I shan't be jealous.'

Fred stammered and looked down, and said, 'I can't read, Jenny.'

'Go on?' said Jane, who had caught this expression from Fred.

'It's a fact, Jenny. Never had no schooling, you see. There's a lot of us the same. Ruth can't read an' write neither.'

'Well, you surprise me!' And indeed, it was a shock. She had never been able to persuade Fred to go to the pictures, and this, she supposed, was the reason: Fred was sensitive about his lack of education.

'Give it to me,' she said gently. 'I'll read it, Fred.'

'That don't seem right, Jenny.' For it seemed strange to have a love-letter from one girl read out by another.

'All right, Fred. It's just as you like.'

'Well, I dunno,' said Fred.

He did not wish Jane to think that there was more between Ruth and himself than there was, and he knew that Ruth's letters, dictated with great embarrassment to a male official, said very little as a rule. And he handed over the letter.

Jane opened it and read solemnly:

'Dear Fred we are loading timber at Marley's for Braunston shall be Braunston Saturday night with luck hoping I may see you Fred as I should like to see you dear Fred hoping that this finds you all well as we are champion Ruth.'

'And seven crosses,' said Jane.

'Mr Oliver puts them in,' said Fred uncomfortably.

'Tell us another, Fred!' She was not jealous, but it did seem strange that Fred could not read a letter; and she had for the second time a sense of class-superiority. 'Well, I'll teach you to read,' she said.

At supper Mr and Mrs Green said little and seemed worried. Jane had seen them muttering together and looking back down the canal. At length they heard the tutter-tutter of a power-boat. Mr and Mrs Green exchanged glances, Mrs Green stood up, peeped out, and, returning, hissed, 'It's him. Don't take no notice of him.' And she said kindly to Jane, 'Another cup of tea, my dear?' Jane guessed that Ruth and her father had caught them up and that trouble was expected. But it was surprising that this should make Mrs Green kinder to her. 'Case of all stick together,' she thought, which was correct; the threat of battle had closed the ranks.

They heard the *Martha* and the *Mary* swish past. A thick voice shouted close to them, 'Where's that young bastard? Afraid to show his face?' Fred made a movement, but Mrs Green, restraining him, said again, 'Don't take no notice of him. He's drunk.' 'Tying up?' asked Mr Green; he cocked his head and there was an anxious silence in the cabin. Mrs Green nodded grimly. The *Martha* and the *Mary* were tying up just in front of them! It was from fear of this and what might follow that Mr Green had kept the horse Beauty handy for a sudden departure. The Greens were respectable and detested 'unpleasantness'.

Presently they heard the same, thick voice, violent and loud. Mr and Mrs Green began to talk, hurriedly, for the voice was hurling abuse at the Greens and their boats, their children, their history, and their professional ability. Mr Walker was of Irish extraction and in the Great War had joined the Irish Guards. He was proud of this, and of his medals, which he always wore; for one good reason or another few of the canal-folk had penetrated to the infantry, and he was fond of drawing their attention to his own valour, especially when he was drunk. The boatmen are a sober lot, but Mr Walker often took too much, and today he had been refreshing himself while his boat was loading. At first he contented himself with shouting, 'Come out, the bastard! Let's see your dirty face!' Then he said something about double faces, and young men who played fast and loose with innocent girls. He said no doubt a common boatman's daughter was not good enough for the 'young bastard', he must have a dolled-up London girl. He stood swaying on his cabin-top, and said that he had fought for his bloody country while the young bastard and his bloody father had stayed at home. Fred was fifteen at the end of the War and his father fifty, so it was fortunate that all this was drowned by the busy talk of Mrs Green. Jane did her part and began to tell them the story of the Derby. Then Mr Walker finding that his taunts drew no response, attacked with a sure instinct the professional pride of the Greens. 'Couple o' dirty horse-boats!' he cried, and 'I'm a bloody soldier, and I never see such dirty boats! Dirty boats, dirty cabins – ' and he developed the theme. No one can pretend for ever to be deaf to abuse of himself, and this awful charge pierced all defences and pricked the Greens in a vital spot. Mr Green sprang up, bumping his head. Mrs Green croaked 'Leave him alone! Don't take no notice of him!' and instantly rushed out into the well herself.

The others followed. It was a fine night, and the moon had risen, nearly full, behind the trees. The last dusk of day was melting into moonlight. There was no wind, no sound of traffic, and Man and Nature seemed at peace. Two pairs of lovers, on their way to the fields, hung over the lock-gates and curiously watched the battle begin. And Jane, the cause of battle, watched curiously too, and, truth to tell, enjoyed it.

Mr Walker still stood on the cabin-top. His two brothers, older men, stood on the path beyond, inviting Mr Walker, now and then, to come off it. The girl Ruth, with her elbows on the roof, stared sullenly at Jane, and said nothing.

Mrs Green shouted, or rather croaked, 'Don't show your ignorance, Henry Walker. You're drunk.'

'That's right,' said Mr Walker scornfully. 'Put the old woman up. There's not a man among you – not a man among you! Who stayed at home? They *all* stayed at home; that's right, isn't it?' He turned as if for confirmation to the lovers, who had never set eyes on any of the parties before, and expressed no opinion.

'Let me flatten him!' cried Mr Green angrily, while Fred used a word which Jane had never heard. But Mrs Green, who had now picked up the coal-hatchet, held it out at arm's length, barring the way.

'Keep back, Tom Green,' she said. 'Don't soil your hands with him! Stay where you are, Fred, and don't take no notice of him, or you're no son of mine.' The two men held back obediently, much more afraid of Mrs Green than of Mr Walker. The old woman dominated the scene. Her lips trembled and her hands, but her eyes flashed fury and power; her croaking voice had grown huskier with her rage, and yet some indomitable force of will took hold of her words and carried them to her enemy. She brandished the hatchet and croaked, 'War, is it? There was never much fighting where you were, Henry Walker. You're a coward, Mr Walker, drunk or sober, and we can all swear to that.'

Mr Walker swayed, and he looked about him, as if to appeal to the testimony of Nature. His eye fell upon the horse Beauty, which was feeding in the hedge, and he said, 'Say that again, Mrs Green, and I'll let loose your horse!'

Undeterred by this threat, Mrs Green yelled, 'Coward, coward, coward, *cow-ard*!' And, as if to meet the challenge squarely, she added in a lower tone, 'Drunk or sober.'

Mr Walker jumped to the tow-path, staggered to the horse Beauty and untied him. But if he expected that the liberated horse would gallop madly down the tow-path he was disappointed, for Beauty remained exactly where he was. Mr Walker gave him a buffet in the ribs with his fist, but at this hour of the day Beauty required some much more powerful stimulus, and he did not move. Mr Walker turned then and kicked into the canal the little fire of sticks which Mrs Green had built on the bank.

This childish exhibition proved soothing rather than enraging to the Greens. It showed the enemy in all his meanness, and put him out of court. The men looked on in silent scorn, and Mrs Green said pitifully, 'There's a man for you; there's a brave fighter – women and horses!' But Mr Walker, on his way back to the *Mary*, turned sharply and stepped on to the prow of the *Adventure*. There he faced Mrs Green and yelled, 'Horse yourself, you dirty old cow!' At once the Greens flared up in a fiercer fury than before – not for Mr Walker's strange accusation, but for his trespass on the boat. Insults they could endure with dignity, but a hostile foot across the frontier was another matter. Their boat was their home, their castle, and temple, and must be inviolate. Fred and Mr Green jumped off the boat, one with a long pole, the other with a landing-plank, and ran along the path towards the bows. But Mrs Green was before them. A long, narrow plank went forward from the cabin-roof, above the cargo, and the old woman ran along this airy track with startling agility, shouting, 'Take your foot off this boat! Take your foot off this boat, you dirty man!' She was the first to come within striking distance of Mr Walker. She halted above him, she raised her hatchet, and croaking, hissing, poured upon him a flood of abuse, threats, curses, blasphemy. She was a terrible figure in the moonlight – a witch, a fury, an avenging shadow on the sky. Her arm sawed up and down with the hatchet; six or seven times it came within a few inches of Mr Walker, and at every swing Jane expected to see it split the offending head. She watched, fascinated and admiring, half-hoping that it would. Fred and Mr Green watched also, holding their pole and plank at the ready, but not interfering; and beyond them stood the two brothers of Mr Walker in similar postures. It seemed to be understood on both sides that this was a battle of champions, at which the main bodies of the tribes were present only to see the right triumphant, and carried arms only as seconds or squires.

Mr Walker stood his ground, too drunk to be afraid, and shouted back at Mrs Green. Jane had not heard much bad language on the canal, nor is it much employed, for the boatmen as a rule are peaceable and gentle folk. But now new worlds of obscenity and malediction were opened to her. The shouts of the two combatants were shocking in the quiet night. Mrs Green's voice weakened, till her curses sounded like the last despairing utterances of a dying woman. Her breath came in gasps, she tottered on her narrow perch. And at last, fearing perhaps that she would soon be reduced to silence, and so deprived of her principal weapon, she raised the hatchet high above her head, as if to give the death-blow. 'Alive or dead, Henry Walker,' she hissed, 'you'll get off this boat.' The hatchet, polished like all Mrs Green's possessions, flashed in the moonlight, and trembled over the hated skull. All the men saw that the possessed woman had arrived at the summit of her rage. Fred called anxiously, 'Chuck it, mother,' and one of the brothers, 'Come off it, Henry. She's potty, can't you see?' Mr Walker at last perceived his peril, and, stepping backwards, slowly left the boat. Mrs Green lowered her hatchet, and without another word walked back along the plank. Mr Walker retired to his own boat, remarking again that he was a bloody soldier.

'Well done, old lady,' said Mr Green, but Mrs Green said to Fred and Jane, 'Take yourselves off, you two. He'll be back again in a minute, and I want no unpleasantness,' as if what had gone before had been no more than a polite difference of opinion.

So Jane and Fred walked down the tow-path, back towards Berkhamstad, to avoid passing the *Martha*. Fred put his arm round Jane, and presently Jane put her head on his shoulder, and so, a little awkwardly, they walked under the moon.

When they had walked a quarter of a mile Fred said, 'Sorry about the turn-up, Jenny'; by which he meant the battle.

Jane said, 'It's all right, Fred. I liked it. Your mother's fine.'

'She's a caution,' said Fred.

Jane felt drawn to Fred by the turn-up, and by all the exciting events of the day; but especially by the turn-up. It pleased her as a 'dramma', so many people worked-up and registering emotion, as people did in the pictures – and all for her sake. That was something new, a fierce battle about Jane Bell. And now here she was, the prize of victory, being carried off by the conqueror. It was exciting and sweet, and she rested her head on Fred's shoulder.

Fred was also excited, and wondered whether he should propose marriage this evening or not. He dimly perceived that this moment, after the turn-up, was propitious; and now he might as well be hanged for a sheep as for a lamb. He wondered what Jane was thinking, and her head gave him courage. But a proposal must be prepared for, he knew; and presently he stopped and stooped and kissed her.

She returned his kiss more warmly than she had ever done. But she said, 'You mustn't kiss me with your hat on, Fred.' He took off his cap and kissed her again. 'You're coming on,' she said.

He put on his cap again, and she put her head on his shoulder, and they walked on, not saying a word. Twice Fred halted and repeated this process, each time a little more boldly, before they reached the lock by the village of Northchurch. From the lock-side they could see the square tower of the church, a little way from the bank, and Fred thought of a plan.

'It's a nice church, that one,' he said.

'Pretty, isn't it?' said Jane.

They walked up the street to the churchyard gate, and stared at the silent tower and the pale monuments of the villagers and the yew-trees throwing shadows over their graves. Jane felt good and solemn and afraid.

'Gives me the creeps,' she said.

This was not quite what Fred had planned; he drew her close with his strong right arm, he cleared his throat, he thought for many minutes, and at last he said, 'Think you might come to church with me one day, Jenny?'

'Sunday?' said Jane.

'Well, any day. You know what I mean.'

'Oh, *that*?' said Jane. 'Well, I dunno, Fred.'

Fred could not think of anything more to say, so he was silent.

Presently Jane said, 'Better go back, perhaps.' So they walked back to the lock.

But at the lock they sat down on one of the great beams which swing the gates open. Fred, uttering at last a question which had fretted him severely, said, 'Are you gone on that Ernest, Jenny?'

Jane said, 'I wouldn't say I was gone on him, Fred.' Then she went on surprisingly, 'I like you, Fred. And I like your old canal.' And she pressed the hand which was clasping her own.

Fred was so much surprised and moved and pleased that he was embarrassed, and did not know what to do next. So he stood up, and they walked back along the tow-path. As they walked, Fred cursed himself, for he saw too late that he had missed an opportunity and should have stayed where he was. Lately he had been asking discreet questions of young men who knew about girls, and he had learned that man must take a thing called the 'Inishative'; and use his opportunities; also that when a girl said 'No' as often as not she meant 'Yes', and when she said 'I dunno' she meant 'Yes, I should say so!' The difficulty was that this might be one of the rare cases when she meant no more than she said. But Fred felt reckless tonight; or, rather, he felt that he ought to feel reckless. So when they came to the gate of a late hayfield, where the hay still lay uncarried, he said, 'Let's go in here,' and, Jane making no objection, they went. Fred thought proudly that he had taken the 'Inishative', and determined to keep it.

They sat down upon an untidy haycock which was a little damp with dew, but they were both accustomed to the damp. And now

Fred put his arms round Jane and kissed her for the first time with a spark of passion. But even as he did so he thought, 'She'll scream or slap me – it's all over now,' and he loosened his embrace just when, as any of his young men who knew about girls could have told him, he should have strengthened it.

Jane thought, 'Fred's a puzzle,' for she had been ready to be hugged, but just as she was yielding herself Fred let her go.

She said, 'You don't like me at all – not really, Fred.'

He was roused, and said eagerly, 'Yes, I do, Jenny,' taking hold of her arm.

She said, 'You're hurting,' and he released her. She said, 'Well, I like you, Fred; only – I dunno.' She looked at the moon and said, 'It's a nice moon, isn't it?'

He stared at her face for a full minute, wondering whether she would say something more. But Jane was thinking, 'Fred can't read and write,' and wondering whether it mattered.

She said nothing, and Fred thought that he should take the 'Inishative' again. He put his hands on her shoulders and gently pressed her back so that she lay flat among the hay. She did not resist. The sight of her lying on her back gave him a sense of power which frightened him. He kissed her reverently, and felt wicked. She lay drowsy in the hay, drowsy with air and the scent of hay and the stillness of the hot night; her eyes were shut and she was half-way to sleep. Fred crouched beside her, gazing tenderly at the beloved face, which was a small white moon in the shadow of his body. So they remained for many minutes. Fred was happy and Jane was contented, and neither wished for anything more. For Fred was in Heaven, alone with his love, alone for the first time, since never before had he kissed her save in a public place; and Jane was in a blissful repose of body and mind, not wild about Fred as he was about her, but liking to be with him, lying cosy in the hay. And her only thought was that she was glad it was Fred, and not Ernest, who would have pawed her about and disturbed the peace.

But poor Fred, conscious always of his inexperience, could not be satisfied that he was doing right, and began to wonder what he ought to do next. He felt that something was expected of him, and if he did nothing he would probably be accused of being backward.

So he put his arms round her and lay down beside her, and drew her gently to his rough blue jersey. The jersey tickled her face, so she put the top of her head against it, and she went to sleep. He was very uncomfortable, for he was resting on one elbow at the edge of the hay, and with the other arm supporting Jane's weight, but he would not move for fear of waking her. He looked up at the moon, and he looked down at Jane curled up in his arms, and he wondered whether she would marry him.

At last his limbs were so stiff that he tried to change his position stealthily, without waking her; but she woke up and rubbed her drowsy eyes, and lying back on the hay stretched out her arms behind her head. The movement inflamed Fred, and suddenly, like a clumsy bear, he rolled over and kissed her long and lustily at last. When he raised his head she smiled up at him and said, 'Well, Fred?' He thought she meant, 'Well, and what next, Fred?' but what she meant was, 'Well, who'd have thought it!' This was the boldest approach which any man had made to her, but she was not excited, only curious. It seemed that nothing Fred could do could excite her, or offend her. He was like a child, or an awkward dog. She thought curiously, 'Is poor old Fred trying to act like Ernest?' and she waited curiously to see what he would do, as one might watch a small child use the telephone. And he was so nice and she was so sleepy that she was not disposed to argue about it, whatever he did. Fred was sure now that something was expected of him, so hugging her again he prepared himself for further boldnesses, though his heart was full of respect and reverence, and while he trembled for love he was already ashamed. Thus the moon and the summer night and the two young people at cross-purposes made mischief together; and Jane came very near to losing her honour, for no better reason than many another of earth's daughters have done. But just then the church bells chimed the hour, and ten o'clock clanged slowly across the fields. Far away though they were, the bells were compelling in the stillness.

'Ten o'clock,' said Fred, and in silence they listened, counting the strokes. They reminded Jane of the churchyard gate, where she had felt solemn and good, and in one of those flashes of her picture-house mind she saw the 'dramma' of the scene – the young girl going astray – 'On the Edge of the Abyss' – but summoned back to safety by the wholesome sound of the bells. There would be a picture of the bell-ringer, and a close-up of the largest bell.

After the last stroke she thought, 'Well, it's true enough – I've been a bad girl, leading Fred on,' though consciously she had done nothing of the sort. And she said briskly, 'Get up, Fred. No more playing about.'

They sat side by side while Jane tidied her hair. Fred took her hand, and said timidly, 'What about the church, Jenny?'

Jane yawned and said, 'Well, I dunno, Fred. I'll tell you to-morrow.'

Mrs Green asked no questions, and kissed her when she came to bed.

In the morning, to avoid unpleasantness, Mr Green delayed starting until the *Martha* and *Mary* had left. But as they steamed away Mr Walker and his brothers all called a polite 'Good morning,' according to the unrecorded custom of the tribes. Mr Walker had set foot on the *Adventure* and Mrs Green had forced him to retire, and now Fred Green was at liberty to marry whom he would. But Ruth Walker was not to be seen.

Beauty plodded across the Tring Summit between high banks clothed with a jungle of bushes and young trees. At Marsworth they began to climb down the hill, and the locks grew thick again. Jane went ahead with Fred or Arthur, and all day she debated what answer she should give to Fred's question. She liked Fred, and she loved the canal; she loved the boats and the business of the locks, the clang of the gates, the rattle of the falling 'paddles', the rush of water, the patient Beauty, the taut rope glistening in the sun, the green fields to right and left, the open air, the quiet, and the wandering useful life. For that life she was fitted by Nature. 'Cut out for it,' she thought. Already, in the two days, had she not done wonders? Mrs Green, who had been her enemy, was now her friend, and had kissed her; and Fred said that Mrs Green had said that Mr Green had said she was a rare one. Already she was one of the family, and they all wanted to keep her. She knew as much about locks as any boat-girl, though she was wearing gloves because of her blisters; and Fred had said that very soon she should go ahead and get ready a lock by herself.

'It's the call of the water,' she thought, and her instinct said that she ought to obey it; besides, she had read somewhere that every one ought to do what they were fitted for. But what would become of Lily and her father? And how about the artist's model, and raising her 'stattus'? What was her Destiny? Could it be her Destiny to sleep in her clothes, and marry a man who could not read or write? Poor Fred! Fred was a puzzle. Fred would be a good husband to a girl, but he was a long way from Love's Bliss. How was it, she thought, that Fred could not excite her, even when he hugged her and crushed her lips, while Ernest with a single touch of his covetous hands could make her tingle, and at the mere thought of Mr Bryan her heart seemed to tremble? Yet Fred, very likely, was the best man of the three.

Thus Jane's little mind went round and round and came to nowhere. The day was lovely, and Jane, with a new rich colour in her cheeks, felt fresh and healthy from the sun. The sun fought for Fred, the smiling country-side said 'Fred', and the thunder of the locks was all for Fred. But in the late afternoon, above Fenny Stratford, which the canal-folk call 'Finny', Fred, knowing not what he did, sent Jane ahead, as he had promised, to get the next lock ready by herself. This was another good mark for Fred, and Jane marched proudly on, eager to do him credit, and thinking only of him. And when she reached the lock the first person she saw was Mr Bryan. The second person she saw was a lovely girl, with a mop of brown hair and a glorious smile, who was talking to Mr Bryan, and smiling at him.

A long house-boat, one of the rare pleasure-vessels seen on the canal, was lying above the lock through which she had just passed. Two of the party were talking to the lock-keeper, and Mr Bryan and the lovely girl were sitting on the roof. Jane felt suddenly weak, her heart raced, and, trembling, she put her hand on the rail of the lock-gate to steady herself. She thought afterwards, 'I know now how Ruth Walker felt.' But that did not matter now. Her dear Mr Bryan, whom she was never to see again, was there before her eyes. She could not think why, but that also did not matter; what mattered was that he should turn and see her, with the fine fresh colour in her face, emptying the lock like a boat-girl born to it. She pulled herself together and crossed the closed gates, trudged up to the top end and dropped the 'paddles', and swung in the half-gate at the farther side; then back and across and up again to close the other half-gate; then back once more to the lower end to begin the heavy winding. She wasted no time, but at every turn, where it was possible, she looked shyly at the house-boat, and the couple on the roof, to see if he had recognized her. But he had not. He glanced at her, as all the party did, but saw nothing more than the usual grubby boat-girl toiling with a windlass; which meant that someone was coming up behind them, so they had better be off. And before Jane had finished they had gone.

She finished just in time, and swung the heavy gate open just as Beauty came in sight. She had looked forward to that moment, and to Fred's approving smile, but now that it was here her heart was so full of confusion and pain that she got no pleasure from her success. There was only one good thing to be said – Fred's question was answered now. For she knew that she could not marry Fred; she could not marry any man unless he could afflict her with the awful weakness which had possessed her at the sight of Mr Bryan. And while she watched the tumbling water in the lock she thanked her stars that she had seen him.

The long day ended at the village of Stoke Bruerne, and that is just below the Blisworth Tunnel, where for two miles the canal runs under the hill. Many boats tie up here for the night, and go through the tunnel with the first tug in the morning. Jane looked eagerly ahead as the boat rose in the lock, and there, sure enough, a little way on, lay the house-boat, with Mr Bryan on the top, making a sketch. It was a very pretty little place, compact and sleepy, and altogether English. The Boat Inn and a few old cottages stood on one side of the lock, the ship-chandler's and the grocer's on the other. An old man fished above the lock, old men sat with their tankards on the bench outside the inn; a few villagers stood gossiping by the doors, or looking idly but politely at the house-boat. The canal was here, the village street and the marine-parade as well. Behind the Boat Inn was the church tower, perched in the tree-tops in the English way, and beyond were the warm, green sheltering hills. The railway was a mile away, and there was no noise nor ugliness nor hurry.

In this charmed corner Jane passed an unhappy night. Fred and Mr Green walked along the tow-path and were soon in friendly conversation with the house-boat party. Jane prayed for Mr Bryan to look her way, and yet was thankful that he did not. She was afraid to meet him now, with women of his own kind about him; the barriers of class were up, and she felt a servant again. He would have to tell his friends that she had brought him his morning tea, and she would have to tell the Greens – there would be difficult explanations and she would blush. No, it was just as well that Mr Bryan was blind. Yet she longed for a single word with him; and helping Mrs Green with the supper-things she was in such confusion of mind that she dropped a plate into the canal.

Mr Green said that they were very pleasant-spoken gentlemen. At supper they could hear the happy laughter of the other supper-party; and presently the two gentlemen walked past the *Adventure* on their way to the inn. Jane, down in the cabin, heard the boots crushing the gravel, and her heart fluttered again. Perhaps he would look in and admire the cabin, as the gentleman did at Fenny Stratford. Fred, outside, said, 'Nice evening, sir.' The steps stopped and Mr Bryan's voice said, 'Fine. You're very snug in here,' and, as he stooped to peep inside, she saw his face for a moment or two. He looked brown and well, and she loved him. She trembled and blushed and looked straight at him. His eyes ranged quickly over the plates and the flowers, the shining knobs and photographs, taking everything in, but from some instinct of courtesy not dwelling long anywhere. Then Jane thought they fell on her face and paused there; she thought he frowned faintly, as if he were thinking, 'Where have I seen that face?' She thought, 'Good evening, Mr Bryan'; in her mind she said, 'Good evening, Mr Bryan,' and 'Hullo, Mr Bryan', and 'How are you, Mr Bryan?' but her lips said nothing. She could not speak. And then, just as she would have spoken, he had gone. Then she felt a fool, and could have cried for her folly. But what was the use? 'Looked straight through me and never saw me,' she thought bitterly. 'Shows what a lot of good I am!' But Jane forgot that she was deep in the shadow, that she wore a handkerchief on her head and the country in her cheeks, and was a different person from the tidy miss who had called at the studio in her coat and skirt.

Mr Bryan, before he slept, wondered again where he had seen that dim face in the dusk of the cabin. He decided that she reminded him of Jane Bell, his model. But that could not be, for surely she would have spoken? A sister, perhaps? Well, in the morning he would go and inquire. But long before the house-boat party woke up the *Adventure* and the *Prudence* were ploughing through the tunnel, and Mr Green was leading Beauty over the hill.

If she had gone to the Boat Inn that evening with the Greens she would certainly have met Mr Bryan; for Mr Green and Mr Bryan played shove-halfpenny together. But Jane was walking out with Fred and explaining gently that she could not marry him. He asked her why, and she could only say, 'I dunno, Fred. I don't feel like marrying, you see.' She could not tell him that she was a born fool, who had fallen in love with a gentleman she would probably never set eyes on again – a gentleman who did not even know her when he saw her. They had a sad short walk and went to bed early.

The house-boat party went to bed late, and she lay awake listening for Mr Bryan's laugh. At last there was silence, but still she did not sleep. A pool of moonlight lay across the cabin floor; she looked up and saw the square of sky which had given her pleasure on the nights before. But now it was nothing; all was spoiled – the canal and the boats and all her joy in them – for Mr Bryan was asleep a hundred yards away and did not know she was there. Would not care if he knew, perhaps. She wondered whether he loved the lovely girl and painted her picture. Never before had she felt so sorely the tyranny of class. The lovely girl would be sleeping in a night-gown, or funny pyjamas, like ladies on the pictures. And she, poor Jane, was sleeping in her clothes, and had not washed all over for a week. It was this which stood between the likes of her and the likes of Mr Bryan, and had stopped her mouth when he had looked into the cabin. A lot of nonsense, Ernest was right. But somehow she would rise above it. The model business had been a beginning; and then Fred and his canal had pulled her down again. For a moment she was almost angry with Fred; and yet she liked Fred, she was sorry for Fred. It was all a puzzle. Mrs Green slept soundly and noisily. Perhaps if she slipped out on to the tow-path now Mr Bryan would be painting a picture of the moon.

Perhaps, after all, he would be glad to see her. She trembled at the thought and pondered it for a long time. She sat up in bed and put one foot on the floor. Mrs Green stirred and stopped snoring, and Jane lay down again, told herself she was a born fool, cried a little, and went to sleep.

13

'MEANWHILE—'

In the morning there was such a shadow of gloom over the Green family that Jane could not bear it. Mr Green was silent and sad, and Fred silent and kind, and Mrs Green silent and sour again. Jane went through the tunnel with them, a frightening passage in the dark. They were the last of a long line of boats hauled through by a tug, which filled the tunnel with sulphurous fumes. The wet walls glistened and dripped. Jane felt the hill heavy over her head, and the water noisome and threatening below, but for a while the little lozenge of light behind them was a comfort. When they turned a corner and were in the dark, she could see nothing but the faint light of a lantern on the tug's smoke far ahead of them. The tunnel twisted, and though Fred was steering the *Prudence* she bumped against first one wall and then the other. Jane, standing beside him, felt the clammy touch of the wall, and clung to him, shivering. At intervals there were air-holes through which a lonely ray of light came down and ghostly water fell on their faces. Fred said that there was eight foot of water in the tunnel and it was full of rats. Jane choked from the tug's fumes; she was oppressed by the blackness, the clammy walls, the dripping roof, the smoke, the noise of the engines, the earth above, the water below, the bumping of the boats, and the swish of the water in the dark. She clung to Fred; Fred put his protecting arm about her and longed to comfort her with kisses, but since all was over between them manfully held off. This nightmare lasted three-quarters of an hour.

On the other side of the hill they met Beauty again and Mr Green in a state of melancholy. Jane told Fred she thought perhaps she had better go home because she could see she would only be a worry to them all. Fred said, 'All right, Jenny,' and lent her the money for the train. Mr Green was very kind and said she was a champion boatman, and only Mrs Green said, 'The tunnel was too much for you, eh? Well, I told you it weren't all roses on the

"Cut", my girl.' Jane said meekly, 'It isn't that, Mrs Green,' and Fred said almost angrily, for Fred, 'You're all adrift, mother.'

Jane watched the tail of the *Prudence* retreating slowly round the corner. Fred waved, she blew him a kiss, and walked miserably to Blisworth Junction. All the way to London, as the train crossed and re-crossed the canal, she looked out of the window and said good-bye to remembered corners, locks which she had helped to fill, and stretches of the tow-path where she had walked with Fred. The train rushed past, despising the little world where yesterday they had crawled with such importance. But Jane envied the boat-girls waiting by the gates, for it was a world which she had lost, had won and thrown away. She told herself that she had made a mistake, and yet, thinking of Mr Bryan, was glad that she had made it.

But 'Meanwhile—' as the pictures said, what were Lily and her father up to, she wondered? It seemed an age since Tuesday and anything might have happened.

Things had happened to Lily, who had gone to work for the first time and was already up to mischief. The Government had moved quickly and transported Lily to a large milliner's shop near Regent Street. The work did not please her, for she was not in the public part where she might have shown off her fluffy charms to customers, but hidden in the background with a number of other girls, where there was never a sight of a man from nine till five-thirty. They sewed on feathers and bits of ribbon, dressed and re-dressed hats, and made all such alterations and additions as might persuade customer A that she was buying something different from customer B. Indoors all day, Lily missed the plentiful fresh air to which she was accustomed and was very tired long before half past five. And to a tired girl not used to it the long struggle home on the Underground was a torment. By the fourth evening Lily had decided that she could not go on with the life. It was hot that evening, and she thought she would try the bus for a change. The moment the clock struck she dropped her work, powdered her nose, and scampered out with the other girls. Like them, she carried an absurd small attaché-case, made chiefly of cardboard. Like them, she wore an absurd small hat of black straw, modelled on the fine ladies' fashions, shaped like a cockle-shell and pinching tightly her golden hair, which struggled out in two protesting clusters in front of her ears. Like them, she walked with quick, short steps on her absurd high heels. Like most of them, Lily was worried about a ladder in her stockings, for now, like the others, she must wear silk stockings every day. They were all dressed too finely for their earnings; nearly all had pearl necklaces; they were all poor and proud and devoted to appearances; they all denied their stomachs for the sake of their looks. Many were silly and some vain. And yet any nobleman idling up Regent Street and scanning curiously that regiment of shop-girls must have seen much to make a nobleman ponder; many more faces that tempted him to turn his head than he saw at Ascot or any gathering of the rich; many more that had courage and liveliness and native humour and what is vaguely called character. Perhaps the good looks were more pretty than beautiful, perhaps the character was rather audacious than strong, perhaps the lively ones were more impudent than thoughtful; but at least there was life in the breed, and the promise of more.

Lily was not one of the plucky ones, but she looked very well in the dark blue coat and skirt which had belonged to Jane. She joined the crowd of women waiting for the bus and feebly fought for a place. From the first she was thrust back easily by elbows and shoulders more experienced than hers. The second was already crowded, and, as if anxious to inflict yet one more exasperation on the women, lumbered past the stopping-place and stopped fifty yards ahead. Lily clutched her bag and ran after it along the road, the sun in her eyes, the hot fumes of the traffic in her nose and throat. She reached the bus among the first, and at last, pulling by the handrail, set both feet triumphant on the step. Then the conductor said, 'Full up, ladies,' and with four or five others she was shaken off, like weary ducklings which strive in vain to mount their mother's back. Lily stamped her foot and could have cried. Tired and angry and hot, she retreated across the Circus to the Tube station. Here was more jostling, more waiting in the queue, more dodging and colliding in the hurrying crowd. A young man in the lift noticed her pretty, flushed face as she came in. They were not far apart in the crowd, and over three or four shoulders Lily noticed the young man. She caught his interested but not bold glances and felt better at once. More and more people were herded into the lift till they stood jammed together as close as sheep penned up for the slaughter. The gates clanged and they descended into the pit, as patient as sheep, and as unquestioning. None asked themselves why they were there, and what they were there for, and to what strange purpose they were carted in droves from one place to another with much discomfort every day of their lives. The sun had shone all day, but not upon them. They began the day in a tunnel, and now they were travelling in a tunnel to see the sun set. All day the sun had been a tantalization through the windows, the sun had done nothing for them but make their work more difficult and the tunnel more tormenting; yet now as they stood sweating in the crush they murmured gratefully that it had been a lovely day.

The gates of the cage clanged again, and the sheep streamed out into the tunnel. Lily as she went took a peep at herself in a square of looking glass which advertised face-cream, and thought that she was looking well enough, considering all things. The young man walked slowly, keeping her in sight. The white-tiled tunnel ran down a slope and curved round many corners. A blast, a gale of wind swept suddenly up it and buffeted the sheep; men caught at their hats, and girls walked struggling against their skirts. The air did not cool or comfort, but was dry and chemical, and irritated without refreshing, like the wind of the desert. The young man, who wanted to write and thought he was a cynic, said to himself that this mode of travel in the tunnels under the town was one of the most artful feats of civilization: and he composed as he walked an ironical couplet,

> *I pity the Arab, the barbarous Nube,*
> *Who rides on a camel and not in a Tube.*

But, cynic or not, he took good care not to lose sight of Lily.

Along the platform the patient sheep huddled together in thick clusters, their obedient toes upon the white lines painted on the floor. There was a roaring in the bowels of the earth, and a train, like a lighted dragon, ran out of the cave, its voracious body swollen with heads and shoulders and uplifted arms.

Lily fought for a place in it, as she had fought for the buses, feebly and crossly and without success. The young man, behind her still, might have won a place, but chose to remain on the platform with Lily, who was left in the front rank, treading the white line. The next train they boarded without difficulty; that is to say, Lily was thrust violently by the press behind into a mass of bodies which seemed impenetrable; the attaché-case was almost torn out of her hands. There were no seats free, and not even a strap untaken. But she was on the train, and she stood gratefully in the middle, in between two large gentlemen who were smoking pipes.

Each of the two gentlemen had an evening paper and was reading happily the story of a murder. Each was securely tethered to the roof by a strap, and each at intervals puffed out contentedly a cloud of thick smoke. Lily swayed between them, bouncing wearily from one to the other. The atmosphere was choking, heavy with smoke and the smell of humanity; at every station the impossible was done, and a few more bodies were squeezed into the car. Men got out, and, fighting their way to the door, trampled her feet or hurt her breasts. Her head ached and her hot hands were sore from clutching the attaché-case. One leg was pressed against the knees of an elderly bricklayer, who had done his day's work and reckoned he had a right to sit down, if anyone had. After Hyde Park Corner the train lurched violently, and Lily would have fallen on to the lap of the bricklayer, but a man's arm caught her and restored her balance. Lily turned her head and smiled into the face of the young man in the lift, whom she had forgotten. He was close behind one of the gentlemen with pipes, and she wondered whether this was accidental; which it was not. Peeping sidelong at his reflection in the window she decided that he was a nice boy. The young man continued to stare at the back of her neck, and was sure that she was a nice girl.

At South Kensington many people left the train, but the seats in Lily's view were instantly taken. Wearily she clung to a vacant strap, hot and sticky from the hand of its last holder. Then she felt a tug at her arm; she turned and saw the young man making faces, and there was the seat next to the bricklayer empty! She sank into it exhausted, the young man raised his hat, and again she smiled her thanks, very prettily and warmly. He had done at the right moment the one service which could commend him most, and already he seemed quite a friend, thought Lily.

Nevertheless, there followed some awkward minutes. She wanted to look at him, but was sure that he was staring down at her, and did not want to be caught. But she grew self-conscious, felt her cheeks burning, and began to be annoyed by the rude gaze which she imagined. At last she decided that she must look at him, if she died for it, but only to give him a cross look and teach him manners. But when she did look up he was looking in another direction, though it was only a moment before that he had turned his head away. Now she was a little piqued by his lack of interest; but she took the opportunity to examine his clothes. His clothes seemed good, but well-worn and untidy. His face was pleasant in a comical way, with a rather pug nose and shaggy eyebrows. His hair wanted cutting, especially about the ears. His soft felt hat was very old and crumpled and dingy. He carried a large book. Lily could not imagine what he was, but anyhow he was a cut above any of the boys she knew, and lately she had remarked to Jane that all the Hammersmith boys were common and used the most awful language.

Then he looked at her, and she looked quickly away, as if this meeting of eyes had been a mere accident. But she had to look again, and there he was, still greedily admiring her. This time she boldly met his gaze, and at last he smiled, a pleasant humorous smile, which very much improved his face, but showed that he had bad teeth. She smiled faintly, and the train ran into Earl's Court. And with this strange wooing the decline and fall of Lily began.

At Earl's Court there was the first real exodus of passengers. Those left in the train stretched their legs and sighed with relief, and the young man promptly sat down beside Lily. He wasted no time, for he was dining with a friend at Baron's Court, which was the next station. The book under his arm was the *Chronicles of Casanova*; that gentleman's adventures were much in his mind, and he was determined in future to conduct his affairs with the same boldness and dispatch. And it was fortunate for him that his first experiment happened to be made upon the pliable Lily. He was a struggling freelance journalist and reviewer; he lived in

Bloomsbury, and his name was Baxter. He had never had any success with women, with journalism, or anything else.

Mr Baxter said, as he thought Casanova might have said it, 'Hot, isn't it?'

Lily fanned herself and replied, 'I should say so. I'm ever so tired.'

He said, 'Where do you work?'

'Fetter & Martin's.'

'Like it?'

Lily looked at him and shook her head. Mr Baxter was delighted by her large blue, innocent eyes and country colour.

'Got far to go?' he inquired.

Lily looked away again, and Mr Baxter transferred his gaze from her large blue eyes to the slight curves of her bosom. Lily, after a moment's thought, said, 'Chiswick', which had a better sound than Hammersmith.

Mr Baxter judged that they were approaching Baron's Court, so with a Casanova ease of manner but a craven fluttering in his heart, he said, 'Care to come out tomorrow?'

Lily faced him, and almost for the first time in her life paused for reflection before making a decision. For this perhaps would be a fatal decision. All the deluded young women in the *Sunday Gazette* seemed to say to her, 'Pause'. For all she knew, this young man might be a schoolmaster, that wicked and dangerous class of person. He carried a large book, and that was suspicious. But he looked her straight in the eyes, which was a good sign, everyone said. And, anyhow, she was very well able to look after herself. Had she not pushed Harry Stratton off his bicycle for passing a vulgar remark? But to gain time she said, 'Pardon?' and Mr Baxter had to repeat his question in louder tones, which embarrassed him, because he felt that everyone in the train was listening and condemning his motives. Casanova, he was sure, had never had to repeat an invitation. Now Lily said, 'It's ever so kind of you,' and Mr Baxter, hurriedly, because the train had stopped, said, 'Meet me at the Café George, six o'clock. My name's Baxter.' Lily nodded, though she had no idea where the Café George was, and Mr Baxter rushed out through the sliding doors just before they closed – not, he was afraid, a very dignified departure.

One of the girls at the shop knew all about the Café George, which, as it happened, was just across the road. It was rather grand, instead of rushing off with the rest, to dawdle before the looking-glass, murmuring that she had an appointment in town; and she doubled her allowance of powder (she had not yet acquired the lipstick).

Excepting, perhaps, the big Royal Picturedrome, the Café George was the most magnificent building which Lily had ever entered. She waited, a little frightened, in the domed entrance hall, where an aspiring fountain strove upwards to the golden tiles, and flunkeys arrayed like the monarchs of the Balkans moved in rubber soles across the marble floor. Mr Baxter came soon, they greeted shyly, and he led her at once into a room all looking-glass and purple plush. They sat down on purple plush with a vast looking-glass behind them and a vast looking-glass before them. Lily examined herself across the room, and thought she looked pale beside the other ladies who were there. The room was full of people, most of them talking; the lights were bright, there was the clink of glasses, and yet Lily thought that most of those present looked tired and unhappy. There were many lonely men who did not talk, but leaned upon their elbows and sipped at little glasses, gazing straight in front of them. There were many couples of gaily-dressed women, some very young, some very robust, whose eyes, while they talked, wandered ceaselessly about the room and rested chiefly on the lonely men. They were thickly painted and made Lily feel anaemic.

She asked Mr Baxter who the ladies were; he looked at her curiously, and said that some of them were artist's models.

Lily said, 'My sister's a model,' and for the first time felt proud of her sister.

'Do you ever sit?' asked Mr Baxter, and added vaguely, 'I know some artists.'

Lily shook her head strongly, saying, 'No, thank you. Strip? Not likely. I'm not that sort,' and for the first time felt superior to Jane.

Mr Baxter, slightly abashed, asked her what she would like. Lily said she would like some of the sticky stuff which the man was pouring the water into, because it looked exciting. Mr Baxter said it was absinthe, and ordered lager beer for himself. Lily looked about her and thought that after this she would be quits with Jane, and more, for Jane's gentleman friend had never taken her to the Café George.

But it was a disappointing evening. When the absinthe came she poured out the water carefully, and thought the little bridge for the sugar was 'Ever so nice', but all she could say for the absinthe was that it was 'Ever so funny. More like cough-mixture.' She took two sips only, while Mr Baxter, bold with beer, began to talk. He said that a lot of artists and well-known people came to the café every evening.

Lily said eagerly, 'Oh, show us! Is Nazimova here?'

But Mr Baxter, looking round, could discover nobody that he had ever seen before, except a certain lady in a green hat whose persistent gaze he was carefully avoiding. 'Funny, I don't see any tonight,' he said.

'Pity,' said Lily, who attached importance to results. 'Do you know a lot of people that a lot of people know?'

'Quite a lot,' said Mr Baxter, wondering which of his acquaintance he had particularly in mind.

'Well, who?'

'Oh, nobody that you'd know.'

'I believe you're a swank,' said Lily, who was also bolder than she had been a few minutes before.

Mr Baxter felt that this could not have been the normal opening to Casanova's nights of pleasure, but he said nothing. The people at the middle tables were beginning to eat – spacious soles, expensive chops, seductive fried potatoes. Mr Baxter would have enjoyed a Dover sole himself, but all the money in his pocket was three and sixpence; and, unless in the morning he received a cheque from the editor of *Chic* for his article on 'The Dressing of the Russian Ballet', that three and sixpence must last him over the week-end. But in his rooms, or rather room, he had, he knew, three rashers of bacon, a kipper, and a bottle of whisky. He debated in his mind whether he should ask Lily to come home with him and share these refreshments. That had been the original intention, but he was beginning to think that Lily might be one of these hard girls who take everything and give nothing. Already she had taken an absinthe and called him a swank by way of return. And from that haughty remark about her 'not being that sort', he judged that she might have strong views about behaviour, though no one would have thought it to look at her. Many people were looking at her – too many, Mr Baxter thought; for while he was proud to be the public companion of such youth and prettiness, he was also a little uncomfortable, for many of the glances, he thought, were as much pitiful as admiring. While he was debating, he began to talk about his ideas for revolutionizing the films by cutting out all natural backgrounds and substituting abstract designs to express the workings of the mind. This did not much interest Lily, who thought that the pictures were quite good as they were, and had no idea of what he meant by abstract design. She had come to the conclusion that there were several gentlemen in the room whom she liked better than Mr Baxter; two in particular, bronzed gentlemen, who looked like explorers. They were talking about her, she could see, but whenever she looked at them too long, Mr Baxter would pop a sudden question at her – 'Do you see what I mean?' – because it was these two whose glances had been, he thought, particularly pitiful, and he disliked them.

At length, despairing of supper, and tired of Mr Baxter's views about the film, Lily said, 'Well, I'd better be going home,' and picked up her attaché-case.

Mr Baxter was still wondering whether he should or should not invite her home, when a robust lady a few feet off said very slowly and clearly, 'Baby-snatching, I call it.'

The conscience, or cowardice, of Casanova, made an immediate decision, and he said, just as loudly, 'Very well, I'll see you to the station.'

On the way to the Tube station he made an appointment for Wednesday, but he went home to his kipper alone, a little, for a few minutes, despising himself, because he was too fastidious to go home with the lady in the green hat, and too ineffective to go home with Lily.

Jane had been so delighted to hear that Lily was at work that Lily had thought it a pity to spoil things by telling Jane that she had made an appointment with a strange gentleman in the Tube. Instead, she had said much about the severity and strain of her labours at the shop, and the fatigue of travelling by the Underground Railway; and Jane had quite coddled her all Sunday. But now, when she strolled on board at eight o'clock, she felt that there were bound to be questions, and she prepared to resent them with dignity. After all, she was an independent girl now, earning her own living.

It was difficult to enter the living-room of the *Blackbird* with dignity, because the entrance was made through a narrow hatch and down a perpendicular ladder, and the feet and legs were the first part of the dignified person to appear. The descending feet and legs of Lily did not look dignified to Jane, but guilty. Jane, who had spent the day sitting to Mr Latimer, was preparing the supper, carving slice after slice of bread, and slabbing on butter generously with a spoon. Mr Bell was lying on his bed in his cabin, reading about the greyhound racing at Shepherd's Bush, which was the new craze of London and was powerfully attracting him.

Jane said casually, 'You're late, Lily. Overtime, or what?'

Late? Late indeed! The guilty Lily discovered a grievance in the word. She could have endured to be blamed if she had had a gay time, but after that unexciting hour with Mr Baxter it was too much. And instinct drove her to choose hanging for a sheep rather than a lamb alone. 'I've been dining,' she said grandly. Jane glanced at her, suddenly maternal.

'Dining, have you? Where?'

'Frascatti's.' It was a name she had seen recently in the papers, and was a good name, she thought.

'Frascatti's? Where's that?'

'Where's Frascatti's?' Lily wondered where Frascati's was. 'Well, it's difficult to say where a place is when you're driving in a car. It's in the Strand or somewhere.'

'In a car? Whose car?'

'A gentleman's.'

'Anyone I know?'

'Oh, no. One of the clients at our place.'

'Oh?'

Jane did not know what to make of all this, and in her father's hearing did not wish to make too much of it.

'Well, did you have a nice dinner?' she said, putting down the loaf.

'Ever so nice, thank you,' said Lily. 'You can't imagine.'

'No, I can't,' said Jane, who was beginning to suspect exaggerations. Lily was cutting more bread and butter, and that was suspicious.

'What did you have?' said Jane.

Lily wished that Jane would not be so particular. She also wished that she had not dined at Frascati's. But now there was no help for it.

'We had *tarble dote*,' she said.

'What's that?'

'It's a kind of fish. Done up with trimmings and a yellow sauce.'

'Well, I never heard of it. What did you have after that?'

'Then we had a partridge. Roast. With chip potatoes.'

'Lucky girl!' said Jane. 'Anything else?'

'Well, I didn't want much else,' said Lily. 'I sat back and sipped my wine.'

'Oh, did you? What about your friend?'

'He had some caviare. And after that he had a plate of olives and some port wine. I took a caramel.'

'What's that?'

'It's a kind of cocktail.'

'Lily!' said Jane, shocked at last, for every reader of the *Sunday Gazette* knew that a cocktail was the beginning of the end. 'Well, you won't want any supper—that's one thing. Come on, Dad, supper's ready. Lily's been dining with a gentleman at Frascatti's, and had partridge. Kettle, Lily!'

Mr Bell shambled out of his cabin. Lily obediently fetched the boiling kettle, filled the teapot, and sat down on the locker and watched them. She was very hungry, but after her expensive meal at Frascati's she could scarcely eat thick bread and butter and damson jam.

Mr Bell made no comment on his younger daughter's behaviour. Since the Derby fiasco and Jane's firm ultimatum he had surrendered the whole conduct of the family to her. Besides, Lily was at work now, and a grown-up girl. The chief thought in his mind was that somehow soon he must go to see these greyhounds and retrieve his fortunes. The horse had played him false; the dog, the friend of man, would perhaps be more trustworthy. There was a dog called Bell's Run, an omen, surely. But Jane had made him promise not to set foot in the White City, not to make another bet; indeed, he could not bet, for she would give him no money.

'Frascati's,' he said. 'I've had many a nice chop there in the old days.'

Lily watched impatiently while he took another slice of bread and butter.

'Perhaps,' he said, 'your friend will take you to see these greyhounds they're all talking about.' And he glanced guiltily at Jane.

'Now then, Dad!' said Jane.

Lily said calmly, 'He's going to. On Wednesday.' Mr Baxter had never mentioned the greyhounds; he was no sportsman, he had never betted. But Lily had suddenly determined that Mr Baxter should take her to the greyhounds, and that she would win a great sum of money. For one thing, it would annoy Jane, who had gone pi-face and was really a little too big for her boots these days. And Lily, in spite of the Derby, had still a secret belief that there was something in this betting.

'A clean sport, they say,' said Mr Bell. 'A fine, clean sport. I'd like to see it.'

'Sport!' said Jane. A sudden panic took hold of her. She had thought her father cured of his madness. If he were to break out again there was no knowing what might happen. 'If you set foot in that place, Dad, she said, playful but firm, 'you shan't come back to this boat – see? I mean it, Dad.'

Mr Bell saw that she meant it, and took refuge in his cup of tea. Lily watched the pile of bread and butter dwindle, and was hungrier than before.

'Any tea to spare, Jane?' she said.

'Want some?'

'I could do with half a cup.'

'How will it go with that wine you had?'

'Chance it,' said Lily shortly.

She sipped her tea and fixed her eyes on the last four slices of bread and butter. Jane did not invite her to take bread and butter with her tea, and Lily did not like to suggest it herself.

The sun was set outside and the room grew dusky. It was hot. The two cats dropped from the hatch and sidled up to the table, begging. Jane gave them a saucer of tepid tea. Mr Bell took another piece of bread and butter. Jane took another piece of bread and butter. They ate in silence, busy with their thoughts. Jane was worried about her family. She was afraid that her father would be too much for her after all. She did not know what to think of this tale of Lily's — whether she was inventing something or concealing something. If Lily's friend was really a gentleman, her own case was a warning; and if he was rich, then, according to Ernest, the thing was fatal.

'You might light the lamp, Lily,' she said.

'There's no hurry,' said Lily, her eyes on the last two pieces of bread and butter.

'Finished, Dad?'

'Yes, Jane.'

Jane rose and scraped the butter off a piece of bread. She put the scraping back in the butter-dish, and began to crumble the bread for the cats.

Lily could not stand this. She said quickly, 'That going begging?'

'Do you want it?'

'I don't mind.'

'Sorry. I didn't think you'd want anything after that dinner.'

'We dined early,' said Lily.

Jane lit the lamp, with one eye on Lily, who was doing her best to eat as if she were not hungry.

'Has your friend got money?' asked Mr Bell.

'Lots,' said Lily, with her mouth full.

'What's his name?' said Jane.

Lily chewed and did not answer for a moment or two. The lamp gathered strength and flooded her with unwelcome light. She turned her head away. It was deplorable, but she had forgotten Mr Baxter's name. After all, he had only flung it at her as he leaped out of the train. She thought there was a 'B' in it.

'Baldwin,' she said at last.

185

Jane smiled to herself, relieved of one worry. Lily was swanking.

'There's a stale half-loaf in the tin,' she said, 'if you're still hungry.'

Lily rose immediately and went to the bread-tin; and Jane smiled again. She took her writing materials, an 'Invicta' writing-pad and a pen from Woolworth's with a magical nib that would write two hundred words after one dip in the ink; she sat on the keelson and wrote to the aunt in Liverpool. For the second time she appealed to the good aunt to find work for her father, and keep him out of mischief, for now that they had taken to betting on dogs a twopenny tram ride away, she was afraid that Mr Bell might break out again any day. Then she said, 'Wash up, Lily,' and slipped across to the Black Swan to earn her nine shillings behind the bar. What with one thing and another, she had her hands full, she thought. On the wharf she looked up at the starry sky, and in starry letters she seemed to see the monstrous legend:

JANE: THE MOTHER-GIRL

14

LILY GOES TO THE DOGS

ON Wednesday Mr Baxter was in good form, and, what was more, in funds. He had received two cheques, one from the editor of *Chic*, and one, much larger, from an American paper for an article on 'Some Personalities of the London Stage', with none of whom he was acquainted. He had paid some debts, and had twenty pounds in his pocket. His professional future seemed secure. Either a great dramatist, a great novelist, or, almost as good, one of those comprehensive, ubiquitous men-about-town who write the gossipy columns in the newspapers, and range daily, like ravening lions, over the whole plain of Art and Literature, Politics and Life.

This was one of Mr Baxter's ambitions, and tonight it seemed not far away. He readily agreed to take Lily to the greyhound races.

They went by the Tube to Wood Lane and were swept down the road by a crowd in torrent foaming towards the Stadium. It was the beginning of the great greyhound fever in London, and thirty thousand citizens were going to the dogs. All kinds and all classes, but mostly the small clerk and shop-hand and the cloth-capped labourer, and their girls. Most of the hurrying, excited men had betted for many years upon race-horses, and had never seen a horse-race. Now at last they could enjoy the ups and downs of fortune at first hand instead of in the Stop Press announcements, and see in the flesh the animal which carried their hopes, their savings, or their weekly wages. Always hitherto their speculations had been criminal because they were cash transactions, not conducted on a race-course, but furtively at street-corners, or through agents frowned upon by the law, and because they could not afford to bet on credit over His Majesty's telephones with commission agents deemed admirable by the law. But now by the mysterious niceties of British Justice they were suddenly permitted to bet in multitudes, three nights a week, at an easy distance from their homes. The greyhound had at last made betting safe for democracy. Already, the papers said, the police courts of West London were reaping a record harvest of embezzlements and larcenies by young employees whom the dogs had disappointed. But the promoters said that the dogs kept the people out of the pubs; and special regiments of police were ranked about the Stadium to make smooth the passage of the people to the book-maker; and that same constable who tomorrow would arrest the defaulting clerk now turned a genial eye upon him and urged him to pass along quickly to his bet.

Mr Baxter wanted cigarettes, and they went into a little shop which sold tobacco, chocolate, barley-sugar, newspapers, stamps, books, toys, and guides to greyhound form. It was five minutes past eight, and the shopkeeper said he could not sell them cigar-ettes after eight, for it was against the law. Another evening he might have stretched a point, but with all these policemen in the street it was dangerous. As he spoke he sold to a small child a bottle of sweets of poisonous appearance, and with the other hand dis-posed of a guide to greyhound form to an unemployed labourer who was existing on the public funds. This traffic he would be conducting until half past nine or ten, when the people came out from the dogs, but a box of matches – no. Mr Baxter made some caustic remarks about this odd piece of legislation, but Lily did not expect the law to be sensible, and it did not worry her. She was more interested in the fine-looking and courteous officers of the law who ushered her into the betting-ring.

Lily found the Stadium thrilling. The vast arena, the murmuring crowd, the babel of bookmakers, and in the tall stands across the course the stippled banks of midget faces sloping steeply up to the roof. But all she said was, 'Coo! What a lot of people!' The second race was almost due, and the bookmakers were loud and plaintive with their last appeals, chalking, rubbing out, and chalking again, their most ungenerous odds. The thirty thousand citizens discussed the amounts of money which they had won, or lost, or were about to win. Lily and Mr Baxter were low down in the five-shilling enclosure, close to the course, where the bookmakers stand. The crowd here was thick, and never still; burly men continually pushed and elbowed them. Lily did not like these men; many were greasy, and most were gross; their faces were sallow, rapacious, hard, and unwholesome, and Lily felt that they had wet hands. As they talked to each other they took from their breast-pockets crumpled wads of Treasury notes, and casually showed their winnings. Many looked disreputable, and all seemed rich. Their talk was not of dogs, but of ponies and monkeys. The sodden ends of cigars hung forgotten from their lips. Their ties were gaudy, and their collars dirty. Their voices were hoarse and querulous, or weakly blustering. They made Mr Baxter feel inexperienced, but superior.

'Too many Jew-boys,' said Mr Baxter.

'What's wrong with Jew-boys?' said Lily, who had just seen one she liked the look of.

Mr Baxter, craving for a cigarette, borrowed one from the nearest man, an obliging young Jew, who seemed, Lily thought, a cut above the others. He had a chubby face, a pale-blue tie, a magenta felt hat, and a purple suit. He readily supplied Mr Baxter, took a careful glance at Lily, and held out his gold cigarette-case to her. Lily did not smoke, but suddenly decided that she would smoke. The few women about her were smoking, perhaps in self-defence against the murky atmosphere. The young Jew crossed Mr Baxter to give her a light, and stood next to her on the other side. 'What are you on for this race?' he said. Lily said that they were not on anything, and felt ashamed. The Jew said that Down Boy was a good thing, and there was still time. Lily looked at Mr Baxter and said, 'Shall we?' Mr Baxter said coldly that they would wait until they had seen a race. The wealth and confidence of the Jew angered him, for he had neither. The Jew said that they were missing a good thing.

A horn was blown, and six grooms in long white coats entered the arena and marched in single file round the track, leading six greyhounds in coloured coats. They seemed diminutive in that vast space, and Lily said, 'Coo! Aren't they tiny?'

The Jew took another good look at Lily and liked very much what he saw. She was miraculously smart – Jane's green hat with a pale parti-coloured ribbon, Jane's green coat with the fur at the collar, 'nude' silk stockings, and shiny smart shoes. No one would have said that her family were insolvent and lived on a barge.

'This your first visit?' he said.

'Yes,' said Lily, facing him for the first time, and her large blue eyes made mischief in the heart of Israel. Lily thought she liked this Jew-boy. He had an air, he had shining white teeth, and he was *so* beautifully dressed.

'My name's Moss,' he said. 'I'll mark your cards for you, if you like.'

Lily looked mystified but said, 'It's ever so kind of you.'

'I marked a friend's card Monday,' said Mr Moss, 'and he went away with nine hundred. Put him on to the good things, you know,' he went on, for Lily still looked blank. 'And he came here with twenty pounds in his pocket.'

Lily at last understood, and almost swooned with astonishment and envy. She turned eagerly to Mr Baxter.

'This gentleman says he'll mark our cards for us; he knows a man who won nine hundred pounds.'

'Very kind of him,' said Mr Baxter without warmth, and stared offended at the advancing dogs. What was the use of taking a girl out if she always showed more interest in other people?

Mr Moss said low and quickly, looking sideways at Mr Baxter, 'Shall I put ten bob on Down Boy for you, as your friend's not betting?'

Lily too glanced at Mr Baxter, who had not heard the suggestion. In the swaying, struggling, vociferous crowd it was difficult to hear anything. She said, 'I haven't got it on me,' and this was true – she had not ten pence on her.

'Well, you can pay me back,' said Mr Moss, and suddenly vanished.

Lily felt guilty but wildly excited. Mr Baxter was silent. He was wondering what Casanova would have done to this intruding Jew. But, after all, he, Baxter, had no rights; he had picked her up himself, and why not others?

The dogs were being inspected before entering the starting-trap. Lily looked hurriedly at her card and saw that Down Boy was Blue. The race – good omen! – was called the 'Hammersmith Hurdle Handicap'. 'That's my dog!' she said, feeling that she owned the animal.

'Which?'

'The Blue.'

'Have you backed it?' said Mr Baxter, surprised.

'Yes.'

'How much?'

'Ten bob,' said Lily glibly. This was Life!

'Good God!' thought Mr Baxter. How could this shop-girl afford to put ten bob on a dog? Was the Jew lending her money already? Quick work! Just the kind of swift efficiency with women which he had always coveted for himself. Mr Baxter boiled, felt shamefully feeble, and wished that he had backed a dog.

The yelping greyhounds, the carriers of countless shillings, were picked up ignominiously, as if they were mere dogs, and bundled into the 'trap'.

'There's the hare!' said a voice.

Mr Moss was at Lily's off-side again. 'I got eights,' he whispered.

The hare – the electric hare – the foundation of the whole proceedings, the real benefactor of the thirty thousand Britons present, the newest portent of mechanical civilization, had appeared mysteriously, modestly, and quietly in a corner. A sudden hush fell upon the multitude; the bookmakers ceased to shout and the people talked in low tones only as the hare began its preliminary circuit of the course. According to Lily's conception of hares it was a very large hare, of unnatural aspect and easily distinguishable from a real hare; she could not understand how the greyhounds, with their wider experience and the famous instinct of animals, could be persuaded to pursue it. But as soon as it began to move the intelligent dogs in the cage set up a pitiful whining, pressed their intelligent noses against the wire-netting, and scrabbled voraciously with their delicate forepaws. The hare was carried on an iron bar, thrust out from the low wall of the arena; sparks flashed under the skirting behind it, the low whirr of machinery accompanied it, and it dashed miraculously through the trap-doors in the hurdles, which closed behind it; but in the sagacious greyhounds it kindled apparently the flaming thirst for blood. The hare gathered speed, until Lily thought that this was the swiftest motion she had ever seen, though in truth the hare was travelling only half as fast as an express train. But, whatever the speed, it was a thrilling object as, with a whirr, it raced along the final straight and passed the waiting hounds. The gate of the trap flew up, and out they tumbled in pursuit. The Red dog, from Number One position near the rails, leapt ahead and was first round the corner. The Orange dog, the favourite, followed him, and the Blue was fourth or fifth among the rabble behind. Lily had no eyes for any but the Blue. Wonders of cunning were done at the second corner, where Red ran a little wide, and Orange, nipping in against the rails, gained several yards. Lily did not see them. She saw only that Blue had somehow passed Black and White, and was now fourth.

The jumping of the hurdles was a marvel of grace and beauty, and Mr Baxter, who had no money on the race, watched every dog jump every hurdle, and in his admiration decided that he would write an article about the poetry of greyhound racing. But Lily missed this. She saw that Yellow hit the hurdle in the 'backstretch', stumbled and fell, so that Blue was now third – the blue dog (she had forgotten its name), which carried her money, or, to be accurate, the money she had borrowed from an unknown Jew. At the far corner Red and Orange were running level. Red snapped at Orange, and Blue came closer. At the last corner Red snapped at Orange again and Blue slipped in past Orange and was second. Blue raced up the straight behind Red, the multitude roared, and Lily felt a little sick. Mr Moss had gripped her elbow and was saying confidently over and over again 'He's got it! He's got it!' but Lily scarcely noticed him. The blue dog was gaining on the red. The crowd yelled, 'Down Boy!' but he was still behind. Crossing the last hurdle the two dogs were in the air together, two flying sprites, two frozen wisps of speed. Red touched the ground first and stumbled. They raced on, neck and neck together. Lily put her hand to her breast and made small ecstatic noises. The blue dog showed a head in front, a shoulder, half his body, and flashed across the line, the winner of the 'Hammersmith Hurdle Handicap'. Orange and Black and White and the other unconsidered dogs followed after, and were caught by the grooms, or, dodging past them, sniffed angrily at the hole in the wall through which the electric hare had gone to ground. Lily did not see them. She was saying rapturously to Mr Moss, 'He *did* win, didn't he?' Mr Moss, with perfect calm, said, 'He did so. Congratulate you,' and again slipped away into the heaving crowd. There were tears in Lily's eyes. She turned to Mr Baxter, eager to share her emotion with somebody.

Mr Baxter said, 'Beautiful sight, wasn't it?' Considering that she had won several pounds – exactly how many she did not know – Lily thought that this was an inadequate remark. She decided that Mr Baxter was a poor fish. How much more admirable was the miraculous Mr Moss, who had confidently foretold which dog would win the race! The first three dogs were being led past the stand, triumphant, panting, and seeming to smile their satisfaction, and Lily, with small, inaudible, but well-intentioned claps, applauded her beloved Down Boy. She thought, 'Wish Dad was here. He would have loved it.' Which shows that greyhound racing is not without merit, for Lily's unselfish thoughts were infrequent.

Mr Moss returned, took from his pocket a bundle of Treasury notes, handed Lily four pound ten, and said, but softly, 'You owe me ten shillings.'

Lily smiled like an adolescent angel at him and said, 'I'm ever so grateful, Mr Moss.' Never in her life before had she held four pounds in her hand; and her opinion of the Jewish race was higher than it had been before.

Mr Moss now easily assumed that he was accepted as the greyhound guide, philosopher, and friend of Lily and her mulish escort. He led them to a higher part of the stand, a place of less jostle and movement, more women, and less noise; more Christians and no bookmakers. Mr Baxter followed, indignant but dumb. Then Mr Moss took their cards and without hesitation ticked off the winners of the remaining races. He also mentioned one or two dogs which might be regarded as possible or outside chances. He explained modestly that he knew one or two boys who were in the game, and that he had followed the form.

He asked Lily what were her wishes for the third race. In Lily the betting blood of her father ran richly. Jane would have clung to the bulk of her earnings and risked perhaps a cautious crown. But Lily said boldly that she would put two pounds on Bluebeard, Mr Moss's choice; and Mr Moss, with a generous display of his beautiful teeth, approved her spirit.

Mr Baxter was determined not to be under any obligation to Mr Moss, and told himself that he would rather lose than bet upon an animal recommended by the Jew. He now recalled a conversation in a Bloomsbury pub where every person had propounded an infallible system for successful wagering on the greyhound. One had said that the dog drawing the Number One position had the advantage, and, if there was anything against him, the dog at Number Four should be followed. Another said that after a careful study he found that the colour red had been more often successful than any other. Another said that he watched the dogs during the inspection, and put his money on the animal which did not yelp, but saved its breath for the race. But most impressive was a didactic old man who said that if he saw a greyhound relieve itself during the preliminary parade nine times out of ten that cautious animal was the winner. Mr Baxter thought that a comprehensive man of the world should bet upon some system, and this seemed as good a system as any other. From the sounding of the horn, therefore, he fixed his eyes on the distant dogs and anxiously watched for the propitious 'sign'. There was no sign until they were at the last corner. Then Mr Baxter looked suddenly at his card, muttered 'Golden Glory', and hurried down the steps.

'Particular friend?' inquired Mr Moss.

'Nothing special,' answered Lily airily. 'A bit sloppy, I think.'

'Some people think they know everything,' said Mr Moss.

Mr Baxter was disappointed to find that Golden Glory was an odds-on favourite, and that he would have to risk three pounds to win two. This was too reckless, omens or not, so he staked thirty shillings to win a pound.

Golden Glory won – Bluebeard a good second. Mr Baxter held up his head again. After all, he was a hard-headed man of the world, able by sheer system and mental power to make a slave of Fortune. Lily was not much impressed. Any fool could back the favourite. And she gave her remaining two pounds to Mr Moss to put on Black Boy.

Mr Baxter, emboldened by success, said sourly, 'Is that fellow going to stick to us for ever?'

'Couldn't say, I'm sure,' said Lily innocently. 'Don't you like him?'

'Seems to think he knows everything,' said Mr Baxter.

'Well, he's got a system, you see,' said Lily.

'So have I,' said Mr Baxter incautiously.

'What's that?'

'Well, it's hard to explain.'

Lily nearly said, as she had said once before, 'I believe you're a swank,' but she refrained, for fear of unpleasantness.

This time Cat's Whisker gave the favourable sign.

While Mr Baxter was investing two pounds in Cat's Whisker, Mr Moss said, 'Coming here Saturday?'

'Well, I wasn't,' said Lily.

'Well, why not?'

'Well, I wouldn't mind.'

'Well, would you like to? Or perhaps your friend –'

'I shan't be coming with him,' said Lily decidedly.

'Well, shall us, then? If you'll pardon the impertinence –'

'There's no impertinence –'

'Well, what about it, then?'

'All right.'

'We might have a bit of dinner first.'

'It's ever so kind of you.' How different he was from Mr Baxter!

'Well, do you know the Clarendon, near the Broadway?'

'I live near there.'

'Well, what about seven o'clock?'

'All right.'

'Well, seven o'clock, then, Saturday, at the Clarendon.'

'Thanks ever so.'

Mr Baxter came back and found them smiling at each other. They did not mention the appointment.

Black Boy won the fourth race; and Cat's Whisker fell at the first hurdle, and was last. Lily won fourteen pounds.

Faint with riches, excitement, and tiredness, she sank down on to the hard stone step. Win or lose, it was a tiring ritual for the women. The races lasted thirty seconds and the betting twenty minutes. The men went about their manly business, the women waited obediently where they were left, standing till their legs ached, or sitting on the cold stone; and when the horn sounded they stood again. Lily ached all over, but she had won fourteen pounds.

All the remaining races were won by Mr Moss's choices. Mr Baxter, though the omens were many times favourable, backed loser after loser. He discovered an unsuspected gambler in him; sullen in defeat, he staked each time a larger sum, enough to recover what he had lost and restore the dwindling credit of the man of the world. He lost seventeen pounds. Lily, under Mr Moss's care, won thirty-five, and Mr Moss displayed with quiet triumph a 'wad' of sixty.

Towards the end the strange figure of Beauty invaded the mercenary scene. Darkness had fallen, and a light mist hung haloes round the lamps. When the horn sounded, by a fine stroke of stage-management, the big lights in the enclosure suddenly went out, and only the green ribbon of the course was left picked out brilliantly by shaded lights from above. The course became a bright green river, the centre of the Stadium a huge island of darkness, the thirty thousand gamblers mysterious, murmuring mountains, hardly perceptible. The course was like green baize. In that light the hare seemed tinier and the greyhounds toys; and seen from high up in the stands, where Lily was, the place might have been some monstrous nursery 'race-game', some inconceivable roulette table – which, as Mr Baxter bitterly remarked, was all it was. Mr Baxter now had no eye for the beauty of the jumping or anything else; the more money he lost, the more sordid and contemptible did the whole affair appear to him. But as Lily's winnings grew, she remarked more and more often, 'Coo! Isn't it pretty?' which irritated Mr Baxter.

After the last race Mr Moss raised his beautiful magenta hat and withdrew, saying nothing of the Saturday appointment except with his little brown eyes. He hoped that Mr Baxter would have better luck next time.

Mr Baxter hoped that Mr Moss would be knocked down by an omnibus. But left alone at last with the nominal partner of his evening he made a despairing attempt to bring Casanova to life again, and suggested to Lily a little supper in the West End. Lily had no thought now but to hurry back to the barge, display her riches, and rest her limbs; and she said 'No'. Mr Baxter protested that he had scarcely spoken to her all the evening. Lily said that was his fault, but, if he liked, he might take her in a taxi as far as Hammersmith Broadway. In the taxi Casanova was bold, but Lily was virginal. Even his arm about her provoked a shudder which might have cooled a Casanova much less sensitive than Mr Baxter. They parted, politely, at Hammersmith Broadway. Mr Baxter, poor again, and surely a much misused man, went back to Bloomsbury by the Piccadilly Tube, reviling Fortune and the feminine gender. And Lily walked to the *Blackbird*, adoring herself and thinking quite kindly of Mr Moss.

Lily's return to the barge with thirty-five pounds in her bag created as much sensation as she had hoped for. Jane was staggered and her father almost delirious. He raised his head again and became a new man; he was as a proud father whose life-work has been justified at last, whose child has bred true to her blood and education. Over thick cups of cocoa, far into the night, the triumphant girl told and retold her adventures, her odds, her winnings, the names of her dogs, and the kind behaviour of her infallible friend. Only Mr Baxter was left out; she let it be understood that the wealthy gentleman of Frascati's was also the prophetic benefactor of Shepherd's Bush.

Jane said no more, but watching her father's ecstasy began to think that Lily's winning at the White City might easily be as disastrous as her father's losing at Epsom. They were drunk with betting; win or lose, it was the devil, she thought. Neither of them, Jane noticed, thought of the thirty-five pounds as a sum sent from heaven for the reduction of the family debt. The one thing in the future was the next visit to the dogs. Lily said that she would take her father to the dogs next Saturday.

Jane said, suddenly firm, 'No, you won't, Lily.'

Lily said, 'What's it got to do with you?'

Jane said, 'Dad's not going betting again; he's promised, haven't you, Dad?'

Mr Bell looked feebly from one to the other and said nothing.

Lily said, 'Well, you can't stop him if he wants to.'

Jane said, 'Can't I?' but she had an uncomfortable feeling that Lily was right.

The next morning Lily very much disliked getting up, and she had half a mind not to go to the shop. But she reflected that it would be fun telling the girls about her riches and the dogs, and she went off grumbling against the hard lot of the working woman.

A letter had come that morning from Liverpool. Mr Bell read it, made no comment, and put it in his pocket. When Lily had gone Jane made him produce the letter. The good aunt had secured him the offer of a job in a music-hall orchestra – to start on Monday; they must telegraph. She would give him a lodging.

Jane was overjoyed, Mr Bell lukewarm. Mr Bell had decided during the night that he was letting Jane boss him too much, that really this ban on betting was ridiculous. He believed that there were persons called 'professional backers' who devoted their whole time and attention to the business, unhampered by the tiresome responsibilities of jobs; and in the night he had toyed with the notion of becoming a 'professional backer'. It would need capital, but with the help of Lily's friend and the beneficent greyhounds that should not be difficult.

Jane also had thought about the beneficent greyhound in the night, and it had swollen into a nightmare, a monstrous terror. She saw her father riding down to ruin on the greyhound, losing, losing – for he always *would* lose – losing, despairing, and then perhaps stealing, arrested, in the dock, one of these larceny and embezzlement cases she kept reading about: 'The prisoner attributed his downfall to gambling on dog-races.' She was obsessed by one thought, that her father must be kept from the dogs. So she said that if he did not take this job and go to Liverpool she would never boil a kettle for him again, she would give him no money, she would make his life a burden, she would leave him and Lily to fend for themselves. Mr Bell became suddenly solicitous for the welfare of his daughters. How could he leave them defenceless on the barge? Jane replied that he was as much good to them as a sick headache, that Mrs Higgins would keep an eye on them, that they could take good care of themselves. Mr Bell was fumbling for another good reason against his going to Liverpool when his eye was caught by the word Liverpool in an old Sunday paper lying on the floor:

GREYHOUND RACING
LIVERPOOL RESULTS

Jane had forgotten that there were dogs at Liverpool. Mr Bell thought cunningly, 'Go to Liverpool – take this job – no fussing Jane – go to the dogs when I like – make a lot of money – give up job – professional backer – come back to London – rich man – show Jane what a lot of nonsense – '

So he patted her cheek and said with resignation, 'All right, Jane, I'll go.'

'And you'll go on Saturday?' insisted Jane. 'Promise.'

Mr Bell hesitated. Saturday? The White City? But he said again, 'All right.' If he travelled in the morning he could go to the Liverpool dogs on Saturday evening.

On Friday evening they all went to the Clarendon Restaurant for a farewell beano, and had fried plaice and chips. They were gay. Lily had given Jane two pounds for a present, and they both had new hats. Mr Bell expressed a little melancholy at the thought of parting from his daughters, but secretly he felt like a boy about to be let loose from the tyranny of home, free to make his fortune on the dogs or horses without interference or nagging remarks. Only Jane remembered that they owed the aunt a hundred pounds and Mrs Higgins many pounds. Afterwards they went to the Blue Halls and saw a picture in which a girl saved her sister from worse than death by slashing a financier in the face with a horsewhip.

They saw Mr Bell off on Saturday morning. Jane had no sitting, and Lily thought it was a good excuse not to go to the shop. Mr Bell had the cornet on the rack above him (the cello was in the van), an old leather bag on the seat, and in his pocket a guide to greyhound form which Lily had secretly bought for him. He had had a private talk with Lily about greyhounds.

'Good-bye, Dad,' she said. 'Best of luck!' and gave him a confidential wink.

'Good-bye, Jane,' said Mr Bell. 'Take care of Lily.'

'Take care of yourself,' said Jane. 'No betting, mind!'

'Oh, no. I dare say not,' sneered Lily as they waved their handkerchiefs. 'Good old Dad! He'll be at the dogs tonight!'

'What d'you mean?'

'What I say. At the dogs. At Liverpool!'

'Do they have dogs there?'

''Course they do, pi-face. Didn't you know?'

'No, I didn't. Does Dad?'

''Course he does. I gave him a fiver.'

'Oh, Lily!' Jane was staggered and hurt. They had been deceiving her. Nothing she planned for seemed to go right. They travelled back to the barge in silence.

The afternoon was fine, and Lily sat on the hatch altering her new hat. At six, after a great deal of preening and preparation, she walked off gaily to keep her appointment. The new hat was a round, tight-fitting object in green felt, lighter than Jane's green, with a small feather lying along one side. She had new shoes. She looked very slender, young, seductive, and bold. She had bought her first lipstick and lavishly employed it. She did not suggest that Jane should go with her. Jane wondered whether she ought to insist, but decided that this would truly be a 'pi-face' action.

'Take care of yourself, Lily,' she said. 'Don't be late.'

'Don't worry, pi-face,' said Lily, and airily departed.

Perhaps she was a pi-face, Jane thought, but what had happened to Lily in these few days? So hard and rude and pleased with herself and superior, keeping things back, telling stories, never helping, not caring what anyone thought. Well, it was true, it seemed, *'Gold is a Curse'*, and if this was what came of Lily winning money, Jane hoped that she would lose it all tonight.

She went over to the Black Swan and took her place behind the bar. Saturday was always a busy night, the two bars were crowded and there were many trayfuls of old and mild to be sent out to the garden. Jane's arms ached from hauling at the beer-engine, her legs ached from the standing, and her mind ached vaguely because of Lily. The jolly, sun-faced Mr Pewter and one or two others chipped her about her solemn looks. In the glib saloon manner which she was beginning to learn she replied that she was as well as some that looked better, thank you, and better than some that had more to say, perhaps. After 'Time, gentlemen, *please*', and the last genial farewells, there were glasses to be washed and put away, and these kept her till a quarter past ten. Glasses were a simple matter, nothing to the complex washing-up at the Ravens' but while she slipped them under the tap and handed them to Harold, the young man who helped Mrs Higgins, she could not help thinking, 'Seems silly, doing all this for nine shillings, when Lily can find a flash gentleman and make thirty-five pounds in a single night.' What was the use of it? What *was* nine shillings, after all? And what was happening to Lily? Harold at one time had hung round after Lily until Lily threw his hat in the river, and he asked after her now. Jane wished that Harold was with Lily, instead of this Mr Baldwin (if that was his name). She slipped out through the street door because she heard that Ernest was in the garden. Ernest never came into the bar, but lately, on his evenings at home, he had taken to waiting for her at the garden entrance and escorting her home. And she had let him kiss her because it was less trouble than refusing. But every time Ernest was a little bolder. She could not stand Ernest tonight. Tonight she felt that all men were alike, and probably Mr Baldwin and Ernest were much of a muchness.

The barge was empty, silent, and dark. It was half past ten. By this time, if Lily had come straight home from the dogs, she should have been there. Jane put the kettle on for cocoa, and sat waiting in the dark. The night was still and sultry, cloudy, with no moon. It was low water; a wide stretch of mud and shingle lay between her and the narrow remnant of the river. At low water she was often depressed—no lively lap against the barge's sides, no friendly sound of siren or motor, no moving lights, nothing to be heard but the remote murmur of the road traffic and the quack of the ducks who came exploring from the island. The river was dead, and Jane was heavy with depression and foreboding. She was a failure, an utter failure. Here she sat alone, the mother-girl, the saviour of the family, and both her charges had spent the evening betting on the fatal dogs. She had sent her father to Liverpool, where she had no control over him; she had kept him from going to the White City with Lily, and because of that perhaps Lily was already up to some serious mischief.

She went below and took the kettle off and brought her cup of cocoa on deck. It was too hot, so she walked across the wharf and looked up the road. There was no slim, hurrying Lily, only a few shadowy couples hugging on the Mall, and one under Fred's elm-tree. Poor Fred!

Probably by this time her Lily was a White Slave. Young girls, she knew, were often lured away by well-dressed strangers and shipped to South America. There were cases about it. On the pictures, she, Jane, would have intervened successfully with a horse-whip, but as it was she did not even know the villain's address. The pictures! And, come to that, where was her own high Destiny? Fred, who loved her, thrown off; Mr Bryan whom she loved, gone away. True, she had raised her 'stattus', but sitting was becoming a weariness already, and her employers were not exciting or particularly friendly. Ernest was after her, of course, but who wanted Ernest? No sign of Queenery or Love's Bliss anywhere.

Jane stared at the sultry sky and for the first time in her life wondered what she was for, what she wanted, and whether anything mattered. Lily knew what she wanted – to have money and a good time and do as little as possible. Lily thought that nothing mattered, and perhaps Lily was right. Ernest knew what he wanted – to break down the capitalist system, establish the Socialist Commonwealth, and go out with girls. But Jane Bell – what was she for, what did she want?

She wanted to be loved by Mr Bryan – but that was foolish; she wanted to keep her family straight – but that was a failure. And beyond these she wanted something high and splendid and exciting. But what? She wanted this forlorn girl sitting by the mud, this insignificant Jane Bell, whom nobody knew, to swell up and be important in the world. But how? When she came to consider the how and what of her aspirations she could think of nothing but highly-coloured events which got obscure people into the papers. A young girl had just swum the Channel – nobody yesterday, now everybody knew her name. Other young girls won beauty competitions, or rescued drowning men. Others made married men distracted, and were found shot with them in bushes after romantic days in the New Forest. Others drove men to suicide, and gave evidence in black, 'feeling their position acutely'. Things happened to other girls, no better than herself. These girls, she thought, must have begun, like Lily, by deciding that nothing mattered. *Did* anything matter? She had thought that working hard and looking after Lily mattered. But if Lily could make all that money in an evening, if Lily could go out with a strange man and stay out like this, after all that Jane had done for her . . . well, what was the good?

Thus Jane pondered, disconsolate and muddle-headed and

leaderless, since all the rich storehouses of civilization, of education, religion, the cinema, and the Sunday Press had been unable to provide her with a single landmark, lifebuoy, or beacon, a single answer to the simple questions, What am I for? What do I want? and, Does anything matter?

She heard the latch of the wharf-door click, and, turning eagerly, cried, 'That you, Lily, dear?'

'It's me – Ernest.'

Jane said, shattered, 'Oh, it's you, is it?' She thought, 'Poor Dad was some use after all, then,' for Ernest had never dared to call so late while Mr Bell was at home.

'You're up late, Jane,' he said.

'I'm waiting for Lily. She's out. With a friend.'

She did not say, 'With a gentleman,' or mention his riches, for fear that Ernest would break out against the *bourgeois*.

Ernest sat down on the hatch beside her, and put his arm round her and kissed her. She did not want to be kissed, but thought, 'What does it matter?' and suffered it woodenly.

She said at last, 'D'you think anything matters, Ernest?'

'Lots of things,' said Ernest. 'What d'you mean, Jane?'

'Well, I mean, what anyone does – '

'How d'you mean – "what anyone does"?'

'Well, I mean, ought a girl just to have a good time, or what? Because it seems to me some people have as good a time as they can and get everything they want' – she delicately refrained from mentioning Lily – 'and others go on trying and everything goes wrong.'

This sounded very much like Socialism, and Ernest with an effort restrained himself from saying so.

'A girl ought to have ideels,' he said, 'same as men.'

'What d'you mean – "ideels"?'

'Well, I've told you many a time – brotherhood, and all that.'

'Oh, *that*!' said Jane, disappointed.

'What d'you mean – "Oh, that"?'

'Well, I dunno.' There was a pause.

'What's gone wrong, Jane?' said Ernest, stiffening his arm.

'Oh, nothing particular. Well, I mean, Dad losing his job – that was the beginning.'

'Things'll go wrong,' said Ernest, 'as long as there's capitalism.'

'Oh, chuck it!' said Jane, impatiently. Ernest again restrained himself.

'You've got no ideels,' he said. 'That's what's the matter with you – nothing to live for.'

'I've got Dad and Lily,' said Jane, and, this reminding her of her trouble, she looked up anxiously at the empty wharf. There was no Lily, no sound.

'That's not ideels,' said Ernest; 'that's personal.'

'Well, what's this?' said Jane sharply, and with her free hand tried to pluck Ernest's hand from her arm.

Ernest strongly tightened his grip, and said in quite a different tone, his wooing, murmuring tone, 'I never said a girl oughtn't to have a good time, did I? A girl *ought* to have a good time. Only she ought to have ideels as well – see?'

After this unimpeachable contribution to the philosophies of life, Ernest put his other arm round her, hugged her, kissed her, and began what Jane called pawing. It flashed through her mind that at this moment, perhaps, some hateful stranger whom Lily did not love was doing the same thing to Lily; and it disgusted her. She tore herself free and jumped up, and said, 'Stop pawing, Ernest! You're a beast! You're all beasts! You and your ideels!'

Ernest, still sitting, said, 'What's that got to do with it?'

She said 'Good night.'

'If you're going to wait for Lily,' said Ernest, 'I'd better stay with you.'

'I'm going in,' said Jane, 'and you're going home.'

'Let me come in with you. Just for a minute. I won't worry you – honest.'

'I don't trust you.'

'You oughtn't to be alone, Jane.'

'I'm better alone than with you,' said Jane, very small but determined. 'And if you don't get off this barge I'll never speak to you again.'

'Don't talk so loud,' whispered Ernest.

'I'll shout in a minute.'

'All right,' he said, suddenly sullen. 'Give us a kiss, Jane.'

'I'll give you nothing.'

Ernest said no more, but climbed up the ladder to the wharf. Jane watched him go, proud of herself, and, somehow, more cheerful, as she always was after a successful tussle with Ernest. She had made a stand, she had been strong, she had not failed for once. Perhaps she had saved her honour. And after this grand but nevertheless quite easy victory her fears for Lily seemed a little foolish. Surely Lily, with all her silliness, could do what she had done. A wave of tenderness for Lily swept over her, and she told herself that she had done Lily an injustice – many injustices. She went below into the cabin, and prepared a special supper for Lily, for Lily would be hungry. She put the kettle on the spirit-stove again for Lily's cocoa. She opened a tin of sardines for Lily; she cut bread and butter and spread some jam for Lily. Lily would be back soon, tired but happy, and they would be happy and friendly together again. She sat down on the wide keelson, with her back against the table, and read last week's *Sunday Gazette*, and waited.

Faint, muffled, through the hatchway, she heard the clock strike twelve. The dogs finished at ten, she believed. Where was Lily? Still, the last train was twelve thirty-five.

She nodded over her paper. She got up and put a saucer over the sardines, because of the cats, now curled up in corners. She sat down, and nodded again, and was soon asleep.

She awoke cold. The alarm-clock had stopped, but she could hear the tide licking along the barge's sides and the soft patter of rain on the deck. If the tide was up it must be late. She went on deck. A breeze had come up with the tide and she shivered in the rain. No one was about. The clock struck two.

Now she shivered inside and all through her, thinking of Lily. She went down into the desolate barge and trimmed and relit the lamp, and lay down without undressing on her bed; and presently she wept, thinking of Lily. 'Oh, Lily! Lily!' she cried into her pillow, and at last fell asleep.

When she woke the sun was on her tiny windows. She lay still for a moment, afraid of what was to come. Then she called, 'Lily, Lily!' There was no answer. But of course the child would be exhausted and asleep. She jumped up and ran into the living-room. The lamp still burned. She saw with joy that the supper had been disturbed, and ran along to Lily's bunk under the hatch. But on the way she saw the remnants of the sardines and bread and butter, mangled and abandoned on the floor. The cats! Lily's bunk was empty. Lily's innocent nightie lay folded on the pillow.

Perhaps a street accident? Perhaps Lily was lying in some hospital. She would wait a little more and then go to the police station. But in her heart Jane knew very well what had happened. Lily had been betrayed, deceived, interfered with, taken advantage of – ruined! Lily, so curious about those cases in the paper, had become a case herself.

Jane made some tea and thought out what she would say to Lily. She would not say anything much; certainly no reproaches – nothing of the 'pi-face' kind. Lily would be 'feeling her position acutely', Lily would be wretched and ashamed and drooping. And Jane would be kind and motherly and understanding, and always look after her better in future.

Perhaps, in a way, it would be all for the best. It would be a lesson to Lily. As the hours passed – nine, ten, half past – and Lily did not come, she began to believe in the street accident again, and was still more troubled. She thought, 'Anyhow, it would be better than Lily being messed up under a bus.' She did not believe that it was worse than death.

At eleven she went down and put on her coat and hat. As she came out of the hatch to go to the police station Lily jumped from the wharf on to the deck. She flung her arms round Jane and kissed her. There were no signs of wretchedness or drooping – she looked fresh and blooming, a gay, laughing Lily, and affectionate again, very different from the superior girl who had called, 'Ta-ta, pi-face!' the night before.

She cried, 'Oh, Jane, I've had such a time! I won thirty pounds – *again*!'

'You didn't!' said Jane.

'I did, my dear. Look!'

Jane looked at the folded notes. 'But where did you sleep?' she said.

'With my friend,' said Lily coolly.

'Not with a *man*!'

'Of course,' said Lily. 'What do you think?' Jane looked at her, puzzled. Perhaps Lily was swanking again.

15

THE EXPLOITERS

LILY was not swanking. She was not drooping. She was not defiant, putting on a bold show. She was happy. She had enjoyed her evening out, and had made arrangements for another.

During the day Jane said frequently, 'Did you *really*?' and Lily replied invariably, 'Of *course*!' And Jane by degrees became more curious and less concerned. Lily's attitude suggested that what had happened was no more deplorable or unusual than a handshake. And since any opinions of Jane's upon the subject had had no bottom in moral belief but had sprung weakly from the conventions of the pictures and the police reports, she began to catch some of her erring sister's ease of mind.

That evening they changed their cabins, Jane moving into the big cabin which had been Mr Bell's and Lily into Jane's. A light partition of wood divided them, and behind this decent screen Lily told, as she brushed her hair, the cheerful story of her evening.

She began with an ecstatic account of the dog races, her immense winnings, and the genius of Mr Moss, who had put her on to six winners out of seven.

'I thought you said his name was Baldwin,' said Jane mildly.

'Did I? Well, you annoyed me, dear. His name's Moss — only I call him Bunny because he can twitch his nose. A Jew-boy, I dare say, only you'd hardly notice it. His father's a well-known furniture-man, he said. Well, after the dogs, you see, Bunny said what about going into the West End to have a bit of supper. Well, my dear, he'd been ever so kind, and after his winning all that money for me I thought it was the least I could do, you see, and besides, I was a bit worked up, you see, well, naturally. So I said I would, only I mustn't be late on account of you being alone, you see, and he said that would be all right, so we took a taxi to some place in Soho, because Bunny said there might be some friends of his, you see. Well, in the taxi he turned a bit sloppy, perhaps, but nothing out of the way — well, I mean, nothing anyone could object to because he's a real gentleman, my dear. You'd be surprised, my dear, the *difference*, after the boys in *this* neighbourhood – well, I don't mind telling you, I'm a bit gone on Bunny, I am really, dear. Well, we got to this restaurant, my dear, but don't ask me the name of it, because I couldn't tell you. Well, we couldn't see any friends of his, so we had supper by ourselves, and he said, "How do you like your champagne, soft or dry?" Well, I wasn't going to say I'd never had any, so I said I'd take a glass of the dry. Well, as it happened, I wasn't very hungry, but I had a bit of everything, because it seemed a waste not to, and the champagne was ever so nice –'

'What's it taste like?' said Jane.

'Well, I dunno: well, it's like fizzy lemonade with the chill off. I didn't have much, you know, because Bunny wouldn't let me, so I never felt the least bit queer with it, but very full of beans, you see, and ready for anything. Well, Bunny drank my health and he said, "I'm very fond of you, Lily," and I said, "Are you? Well, I'm a bit gone on you, Bunny." And then we sort of clinked our glasses together, which is an old custom, he says, and he held my hand under the table, but no knee-grabbing or anything. Well, I tell you that to show you what I mean about Bunny being a gentleman, you see – he's *different* from the West London type of boy, and that's all about it. Well, we hadn't half finished the champagne when the waiter came and took it away because it was after hours, you see, and I said that it was a rotten shame, so he said, "Well, if you want any more, we can go back to my place and have some there," and he said perhaps he would ring up a few friends and play some tunes on the gramophone. Well, I said it was about time I was going home, on account of you being alone, you see, and he said he was quite sure any sister of mine could take good care of herself, and if I had no father or mother I shouldn't get into a row if I was late. So I thought, "Oh, well, it's Saturday night, and we've only got one life," and I thought you wouldn't mind, because I thought you'd be out with Ernest or some one perhaps –'

'What time was this, Lily?'

'Well, I dunno. About twelve, I suppose.'

'When was I ever out with Ernest as late as that?'

'Well,' said Lily, 'you might have been. How was I to know?

Anyhow I only said I'd go along for a couple of minutes; so we took a taxi to this place, which was some sort of a hotel, because we went up in a lift, and when we got up into the room I said, "D'you live here?" and he said, "No; I'm only staying here for the week-end," so I said, "You oughtn't to bring me up to your bed-room, ought you?" and he said no, perhaps he oughtn't, but it was all right, we'd just have a drink and I could go home as soon as I liked, because he could see I was tired, and I suppose I was, only I didn't notice it because I was having a good time – but that's the kind of man he is, you see, always thinking of others. Well, my dear, you never saw such a room in your life. Grand? Grand's not the word; my dear, the bed was the size of this barge, about, and there was a nice fire burning, and as for the bathroom – yes, there was a bathroom belonging to the room, you see, all white, my dear, like the passages in the Tube, and, my dear, the *taps* in that bath-room, there must have been *twenty*! I went in and turned on every tap I could see just for a lark – shower-bath and all. My dear, you ought to have seen Bunny laugh. Well, I like anyone that likes a good laugh, don't you?'

Lily could be heard creaking herself into a comfortable position in the narrow bed.

'Well, then, my dear, there was a long looking-glass on every wall and *both* doors – I mean long ones, dear, like they have in shops, so that you can see yourself all the way up, hindside, fore-most, and all the way round. And *cupboards*? There was a cup-board in every corner; room enough for forty women's clothes. Well, I opened them all to see, so I know – Bunny *did* laugh, and then I jumped on to the bed to see what *that* was like, and my dear, talk about *beds* – I sank up to my neck in it; it was like – like – well, ever so soft, and all velvety on top. I only wish I was in a bed like it now. Was this bump here always, dear?' Lily could be heard creaking again.

'Which bump?' said Jane.

'The one in the middle.'

'It's all right if you lie on your side.'

'Oh, is it?' said Lily. 'Well, I've a good mind to go back to my bunk. Well, my dear, in a minute they sent up champagne and sandwiches, and we sat in front of the fire, and it was ever so cosy, because Bunny turned out the lights, you see, and I suppose we got a bit romantic, or something, because I sat on his knee, which I've always thought was a bit silly before; only I dunno – with Bunny, it seemed ever so natural.'

'What about the gramophone?' said Jane.

'What about it?'

'Well, you said he said he was going to play some tunes on the gramophone.'

'Oh, yes. Well, I expect he forgot about it. I know I did.'

'Did you see any gramophone?'

'Don't know that I did.'

'That's funny.'

'What d'you mean – funny?'

'Oh, nothing,' said Jane. 'Go on.'

'If you're going to be nasty, dear, I'll go to sleep. I'm quite ready.'

'No, Lily,' protested Jane. 'I never meant anything. Go on, dear. Don't be so touchy.' Jane felt somehow that she, and not Lily, was the guilty party.

'If you didn't mean anything,' said Lily in an injured tone, 'why did you say anything?'

'What happened next, dear?' said Jane in a meek voice. 'Did he kiss you, or what?'

'Well, of course he did! What do *you* think?'

'Are you in love with him, Lily?'

'Well, I dunno, Jane,' said Lily, suddenly serious. 'Anyhow, I was then, I can tell you that. But I suppose you'll be saying it was the champagne and everything.'

'I never said any such thing.'

'Well, it wasn't. All I know is I was never so happy – well, I mean, sitting by the fire and that, talking about the dogs, it was ever so nice, and I didn't want to go one little bit. But at last I said I ought to be going, so I said, "Give me one more Bunny-hug for good night," you see, and we had a good hug, and after that it was harder to go than ever, you see, because he said he was ever so fond of me, only he was ever so nice, you see. Well, he said he was ever so sorry he had taken me up there because I was so young, you see, and he ought to be ashamed of himself and everything, and he'd only done it because he was so fond of me; and, would you believe it, my dear, there were tears in his eyes. Well, of course, the more he said that, the more I thought, "Well, I must stay a little longer," because I didn't want to put him in the wrong, you see; so I stayed a little more, and he said he'd never met anyone like me and he wished we could be together always, only his people would never let him marry me because I was a Christian; so I said, "Well, that's the first I've heard of it; but anyhow," I said, "I wasn't for marrying anyone just yet, but thank you kindly all the same." Well, then I said I'd better be going, and I looked at his watch, and, my dear, it was half past one, so he said he'd get me a taxi, but we'd better finish the champagne first; so he put some more coal on and we had half a glass each, and then I said it was quite time I was going, so we said good-bye again; and by that time, my dear, it was two o'clock, though it didn't seem like five minutes. Well, he said he'd get a taxi and take me home, and I said I wasn't going to drag him out at that time of night, and he said well, he wasn't going to let me go all that way alone, and while we were arguing, my dear, we happened to look out of the window and it was raining *cats* and *dogs*. My dear, you never *saw* such rain – my dear, it was coming down in *sheets* –'

'What time did you say it was?' asked Jane.

'Two o'clock, dear, I told you.'

'There wasn't much rain here – only a drizzle.'

'Well, I tell you, it was coming down in sheets in London.'

'Not this part.'

'How do *you* know, dear?'

'Because I was on the deck, dear, waiting up for you.'

'Well, I'm very sorry, dear, but you ought to have had more sense. Anyhow, it was pouring where we were, and you know well enough you can have it pouring in King Street and not a drop here. . . . So how was I to tell it wasn't pouring *here*?'

'That's right,' said Jane pacifically. 'It's local. I didn't mean anything, Lily.'

'All right, dear. No offence. Well, where was I?'

'From what I can make out you were nearly in bed,' thought Jane; but she said, 'You were just saying good-bye.'

'Yes. Well, my dear, there it was, raining, and I was so sleepy

I didn't know what to do, and he said what a pity I couldn't stay in that nice warm room and have a nice hot bath, instead of going out into the wet, and I said, "Yes, all very well, but what would the hotel people say?" Well, he said, as a matter of fact he'd put me down as his wife, so that was all right, and he'd only taken the room because he thought I might like it, you see. So I said, "Well, you've got a sauce," and he said he was ever so sorry but he hadn't meant any harm, and anyhow he'd thought better of it now. So then I said that was all right, and he wasn't to upset himself. So of course we had to kiss and make friends after that, and he said well if I liked to stay there for the night after all, he'd sleep in the arm-chair or somewhere and not do me any harm, and then I could have a nice hot bath and a good night's sleep, you see. Well, my dear, think what you like, but by this time I didn't much care *what* happened, because I was feeling like that, you see, and I was just longing to try a bath in that bathroom, so I said, all right, I would, only I did think of you, Jane – really I did; and if I'd known you were sitting up for me I'd never have done it. Well, he lent me a dressing-gown and some silk pyjamas – you know, like Dad wears, only silk – and I went into that bathroom and turned on all the taps again, and put some bath-salts in for a lark, and my dear, I did enjoy it; well, I've never enjoyed a bath before. Of course you've had proper baths before at the Ravens', but I never did; only, of course the water was so hot I couldn't get into it for an age. Well, then, Bunny undressed in the bathroom while I got into bed, you see, and then he came out in his pyjamas and he tucked me up and kissed me good night – my dear, ever so gentle he was, more like a mother. Well, then he sat down in the arm-chair and we said good night again, only I didn't feel like going to sleep somehow. Well, I suppose the bath woke me up, you see, and it was ever so nice lying in that lovely soft bed, my dear, looking at the firelight, only it seemed a bit silly, me with a great bed like that all to myself and Bunny sitting up all by himself in the chair; and of course after a bit the fire went down, and, my dear, he looked that cold and lonely in the chair I felt ever so mean, because, after all, it was his bed and not mine, wasn't it, dear, so I said, "Aren't you cold, Bunny?" and he said he was all right, you see, but he sounded a bit down, and I was ever so sorry for him, you see, because, really, my dear, I'm ever so fond of Bunny; so I said, "Oh, well, Bunny, it isn't sense – there's room for forty in this bed, and if you're a good boy you're welcome to a corner – see?" So he said all right, he wouldn't do anything I didn't want, and what's more he meant it, my dear – I'll swear to that; and I don't want to hear anything against Bunny, Jane, because he's a real gentleman, and ever so gentle, and if you *want* to know, dear, that's how it happened, and if you *want* to know, dear, it was as much my fault as his, and I don't care.'

Jane asked a few questions, to all of which Lily made frank and unashamed replies. Jane, with the *Sunday Gazette* in her mind, said, 'Suppose you have a baby, Lily?' But Lily replied emphatically that there was no danger of *that*. Very soon the guilty girl fell happily asleep. But Jane, the innocent, lay awake a long time, and her head went round and round.

From thenceforth many things were different on the barge. Lily was different, and in the strangest way. On the Monday morning she did not get up at seven-thirty, but announced through the partition that she was not going to the milliner's again. She had had enough of being trampled to death on the Underground. That was only natural. With the money she had won, with the money she was going to win that very evening with Bunny Moss, why should she waste the whole day scraping together a shilling or two? But there were other differences, less to be expected. Lily was improved: less snappiness and temper, more thought for others. By all accounts, a betrayed girl should be a nuisance in the home, constantly weeping, often attempting suicide. But Lily was less of a nuisance on the barge; she would not work at the milliner's, but she worked more at home than she had ever done. True, she did not complete all the tasks she took in hand; but she took more in hand. Perhaps it was that she had expected reproaches from Jane, and, having received none, was trying to show gratitude or buy Jane's continued silence with good works. But whatever the cause, there were the good works. Three times in one week she had supper ready when Jane came back from a long day in the studio and a stuffy evening in the shops. She seemed to have picked up some of Bunny's generosity, and voluntarily paid off the debt to Mrs Higgins, which Jane had regarded as her own personal burden.

With some of Lily's money-present Jane had determined to brighten up the *Blackbird* and paint the barge as nearly as possible in the likeness of the *Prudence*. Lily actually trudged up to King Street and bought the paint and brushes for her. She was quieter, kinder, and no longer went rolling along the Mall with the rough Hammersmith boys. The ruined Lily was a great improvement.

Jane had now a strange impression that Lily was the older and superior of the two. She, Jane, felt somehow childish in the presence of Lily who had had this great adventure and passed easily into the ranks of experienced women. She had not reproached Lily; she almost looked up to her, certainly envied her. She thought often of the grand bedroom, the soft, enormous bed, the bathroom with the multitudinous taps, the shiny tiles, the bath-salts, the champagne, the firelight, the silk pyjamas, and the encircling arms of the rich but gentle adorer. She lay awake and imagined herself in those delicious surroundings, not with Fred and not with Ernest, but with Mr Bryan. She had never heard of anything so like the pictures; and it had happened to Lily. Why not to her?

But all she had was Ernest. Every time she went out with Ernest he was a little naughtier, and every time she half-hated, half-enjoyed it. But perhaps even Ernest, she sometimes thought, might do for her what Mr Moss had done for Lily – remove her vague wishings for she knew not what, and make her as comfortable and as happy as her little sister.

Meanwhile the two of them were peaceable and friendly together. September slipped away. The midday sun hung lower and shone through the little windows again, the evening sun each day passed earlier behind the factory. The high tides of the equinox covered the island and Chiswick Mall. One Saturday Jane and Lily went out in their boat and rowed up and down the highway for a lark.

One Monday morning the first mist of autumn eddied through the hatch; and on the following Saturday the Yacht Club held their last race of the season in a gale of wind. Jane, whenever she could, went out in the boat and fished for firewood, which would soon be needed. Winter was coming; no more sitting on the deck, and much less clinging under the elm-trees, except for those who were ready to cling in the cold, in the rain, or in any weather. The poor are more the slaves of the seasons than are the rich; Jane felt that the year was almost finished, and finished, for her, in failure. She stuck to her wearisome sittings and earned a steady wage; for the artists liked her; she sat still and kept her appointments. They were kind and polite, but no one showed any personal interest in her, and none of them could displace Mr Bryan from her mind. She took off her clothes in their studios with as little thought as she took them off at home, except that now it was beginning to be chilly. Lily said, 'Why not give it up and bet on the dogs?' But Jane was sure that she must have work, a profession, a 'stattus', a sheet-anchor. Besides, she was not like Lily; she was like her father, and would never win money if she went to the dogs every night for a year. And in spite of Lily's wealth Jane would not even give up her evenings at the Black Swan. She was not going to abandon Mrs Higgins who had been so kind when they were in trouble. Besides, Lily might lose it all.

Lily continued to win, though less largely. Twice a week she went to the dogs with Mr Moss, and every second Saturday they went to the grand hotel and Lily had a lovely bath. Jane wondered whether she ought to tell somebody about it. But what was the good? By all accounts – books, papers, the pictures – it was the first step which mattered; once a girl was ruined, she was ruined, and nothing could be done. To tell anyone now would be to go back on Lily, cause a terrible unpleasantness, and perhaps make Lily go off and leave her, as Mr Moss wanted. Her father wrote happily from Liverpool, and he was much better in work there than out of work in London. Lily said confidently that she would never have a baby, and that was what mattered now. The only sensible thing was to pretend that Lily was confidentially married.

And besides, Jane thought, if it was Mr Bryan, wouldn't she do the same perhaps?

So whenever Mrs Higgins asked vaguely how they were doing, Jane answered, 'Nicely, Mrs Higgins, thanks all the same.'

On the last Sunday in September, Ernest took Jane to a Socialist Sunday School in the Fulham Palace Road, and afterwards to Richmond on his motor-bicycle. The regular teacher of the school, a friend of Ernest's, was sick, and Ernest, who was an old pupil of the school, had kindly agreed at the last moment to take his place. This was kind of Ernest, because he had booked the afternoon with

Jane a fortnight before, and the afternoon was fine. It would have been kinder still, Jane thought, if Ernest had said, 'Well, you don't want to waste your time, Jane; don't you bother about me.' But Ernest assumed that it would be a treat for Jane to spend her Sunday afternoon at a proletarian Sunday School.

In a way she enjoyed it. In a way she always had to admire Ernest's strange enthusiasm, as in a way, she admired the people who plunged into the Serpentine every morning of the year or otherwise exposed themselves to unnecessary discomfort with the best of intentions. And, in a way, she was glad to share in Ernest's sacrifice. Besides, from what the papers said, it might be violent and lively. She had read in the papers that these schools were 'hotbeds of revolution'; Lily said they drank blood.

The school met in a small room over a tobacconist's shop. Sixteen small children were ranged in a single row against the walls. Most of them were girls; one carried a baby in her arms. All were neatly dressed and seemed well-fed; none looked like what Ernest called 'the starveling wage-slaves of the capitalist domination'.

When Ernest entered the room, followed by Jane and an anaemic youth who played the harmonium, all the children stood up respectfully and said in a piping soprano, 'Good afternoon, Comrade.'

Ernest said with dignity, 'Good afternoon, Comrades,' and everybody sat down.

Ernest said, 'Now which little Comrade will recite the text of the week?'

A young chubby girl with long plaits stood up and said, 'If you please, Comrade, Comrade Slatter don't allow us to be called little because he says we're all Comrades same as others and there's no little about it.' And she sat down.

Ernest said gravely, 'That's right, Comrade. What's your name?'

'My name's Hattie. I know the text of the week, Comrade.'

'Go on, then, Comrade Hattie.'

Hattie, who seemed to be the star and spokesman of the school, folded her hands and recited rapidly:

'Love-learning-which-is-the-food-of-the-mind-be-as-grateful-to-your-teachers-as-you-are-to-your-parents.'

'That's good, Hattie. Now all together,' said Ernest.

The sixteen children stood and gabbled the revolutionary text in a mechanical unison. The baby wailed.

Ernest paused, not quite certain of the next step in the ritual. But the admirable Hattie came to his rescue and handed round the class the little Socialist hymn books, bound luridly in scarlet. Jane already had formed a strong dislike for Comrade Hattie. As she explained afterwards to Lily, 'I don't bear malice to anyone, not as a rule, but I wanted to shake that kid.'

The harmonium panted out a disconsolate tune, and they sang hymn Number 66:

> *I deem that man a nobleman —*
> *Yes, noblest of his kind —*
> *Who shows by moral excellence*
> *His purity of mind.*
> *Who is alike, through good and ill,*
> *A firm, unflinching man,*
> *Who loves the cause of brotherhood*
> *And aids it all he can.*

The voices of Ernest and Hattie supported the main burden of the hymn, in which there were five verses. At the end, after an encouraging nod from Hattie, Ernest rose and delivered his address. His theme was 'Brotherhood and the Exploiter'.

'Boys and girls, Comrades,' he said, 'some of you may have read in the papers attacks on the Socialist Sunday Schools. It is said that we are in the habit of inculcating class-hatred and animosity. This is not true, boys and girls, as *you* know. Our gospel is the gospel of peace and love. If I had been born the son of a duke, I don't doubt I should have had the same outlook and mentality as *he* has. We don't *blame* such people,' said Ernest, with infinite understanding, 'we don't *hate* them, boys and girls, we *pity* them. For we believe in the Brotherhood of Man, and we must never forget that dukes and exploiting capitalists are human beings same as ourselves. I ask you, Comrades, do you ever remember an occasion on which Comrade Slatter has attempted by word or deed to inculcate class-hatred or animosity?'

There was silence. The children continued to stare at the floor. The baby wailed again, and at last Hattie, the infallible, said, 'No, Comrade, never!'

'Thank you, Hattie,' said Ernest, and having paid this loyal tribute to Comrade Slatter, he passed on with more conviction to a more polemical explanation of the nature of exploiters.

Ernest was enjoying himself; he liked talking, he liked the sense of power, he had a burning faith, and he believed that what he, Ernest, was saying would seed and multiply in the minds of these sixteen children (if not the baby), so that they would grow up into sixteen Militant Socialists with a proletarian outlook. Nothing in their appearance supported this view; for Comrade Slatter had implanted in them nothing more militant than a gentle priggishness. They sat staring at the frayed carpet, or fidgeted with their fingers on their knees, except Hattie and one other, who gazed blankly at the preacher's face as they would have gazed at some strange animal in a cage. Jane thought again that it was nice of Ernest to give up his afternoon to these smug little lumps, though she could not imagine what was the use of it. Outside the warm sun was shining, they would be much better playing in the streets or walking along the tow-path. The only reason she knew for shutting oneself up on a fine Sunday and singing was God. But God did not seem to have any place in these proceedings. Cautiously she turned over the pages of the hymn book to see if she could find any reference to God. She found a number of the long words with which Ernest had made her familiar. There was a hymn about the Proletariat:

> *Who strives from earliest morn,*
> *Who toils till latest night,*
> *Who brings to others wealth,*
> *Ease, luxury, and might?*
> *Who turns alone the world's great wheel,*
> *Yet has no right in commonweal?*
> *It is the men who toil,*
> *The Proletariat;*
> *It is the men, the men who toil,*
> *The Proletariat.*

But there was no mention of God. The only hymn which reminded her of her rare visits to church played alternately, as Ernest was doing, on the two notes, pacific brotherhood:

> *One heart, one home, one nation,*
> *Whose king and lord is love,*

and well-intentioned militancy:

> *So on we march to battle*
> *With hearts that grow more strong,*
> *Till victory ends our warfare,*
> *We sternly march along.*

That had a Christian sound – a hymn-like sound; and Jane liked it better than:

> *Democracy! Democracy!*
> *Our sordid lives take thou in hand!*
> *Transmute them to a symphony*
> *Of organ-music grand!*

or the hymn about sabotage and industrial despots, thralls, tyrants, and economic pawns.

Ernest was nearing the end of his address. By raising his voice to a pitch which Comrade Slatter never attempted he had gained the attention of many of his audience, and he was rubbing it into them that, one day, sooner or later, all these girls and boys would be exploited by the capitalist classes – exploited in the workshop, at the loom, and in the home. The capitalists would take them and use them, suck them, squeeze them, grind them, tear them, their souls and their bodies; and at last, when they were no more useful, fling them aside, mere husks or skeletons, to rot and be trampled under the wheels of a soulless civilization.

The children did not appear to be much alarmed by this unpleasant prediction; for they had heard it before, though in milder terms, from Comrade Slatter, and they knew that there was a catch in it. They knew that, as Ernest now proceeded to explain, these evils would be averted if only they stood shoulder to shoulder in the onward march to Socialism and were prepared to fight in the vanguard of the battle to secure the reign of brotherhood and peace. And this they had all undertaken to do.

But Jane was moved, as she had been moved in Hyde Park, by the hot fire and sincerity of Ernest. Whatever it was that he meant, he meant it. It made her think of Lily, who perhaps was being exploited by the capitalist Mr Moss. In a way, perhaps, she had herself been exploited by Mr Bryan. He had painted her picture twice, and then flung her out of his life like a mere pawn or husk.

Anyhow, when Ernest talked like that, he was really rather a wonder. When Ernest stopped talking the baby began to cry, and they sang a hymn, selected by Comrade Slatter before his illness, and hardly suitable at that moment, for the burden of Ernest's address had been, 'Look out for yourselves', and the hymn was about 'Thinking of others':

> *And we practise as we go*
> *On the little things we meet,*
> *Carrying Granny's parcel for her,*
> *Guiding blind men o'er the street;*
> *Lifting up the fallen baby,*
> *Helping Mother all we may;*
> *Thus as little duties meet us,*
> *We perform them day by day.*

After this fraternal messages were moved and carried to Comrades who were absent having measles, or about to have birthdays; and the service closed with a hymn about the Red Flag sung to the tune of 'Auld Lang Syne'. Before the last verse Ernest clasped Jane's hand and Hattie's on the other side, the children clutched each other laboriously, shyly, and with many whispered arguments about the crossing of hands, and they all sang:

> *And now we'll clasp each other's hands,*
> *And by the dead will swear*
> *To keep the Red Flag waving high*
> *Through all the coming year.*

'Good lot of kids,' said Ernest in the street.

'You spoke splendid, Ernest,' said Jane.

'Think so?' said Ernest, pleased. 'What'd you like to do, Jane?'

Ernest, conscious of a good deed well done, felt an urge toward some compensatory indulgence. He eyed Jane up and down and thought that she looked unusually nice in her green coat and the little new hat.

She said, 'I dunno, Ernest.'

He said, 'Well, what about running down to Richmond on the bike?'

'Well, I dunno.'

'Well, I think you might, Jane. I've give up my afternoon.'

'Well, I don't mind, Ernest.'

'Might go on the river, or something.'

'All right, Ernest.'

Ernest had recently read in the papers a letter of protest by a moral citizen against the disgraceful goings-on in hired boats on certain parts of the river on Sundays; and, as moral protests in the newspapers often do, it had roused in him an agreeable curiosity and had even 'put ideas' into his head. He had only once taken Jane out pillion-riding on his motor-bicycle because he preferred a more intimate contact and did not care to waste his time with her on dodging the traffic. But on this occasion it seemed worth it.

Jane seated herself astride the carrier (now dignified by the name of pillion), and clutched with both hands Ernest's leather belt. The little Comrades, who had decided that they liked Ernest because of his lusty voice and his motor-bicycle, clustered on the pavement, and gave them a parting cheer. Ernest swung round the corner into the Fulham Road, charged across the bows of a motor-omnibus, and, leaning over at a frightening angle, turned sharply to the west.

Jane clung to the belt and prayed. She hated and feared this pillion-riding; but to all the young women she knew it was an envied pleasure, and almost the greatest known adventure. It was now perhaps her only point of superiority over Lily; for Lily, with all her experience, had never had a boy with a motor-bicycle. So she determined to enjoy it, and told herself repeatedly that one could only die once, and probably it would be instantaneous.

Ernest drove fast, for it was Sunday and the traffic was light. And all thought of equality and fraternity fled out of Ernest's mind as soon as his engine started. The capitalist car, the municipal tram, were all equally his enemies now and must be left behind. Jane was terrified. The noise, the vibration, the jogging up and down, the heeling over, the agonizing scrapes past omnibuses, the involuntary leaps heavenward when they crossed a tramline or a bump, the feeling that if she relaxed her grip upon Ernest she would fly backwards through the air at fifty miles an hour; the certainty that her hat was coming off, her stockings coming down, and nothing could be done to save them; the rush of wind, the shouts of bus-drivers, the mere pedestrians flashing by, the half-seen persons who turned to look at her and marvel – everything was terrible. At Turnham Green a thin drizzle of rain began, and in the shelter of the great Tank which Chiswick has set up to be a perpetual memorial of the Great War Ernest unstrapped his raincoat from the pillion and she put it on. After this, on the wet blocks, it seemed inconceivable that the flying bicycle could avoid collapse. The Bells' boat, in a high storm, with too much sail up, was more stable, Jane thought, and far less frightening. Ernest himself was solid enough, but the machine was no more secure than a drunken man on a tight-rope. But the machine sped on, sliding awfully back and forth across the tram-lines, squeezing between trams, roaring and reeling. Jane longed to shout in Ernest's ear, 'Go slower! Go slower!' But she clung on and said nothing, wondering what would happen when they fell – would she be pinned under the bicycle, would she be flung under a tram, or pass like a rocket through a plate-glass window? And Ernest, his eyes screwed up, his cap the wrong way round, and his thin lips set and smiling, was thinking, 'She'll enjoy this. She'll think the more of me after this.'

But by Kew Bridge the rain had stopped; there were no more tram-lines. Jane decided that, after all, she was not going to be killed, and so strong was her belief that she swung across and began almost to enjoy herself. Clinging, bobbing, aching, half-blind, she was swept past Kew Gardens, saying to herself that it was certainly exciting, though not exactly fun. And she began to wonder what would happen at Richmond. This swift and furious motion, now that it was no longer frightening, seemed to let loose something in her which asked for more excitement. She felt, as Lily had said, 'ready for anything', and wished that it was not Ernest Higgins to whose vibrating frame she clung.

Ernest also was wondering what would happen at Richmond, but he had definite ideas of his own. Ernest was pleased with himself. The taste of his own eloquence was still in his mouth, the bike was running gloriously, and he was speeding into the west with the woman of his choice behind his saddle and bold intentions in his breast. Thus did the old knights carry their ladies about, though not on motor-bikes, and thus, not less noble, the sheikhs and cowboys of Ernest's own times; and possibly at this moment Ernest, the heir of the ages, racketing to Richmond on a shameful quest, dimly connected his mission with theirs, and saw himself as a figure of romance.

It was very remarkable, Jane thought, Ernest proposing to go out in a boat; for Ernest was as little fond of boats as she was of motor-bicycles. However, passive and sleepy after the ride, she made no comment on this sudden enthusiasm for rowing on a rainy day, and let him arrange what he would. He knew what he wanted. Rain was threatening again and he was easily persuaded by the boathouse man to hire one of the rowing skiffs with the nice green waterproof covers which in case of rain could be let down on both sides and keep the lady as dry as a bone.

Ernest rowed with a pair of shiny yellow sculls, and Jane, lying on velvet cushions, held an unaccustomed pair of tiller-ropes, soft, white, and ladylike. It was her first taste of ladylike boating, and she despised it.

Ernest rowed very badly. The buttons of his sculls slipped out through the rowlocks till they were almost in the water, or, having been rescued, hovered foolishly over the centre of the boat. He rowed too strongly with his right or too weakly with his left, and the boat was continually heading for the Surrey shore. Sometimes he missed the water with his left oar, and sometimes his right plunged steeply into the depths. Sometimes one of the oars jumped out of the rowlocks altogether and trailed in the water like a broken wing. The foot-board was never quite right, and often had to be readjusted. But the tide was with them and they travelled slowly and in zigzags in the direction of Twickenham. It began to drizzle again. Ernest swore, mildly but often; he looked first at his right blade and then at his left, to see what they were doing, and then at Jane to see if she was laughing at him. Jane did not laugh, but gave him directions in a calm, kind tone which irritated him. Jane did not laugh until he took off his coat and waistcoat and it was revealed that he wore red braces. Rowing in the red braces and stiff white collar and little bow-tie, Ernest was pathetic, she thought –

killing. There never can have been a marauding lover less equipped with dignity and glamour; there never can have been a couple less marked out for the high extremes of passion and romance – he in red braces incompetently rowing a hired boat through the rain, and she repeatedly assuring him that he looked ever so funny. Not thus, surely, have the high seducers of poetry and their victims approached their celebrated sins. But Ernest, the heir of the ages, the vanguard of the Socialist Commonwealth, did not care; he did not know that he was ridiculous, pathetic, almost tragical in the small squalor of his designs. He knew what he wanted, and he thought that the sooner he stopped this rowing the better.

There was a small island round the corner, about a quarter of a mile above Richmond. Against its banks, under the trees, lay a number of long, low, whale-backed, pale-green shapes, boats and punts with their hoods let down, floating islands, hidden kingdoms, under whose all-embracing canopies invisible citizens celebrated the Sabbath in mysterious silence or with tantalizing laughter, with noisy gramophones or the popping of corks.

Ernest said, 'This looks snug,' Jane steered the fated vessel into a gap in the line, and Ernest tied her up. He began to let down the green sides of the canopy, which were now hitched up above their heads. Jane said quickly, 'Leave one side open, so's we can look at the river.' Ernest grumbled that the rain would come in, and just then, fortune favouring him, the rain quickened and a sudden gust sprinkled her face; she protested no more.

The last flap fell into place, shutting out the last sight of day.

'Coo!' said Jane, catching her breath. The world had suddenly gone green, the world had suddenly dwindled into a long, green lozenge in which Jane Bell and Ernest were somehow imprisoned, the last people alive. It was lit by a strange green, sickly radiance, the light the fishes see. Ernest's white shirt had gone green, and Ernest's red braces had lost their glory, and Ernest's face wore an unearthly hue. Under their low, translucent roof they were as secret, as solitary, as if above them rolled the ocean. It was like a child's perfect hiding-place, stumbled on without warning; and Jane felt a childish, pleasant thrill of apprehension. But all she said was, 'Coo! Ernest, you've all gone green. Your braces look funny.'

Ernest was tired of being funny. He lay down beside her, and muttering with a fierce fondness, '*I'll* teach you to laugh at me, my girl,' hungrily seized the prey. She had not thought of his kissing her like this, suddenly, roughly, and without leave; she was angry, taken aback, she turned her hunted head this way and that – the old and fatal trick – a hot little struggle, hot little whispers. She did not like to be rushed like this, but now she could not struggle much because the boat rocked, and soon she lay panting, with hurt lips –could not resist any more. Why should she resist? It was the old story; when Ernest began his tricks she was always angry, but after a little she was not really angry at all. Ernest inflamed her, made her as bad as himself, though she might like him no better than before. But what did it matter? Why worry? Lily didn't worry, and Lily was happy.

'Don't be so rough, Ernest,' she whispered. 'What's the matter with you?'

'You know what's the matter with me,' said Ernest.

The green, desirous face of Ernest hung over her like a confident hawk, waiting in a pale-green sky. It was darker now, and the rain was heavier, hammering on the roof. There was a hole on one side where the water dripped in. A steamer passed and the boat tugged at her moorings and was swirled back alarmingly against the bank. Jane kept thinking of Lily. The green hawk swooped down upon her, pillaging her lips again, and this time she lay quiet, thinking of Lily. Why worry? What was all the fuss? Lily had made no fuss, and now Lily knew everything. Anyhow, she was too tired to struggle any more; she was always struggling, and nothing went right. Now she was sleepy – that rain made her sleepy, and the rocking boat; darker and darker too. Now she was going to let things slide at last, lie like a log and let Ernest hug her; it was nice to be hugged, whatever anyone said.

Thus without passion, without affection, without much satisfaction to anyone, squalidly, crudely, and even ridiculously, Jane lost her honour.

The boat rose up on the tide, the trees came down to meet them. The rain stopped. A voice in the outside world, far away beyond the pale-green canopy, said 'Oy! You'd better be moving!' Ernest had forgotten about the tide. The ring to which he had made fast was now submerged, far out of his reach; the rope, taut as steel, was straining to pull them under. Ernest cut the rope and the released boat jumped skyward alarmingly among the branches. Pressed between tree and tide they had a struggle to escape. Ernest swore incessantly, punting clumsily with the end of an oar, cursing the canopy, the trees, the tide. When they were free at last he rowed so badly and swore so much that Jane made him give her the oars, and without a word she rowed her seducer back to Richmond. 'Just like Ernest,' she thought – a fitting end to it. She would not look at Ernest, nor he at her. She despised him. She did not feel wicked; she felt cheated, bewildered, and a little disgusted. She had been hurt and made ashamed, and there seemed to be no joy or meaning in it. So *that* was the famous love-business, was it? *That* was the end of everything, *that* was what the papers and pictures and books were about? She could not understand it. Anyhow, she *knew* now. And once bitten, twice shy. Never again! How *could* she have? For she wasn't like Lily; she was a good girl, really – had been – and now she was a good girl no more. As for Lily – she could not understand it. Lily had enjoyed herself. But Lily had had the firelight, the champagne, the bath, and everything. Lucky Lily! And Lily was fond of Mr Moss – really fond of him; perhaps that was the difference.

Ernest said nothing. But he had words with the boathouse man about the cut painter. Then Jane refused to go back on the pillion, and he rode home sulkily alone, very angry with the world.

'What's the matter with you, Jane?' he protested. 'I thought you *wanted* . . .'

'You've exploited me,' said Jane, and climbed on to a 27 bus.

16

TROUBLE

JANE was quite certain that she would 'get into trouble'. Everything had gone so wrong this year that it was too much to hope for a change. She was not like Lily, who lived in the present and could put the future out of her mind; Jane was always living ahead. She expected the worst now, and thought of it always. In a few days it was as firmly fixed in her head that she was going to have a baby as if a doctor had told her so. The idea horrified her and terrified her, and she could not imagine what she would do: something desperate, probably, for her mind moved naturally along the lines of the *Sunday Gazette*, and she nourished her nightmare with a hundred dramatic pictures, all of which included, sooner or later, the police court or the mortuary, and sometimes the gallows. She never said to herself, 'Well, it wasn't my fault; and after all it isn't a crime. Lily's got plenty of money now, she'll pay for me to go somewhere.' The unmarried mothers she read about never behaved sensibly; they behaved tragically and insanely, as if they had murdered somebody, and everybody else behaved as if this were right and proper; for, indeed, to bring a life into the world was as bad as taking one away — worse, for a young girl. If she murdered Ernest everyone would be on her side, and a lot would be said about the Unwritten Law; but to have a baby was wicked. Ernest might marry her, though she doubted that; perhaps if she went and told Mrs Higgins he would have to. But she did not want to marry Ernest. The very thought of Ernest disgusted her. She dreamed of that green, leering face hovering over her, the sickly green light, the sickly green-red braces. When Ernest waited for her in the evenings by the garden gate she walked straight past him and said, 'I don't want to speak to you.' Probably, she thought, she would commit suicide — jump into the river on a cold night — as soon as she knew for certain. Meanwhile she went to a chemist and bought some stuff which she remembered Florry had said girls took.

She said nothing to Lily. She could not go to Mrs Higgins. There was nobody else.

She did not think out clearly the actual suicide; it was a vague picture of a midnight leap from the Embankment at Westminster – always the Embankment, though she could not have explained why the river at Hammersmith would not do as well. The Embankment seemed right. But often she read over in her mind the account of her inquest in the *Sunday Gazette*, until long passages of the evidence were familiar. Lily and her father 'identified the remains', . . . 'both dressed in black and unable to conceal their emotion. . . .' 'The Coroner asked Mr Bell if he would like to sit down. . . . He declined the courtesy, and in quavering tones spoke of the deceased girl's condition of mind. . . . Lily Bell, the dead woman's sister, a pretty girl with bobbed hair, smartly dressed . . .' 'Was the deceased of a cheerful disposition?' . . . 'To your knowledge, had she anything on her mind?' . . . 'Seemed worried lately, but didn't mention anything.' . . . 'Had she any men friends?' . . . 'Oh yes, one or two, but always a good girl, Jane was . . . ever so quiet.' . . . 'At this point the witness gave way to her emotion . . .' and a lump of infinite tenderness swelled up in Jane's own throat. 'The doctor . . . in a certain condition . . .'

Jane was never clear whether Ernest would come into it: not, certainly, through anything that she would say – she would give no one away; but she'd like to think that Ernest would be there, downcast, guilty, and feeling his position acutely . . . and sometimes she played with the idea of a few severe words from the Coroner:

'Morally you sent this poor girl to her death.' . . . And even a 'rider' to the jury, whatever that was.

But generally there were no severe words, for her inquests always left her very pitiful and tender and nobly resigned towards the world. They did her good, drugging her fears, softening her resentment; and she would fall asleep at last, not happy, but comforted.

She was very gentle and loving with Lily, and thought much of what would happen to Lily when she, Jane, was gone. Perhaps after the inquest Mr Moss's parents would let him marry Lily after all, and they would live on the barge. She went on with the painting whenever there was time; half the living-room was clean white already. The paint was patchy and disappointing when it was dry, and Lily thought it was a mess. But Jane, as she worked, thought that it was for Lily's wedding-present, and her lip would tremble, and once she cried.

The days passed. She slept late and light, and would wake up trembling, saying to herself, 'I feel sick. This is it.' Mrs Higgins said several times that she was not looking the thing, and told her to keep away from the bar for a day or two. Ernest heard of this, and he too feared the worst.

Ernest, though she did not know it, had been 'feeling his position' acutely enough. At first he thought bitterly of the female sex, and was inclined to consider himself an injured party, and wished never to see Jane again. After a few days he found himself anxious to see Jane again, and decided that they had both made mountains out of a mole-hill. They had had a pleasant afternoon, and he was ready for another. Then Jane avoided and insulted him, and this annoyed him. Then he heard that she was looking ill, and this frightened him. He began to think that perhaps he had done the wrong thing. He was by no means eager to marry her, but it had to be thought of. The latest opinion of his school of thought was that marriage was a *bourgeois* conception; and Comrade Watkins, who was in with the Russians and had visited Moscow, had told him at a meeting of the Minority Lift-workers at the Eat-Less-Meat Restaurant in Oxford Street that every Comrade who was to be in the vanguard of the revolution was a fool to marry, because in the revolution wives and other female appendages would only encumber, poisoning the pure red faith with pacific sentiment and pallid loving-kindness.

Still, he was sincerely fond of Jane, and one night in late October, meeting her in the passage as she went home from the Black Swan, he was shocked to see her white little face and hollow, frightened eyes. She tried to slip past him, as usual, but he caught her arm, stopped her, and said, 'Hullo, Jane!'

'Hullo, Ernest! Let go of me.'

'What's the matter, Jane? You're looking poorly.'

'I shouldn't wonder, Ernest. Whose fault's that?' said Jane, consciously tragic, and in a strange fashion enjoying it.

This seemed a certain confirmation of Ernest's fears. He said, 'Jane, you're not – you're not going to – '

'Have a baby, Ernest? Well, what d'you expect?' She was certain now.

'Jane!' The true spark of compassion and humanity which had first made Ernest a Socialist flashed in him again. It was not his way to pass over a bitter word against him, but now he did it. He forgot the revolution, and he said, 'Don't worry, Jane. I'll stand by you. I'll marry you, if you like.'

'S'pose I don't like?' Jane said, her lip trembling. 'I wish I was dead!'

'Don't talk silly, Jane,' said Ernest gently.

'Yes, I do. And what's more, I'll do it!'

'Jane!' Ernest was frightened.

The little face was fierce, and almost ugly with strain. From that muddy corner of her mind where the dregs of the *Sunday Gazette* reposed there had oozed up a new thought. This was the sort of situation which was generally concluded by a 'Death Pact'. She and Ernest with their heads in the gas-oven. A letter left on the kitchen-table. 'Boy and Girl Drama'. Then she laughed aloud – a bitter little laugh. The idea of Ernest doing away with himself for the sake of a girl was funny.

'What you laughin' at?'

'Who's laughing?' Jane felt contrary – contrary and cruel. She would like to hear what Ernest had to say to a death pact. She would like to see his face.

'Ernest,' she said, 'would you do anything for me?'

''Course I would, Jane. Well, anything in reason.'

'Well, Ernest, let's – let's – ' 'Let's end it all,' she would have said, 'you and me together, Ernest.' But she found she was too unhappy to pretend, even to punish Ernest. 'Oh, Ernest,' she sobbed instead, 'I'm so tired.' And she put her head on his shoulder and cried.

Ernest was embarrassed but deeply stirred. He said to himself that he was very fond of Jane, and would marry her. He could not have her weeping on his shoulder in public places. And although he challenged on principle almost all the laws, customs, and conventions of the land, he found that he was anxious to do what was accepted and customary in his present position. Jane was a dear little thing, he was really gone on her, and, if he must marry, there was no one else that he would choose. He patted her back and looked anxiously down the passage. A couple came under the lamp at the corner, arm in arm. Ernest stooped low over his love, and thrust her into the darkness of the corner, murmuring entreaties to be quiet.

When the couple had passed he said, 'Cheer up, Jane! The world won't come to an end if you do have a kid. Are you sure?' he added; there was still hope.

'Quite, Ernest,' sniffed Jane, wiping her eyes; and she gave him her reasons. Ernest sighed; but he was not going back.

He said comfortingly, 'Well, it's all right. We'll get married, you see?'

'All right, Ernest.'

'Well, that's all right, then.' He kissed her gently.

She had never known Ernest so nice and gentle before. She was so tired, her spirit had gone; it seemed that she had arranged to marry Ernest, but she was so tired she could not think. She was so tired, it would be nice to have someone to look after her, some one to lean upon. She laid her head upon his overcoat and closed her eyes. Ernest held her tenderly, and was quiet. So they stood in the darkness for many minutes, and were nearer to each other than they had ever been.

At length they went back to the Black Swan and told Mrs Higgins. Ernest's mother was surprised and pleased to hear the news, for she knew Ernest well, and she was familiar with his opinions about the *bourgeois* institution of marriage. She liked Jane, knew she was capable, thought that she might do Ernest good, but was sorry for her. When she heard that they wanted to be married immediately, she drew what the police reports would call 'conclusions of a certain nature'; for long engagements were the general rule. But it was no business of hers. The young folk were up to everything these days. She went into the bar and fetched a bottle of Rich Old Tawny Port and two fizzy lemonades.

Ernest was teetotal, and even now would have nothing but lemonade.

'Quite right, boy,' said Mrs Higgins; 'begin as you mean to go on.'

The port revived Jane for a minute or two. She said, 'All the best, Ernest!' and clinked her glass against his, for Lily had said that this was a custom. During all the talk and thought a reservation had been struggling for utterance, and now at last it was released. 'We'll live on the barge, Ernest, won't we?' she said. 'I couldn't live in a house.' She spoke firmly but with doubt in her heart, since Ernest, as she knew so well, was not much of a one for boats.

'All right, Jane,' said Ernest kindly, looking at the tired face. He would have agreed to anything then.

'Saves the rent, don't it?' said Mrs Higgins; 'and rent's half the battle.'

Jane was content, and, leaning against Mrs Higgins, was very soon asleep.

Next evening at the Black Swan there was toasting and teasing, and Jane had to refuse many a glass of port wine. They made her blush, some of the teasers, but they made also a warm glow in her heart with their kindness. The elderly men who whispered good wishes over the bar, their wives in the corners raising their half-pints of stout towards her, old Mr Pewter, who gave her an earnest little homily on the blessings of the married state, Mrs Fox, who had nine children under fifteen alive and a husband out of work — they were all, she knew, truly happy in what they thought was her happiness; for that was the way of the Private Bar. She knew that, if the need came, every one of them would do anything they could to help her in trouble (except, perhaps, the particular trouble in which she happened to be). It was warming to have friends, and she was glad she had served these friendly, sober people behind the bar, which Lily had once said degraded a girl. The wives, against the wall, may have whispered that 'the young couple seemed in a bit of a hurry', but nothing of this reached Jane's ears. At the other end, in the Public Bar, where darts was played and few collars worn and old and mild was threepence instead of threepence-halfpenny, the congratulations became a little noisy, and more than a little 'saucy' as the evening advanced. But Jane had always been able to keep her end up with the rough boys; and the cure for 'sauce' was easy; Jane became blind and deaf, and the culprit's next order was unaccountably delayed.

Ernest, who seldom entered the bar, sat in the parlour behind it, and listened on the wireless to a talk on the League of Nations, about which he hovered between two opinions – that it was an active conspiracy of Capitalist Governments, led by the British, and that it was a noble ideal shamefully neglected by the Capitalist Governments, especially the British.

But at ten minutes to ten, when Harold shouted, 'Last orders, please, gentlemen,' and vaulted over the bar to collect the empty glasses, a cry was raised, 'Where's Ernie Higgins?'

'Ernest! Ernest!' cried Private and Public together, and Ernest, almost blushing, was led out from the parlour by his delighted mother, who had never seen her son in such general favour.

'Drinks all round!' 'Speech!' 'Mine's a bottle of champagne, Ernie!'

Ernest stood smiling in his shirt-sleeves at the parlour door, while his mother and the staff worked busily at the beer-handles and poured out ports and porters for the ladies. Several friends of the family ordered festival liquids for the son of the house, but Ernest would take nothing but his lemonade, though he was pleased by the general goodwill. As a rule he suspected his mother's Private Bar customers at least of having a '*bourgeois* mentality', but he forgot this now.

When everyone was served, the red-faced, genial Mr Pewter called for silence, and made a rambling speech, which continued so long that everyone was afraid that it would be closing time before the toast was drunk.

'Tell us the tale afterwards, Bert!' A confused hubbub of 'Good old Ernies!' and 'All the best, young Janes!' overwhelmed the orator, and Mrs Higgins, to applause, handed Ernest a tray on which were the five port wines and two whiskies generously ordered for him. But Ernest waved them away and lifted his glass of lemonade to the company. The company yelled in friendly derision, but Jane admired him for sticking to his guns.

'Well done, Ernie!' she whispered, and it was the first time she called him Ernie.

Ernest stood with his arm on her shoulder and made a little

speech. He said, 'Well, ladies and gentlemen all, thanks one and all. Here's all the best to all present, one and all, which you've all wished the same to me and Jane here – '

'Not in lemonade, Ernie!' said the incorrigible Mr Fox.

'Well, there's worse drinks than lemonade – '

'Only water – and ink.'

'Well, anyhow,' said Ernest, confused by the laughter – as a speaker he was best with preparation and a clear run – 'I dare say some of you's thinking I'm a lucky man, and there's no argument about it, not to my thinking; so here's my very best respects, ladies and gentlemen, and thanking you one and all.' Ernest retired into the parlour, annoyed because he had spoken badly. He would have to do better than that if he became a councillor and opened bazaars.

But his audience were not fastidious about phrases; Mr Pewter cried, 'And now for a little harmony!' and throatily broke into 'For She's a Jolly Good Fellow'.

At that moment, pumping a final ale for Mr Fox, Jane saw the door of the Private Bar open, and Mr Bryan came in.

Her heart leapt, and she turned pale. He was with Marrow, the longshoreman, who looked after the moorings, but he wore one of the 'smart' suits in which he used to go into London. She was suddenly enraged. Why must he turn up again at this moment to see her the centre of this noise? She was for the first time ashamed to be drawing beer behind the bar. She would not look at him. Upsetting her again! She would not look at him. But old Mr Pewter had cleared a way for him to the bar, and was ordering refreshment for the gentleman, and Mr Pewter had to shout, because of the song they were singing in her honour. But she could hear that strong, quiet voice, which she loved, inquiring what it was all about; and she could hear Mr Pewter at the top of his husky voice explain that they were celebrating the engagement of Ernie Higgins and 'our young Jane'. 'A nice Burton, Miss Jane, please.' As she pumped the Burton for Alf Edwards, she imagined those amused eyes curiously examining her. Patronizing, very likely. Blast him! This time he must recognize her. She felt pink all over. She would not look at him. Class was class, and she was going to marry Ernest, and have a baby.

But old Mr Pewter was shouting through the funny little windows over the bar, 'Jane, my girl, here's a gentleman wants to drink your health!' Then she had to look. And there was his face, framed in one of the little windows, patronizing, amused, and curious, just as she had expected. No, it was not superior – faintly mocking, perhaps, but friendly. He raised his glass; for a moment their eyes met, she flushed scarlet, smiled like a born fool (she thought), and turned away.

It was three minutes past ten. 'Time, gentlemen, please' had twice been called, and Mrs Higgins was anxiously attempting to silence the song; for she knew of a dreadful case in which a publican had been prosecuted for permitting the singing of a cheerful chorus on licensed premises, on the ground that he had no music licence. 'Time, gentlemen, *please*. Will you kindly finish up your refreshments, please?' 'Good night, Mrs Higgins.' 'Good night, Jane.' With salutations and handshakes all round the company oozed out into the night. Jane already was rinsing glasses under the tap, and would not look up; so she did not see Mr Bryan go out with a backward glance. 'Class is class,' she was thinking savagely.

Mrs Higgins would have prolonged the celebrations in the parlour, but Jane, saying she was ready to drop, slipped away to the *Blackbird*.

Lily wanted to know what the noise at the pub was about. 'Coo!' said Lily, 'is that all?' Lily was still stupefied with wonder that anyone should think of marrying the disagreeable Ernest.

'But you can't be *gone* on him!' she said for the seventh time, as if Ernest were a spider. Then Jane, tired of bottling things up, told Lily all about it.

'Coo!' said Lily, impressed. 'A dear little baby? Well, if that's it, I suppose you've got to.'

But the next morning Jane knew that there was to be no baby after all. She had imagined the baby.

'Lily!' she cried, sitting up in bed and hammering excitedly on the partition. 'It's all right, Lily!'

'What's all right?' said her little sister, muffled and resentful.

'The baby,' said Jane, 'it's a false alarm!'

'Coo!' Lily yawned. 'You do chop and change. What next?' And she went to sleep again.

17

SOLEMNIZATION OF MATRIMONY

WHAT next?

The next thing, nearly, was that Jane and Ernest were married at a Registry Office in the Goldhawk Road.

There seemed to be no going back. Ernest had been relieved to find that he was not going to be a father; but he wondered once or twice whether he would ever have thought of marrying Jane if she had not made her unfortunate mistake. He had been a fool; he should have sent her to the doctor. But she had been in such a state, and he in such a panic, he had been rushed into it. Still, he was gone on Jane, and it would be all right to have her all to himself every night. He lay awake often, imagining the joys of Matrimony.

Jane also had wished once or twice that they had kept quiet a little longer and not provoked the celebrations and speeches at the Black Swan. That evening seemed to make the thing so final, it was almost a wedding. What a lot of talk if they said they had changed their minds! She would be ashamed to show her face in the neighbourhood. Besides, who wanted to change? She gave Ernest the chance – told him that if he liked to think it over she'd quite understand. But she was in Ernest's arms at the time, clinging under the elm-tree, and Ernest only said, 'Not much!' hugging her possessively. He was a fine boy, Ernest, after all, and now that she was not going to be an unmarried mother she was not angry with him any more. Who cared? There was no sign of Mr Bryan, and Mrs Staples, the char, had said she had heard the studio was to let. So that was the end of that. 'You're a born fool,' she said to herself.

Mrs Higgins wanted a grand wedding at the church in the square. But Ernest insisted on a Registry Office and grieved his mother bitterly. He said her attitude was a lot of humbug, for when did she ever go to church? Mrs Higgins had to admit that she had not been inside a church since the day he, Ernest, had been christened. 'Still,' she said, 'I never feel a person's properly married if it isn't in a church; what I mean to say, it isn't the same thing, is it, not reely.' And she had a vague notion that the church and the public-house were two threatened institutions which ought to hang together.

All the ladies in the Private Bar agreed with her; but Ernest was immovable. Ernest's position was quite clear. He was thinking of his principles and the League of Red Youth. Already, he felt, he was risking his revolutionary reputation by contracting a marriage. He would like some of the Hammersmith Branch of the League of Red Youth to be present, nevertheless; but if they were invited to attend a Church of England ceremony in a parish church he shuddered to think what would be said of their secretary. As like as not he would be accused of having a *bourgeois* mentality at the next meeting of the plenum. Besides, the Registry Office fitted into his picture of the Socialist Commonwealth, in which everything would be registered by the State, run by the State, and (in the case of marriages) unregistered by the State. The State was his God and should have the marrying of him. He thought it vain to explain all this to his mother; what he did say was that weddings in church was a lot of dope.

Ernest appealed to Jane, and Jane said, 'Who cares?' (which words were often on her lips at this time). She had never been present at a wedding of any kind. But, after one of the wrangles, she took down the dusty prayer book from the *Blackbird*'s shelf of books and read through the Marriage Service. She could not find it at first, not recognizing it under the name of 'Solemnization of Matrimony'. Lily read over her shoulder, and said it was disgusting.

'Carnal lusts and appetites! Coo! what language!'

'Shurrup!' said Jane. She was reading with some alarm that the first purpose of marriage was the procreation of children. According to all that she had ever heard about marriage, that was the first thing to be avoided. She was quite sure that was not Ernest's idea of marriage. (Perhaps that was why he wanted to be done at the Registry Office.) She read on. 'Secondly, it was ordained for a remedy against sin, and to avoid fornication –'

'What's fornication?' said Lily.

'You and Moss would be fornication, because you're not married – see?'

'Well, what a word and a half!' Lily was skipping. '" Till death us do part." Coo! Fancy cherishing Ernest as long as that! "With my body I thee worship." What a way to talk! D'you have to say that, Jane? "Worship", eh? Worship *Ernest*!'

'The man says that.'

'Oh, does he? Well, if that's the church, it's me for the Register every time. My dear, say those things before a crowd of people? 'D make me feel half naked.'

Jane agreed; and she supported Ernest. This 'Solemnization of Matrimony' seemed far too solemn a business for the joining of Ernest Higgins and Jane Bell.

*

Nevertheless, she felt there was something missing from the drab proceedings in the Goldhawk Road. It was like buying a ticket for a railway journey. The room was like a railway waiting-room, with its bare, cold walls and floor: the only furniture a bench, a table, and two high desks, behind which sat two little pale men writing in ledgers. Mr Bell had come down from Liverpool in a frock-coat which was shiny and a top-hat which was not – both the property of the Liverpool aunt's late husband. Mrs Higgins carried a bunch of chrysanthemums, Ernest had a red buttonhole, and everybody present wore their best; but the scene lacked brightness. Jane had always imagined that she would walk to her wedding over a red carpet. As it was, she had to step over a puddle, for it had rained in the night. But the League of Red Youth had sent her a bunch of artificial flowers, which were extremely red, and these she carried, which pleased Ernest. Only two of the League were present, for it was Saturday morning, and most of the League had jobs.

The bride and bridegroom sat in a row on the bench till the little men were ready. Then Jane and Ernest were called for sharply by the first little man, as if they had been the next case at the panel doctor's. Their names and addresses and 'Other Particulars' were taken down, and they passed before the second little man, who had not till then so much as glanced at them. He read rapidly from a printed card and then made the happy couple repeat some words after him. At this point the company on the bench realized suddenly that the wedding was in full swing and stood up sheepishly.

So far from impressive were the proceedings that Mr Bell had absent-mindedly taken his pipe from his pocket, and he now stood guiltily with the pipe held behind his back.

The fatal words were a strange compromise between the secular and the ecclesiastical. But Jane thought they were less alarming than the words in the prayer book, and seemed to make sense. There was no talk about bodies or the procreation of children. It was all very simple. Mrs Higgins and Mr Bell wrote their names in the book as witnesses, but were not required to give their addresses. Ernest paid the bill, and they went out married, till death did them part.

The two members of the League (who had remained outside) raised a small cheer and waved two large red handkerchiefs. Jane thanked them prettily for the artificial bouquet; then she and Ernest, Lily, Mrs Higgins, and Mr Bell squeezed somehow into Mr Ewer's taxi.

'Just like the Derby!' piped Lily, 'only Fred's not here, and Ernest's in a good temper.' An unfortunate remark. Ernest scowled, and Mr Bell sighed heavily, thinking of the Derby. Jane thought of Fred and wished that he was there.

They drove to the Black Swan, where Mrs Higgins had prepared a 'little luncheon' in the skittle-alley: cold ham and chicken, a bowl of pickled onions, bread, cheese, two jugs of beer and one of lemonade. The skittle-alley, the largest room on the premises, was often used for festal occasions. The big horn-beam nine-pins at the far end looked strange in the daytime with a patch of sun upon them, and no electric light. Everything seemed strange, Jane thought. Someone offered her the onions, and she took an onion in her fingers; and that was strange, for she did not like onions. Now she would smell of onions, and presently someone would say that Ernest must have an onion too. Nothing seemed to matter. She felt flat and acquiescent – not excited and not unhappy.

The Foxes came in, and Mr and Mrs Pewter with their two daughters, all looking strange dressed up, and Mr Pewter especially strange with a collar on. Everyone was subdued and talked more quietly than usual. 'Might be a funeral,' Lily whispered. Jane sat on a bench by the wall, slowly nibbling her onion and sipping her lemonade. The two boys from Ernest's League arrived presently, having walked from the Registrar's, and were introduced by Ernest. Jane watched him and thought without excitement that tonight she would be going to bed with Ernest at Brighton. She wondered idly whether there would be a grand bed like Lily's and a bath with a great many taps.

Mr Pewter generally cheered things up, with his loud laugh, happy face, and incoherent geniality; and very soon he said that Ernest must have an onion to be even with Jane. Ernest, with a flourish, bit a large lump out of the largest onion; everybody laughed, forgot about their clothes, and became natural and talkative. Mr Pewter explained to one of the Red youths the mysteries of skittles, and showed him Ernest's name on the Roll of Fame. To win a place on the Roll of Fame a player must score three 'floorers' in succession. A 'floorer' knocks down all nine pins with one blow. Ernest's name appeared twice on the Roll. Lily made eyes at the other revolutionary and Mr Bell sat down beside Jane. Jane's almost only positive sensation that day had been her pleasure in her father's appearance. He looked more sure of himself, cleaner, neater, and better-fed. He told Jane that he was doing well and had paid back sixty pounds of the debt to the aunt; but he did not tell her that this had been made possible by one big bit of luck at the dogs and a run of smaller successes. Jane thought his improvement was the work of the aunt, and she congratulated herself on her wisdom in sending him to Liverpool. No failure *there*, anyway.

And yet, if her father had been at home, perhaps she would not now be married to Ernest. He would have taken her to a doctor, perhaps. . . . Well, there it was, you couldn't have everything.

She looked up and saw Fred standing at the open door, gazing at her across the crowd.

No one else had seen him, and they stared at each other for a moment or two in silence. From the look in Fred's eyes she knew that Fred was just as gone on her as ever. And she found herself delighted to see him – almost excited for the first time that day.

'Well, what a surprise!' said Mrs Higgins. 'If it isn't Mr – ' But she had never known Fred's name.

'Hope you'll pardon the liberty,' Fred mumbled. 'I only just heard.'

Then he came straight down the alley and sat down beside Jane, without saying a word to anyone. He was in the old blue jersey and the worn brown coat, with a blue scarf round his neck; and she thought he looked nice.

'Hullo, Jenny!' he said.

'Hullo, Fred!'

'Bit of a surprise, this, Jenny. I just been to your boat. Then Mr Marrow told me.'

'We didn't know where you were, Fred. You're looking nice, Fred,' she said, smiling at him. She was suddenly alive again; and Ernest, with one eye on her, noticed the change.

'Think so?' said Fred. 'So are you, Jenny.'

'Down here for long?'

'Morning tide Tuesday, I dare say.' Fred looked cautiously behind him and then spoke low. 'You never told me it was this one, Jenny.'

'Well, it wasn't, Fred – not then.' She hung her head. She was wondering why it was Ernest she had just married and not Fred. Fred had brought back the canal, the ripple at the *Adventure's* bow, the clip-clop of Beauty's feet, the silent country gliding by, the roar and gurgle of the locks. That Bryan had a lot to answer for! And if Fred had been bolder that night in the hay-field it *would* have been Fred. Poor Fred! she thought, that's what you get for being good. Well, well. . . .

'You was too slow, Fred,' she said.

'I'll be quick enough another time,' Fred said grimly.

'There won't be no other time. You better get off with Ruth. How's Ruth?'

'Ruth's all right.'

'How's your mother?'

'Ma's all right. She was asking after you.'

'How's your father?'

'Dad's all right. Here, Jenny,' said Fred earnestly, looking over his shoulder again, 'if you're ever in trouble – *you* know, if he knocks you about or anything – you've only got to say the word, you see –'

'I'll be all right, Fred. Thanks all the same.'

She was touched by Fred's words, and by the most unusual energy he had put into them; but it struck her that this was strange talk for a girl who had been happily married exactly an hour ago. She looked up and found Ernest watching her; and she knew (what indeed she knew already) that she had a very jealous husband.

Ernest came down the alley with a touch of swagger, and said, 'Well, kid, what about making a move?'

'You're right,' said Jane, rising. The evenings were drawing in, and she did not want to travel on the back of Ernest's motor-bicycle in the dark. Mr Pewter, as usual, tried to make a speech, and, as usual, was soon silenced. They drank the happy couple's health and called 'Speech!' But Ernest, half sulky and half superior, said, 'No more speeches; but I'll tell you what I'll do – I'll throw you a "floorer".' There were approving cries from the ladies, and Mr Pewter said, 'Make it three, boy.'

Ernest took his heavy 'cheese' from the box. It was like a Dutch cheese which somebody had sat upon, a sort of wooden discus, round and flat; it was made of lignum vitae and weighed twelve pounds. Ernest carefully arranged his feet, stooped, balanced, swung back his arm, took one step forward, and flung the awkward missile fast and low. Suddenly all the nine-pins were rolling noisily on the floor.

A 'floorer'! Everyone cheered. 'Not bad for a married man!' said Mr Pewter. 'Now the other two, boy!'

'That's enough,' said Ernest; then, looking at Fred, 'Here, sailor, like a throw?'

'I can't play skittles,' muttered Fred.

'Well, have a try, mate. There's nothing to be afraid of.'

'Come on, mister. There's no harm done, anyway.' Mr Pewter was always anxious to instruct the novice.

'All right,' said Fred good-humouredly. 'Only mind your-selves.'

Ernest sat down by Jane while Mr Pewter took Fred in hand. Jane thought that if Ernest was trying to show her that he was the better man he was wasting his time; for she knew very well that the best man in the world cannot throw a 'cheese' correctly except after long practice, not if it was the Prince of Wales. Moreover, the first attempts are generally rather ridiculous.

Fred was strong, but he could not at once get the knack of the grip. His first ball never reached the pins at all, but flew off side-ways and crashed alarmingly against the benches. The second was straight, but flew too high and shattered an electric lamp. Fred stepped out of the alley blushing, and Jane blushed for him. 'Well, now I hope you're satisfied,' she said to Ernest.

Ernest did indeed seem pleased by this absurd demonstration, beamed with good humour, and spoke kindly to Fred. Then he carried off his bride on the back of his motor-bicycle.

Fred managed to whisper a hurried word to Jane. 'I see you been painting the boat,' he said.

'I done a little bit, but it's a puzzle to get it nice.'

'Well, I've got a surprise for you,' said Fred mysteriously. 'Sort of present, you see.'

'Come on, Jane,' cried Ernest, and she heard no more. She perched herself on the small case which carried their belongings, and gripped Ernest by the belt. Many kisses, three loud explosions, tears in Mrs Higgins's eyes, another explosion, a roar, the smell of petrol, cheers, a glimpse of Fred, a glimpse of Mr Bell, a jerk, cheers, the rattle of a tin can tied to the saddle by Lily, and they were off to the New Life.

The journey to Brighton was safely and swiftly done. Jane was tired and sore by the end of it, but it was rather a lark, this trip to Brighton, for she had never been to Brighton – indeed, she had never seen the sea – and she kept forgetting what the trip was for. She was a little disappointed with the Russell Hotel (which Mrs Higgins had recommended), a small 'commercial' in a back street off the King's Road, for, against all reason, she had imagined a place such as Lily had visited with Mr Moss. Their room was low and shaped like an L. The bed was large enough, certainly, after the *Blackbird*, and stuffed with feathers; but its accoutrements were dingy and rough. There was an electric lamp beside the bed, such as Lily had described, but it seemed to be broken. The other light was round the corner, at the far end of the room. So Jane said, 'Oh, Lor', no reading in bed!' for reading in bed was a favourite custom on the *Blackbird*.

Ernest said, 'Well, that don't matter much!' in a tone that made her blush. Ernest never seemed to forget what the trip was for.

There was also a bell-push behind the bed. Jane said, as casual as she could be, 'I think I'll ring for some hot water,' as if about this hour in the evening she always rang for hot water.

Ernest said, 'That's right,' though his principles were all against the ringing of bells for domestic servants.

Jane rang the bell several times. Nobody came. She said at last, 'Well, I'll slip along to the bathroom'; for secretly she was longing to see the bathroom with the bath-salts and the numerous taps.

Ernest said, 'That's right,' and continued to struggle with a clean collar.

Jane wandered round many dark corners and along several dark passages, past rows of numbered doors and dirty pairs of shoes, bumped her head twice and once fell down a small flight of steps, before she found a door labelled 'Bath'. She opened it timidly, groped for a switch, and turned on the light. And her heart sank. The bathroom was small and steamy. There were no bath-salts. There were only two taps. The paper was peeling from the walls. The enamel of the bath carried a thousand scars; below the hot tap was a long, red streak terminating in a large, red patch the shape of a pear; and all round the bottom of the bath was a line of dusky soapsuds, the relics of a bath but lately enjoyed by the commercial gentleman in Number 52. A small piece of sodden yellow soap lay at the bottom. A cork mat labelled 'Welcome' lay on the floor; and on the mat lay a very wet towel.

Jane gazed at this depressing scene; and not till then did she realize what hopes she had hung upon the luxurious bathroom. She shut and bolted the door; she sat on the edge of the bath and cried.

She knew it was silly to cry, and very soon she was rebuking herself for this weakness. She washed her face under the tap and returned to Number 25. She put on her new cherry-coloured artificial silk. Ernest embraced her fiercely and they went downstairs.

Dinner in the coffee-room was a quiet affair. Both were shy of the commercial gentlemen who talked so confidently or ate so silently at the other tables. Ernest was anxious to make a splash, and though he did not drink himself insisted on Jane's beginning the meal with a *crême de menthe*, which he thought was a cocktail.

There were no cocktails at the Black Swan, and Jane knew no better. She liked the look of the green drink, but it took away her appetite.

It was funny, she thought, she had never felt so lonely as she felt now with the partner of her life. The eloquent Ernest seemed to have nothing to say. He ate his soup hungrily and eyed Jane greedily from time to time. Then there was a long wait. They crumbled their bread and looked guiltily about the room. Both were afraid of the waiter and fearful of doing the wrong thing with their knives and forks.

'This is fish,' said Jane at last.

'Of course it's fish.'

'Well, you've used the wrong knife.'

'Don't matter,' said Ernest airily. But he knew perfectly well that it mattered tremendously, and he picked up his fish-knife at once. The problem was what to do with the fishy meat-knife. First he laid it on the side of his plate; but that looked funny and would draw attention to his mistake. Then he laid it on the tablecloth, where it made a mess.

'Dirty boy!' said Jane.

'Well, I dunno,' said Ernest irritably, and rested the blade of the knife on the edge of his plate. That looked wrong too in this capitalist hotel. All this red tape, he thought, would be swept aside one day, when the workers ruled.

'Wipe it on your bread,' said Jane. Ernest obeyed, but he was cross. She had solved the problem, certainly; but this was all wrong, Jane giving him orders.

They were silent again. She thought, '"Solemnization of Matrimony". Well, this is solemn enough.' At last she could endure it no more. She said: 'Ever been to Brighton before, Ernie?' (She was doing her best to call him Ernie now, though it never came easily.)

'Yes, I come here once. Day-trip. With a friend.'

'Girl?'

'Well, I believe it was. No harm in that, is there?'

'No offence, Ernie. Who was it? Maud Barnett?'

'Pearl Watson.'

'Oh, that?'

Pearl Watson sold tobacco at the District station, and made eyes at the City men. Jane did not think much of her.

'What d'you mean – "Oh, *that*"?'

'I dunno. I went to Folkestone with Fred once.'

'You never told me.'

'Didn't I? Folkestone's ever so nice,' she continued dreamily; and wondered why in the world she had suddenly invented this mischievous story? She was as bad as Lily with her 'Mr Baldwin'. But then, why was Ernest so touchy?

Ernest was silent, picking his chop, and brooding suspiciously. 'D'you ask Fred Green to come to the wedding?'

'No.'

'D'your father ask him?'

'Not as I know of.'

'Well, he came.'

'Yes, I saw him.'

'Mother didn't invite him – I know that.'

'Well, what of it?'

'Bit of a sauce, I call it.'

'Well, if an old friend can't come to a person's wedding without a lot of fuss! Whatever next?'

'Old friend, is he?'

'Yes, he is!' Jane realized that she was flushed and angry, and it seemed extraordinary; but she had to go on. 'If you want to know, I walked out with Fred Green a long time before I met you.'

'Did you? Well, there's no need to raise your voice,' said Ernest, looking anxiously about him.

'I know that, because you was gone on Maud Barnett at the time.'

'Oh, was I?'

'Yes. And probably one or two others, if the truth was told.'

Ernest was now alarmed by the storm he had himself provoked. He said pacifically, 'There's no need to be nasty, Jane. I didn't mean any harm.'

'You've put your sleeve in the gravy,' said Jane.

They sat in silence for the remainder of the meal. Both of them thought, 'Well, this is a nice thing – sparring and snapping already at the first meal of our married lives!' Jane thought perhaps it would be better when they went to bed. But, then, looking at Ernest, she said to herself that she did not want to go to bed with Ernest. Not a little bit. If the truth was told, she saw now she was not really fond of Ernest at all. She could not be, if she could snap at him as she had just now. She had never kidded herself that she and Ernest were a case of Love's Bliss. But she had been, she thought, sort of fond of Ernest. They had hugged and kissed and cuddled so much, to say nothing of Richmond. But that was about all there was to it. 'Case of "carnal lusts and appetites",' she thought; and not always that. Not even that now, perhaps. She thought Ernest looked a bit skinny, after Fred, though he could throw 'floorers'. But were they to go on like this for the rest of their born days – sparring and snapping, 'till death us do part'? No, said Jane; she had made her bed and she must lie on it, even if Ernest lay on it too.

When they had both finished their stewed apples she said, 'Sorry, Ernest. I didn't mean to be so sharp.'

'That's all right,' said Ernest gruffly, equally penitent. 'What'll we do now? Go to the pictures?'

'I dunno, Ernie.'

'Just as you like, Jane.'

'No, *you* say.' Jane thought it might be a good thing to go and look at the sea; but this did not occur to Ernest, and she was not going to suggest it. The waiter said, 'Will you take coffee in the smoking-room?' and solved their problem for them.

The smoking-room was furnished in dark leather and decorated with hunting pictures and caricatures of racing-men. All the picture-papers in it were at least six months old. Jane picked up a number of the *Sketch* dated December of the year before, and studied it avidly, as if she might find the photographs of her own family on any page.

The waiter served coffee, and said, 'Will you take any liqueurs, sir?'

Jane said suddenly, 'I'll take a brandy, thank you,' and blushed all over. It was alarming, the way she kept saying these sudden things – things she had never thought of till they popped out. Lily was responsible this time. Lily had had a 'brandy' on the famous dog-night.

Ernest gasped; but, anxious to keep the peace, said nothing.

'Cigarettes or cigars?' said the waiter, encouraged.

'Have a cigar, Ernie,' Jane pleaded, she could not have told why.

Ernest smoked a cigarette now and then, but never in his life had he tried a cigar. But he was still anxious to please, and he had a rankling suspicion that Jane did not consider him to be a male man – like Fred, for instance. Just because he disliked liquor. Well, he would show her. As for the expense, Mrs Higgins had given him a nice lump sum for the honeymoon. He took a large cigar.

Jane did not much like her brandy, and Ernest detested his cigar; but neither was going to be beaten. Jane sipped steadily over her *Sketch*, and Ernest puffed away over an *Illustrated London News* of even greater antiquity. Two groups of 'commercials' talked earnestly about the state of business in two corners, but the bridal pair said nothing. Jane, as she read, kept thinking, 'Oh, Lor', this going to bed!'

About ten both the brandy and the cigar were finished. Ernest said, 'Tired, Jane?' and Jane said, 'Well, I dunno, Ernie, s'pose I am.' She did not feel so much tired as stupid, sleepy, and rather sick. She lingered a moment over a picture of Lady Ponsonby chatting with a friend at Gatwick. Then she thought, 'Well, better face it,' put down the paper, and went upstairs.

As she undressed she thought, 'Coo! I don't feel like a "Night of Love".' Ernest, coming up the stairs, was conscious that his ardour was less than it had been at dinner-time. Like Jane, he felt rather sick.

With only that one light round the corner the room was gloomy.

'Put a match to the fire, Ernie,' said Jane.

'Feel cold?'

'No, but this room gives me the creeps.'

'All right, Jane.'

Ernest lit the fire, thinking it would be a nice thing to be sick on one's wedding-night.

Jane was standing before the dressing-table in her pink nightie, doing her hair. It was her first silk nightie, and she thought it was rather shocking. Ernest went up behind her and put one arm round her gently, suddenly afraid. Jane wished that she could feel more excited.

'Give me a kiss, Jane,' he said humbly, as if they were walking out for the first time.

'Half a mo',' said Jane. 'That fire's going out.'

'Damn the fire!'

'Oh, naughty!'

Ernest went back to the fire, which was crackling feebly and smoking fiercely.

'I tell you what, Ernest – let's have some champagne.' Lily's 'Night of Love', with all its exciting comforts, was still in her mind.

'Champagne?' echoed Ernest, astonished, from the grate. 'Whatever next?'

'I dunno. I feel a bit sick, Ernie.'

'Do you, Jane?' said Ernest, rather pleased. 'Well, if you want to know, so do I.'

'That's funny. Them onions, I dare say.'

'Dare say it was.'

'Champagne's a pick-me-up, they say.'

'Yes, I've heard that.' Ernest hesitated. The expense would be tremendous, but it might make Jane more affectionate, from all accounts.

'But I forgot – you're teetotal.'

'That's all right, Jane. You have some if you like it.'

'Oh, I couldn't drink alone, Ernie.'

'Well, I don't mind tasting it, if it makes you any happier.'

'Do you good.'

'All right, then.' Ernest rang the bell, and Jane climbed into the squashy bed.

'Coo! it's ever so soft! Which side d'you like, Ernie?'

'I'm not particular, Jane.'

'Well, I'll have this side, away from the door. Why don't nobody come?'

Nobody came. Ernest rang again, took off his coat, and washed his teeth.

'This is a one-horse place,' said Jane. 'The light's broke, the bell don't work, and now that fire's gone out.' It was all so different from Lily's fabled hotel. She jumped out of bed and tackled the fire, cleared the grate, and laid it again with a bit of newspaper she took from the chest of drawers.

'Well, this is a nice thing!' said Ernest, infuriated by the sight of his bride at work on the grate; he stepped to the bell angrily and rang and rang and rang again – the just man roused to action.

'Don't worry, Ernie. Dare say they think we're not worth the trouble.'

This thought had already come to Ernest; and now, openly expressed, it maddened him. Through him the toiling masses were being deliberately insulted. He said, 'Oh, don't they? Well, I'll soon show them!' He put on his coat and marched fiercely to the door.

Jane said, 'That's the stuff, dear. You make a scene.' But she could not help laughing, for Ernest had forgotten that his red braces were hanging down behind.

'What's the joke?'

'Your braces, Ernie! You look ever so funny.' Ernest made an angry sound and went out. If she were really gone on him, she thought, as she blew at the fire, she would have told him about the braces without laughing at him. But she could not help it; she always saw the comical side of Ernest. She got the fire going and again sank into the great bed. When Ernest returned, the strong man justified, she was nearly asleep.

'It's all right,' he said shortly. 'I told him a thing or two.'

The fire was burning brightly now, but from time to time expelled a heavy cloud of smoke into the room. Jane lay and stared at the leaping flames, thinking that this was better. She hoped she would not be sick, wished she might be allowed to go to sleep in peace, and dozed. Unfortunately, when the waiter knocked at last, Ernest had nothing on but a woollen vest; and as Jane opened her eyes, she saw him most cautiously opening the door in this costume, and laughed again.

'I'll make you laugh, my girl,' said Ernest strongly, as he filled the glasses. But he did not feel strong; he had an empty sensation in the stomach, which he hoped the champagne would remove.

They sat up side by side in the bed with their golden glasses.

Ernest said, 'Well, all the best, old girl.'

'All the best, Ernie.' Again remembering Lily, she clinked her glass against his. In silence they sipped at their wine.

'Oo! Fizzy! Like soda-water!'

'Funny stuff,' said Ernest.

'Fancy you taking anything, Ernie! What would they say at the pub?'

'Oh, well; once in a lifetime don't matter, I dare say.'

They both sipped again, both wondering secretly what there was in this expensive liquid that caused all the talk about it; but it was grand, nevertheless, to be drinking the celebrated drink of the rich. And Ernest was pleased because he had satisfied his wife's desire, and asserted himself victoriously against a hostile hotel.

Jane said dreamily, gazing into the fire, 'I'd as soon have stone-ginger any day.'

'Would you?' said Ernest, damped. 'What d'you ask for it for, then?' He refilled his glass, determined to like champagne.

'I dunno. Woman's whim, I suppose. I was feeling so queer.'

'How're you feeling now?'

'Not so grand, Ernie.'

'Have some more.'

'Just a drop, then. Woa!' Jane sipped, staring at the fire. Ernest drank more largely. He did not like the stuff, but he must throw off this feeble, sick sensation in his stomach. He was feeling better, and he wanted to embrace Jane; but as they sat there with the delicate glasses in their hands it seemed difficult.

'I'm ever so sleepy,' said Jane at last. 'You've forgotten the light, Ernie.'

Ernest had not forgotten the light, but he did not like to say so. He put down his glass and got out of bed.

'And you might make up the fire.' Ernest obediently plucked coal from the scuttle, and then turned on the light again in order to wash his hands.

'Not much of a pick-me-up,' he heard Jane say drowsily. When at last he returned to the wife of his bosom she was lying down with her back to him; bending over her he saw that she was asleep.

'Well, this is a nice thing,' thought Ernest, and meditatively drank some more champagne. Later she would wake, or he would wake her. There was no hurry. He was feeling warm and generous, though still rather sick. He bent over his young wife again. Her face looked childish and pathetic in the firelight. Tired out, poor girl. It would be a shame to wake her.

Still, it was a nice thing – not even to say good night to your wife on your wedding-night. And there was half a bottle of champagne left. He wondered if it would keep. Fizzy drinks seldom did, and this was expensive. He drank some more and felt better, but very funny in the head.

He pulled down the bedclothes very gently, and gently, with his free hand, stroked Jane's arm. It was wonderful to think that this girl belonged to him, that he could wake her up and do what he liked with her. But he would not wake her up for the world. He would sit there and watch over her. He drank some more champagne and his eyes filled with tears.

There was something to be said for this champagne after all. He felt much better, but very sleepy after the ride from London and the long day. There were two or three inches of champagne left and it would be a pity to waste them. Ernest sipped his wine, stroked his wife, and dreamed dreams. He and Jane would do big things. One day he would be secretary of the Union. Then member of the T.U.C. The strong man who made and unmade general strikes. A Labour Government – and he would be Minister of Transport. Ernest emptied his glass and became Prime Minister.

He would have to educate Jane. But he would not wake her up. His head was buzzing a little and he was extraordinarily thirsty. This was the last glass of champagne now. It had been splendid, going down like that and raising hell in the hotel, because they thought that he and Jane were not worth the trouble. All for Jane's sake. She had wanted her champagne and she had got it. Why not? She was as good as anybody. Better. And that was the end of the champagne. It was a good pick-me-up, certainly, but he must lie down at once.

He lay down beside Jane and gently put his hand upon her waist. It was not quite what he had expected on his wedding-night; but he was happy.

Jane stirred and muttered something in her sleep. Only one word was intelligible: and that was 'Fred'.

18

MATRIMONY

It was a very different Ernest who lit the fire on Sunday night. Jane again said something about champagne. But Ernest said 'No'.

They had had a lazy day. They lay in bed till eleven and read the *Sunday Gazette*. Then they went out and walked up and down the Grand Parade. It was Jane's first sight of the sea, and she said so. Ernest said, 'I thought you'd been to Folkestone,' and Jane said that was only her teasing.

She was disappointed in the sea, which was muddy and grey, for she had always understood that the sea was blue. She had seen the river at Hammersmith bluer than that on windy autumn afternoons when the sky was clear. But the distant steamers, the huge hotels, and the sauntering crowds pleased her; and the sharp east wind gave her a pretty glow. The vast red Metropole was wonderful. 'Cool' she said, 'I'd like to go in there, Ernie.'

Ernest was about to say something about the idle rich, but thought better of it, for he was anxious not to annoy today. They were both thinking twice before they spoke; so not much was said, but the peace was kept.

After lunch Ernest wanted to go to bed; but Jane said, 'In the daytime? What an idea!' and would not hear of it. So they went on the pier and put pennies in the automatic machines. Jane loved these. She played golf and football, and shot pennies out of pistols, and with a little ship's wheel steered a magnetic little ship past rocks and under bridges. This was her favourite, and many times, with little chirrups of delight, she steered her vessel into port and won her penny back. Ernest watched her, a little superior; but he consented to 'Try His Grip' and 'Guess His Weight', and he readily provided Jane with coppers so long as she kept to the machines which held out hopes of returning them. But he was alarmed by Jane's extravagant ways of thought – the gambling blood of that father, he judged. There would be no champagne tonight.

Ernest brightened up when they went into the 'Hall of Fun' and looked through the 'Peeposcopes' at a penny a time. These had alluring titles, such as 'What Tommy Saw in Paris', 'What the Butler Saw', and 'A Night in Bloomsbury'. Ernest said that he must look first, to make sure that they were respectable; but he hoped they were not. He began with 'What Tommy Saw in Paris'. The penny clanged, a bright light shone, and Ernest saw a young woman in the costume of 1890 and a large, round feathery hat, holding a bicycle. One foot was on the pedal, and her ankle, clothed in an open-work black silk stocking, was daringly exposed. The vision passed with a click. It was succeeded by a picture of the same young lady sitting in an apple-tree and dangling from a bough a single foot on which was no shoe, but a stocking only. Next Tommy saw her well wrapped-up upon a stony beach (doubtless the shores of the Seine) and, at a little distance, a man with a very large moustache and an open umbrella. Again, sitting on a stool, with one foot in a hip-bath. Again in walking-dress, but upside-down. Again, sitting in a boat and a Victorian blouse, the hair falling boldly about her ample shoulders.

These glimpses may have shocked or delighted some ancestral Tommy; but Ernest said angrily, 'A proper sell,' and he would not allow Jane to waste a penny on the 'Butler'.

It was cold on the pier; so arm in arm they went to the Aquarium, saw the sharks fed, and had tea, while the band played 'Lohengrin'. Then they went on the West Pier, where the automatic machines were not so amusing; but Ernest played skee-ball because it was the nearest thing to skittles, and he won a china dog. It was dark now, and the wind was bitter, but the long, shadowy pier was exciting. Jane suddenly stamped her cold feet and scampered off round the corner of the theatre; she ran to the end of the pier, where tomorrow a man was to dive into the sea in flames; and Ernest chased her over the noisy planks, and caught her, and hugged her in the dark, above the swishing water. They looked out into the darkness of the sea, panting and clinging close; and Jane felt the old fever and flame in her again. After all, she was rather fond of old Ernest, she thought, and tonight she would be quite ready for a bit of love.

After dinner they went to the pictures and saw a film about a girl who was constantly undressing and showing her under-clothes. Ernest did not think she was as attractive as Jane, even in her underclothes, though Jane told him her legs were insured for thousands of pounds. Ernest grew restless, and after the girl had lost her honour they went home.

The fire burned better tonight, the light by the bed had been mended, and the room seemed more cosy and home-like. But it was funny, Jane thought, she did not feel any less wicked because they were married now. She just felt she was enjoying herself, and had no business to be. It was she and Ernest misbehaving, as they had misbehaved before. 'A remedy against sin', indeed? This was better than Richmond, of course; though, as to that, there was something to be said for getting the first and worst over before one was married. She wished it was more than misbehaving, she wished it was Love's Bliss; she wished she felt wild, as Ernest was. If it had been Mr Bryan, now, she would not be lying in his arms, calmly thinking things out; she would be half mad. It was shocking to be lying in her husband's arms thinking about another man, she thought, and she hugged Ernest penitently. Ernest tightened his ferocious hold, and she said, 'Oo, you'll squeeze the breath out of me!' She would not have complained to Mr Bryan; he might half kill her and she would never murmur. Ernest raised his head, and she saw his face, animal, rapacious, excited, and strange. She laughed aloud.

'Coo! Ernie! You look ever so comical.'

'I'll teach you, my girl!' said Ernest fiercely.

'Sorry, Ernie,' she whispered, penitent again. 'I'm a bad lot; you're right.'

*

On Monday they walked on the Parade, and walked on the pier, and went to the pictures, and went to the Palais de Danse. The wind was still in the east, and Jane had a snuffly cold. They had a small quarrel at dinner because Jane wanted to try oysters, and Ernest said oysters were parasites' food and did Jane think she had married a capitalist? And Jane said he was talking silly. Next morning Ernest had caught Jane's cold, and in the afternoon they went back to London.

Mr Bell had spent the week-end on the barge with Lily. On Saturday evening they went to the dogs together and met Mr Moss, who put them on to many good things. On Sunday he was invited to take a cup of tea with Mrs Higgins, and they had a nice talk. Mrs Higgins was impressed by his neat clothes and by the quiet air of affluence with which he stood drinks in the evening. Evidently Mr Bell was doing well in the north. And Mr Bell, sitting by the fire in the cosy corner of the Private Bar, admiring the ferns and the stuffed fish and the old photographs, the pewter and the copper and the beautiful rows of bottles, saw himself again the master of Mrs Higgins and the Black Swan. 'When I've put by a little more,' he told her with an earnest look. 'I'm coming back to Hammersmith.'

'That's right,' said Mrs Higgins warmly; and Mr Bell felt that he was practically engaged to be married.

During the week-end there was great activity on the barge. All Sunday Fred and his father were there, busy with paint-brushes and many pots of paint. Mr Bell assisted for short periods, and Lily stood about and complained of the mess. When the bridal pair returned the barge still smelled of paint, but Fred's 'surprise' was ready.

They had made the *Blackbird* as like the *Prudence* as paint could make her. The long cabin was gay with castles and hearts and roses. At the far end was a vast red heart on a white ground. There were castles on each wall, and clusters of roses and diamond squares on the doors. Castles and hearts and roses. Greens and yellows and reds. Crude but gay. The biscuit-tin, the bread-tin, the kettles, the water-can were green too, and decorated with roses. By the stove hung a number of shiny brass ornaments, and near the ladder were seven shiny brass knobs, screwed into a bulkhead.

'Coo!' said Jane, 'whoever done this?' and stood entranced at the bottom of the ladder.

'Fred and his father, of course,' said Lily. 'Who d'you think?' Fred, far away at the Cowley Lock, was wondering what Jane would think of their loving labours. If he had seen her happy face he would have been satisfied.

Ernest, who was waiting half-way down the ladder, said, 'Go on Jane. What's the game?'

'Look what Fred's done,' she said, almost in awe, and ran

through into the bedroom. Here was another red heart on the white wall facing the bed, and on the other a splendid chocolate-coloured castle rising from the banks of a silver stream. A black barge of the build of the *Blackbird* was disappearing under a bridge, and two figures stood side by side at the tiller – a boy and a girl.

'Would you believe it?' whispered Jane to herself. 'Fred!'

Ernest, in the living-room, was looking at Fred's handiwork a little sourly.

'What d'you think of it, Ern?' said Lily, watching him.

'My name's Ernest.' He disliked being called 'Ern' by Lily; and he wished he had not consented to have Lily on the barge 'till something turned up'. It would never do; she was always 'getting at him'. And now all this fuss about Fred's painting! A nice way to come home, he thought.

'Sorry, I'm sure,' said Lily. 'Fred's clever, isn't he?' She had not thought much of the Greens' paintings till now, when she saw that they annoyed Ernest.

Ernest said nothing, but followed Jane into the little bedroom. He looked critically at the red heart, and at the two figures on the tiller of the barge; and he said, pointing, 'Who's that?'

'You and me, I s'pose, Ernie. That's our barge, you see.' But in her heart she thought the figures were Fred and Jane. Ernest grunted. 'Don't you like it, Ernie? I think it's ever so nice.'

'I like the red,' said Ernie grudgingly. But all through supper he saw Jane's eyes wandering to her lovely castles and roses; and he decided that he must keep a close eye on this Fred.

After supper she sat down and slowly composed a long letter to Fred. She began: '*Dear Fred the castles and everything is ever so nice you are a dear to think of it* – But she thought of the lock-keeper reading out her letter while the lock filled, and Fred standing embarrassed at the office-door; so she scratched out 'you are a dear' and wrote '*it was ever so nice of you to think of it you are a one –*'

Ernest, watching her, said, 'Who're you writing to?'

'Fred, of course.' Ernest said, 'Huh! Well, I'm going over to the alley.' And he went off to play skittles. They heard him swearing as he stumbled against the hatch.

'You and Ernie's going to fall out,' said Lily.

'Don't you believe it,' said Jane. But she wrote, '*I don't know as*

Ernie's so gone on them Ernie's a bit jealous if the truth was told so mind out when you come and see us.'

But then she remembered the lock-keeper and scratched out the last words and wrote: *'But we are doing nicely thanks.'* This sort of correspondence was not so easy.

They 'did nicely' enough for three or four weeks. Ernest had said there was to be no more sitting for artists and no more serving in the bar; but Jane, very houseproud now, had plenty to do, cleaning, sweeping, tidying, and cooking. November was near, the nights were cooler, and whenever the water was up and the wind blew she hoisted sail and went hunting for wood. It was a good year for wood – Jane had never known a better – and soon there was a great, untidy pile of it on the wharf; but it must all be chopped up, small enough for the stove, and carted in baskets down the ladder. Ernest was not much of a help in that sort of way. He would sometimes consent to fill the heavy jar of water at the tap on the wharf, but when any prolonged and patient job, like wood-chopping, was at hand, he was generally resting from his labours on the railway, or preparing for those to come. Ernest had three alternative shifts of duty – five in the morning till one, one till nine, and five till one at night; and he did a week of each in turn. He liked the early morning shift best in the winter, since it left the evening free for skittles or the committee meetings of the League of Red Youth. Jane preferred it too, for she was less pestered at night, and in the morning had the boat to herself, without Ernest rolling about and getting in the way.

Ernest tried hard, but he could not fit himself into life on the water. He was one of those who will always be clumsy and impatient in boats. Jane took him out in her boat many times, anxious to share her skill and her pleasure. He would shock her at once by jumping heavily into the bottom of her boat, or stepping dangerously on the gunwale. She cured him of these horrid practices, but she could not teach him to sail. He wearied soon of tacking back and forth across the river, and changing his seat when they went about. He would put the tiller the wrong way, and become flustered as they charged towards the bank; with legs and arms entangled in the sheet, he would forget to duck his head as the boom swung over, and catch a smart blow on the ear, and swear bitterly. This happens at first to all recruits to the water; but Ernest, the owner of a motor-bicycle, had not enough respect for this ancient method of travel to suffer its difficulties gladly. When they ran before the wind, straight down the river, sensibly, like a motor-bicycle, he understood and enjoyed it, so long as the wind held and there was a hint of speed. But when the wind fell light and they hung motionless against the tide, he had not Jane's patience – the patience of the sailor who loves his vessel in all her moods and can find contentment even in a calm. Then Ernest would begin to fret and mutter, thrashing the tiller this way and that, and shaking what breeze there was out of the sails. Once in a high wind, refusing to heed Jane's instructions, he rammed the *Blackbird*'s ample flank, and started a new leak in the small boat; and they had words. So Jane gave up asking him to go with her; and this annoyed him, though he had no wish to go. Also, she never wanted to ride behind him on his motor-bicycle now.

Poor Ernest! It was a fortnight before he learned to go up the ladder without bumping his head; always when he did this he swore and Lily said he was disgusting. On the deck he always seemed to stumble against something in the dark; and Lily sometimes shouted up that he'd better learn to swim, for he'd be over one night. The night noises of the river, which Jane loved, and Lily did not notice – the lap and chuckle of the rising tide, the *Blackbird* heaving and straining at her ropes on the wash of a string of barges, the quack of the ducks exploring in the night, the raucous cry of the heron, the hoot of owls and of tugs, the very creaking of the *Blackbird*'s timbers – woke Ernest up and kept him awake sometimes and angered him. If he lay awake for long he would want to make love to Jane, and Jane was less and less ready for love-making.

Then there was Lily, yapping at him always like a golden bitch in his own home. Lily was intolerable. She was generally out in the evenings, at the pictures or the dogs; and on many afternoons she would go shopping in Oxford Street, or meet Mr Moss at a Palais de Danse. But night and morning she was there, passing remarks and making Ernest uncomfortable. Whenever Ernest talked politics, Lily said, 'Chuck it, Ernie!' In the morning, when he walked about in his shirt, she made remarks about the hair on his legs; and at night she would lie with one ear out of the bedclothes, listening for kisses. And if she thought she heard love-making she would cry out, 'Leave her alone, can't you, Ernie?' He told Jane often that Lily must clear out; but Jane said in that case she would only go and live in sin with Mr Moss, and Ernest did not like the idea of that. He thought he could have got on with Lily very well himself, if only she would not dislike him so. So Jane lectured Lily about nagging, and Lily stayed on the *Blackbird* and nagged.

November came, with the wild winds from the south-west, and driving rain, and mud in the cabin. A leak started in the roof, and at night the river was as noisy as the sea. But the skittles season had begun, and Ernest, every evening, found refuge in the cosy alley. On match-nights, Jane would dutifully attend with the other wives and watch the Black Swan team battle with the Man in the Moon from Chelsea, or the Freemasons' Arms. She was proud of Ernest, who always won his match, but she soon tired of watching. It was better when the match was away from home, and they all went over to Putney or Roehampton in a charabanc, singing silly songs.

One day there were three heavy knocks on the hatch, and Fred came down the ladder. It was tea-time; Ernest had gone off to Down Street, and Lily was choosing a necklace at Woolworth's. Jane was glad to see Fred and the old wet oilskins; but all she said was 'Well, stranger?' She was shy.

Fred said, 'How's the happy home?'

'Mustn't grumble, Fred. Take off your oilies.'

Fred took them off and stood looking round the room at his castles and roses.

'Nice, isn't it?' said Jane.

'Dad did a lot of it,' said Fred modestly.

She put her arm under his and showed him round the barge. In the bedroom they stood and looked at the red heart over the foot of the bed.

'I like that heart, Fred,' said Jane.

'I did that.'

'Well, you ought to put your name on it. Like the artists do.'

'I can't write, Jenny,' he said. 'You know that.'

Jane blushed. She had forgotten that. 'Well, I'll write "Fred",' she said, 'and you can put your mark – see?'

She ran out and fetched the barge pen and the inkpot, made out of the fuse of a shell, which Mrs Higgins had given them; and she wrote a sprawly 'Fred' at the bottom of the red heart.

'Now then, Fred, your mark.'

'What sort of a mark?' said Fred.

'Just a cross. Same as a kiss, you see.'

Fred made a laborious cross, and stood up, blushing. 'Same as a kiss,' he muttered, and looked at Jane, and put one timid great hand on her shoulder. It was strange to be looking at a married Jane. This was the room, and this the bed, where Ernest hugged her. He felt she ought to look different; but she looked the same. He wondered if he dared to kiss her now. He said, 'How d'you like being married, Jenny?'

'Mustn't grumble, Fred,' said Jane, with her head on one side. 'Give me the pen.'

Fred gave her the pen, and stooping, kissed her, shyly and clumsily.

'Mind out, you'll spill the ink,' said Jane, but her heart fluttered pleasantly.

Fred felt profoundly wicked. 'I beg pardon, Jenny,' he said humbly; 'but I can't help being gone on you, can I?'

'You're a dear old goat,' said Jane, affectionately. 'What about a nice cup of tea?'

Fred sat on the keelson and watched Mrs Ernest make tea, and told her all the news of the canal: how somebody's horse had gone to sleep and walked into the 'Cut', how the Dixons had given up their horse and bought two power-boats, and how they had put in a new lock-gate at Cowley, and many other exciting things.

Jane listened wistfully, and said, 'Wish I could come up the "Cut" with you again, Fred.'

'Wish you could, Jenny.'

'It's never no more,' she sighed. 'Ernie isn't so keen on the water, you see.'

'Blast Ernie!' thought Fred. But he drank up his tea, and said, 'Well, I'd better be getting along.' He did not want to see the insufferable Ernie in possession.

'What's the hurry?'

'I dunno.'

'Ernie'll be sorry to miss you.'

'Back soon?'

'No. He's on the night-shift. Don't get back till two in the morning sometimes.'

Fred paused, one foot on the ladder, revolving a desperate thought, and trembling at his own audacity.

'Ever go to the pictures, Jenny?'

'Not so often, Fred.'

'Anything on at the Blue Halls?'

'Novarro's good, Lily says.'

'You seen him?'

'Not this time. I saw him in "*Rosebuds*". That was a nice picture.'

'I never saw that.' Fred could not quite say what he wanted to say; and Jane, the married woman, was not going to help him now, though she was longing to see Novarro with Fred.

'S'pose you're busy tonight?' Fred went on, taking his foot off the ladder.

'Nothing to mention,' said Jane, busily clearing up the tea-things.

'Well, I was wondering – S'pose you couldn't come out tonight?'

'Well, I don't know why not.' She knew very well why not. She would have words with Ernie. But she did not care.

'Well, that's all right, then,' said Fred, and sat down on the keelson, where for ten minutes he pondered silently the enormous boldness of his act.

Jane washed up the tea-things and put on her best. Then they went to the Blue Halls and held hands.

That night Ernest came home at about a quarter to two. It was one of the regular south-west stormy nights. Jane was lying awake, listening to the wind and the water, and thinking fondly (but not excitedly) about Fred, and wishing rather that she had a bed to herself. When Ernest came in she jumped out dutifully and made his tea, then hopped back, shivering, into bed, and was asleep, or seemed to be, before Ernest had finished undressing. This always annoyed Ernest, especially on stormy nights, when all these noises kept him awake. But it was only natural, he supposed, and he crept into bed with considerate stealth. He was sure he would not sleep tonight – there was too much noise – so he left the candle alight on the chair and stared gloomily up at the whitewashed beams over his head. He had had a bad day: there had been trouble with three passengers, and one military man had promised to report him for preventing him from rushing on to the train just as it moved off. This often happened, but it always upset Ernest. Passengers did not seem to understand that he was only acting in their own interests – particularly the kind of passenger who frequented Down Street. They were always intimate friends of the manager or one of the directors. And in this unjust world Ernest could never be sure that one of these important passengers might not one day cause real trouble for him. And now this noise, this creaking and whistling and banging and thudding and splashing! It was a mad place to live in, cheap as it was; good enough in the summer, but in these wild winters one should live in a house where one could shut the windows. The windows of the *Blackbird* were permanently open.

Ernest's eye travelled down to the red heart on the wall in front of him; and he thought for the hundredth time that it was a bit of sauce, that fellow Fred Green coming in and painting silly pictures in his home. The heart, though it was red, annoyed him most of all, for he thought it the silliest. And now, at the bottom of the heart, he saw with amazement the word 'Fred' – and after 'Fred' a cross, such as he had often put at the bottom of letters, meaning a kiss.

'Talk of the devil!' muttered Ernest, and jealous suspicions flamed in his mind.

He was quite sure that Fred and his cross had not been there the night before. But he would go carefully; he had learned that it was best to go carefully with Jane. She was lying curled up against the partition, with her back to him. He sat up and pulled her over, and when she opened her eyes, said, 'What about a bit of love, my girl?'

Jane said sleepily, 'Not tonight, Ernie. I'm tired.'

'Tired, are you?' said Ernest. 'Anybody been here today?'

'I dunno,' said Jane, her eyes closed again. 'Oh, yes, Fred looked in.'

'Oh, he did, did he? Funny thing you didn't say nothing about it?'

'I was half asleep when you come in.'

'What did you do?'

'What d'you mean – what did I do?'

'You and Fred.'

'Well, if you want to know, we went to the pictures.'

'Friday, when I wanted to go to the pictures, you was too tired.'

'Dare say I was.'

'And now you're too tired.'

'So I am. Go to sleep, Ernie.'

'Here, my girl, you open your eyes and look at me!'

Jane opened her eyes and looked up, a little frightened, into her husband's scowling face. 'What's the matter with you, Ernie?' she said.

'What else d'you do?'

'What else d'we do? Nothing, of course, only had a cup of tea.'

'Fred bring you in here?'

'Bring me in here? What you talking about?' Jane was really frightened now. Ernest was terrible. 'Just on the boil,' she thought.

Ernest pointed a fierce finger at the red heart, and said, 'Did Fred What-is-it write his name there, or did he not?'

'No, he didn't. If you want to know, *I* did, Ernie.'

'Oh, did you? A nice thing! And you expect me to believe that, do you?'

'Fred can't write; you know that, Ernie.'

'I don't know nothing about him. And I suppose,' said Ernest, sarcastic, 'he never come in here at all, eh?'

'Yes, he did,' said Jane, defiant now.

'Oh, he did? And what for, may I ask?'

'To look at his pictures, of course.'

'Pictures!' shouted Ernest, and raised his fist, so that Jane thought 'He's going to strike me.' But Ernest did not strike her. 'Pictures!' he said again, throwing off the bedclothes. 'I'll give him *pictures*!' He rushed out into the living-room and came back with a screwdriver.

'Ernie!' cried Jane in terror, 'what's the matter with you?' And she pulled the bedclothes up to her eyes as if that would protect her from the murder she half expected. But even at that moment the words 'Girl Slain with Screwdriver' flashed across her mind.

But Ernest did not intend murder. He ran past Jane and slashed with the screwdriver at Fred's name and Fred's mark, and made fierce diagonal gashes across the red heart.

'What's the matter with you, Ernie?' cried Jane again, peering over the sheet with eyes of horror; for this was worse than murder – it was madness. Ernest went on slashing and talking swear-words to himself. And when he had done with the heart, he knelt on the bed and attacked the castle picture, beginning at the couple standing in the stern of the barge, at which he directed not slashes only, but deep vindictive stabs.

'Ernie!' shouted Jane, angry herself now. The heart was nothing much, but to see Fred's barge being slashed and stabbed, and those two figures, who of course were Fred and Jane – it hurt.

'Ernie!' she cried. 'You *beast*!'

At that moment from the after end of the boat came Lily's voice, sleepy and angry. 'Oy, you two! What's the game? If this is wedded bliss, give me the old maid!' Lily's voice succeeded where Jane's had failed.

Ernest ceased his murderous assaults on the painted bargees, rushed to the door, and shouted down the long, dark living-room some eloquent abuse at Lily. 'As for you, you —,' said Ernest, 'you can pack up and clear out tomorrow morning, for I've had enough of you. You —!' And Ernest proceeded to describe Lily in terms which had better not be repeated.

Lily was not the one to lie still and listen to foul language about herself. So she left her bed, and slowly approached Ernest, a ghostly figure in her nightie, giving Ernest as good as she got.

Jane was amazed and shocked by the words which Lily knew and used so easily. Fearing violence, she too left her bed, came to the door of her bedroom, and shouted at them, 'Give over, you two. Ernie, you ought to be ashamed of yourself.'

Ernest turned and said brutally, 'Here, none of that – you!' He put his arm on her shoulder and gave her a push, so that she fell back through the door on to the bed.

She felt ridiculous, and she thought 'He's struck me!' It was only a push, but it was violence, and she thought 'He's struck me!' It was a turning-point.

Ernest returned his attention to Lily, who had now come close to him. Through the door Jane could see their two faces together, spitting venom, like two cats on a wall. As they drew closer, she was sure that presently Lily would be struck, as she had been struck;

and she could not bear the idea. She shouted again, more urgent and louder than before, 'Ernie! You *beast*! Give over!'

A strange feature of Ernest's state of mind was that direct address seemed to pass over him, but an interruption made him furious. The moment he heard Jane's voice, he left Lily, shouting abuse in the dark, rushed back into the bedroom, took hold of Jane, roughly turned her over, and violently spanked her. Jane, her face in the blanket, made muffled, indignant cries, and struggled and kicked, but Ernest took no notice. The ungrateful Lily came on to the door, and, leaning against the doorpost, watched Ernest's proceedings with interest and mild approval.

'That's right, Ernie,' said Lily. 'That's what she wants. Go on, Ernie, give her some more!' These remarks she repeated, with variations, several times. Ernest at last, moved, not by Jane's cries, but by Lily's comments, dropped Jane suddenly and turned on Lily. Lily, not wanting to be spanked herself, retreated nimbly down the living-room towards her bunk. Ernest gave chase, with half a mind to punish Lily in the same way; but he fell over the keelson, as he usually did in the dark, and, being half ashamed of himself already, he struck a match, lit the Aladdin lamp, and sat down in front of the stove.

Silence fell on the barge. The two sisters crept into their beds without a word. Jane was bewildered, ashamed, and implacable. Strangely, it was not the spanking which governed her thoughts, painful and humiliating though that had been, but the push which had thrown her on to the bed. The violent spanking did not somehow, count as a 'striking' in her mind, but that push was a landmark. Ernest had struck her; and now, she was quite clear, she hated him. He should never love her again.

Lily's thoughts dwelled with pleasure on the spanking of Jane, which had amused her; but she decided that Ernest, in this frame of mind, must be obeyed. The end had come; she would go to Mr Moss; and she would tell her father and everyone they had been married secretly, to avoid fuss.

Ernest coaxed up the fire, boiled a kettle, and made some more tea. He peeped uncertainly into the bedroom, but Jane seemed to be asleep. So he drank up his tea, and marched up and down the room in his bare feet for half an hour, thinking. He was pleased with himself, though in a vague way ashamed. He had lost his temper and done more than he intended; but still, he had asserted himself. He had been the strong male at last, and in future he would be master in his own house. Tomorrow Lily should pack up and go – there should be no doubt about that; he did not care if she went 'on the streets'; he did not care where she went: the 'streets' might do her good. As for Jane, he did not really think there was anything wrong between her and Fred; but he was not going to have every man who liked his wife hanging about the place and taking her to the pictures. In future, if she was too tired for him, she would be too tired for Fred.

In the morning neither of the two girls would speak to him, but addressed their remarks ostentatiously to each other. Jane would not even look at him. This was a pity, for Ernest had woken in a less uncompromising frame of mind, and was almost ready to say he was sorry. But these sulks angered him, and he said to himself that when Lily had gone he would teach Jane a lesson.

Lily went ashore and telephoned to Mr Moss, borrowed Jane's leather case, and let Jane pack for her. After lunch she departed.

Ernest might perhaps have offered to carry her bag to the Underground; but she said, 'Good-bye, bully-boy. You touch her again, and I'll bring the police.'

Ernest said, 'You shut your mouth!' and decided she should carry her bag herself.

The two sisters hugged tenderly on the deck, and Jane cried, but not Lily. When they had done and Lily was climbing the ladder to the wharf, Fred came slowly through the gate in the fence. 'Come on, Fred Green,' cried Lily cheerily. 'Ernie's crazy to see you.'

Fred came forward uncertainly to the wharf's edge, and looked down at them. 'And this,' thought Ernest, 'is where I show the lot of them where they get off.'

'Anybody send you a card of invitation, Fred Green?' he said sarcastically.

'What d'you mean?'

'Anybody ask you round?'

'No,' said Fred. 'I just thought –'

'Well, you thought wrong You can clear out – see?'

'Behave yourself, Ernest!' said Jane, white with anger.

Ernest turned on her fiercely. 'Shut up, you! You heard what I said, Fred Green. Clear out of this wharf. I'll have no tampering here.'

'Dunno what you mean,' said Fred, and he looked inquiringly at Jane.

'Go on, Fred,' said she, bitter and sullen. 'This is no place for a decent boy. Perhaps next time you come somebody will have learned manners.'

'You've been crying, Jenny,' said Fred suspiciously.

'What's that to you?' said Ernest truculently, with his head back.

'Go on, Fred,' said Jane.

'Last night he struck her,' put in Lily calmly.

'Is that a fact?' said Fred heavily.

'No, it isn't a fact. Go *on*, Fred!' said Jane with urgency, for she feared another scene.

'Well, I'll go if you say so, Jenny,' said Fred slowly, and he turned to Ernest. 'But if you treat her bad, I'll murder you – see?'

Ernest folded his arms and said offensively, 'You mind your own bloody business – see?' And if he had not been six feet out of reach, Fred would have hit him then; for the effort of thought was becoming too much, and he did not know what to do or say.

Lily, who had been enjoying the scene, said suddenly, 'I tell you what, Fred Green, you can carry my bag.' Fred was almost relieved to find some definite thing he could do, and with a last puzzled look at Jane he walked slowly away. Lily tripped beside him, and told him, with embellishments, the story of the night's goings-on. When she came to the spanking, Fred stopped dead in the middle of the pavement, and swore; and all Lily's arts of persuasion were required to prevent him from going back to the barge at once.

As soon as they were out of sight, Ernest went below, and, with the screwdriver and an old file, methodically scraped at Fred's castles and hearts and roses, till nothing was left of Fred but a few scars on the wall. Ernest was determined to decorate his dwelling-place himself; and he knew a man in the Advertisement Department who would get him some of those fine coloured Underground posters. Pictures of Kew and Hampton Court – they would be something like.

Jane came down and found him at work; and she was so sick at heart and dazed in mind that she did not even protest. Without a word she went up the ladder again and sat on the hatch and cried. She had lost Lily, she had lost Fred, she had been struck and spanked and humiliated, and now she was left alone with this terrible angry Ernest, whom she hated.

As she dried her eyes she noticed idly that old Mrs Staples, the char, was unlocking the door of the studio.

19

MR BRYAN AGAIN

Two days later Mr Bryan returned to the studio. A week later Mrs Staples was knocked over by a motor-bus in King Street, and Jane 'did for' Mr Bryan instead.

This came about easily enough, although Ernest had his objections. It was natural for Mr Bryan to cross the wharf and ask if Jane could tell him of another charwoman who could cook a little. It was natural for Jane to say that she could not think of anyone just then, but that meanwhile she would come over herself, sweep out the studio, and get Mr Bryan some tea. He had not, it seemed, bothered to get himself lunch. It was not so natural, perhaps, to offer herself as a 'permanent'; for Ernest, she knew, would be against her returning to the 'degrading thraldom' of domestic service. Yet she had made up her mind before she had finished the sweeping. The opportunity thrilled her. Only once had she spoken to Mr Bryan since his return – a polite hurried word as they passed on the wharf. Too polite, she thought – she might have been anybody – they might never have met before – '*Ships that Pass in the Night*'. Yet she had trembled and felt a fool; and she thought she had blushed. She was as mad about him as ever, she found, polite or not; and all that week she had envied Mrs Staples. It was a case of so near and yet so far.

Now, she thought, as she put his kettle on the gas-ring, she would make his tea every morning, and pull the curtains back, and say, 'Good morning, Mr Bryan,' as she had in the old days.

She thought that Mr Bryan might show some excitement when she made her offer: he would smile delightedly and say something about it being quite like old times. This did not happen, for Mr Bryan was deeply occupied in the painting of a lady's ear, which, after several attempts, was not the desired shade of blue. Not looking up from the ear, he said it was very good of Jane, and what should he pay her? He would rather be 'done for' by a young woman than an old, but he did not much care what young woman it was. Jane did not know this; and though she was disappointed by her cool reception, she said to herself wisely that these artists were never quite all there when they were at their pictures. Now there was only Ernest to get round.

Ernest growled at the proposal, but, surprisingly, said nothing. For Ernest was frightened. He had gone too far on that victorious night of the spanking, and he was afraid that Jane would never forgive him. It was not in her nature to maintain the silent sulk after the first day; but, though she spoke to him now, it was a strange young woman who spoke, a polite young woman in a shop or post office. And she had gone off to sleep in Lily's little cubbyhole, and would not let him come near her. He thought she would come to her senses soon, and he was biding his time; therefore when she told him of her new job (she did not ask his permission, but calmly said it was all arranged), he growled only, thinking it better not to provoke another row. Poor Ernest was discovering already that the dictatorship of the proletariat was not so simple as it sounded.

But Jane thought that she had come to her senses already. It was plain to her now that she did not love, but even disliked Ernest. Ernest had spoiled Fred's pictures and struck her. Of the two offences perhaps the first was the worse, but the striking rankled. That was what had 'done it'. Something had happened to her that night, and the thought of sleeping with Ernest again was hateful.

*

Mr Bryan was working very hard, preparing for a Spring 'Show' of his pictures at the Atalanta Galleries. He had spent the late summer and autumn wandering with friends about the coasts of Brittany, and now he was painting nothing but the fishing industry – the fishing fleets of Concarneau and Belle Île, blue spars and cinnamon sails, sturdy Breton fishermen in scarlet trousers, blue sardine-nets drying at the masthead, disembowelled tunny-fish hanging in steely green rows, anchors and bollards and quays and lobsterpots. Jane liked these pictures because of their subjects; the boats were like boats, and even the fishermen were more like men than most of Mr Bryan's human beings. She decided that one day the sails of her boat would be copper-coloured or a faded blue, with pale-green spars, perhaps.

During these weeks few visitors came to the studio, and Mr Bryan went seldom into the town. He was excited about his 'Show', and when the light had gone would sit about staring at what he had done during the day, carve a walking-stick, or visit some neighbouring artist and enjoy an argument about significant form. As a rule, about seven, Jane cooked a kipper, sausages, or bacon and eggs for him; and afterwards, very often, he would go over to the Black Swan, have a beer or two, and play skittles. Potts and Latimer and one or two other local artists were members, and played spasmodically but not very well. Mr Bryan was the most promising of what the regular members called the 'gentlemen novices'. The working men members were perfect gentlemen themselves, and warmly welcomed anyone who paid his dues and did not put on airs. Ernest alone was 'class-conscious', and sometimes inquired sarcastically if this was a working man's club or not. But Ernest, though a vocal member of the committee, was not the secretary, the gentlemen's subscriptions were useful, and most of the artists were so much less well dressed than the working men, and looked so much less well fed, that even Ernest could not feel bitterly class-conscious about them. Besides, they listened humbly to everything Ernest told them about the playing of skittles, and most of them played so badly (compared with Ernest) that their visits to the alley gave him a taste of the dictatorship of the proletariat, such as he did not find anywhere else.

Mr Bryan was another matter. Though he was friendly and modest and had no swank, there was an air of 'class' about him. He did not make himself out to be superior, but Ernest felt that he *was* superior – which was still more annoying. Besides, he was Jane's boss, and in the old days Jane had sat to him, Ernest remembered, with nothing on. So Mr Bryan wanted watching, and when he began to come regularly to the alley Ernest watched him very carefully. But Mr Bryan's behaviour gave no ground for offence. Tenaciously pursuing his plan for the winning back of Jane, Ernest shrank from showing open hostility to her boss without good cause, and he contented himself with 'passing remarks' when Mr Bryan was in the alley – the kind of remarks that Lily would have passed if she had ever watched Ernest playing. If Mr Bryan made a good shot, Ernest would remark that skittles was easy enough if you hadn't a hard day's work behind you; and if Mr Bryan 'went five' (for which a forfeit of a halfpenny was charged), Ernest would say, 'That's all right – he's plenty of money.'

But Mr Bryan was popular, and these remarks shocked the sensitive taste of the rest of the club, as Ernest soon discovered. They did not escape Mr Bryan; he was charmed by the friendliness of the majority, did not know why he should be offensive to the husband of his 'help', and set himself to conciliate the enemy. He made a point of asking Ernest's advice about the subtle arts of skittle-play, although Mr Pewter, for example, was a more experienced and congenial tutor. This pleased Ernest, who patronized the novice gladly; and since the 'novice' soon gave promise of throwing 'a very good cheese', Ernest began to take a personal interest in the progress of his pupil. Old Mr Pewter had hitherto regarded Mr Bryan as *his* pupil, but gracefully retired. Mr Bryan contracted a sort of fever for the game, as novices often did, and having a good eye, and the native ball-game sense of the aristocracy, rapidly improved. After three weeks he was mad about skittles; said it was a grand game and promised to paint a picture of the alley. Indeed, it was the geometrical aspect of the game which had first attracted him – the long parallelogram of the 'run', the nine elliptical pins at the end under the bright light, and the squares of the thick rope-netting behind. The members were delighted by his enthusiasm. Mr Pewter said he would soon be playing for the 'Black Swan' in the matches, and Mr Fox said he should order a private 'cheese'. All the crack players had their private 'cheeses', which were as carefully preserved as Mr Hobbs's bats. But Mr Bryan thought that a private 'cheese' would be presumptuous, and continued to play with the novices' ten-and-a-half pounder.

One night Ernest came back to the barge and said, 'Got the makings of a champion, that Bryan.'

'Bryan?' said Jane, pricking up her ears.

'Bryan. Your boss.'

'Go on?' said Jane, as calmly as she could.

'Yes,' said Ernest. 'I've been taking him in hand. Throws a very nice ball now.'

'Go on?' said Jane again, afraid to say more, for she was absurdly pleased. Ernest throwing bouquets at Mr Bryan! Wonders would never cease.

Two nights later, after a long lecture from Ernest, Mr Bryan scored his first 'floorer'. A little lucky, perhaps, but there it was – down went all the nine pins, and Mr Bryan had won three chalks to Mr Pewter's two. (Mr Pewter never played quite his best against a novice, though, perfect knight, he always seemed to be trying his best.) It was a great moment, the alley rang with cheers, Mr Pewter said, 'Drinks all round, sir,' and Ernest, beaming proudly, shook his pupil by the hand, quite forgetting that he was a capitalist.

'Well done, Ernie,' said the generous Pewter. 'You'll make a champion of him yet.'

Ernest and the coming champion walked back to the wharf together, and Ernest, still warm with the evening's events, said, 'How would a cup of tea go down, Mr Bryan? You've never seen our place, I believe?'

'Thanks, I'd like to,' said Mr Bryan truthfully. He had often wondered how life was lived in that strange dwelling-place.

Ernest led the way down the ladder, jocular. 'Here, Jane, tea for two. Gentleman to view the floating hotel.'

Jane emerged in her dressing-gown, and when she saw who 'the gentleman' was, blushed scarlet, and protested 'Ernie! I'm not fit to be seen!' But Mr Bryan bowed grandly and said, 'Good evening, Mrs Higgins,' as if she were in evening-dress, which pleased Ernest. But Jane ran back to her cubbyhole and threw on a skirt and jumper.

While she was getting the tea Ernest took his guest round the barge, and showed him proudly the Underground posters. Since the destruction of the Greens' castles and hearts, Jane had lost a little of her house-pride; but the brass knobs were still polished and the white walls clean. Mr Bryan thought it was a fascinating dwelling, though he bumped his head once or twice; and he duly admired Ernest's artistic posters. .

'Funny thing,' thought Jane. 'Ernie showing him round *our* barge, with his "*We* do this" and "*We* do that". Might belong to him. No one wouldn't think he was always turning up his nose at it.' She wished bitterly that *she* could have shown Mr Bryan her barge – as it had been, with Fred's pictures and all. Still, wonders would never cease – Ernest bringing Mr Bryan home, and ever so matey. She was delighted, though she had been caught in that rag, and still felt hot and bothered. As soon as the tea was ready she slipped away to bed.

Ernest and Mr Bryan sat long over their tea and talked, and liked each other. Mr Bryan asked Ernest about his work, and Ernest told him about his ambitions and (Mr Bryan leading him on) his politics. But having forgotten, or forgiven, Mr Bryan's class, and having no other audience, he was less aggressive than usual, more human, and more convincing. He talked about unemployment and casual labour and slums, and Mr Bryan agreed that there was something wrong somewhere. Jane listened anxiously in her bed, afraid that Ernie would talk his usual talk – say something silly which would lead to a row or something awful. But, hearing with growing astonishment Ernie's reasonable tone and Mr Bryan's quiet agreement, she began to be queerly proud of the pair of them.

Ernest made some fresh tea, and talked about the mines, about Keir Hardie, and about Russia. Mr Bryan admired his enthusiasm and the spirit of it all; his artistic sense appreciated the spectacle of this liftman sitting in his shirt-sleeves on a barge gravely remodelling the structure of society. Beyond that, whether Ernest was right or wrong about the mines, he felt himself in a sort of sympathy with Ernest, for were they not both rebels against Society? Also, he was on the side of the 'producers', for he knew what the 'producers' of pictures had to put up with. But though he had leisure and money, he had never given an active thought to the reform of society, the relief of unemployment, or the future of the coal-mines, did not even know the orthodox answer to Ernest's arguments; and he felt almost ashamed. Perhaps in unconscious apology, he began to tell Ernest something about his own life, how he had rejected the silver spoon and refused to live among Society. Ernest nodded approval, and Jane listened eagerly. Encouraged, Mr Bryan continued, and found himself, to his surprise, relating to this stranger how his engagement to a Society girl had been broken off, chiefly, Ernest gathered (Mr Bryan became a little confused), because he disliked top-hats and dance-clubs. 'Flummery,' said Ernest wisely. 'That's right.' Jane, listening to this recital, became strangely excited; if he did not like girls of his own class, perhaps she had not been such a fool after all to think about him. But now she had been fool enough to marry Ernest, and that was the end of it. Mr Bryan, more and more surprised at himself, and feeling that he had said too much, was suddenly silent.

'Well, sir,' said Ernest (and that tickled Jane, for Ernest never said 'sir' to anybody), 'you ought to be one of us, and that's the truth. You're a born Socialist, that's what you are.'

'Perhaps,' said Mr Bryan. 'I've never thought much about politics.'

'Ah,' said Ernest profoundly, 'that's the trouble. That's the reason why nothing gets done.'

And then Mr Bryan, after an exchange of many compliments, and a promise that Jane and Ernest would return the call, went off to bed.

Ernest tapped gently on the door of Jane's cubbyhole. 'Awake, Jane?'

'Come in,' she said. 'Well, you're a wonder, Ernie!'

Ernest saw that he had pleased her and seized his chance.

'What about your coming along to the other room, Jane?'

'I'm nice and warm here, Ernie.'

'Come on.' The old wheedling Ernest. Oh, well, why not? She did not want to go, but certainly he had behaved very well.

'Oh, all right,' she said. 'Only you behave yourself – see?'

'You're not sore about the smacking, are you, Jane? It was only a lark.'

The subject had not been mentioned between them before, and Jane was not going to yield about that.

'Yes, I am,' she said with spirit, 'and don't you forget it.'

'All right,' said Ernest penitently, thankful for small mercies.

Jane's kisses were cold. 'A funny thing,' she thought, 'Mr Bryan being the one to bring us together again, if it's only for the one night.' For tomorrow she would go back to her cubby hole, she was determined.

*

The next morning, as she swept out the studio, Jane said, 'Well, what d'you think of the barge, Mr Bryan?'

'Very nice. Delightful. You keep it very clean.'

'You ought to have seen it before, Mr Bryan.'

'Before?'

'Before it was spoiled.'

'How d'you mean? What spoiled it?' Mr Bryan looked up from his work, caught by the intensity of her tone. He saw a face set and bitter. At the thought of that outrage she was implacable again.

'*He* did – Ernest – my husband, Mr Bryan. You see, Fred and his father painted it all for my wedding – a surprise, you see – all castles and hearts and roses, like they have on the canal, you see – and it was ever so nice. Fred can't read or write, you see, but he can paint beautiful; but then my husband don't like Fred very much – a bit jealous, you see – so we had words, and my husband lost his temper and beat me, and he scratched them out with a file. And then he put up them rotten old posters you see last night, and it isn't *half* so nice. So, you see, I was wishing you could have seen it like it was before, Mr Bryan.' And then Jane quietly began to cry.

Mr Bryan had listened with amazement to this tragical narrative. Wild and gabbled though it was, he had got the gist of the story. 'How the poor live!' he thought. All these awful things had happened in the quiet room where he had tea last night with the quiet Ernest. 'A happy home,' he had thought. Works of art destroyed by a jealous husband. It was like medieval Italy. And the vandal act had been done by the same quiet, reasonable, philanthropic Ernest who wanted to reform the world. Ernest – Jane – and then there had been something about a mad father who betted on horses – not to mention Fred, who could not read and write, but painted beautiful. He would like to meet Fred. The more he heard of these strange people, the more he was interested in them.

Meanwhile, he must stop this girl crying or there might be trouble. He put his hand on her shoulder and murmured vague words of comfort. His touch thrilled her. She dried her eyes, gulped, murmured, 'I'm sorry, Mr Bryan,' and looked up at him adoringly. Adoringly. There was no mistake about it. Once before, he remembered, she had looked at him thus, and he had not thought much of it. But now she was the wife of Ernest, with whom he had made friends only last night, and he felt himself on the edge of perilous ice.

He said, 'What's the matter, Jane? Aren't you happy? You're only just married.'

'I hate him! I hate him!' she said, with a fury which shocked him. 'He's a beast!' She clung to his arm. 'Oh, Mr Bryan –'

But fearful of more tears, or worse, he said firmly, 'Come, you mustn't talk like that,' and this steadied her.

She said, 'I'm sorry, Mr Bryan. You've been ever so kind,' and picked up her broom.

She had made a fool of herself, she thought, but she went back to the barge comforted, in a way; she had become a person to him again; he had talked to her like a person, and that was something.

She thought Ernest would be still in bed, but he was prowling about in a shirt.

He looked at her suspiciously, and said, 'What you been crying about?' She made no answer. He seized her arm and peered into her face. 'That fancy-bloke being playing any tricks?'

'Let me go,' she said. 'He's a better man than you are.'

'Answer a straight question, can't you?'

'What question?'

'What I said.'

'Well, what did you say?'

'I said, has that bloke been interfering with you?'

'No, he hasn't. He's a gentleman.'

'Gentleman!' Ernest almost spat out the odious word.

'Yes, he is; and it's a pity some I know isn't more like him. Leave go of me; I've got the potatoes to peel. And it's time you dressed yourself.'

Ernest withdrew, muttering, all his suspicions of the artist revived. When he had dressed, he sat on deck and gazed darkly at the studio. These painting blokes – Fred Green and Bryan – all tarred with the same brush, probably, if the truth was told. He would have to be careful; and yet he liked this Bryan.

A few days later, shifting some old canvases in the course of sweeping, Jane was confronted with her own face, the unfinished picture which was to have been called 'The Blush'. She blushed now to see it, but thought that it was quite 'like', and the pearl necklace looked nice. She remembered the hopes she had had then – she was going to be a famous model, her pictures would be everywhere, she would marry Mr Bryan. And then he had gone away, Ernest had taken her to Richmond, and everything had gone wrong.

Trembling, she said, 'Aren't you going to finish this, Mr Bryan?'

'What's that?' said Mr Bryan, looking up. 'Oh, that. Well, I might. I'd forgotten all about it. What happened? I went away, didn't I?'

'I wouldn't mind sitting, Mr Bryan, if you liked.'

'Oh, thanks.'

He did not sound very grateful or even interested. But then, ever since the day she cried he had been rather distant and boss-like, and she had not once felt herself 'a person'.

Mr Bryan was reflecting that he must be cautious and wise. The last few evenings Ernest Higgins had not been so friendly in the alley, and Mr Bryan had wondered why. He said, 'What about your husband?'

Jane decided instantly to lie. 'He don't mind. I've sat for several since we was married.'

'Well, we'll see.'

'It wouldn't be in the Exhibition, I suppose?'

'Might. Would you mind?' Quite an idea. Jane, if she turned out well, might provide a patch of variety among the fishing subjects.

'Not if nobody didn't know who I was,' said Jane. But really she was thinking that it would be ever so grand to be in an Exhibition. She had never seen one, but she had read about them in the *Sunday Gazette*; and sometimes there were interviews with the famous models, who had a habit of committing suicide.

There was a knock on the door, and a man's voice, 'Beg pardon?'

Ernest! What a cheek! If he was going to hang round! She would tell him off, and make sure this did not happen again. She turned 'The Blush' face to the wall, and hurried to the door.

'You're wanted,' said Ernest shortly.

Jane scowled at him, slipped out, and shut the door behind her. 'You've got a cheek,' she said.

'Here, less of that!' said Ernest. 'Mrs Raven wants you.'

Mrs Raven was waiting on the wharf. She was in a hole again. Margaret had the mumps, Florry was in the West London Hospital with chest-trouble, and she could not get a cook. Would Jane come and cook for her? A pound a week.

Jane was solicitous, but firm. She was sorry for Mrs Raven and anxious to help. But she thought quickly – cooking, illness in the house – that would mean the whole day. She could not do that and look after Mr Bryan as well, to say nothing of Ernest. Mr Bryan might get somebody else, and she would lose the job.

She told Mrs Raven that if it was a couple of hours a day charring or anything she would be glad to oblige, but not the cooking, because she was doing for Mr Bryan, and then there was her husband, 'you see.'

Mrs Raven, sighing, looked towards the studio. 'Is Mr Bryan in?' she said.

'Yes,' said Jane, in a panic. She was afraid that Mrs Raven would go to Mr Bryan and ask him to release his 'help'; and she was sadly sure that Mr Bryan would agree at once.

Mrs Raven looked towards the studio again, sighed again, hesitated, smiled sweetly, and went away.

The odd thing was that Ernest seemed to think she ought to have taken the job. 'Well, why didn't you?' he said.

'Well, I've got one job, haven't I?'

'I'd rather it was that than this – see?'

'When I was there you was always on at me to get out of it,' said Jane; and she nearly added a remark about 'domestic thraldom'.

'That was different.'

'How was it different?'

'You know very well,' said Ernest darkly.

Jane did know very well: Ernest was on the way to make trouble about Mr Bryan, and she must steer clear of that. 'All I know is,' she said, indignantly, picking up Ernest's pyjamas from the floor, 'I've got two women's jobs clearing up after you.'

'That's a wife's job, isn't it?' said Ernest. '*I* never asked you to take another, did I?' Jane was silent; another word and there would be a scene.

That Saturday they were both to go for tea to the studio – a return visit; and she hoped that this might help to keep Ernest in a good temper. The invitation had been made on the day after Mr Bryan's successful call on the *Blackbird*. Now that his suspicious animosity had returned, Ernest did not quite know why he was going to have tea with the *bourgeois* artist. Perhaps to spy out the land; and since the fatal night of the spanking his instinct now was always to avoid open or active unpleasantness. He had learned more than one lesson that night.

Ernest put on the respectable dark-blue suit which he wore for revolutionary meetings, and Jane too put on her best – the green coat with the fur, 'nude' silk stockings, pearl necklace and all.

Also, for once, she lightly powdered her face. Lily had long ago given her a 'vanity set', and taught her the mysteries of powder, but she had used it rarely, for Ernest disapproved.

'Here, what's the game?' he grumbled now.

'Better look the little lady,' she said, intently studying her appearance in the cracked looking-glass. 'I want to do you credit, don't I?'

'Well, you paint your lips my girl, and the bet's off – see?'

'No fear, Ernie,' said Jane soothingly. 'Powder's one thing, paint's another.' And indeed she agreed with Ernest that all this paint on the lips was disgusting.

'Come on, then,' said Ernest, jealously watching the long preparations. 'You don't get yourself up like this to go out with me.'

Jane realized her mistake and put away the puff. 'You never know who you'll meet at a party, do you?' she said.

'Party!' sneered Ernest. 'Anyone would think you was a "Bright Young Thing".'

They met nobody but Mr Bryan; but the party proceeded easily and pleasantly. Jane made the tea, while the two men talked skittles. Very soon they were deep in a discussion about the misdeeds of the Amateur Skittle Association, which was making new rules for the championship matches, most of them aimed, it was thought, at the Black Swan Club. Ernest found that in spite of everything he liked Mr Bryan, and liked talking to him. Mr Bryan decided that he had imagined Ernest's unfriendliness at the alley; and Jane once again enjoyed the sound of her two men (for thus she thought of them) getting on well together.

She said very little during tea – did not have much opportunity to speak; for skittles, among enthusiasts, is as rich a food for conversation as golf. Mr Bryan thought she looked surprisingly smart and attractive, and wondered, as he had wondered before, how the poor did it. After tea, from force of habit, he offered her a cigarette, and Jane, living up to her best clothes, accepted it, though she caught a disapproving glance from Ernest. 'Drat Ernest!' she thought – would he always be in the way?

'Like to have a look round the studio, Ernest?' said Mr Bryan He had been calling Ernest 'Ernest' for some time; and Ernest, democratically called him 'Bryan'.

'Thanks,' said Ernest. 'I never been in one before.' So Ernest strolled round the studio, peering at Mr Bryan's extraordinary pictures, and examining with wonder the messy paraphernalia of the painter.

'Are you going to get a new boat, Mr Bryan?' said Jane; and she and Mr Bryan talked about boats. Here, her instinct told her they were on common ground; she knew almost as much about small boats as he did, and at least could talk as confidently. Mr Bryan was thinking of buying a 'cabin-cruiser' for trips down the tide-way, and they discussed the points of his design. He thought her remarks showed sense and knowledge; and he thought her keenness delightful. At the studios and parties of his friends people were keen, not about boats, but motor-cars. He could think of no one in Bloomsbury who could handle a boat or talk about sailing so well as this little 'daily help' of his. Funny.

The sense of 'class' slipped away from Jane; she felt herself a person again; and both of them almost forgot Ernest, prowling about in the shadows at the back. Ernest kept quiet; from time to time he looked over his shoulder at Jane's eager face or scowled at the sound of her lively laugh; but he felt that he was not wanted, and bided his time. He was almost sure now that there had been something 'between' these two, and if they kept quiet they might give themselves away.

Mr Bryan said something about the canal, and Jane said impulsively, 'I saw you up there, Mr Bryan!' She had never dared to confess this before.

'Where was that?' said Mr Bryan.

'Do you remember the lock at Stoke Bruerne? You put your head into the cabin and you played dominoes with Mr Green.'

Mr Bryan remembered putting his head into a dozen cabins.

There were eager questions, explanations; and he remembered seeing a face which had reminded him of Jane. 'But why didn't you sing out?' he said in astonishment.

'You was with your friends,' said Jane shyly, and that 'class' feeling which had kept her silent came back as she spoke, and she saw again the picture of the lovely girl laughing on the house-boat roof.

'But how absurd!' said Mr Bryan, with a note of disappointment which sounded so genuine that it thrilled her. She was at her ease again. He asked her about the life of the canal, and what it was like to sleep in those little cabins.

She said, 'It's a bit stuffy, Mr Bryan, 'specially sharing a bed with Mrs Green – that's Fred's mother.'

He asked her more about that, and laughed, and admired her pluck. Certainly, he thought, this girl is a character. Jane thought happily, 'I shall always be a "person" to him after this, surely.' Here they were, talking away, just like old friends. And Ernest, scowling at a picture of two anchors and a hurricane-lantern, thought that all this talk about meetings and cabins was a bit too thick. And if they were as thick as this in front of him, how thick, he asked himself, might they be when he was not there?

Now they were back at the 'cabin-cruiser' again. 'Blast all boats and barges!' thought Ernest. Mr Bryan talked about anchorages and Canvey Island, and Jane said she had always wanted to sail down the river and see Canvey Island. 'Throwing herself at him, the bitch!' thought Ernest. And then he heard her say gaily, 'I'll be your cabin-boy, Mr Bryan!'

This was too much. Ernest turned sharply, thinking with reason that it was time for some attention to be paid to Ernest Higgins. And as he turned his foot caught three or four canvases standing face to the wall, and two of them clattered over. Ernest looked down in confusion and found himself gazing at an unfinished por-trait of his wife, with, so far as he could see, nothing on. So far as he could see – for most of the thing, fortunately, was still shadowy and vague; and, hot and angry as Ernest was, he was not so angry as the finished picture might have made him. Indeed, at the mo-ment, anger was not uppermost in his mind, but embarrassment; it would look silly to be found staring at the thing; and some sense of delicacy told him that he could not say anything about it here and now, when he was the artist's guest. Besides, he had always known that Jane had sat before they were married, and as long as she had not sat since he had no right to say anything to Mr Bryan perhaps. He would say nothing now, and say a lot to Jane later. And with some such jumble of thoughts he picked up the picture and hid its face.

The clatter had broken the spell of the yachting conversation. Mr Bryan said, 'Hullo, what's up?' crossed to the door, and turned on more light. And Jane came to Ernest, conscious suddenly that much of that conversation might have displeased her husband. Also, she remembered very clearly where she had concealed that particular canvas, as she thought, out of harm's way. From Ernest's position she feared that he had chosen to upset that one particular picture, and the one fierce look which he gave her told her that something was certainly up.

But Ernest, strange man, was apologizing nicely to Mr Bryan, thanking him warmly, and saying that they must be getting home. Ernest was a puzzle.

At that moment there was a heavy knock on the door, and a babel of cheerful voices outside. The door opened and four people rushed in, laughing – two young women and two young men, the women in evening coats and the men with the scarves and stiff collars of evening-dress showing above their overcoats.

Jane, at the sight of them, felt small and cold; for the first of the two girls was the lovely creature with the cloud of hair who had sat on the roof of the house-boat with Mr Bryan and laughed.

'Sorry, my dear,' said this vision; 'but we've come to *extract* you. *Definitely*, darling. You can't stay here and die among your *fantastic* pictures! I've *no* rehearsal, and you're coming *out*!' And then, suddenly seeing Jane and Ernest, she smiled divinely and said, 'Oh, I *beg* your pardon. I thought you were always alone.'

Mr Bryan said, smiling, 'Granted, Moon of my Night,' and then, with ease, introduced the four to Ernest and Jane. Ernest was no less abashed than Jane, but it was against his sturdy principles to show it. He stepped forward and strongly shook hands with each of the newcomers, embarrassing all of them, and paining two. Jane smiled timidly, said, 'Pleased to meet you,' and did not move.

Only one of the names reached her, and that was the name of the cloud of hair. Miss Fay Meadows, an actress, it seemed. This vision was taking off her fur coat; and with her white frock, her lustrous eyes and ivory shoulders, her glossy hair and brilliant smile, her voice, her pearls, her assurance, she dazzled and stupefied Mrs Ernest Higgins.

Fay Meadows was slender, but she seemed to fill the room. All the happy glow about boats, which had survived even the freezing glance of Ernest, departed from Jane when Fay Meadows looked at her with those teasing, beautiful, commanding eyes. And Ernest, who, angry or no, had a moment earlier been easy and confident before his *bourgeois* host (man-to-man-and-I'm-as-good-as-you-are), had utterly collapsed. The strong air of 'class' oppressed and stifled him; the pearls, the dresses, the white skins, the stiff shirts, the superior voices enraged but frightened him.

He said, 'Good night, sir,' and he and Jane crept awkwardly out, feeling, as Jane afterwards expressed it to Lily, like 'two balloons gone bust'.

Even before they had carefully closed the door, the voices broke out behind them. 'Who's your friend, Gordon?' '*Delicious* people!' 'Is that a model, or what?' 'My dear, she's *exquisite*!' And then Mr Bryan's voice, very stern, '*Manners, manners!* My God, have you got no manners?' Mr Bryan, in fact, was very angry, and said more than that, but Ernest did not hear it.

'Blast them!' said Ernest (but in stronger terms), and hurried Jane across the wharf, out of the reach of those mocking voices.

For a little they were united in the common shock of deflation; but while Jane got ready the evening meal they had time to think. Jane wondered first of all what exactly was meant by 'exquisite', and, if it was a nice word, whether the speaker had meant it nicely. Ernest regretted first of all that he had broken the habit of a lifetime and the rules of a Socialist by suddenly addressing Mr Bryan as 'sir', simply because a lot of good-for-nothing poops in evening-dress had come in.

Even now, to his surprise, he was not ferociously angry with Mr Bryan, in spite of his class, his picture, and his offensive friends. In spite of everything, Ernest still had the idea that Mr Bryan was a decent bloke, one of the very rare specimens of the worth-while *bourgeois.* After all, there was no swank about him. He had introduced Jane and Ernest as if they were members of his family, and he had ticked off those squawking friends the moment they squawked. But Jane! It was all coming back. Jane, his wife, who had thrown herself at the man's head! Cabin-boy on his boat, or something. Sitting in the nude. All Ernest's original anger returned.

He stood up and went to Jane, who was frying bacon and thinking of Mr Bryan, and, gripping her arm, he said fiercely, 'Here, my girl! I seen that picture tonight.'

'Let go of me. What picture?'

'You know what I mean. You in your birthday suit.'

'Let go of me. What of it? That was donkey's years ago.'

'Before we was married?' said Ernest, suspiciously, not loosening his grip.

'Yes, of course!' snapped Jane. 'I told you about it, didn't I?'

'Swear it? On your Bible oath?'

'Oh, chuck it! The bacon's burning.'

'Do you swear you've not stripped for anyone since we was married?'

'*No, I tell you! Will you let go?*' screamed Jane in a sudden fury.

Ernest let go, and stepped back. He had learned to respect the tiger in his wife. But this time he was not going to accept defeat without a struggle. He said deliberately, 'Well, I told you before — if I find anything I'll *kill* that bloke.'

He did not mean it; he did not at the moment feel at all anxious to kill Mr Bryan, but he very much wanted to frighten and hurt his wife, and he intended this to be the last word, for the bacon was ready.

But Jane took the frying-pan from the stove and turned and faced him, frying-pan in hand; and she said with cold intensity, furious and fearful for her Mr Bryan, 'Well, let me tell *you*, Ernest Higgins, if ever you say that again, I'll do for *you*!'

The frying-pan swayed up and down in her trembling grasp, and they looked at each other for many seconds, appalled; for each of them realized, in a blinding flash of conviction, that she had meant what she said.

'Tea's ready,' said Jane at last, and moved to the table; and Ernest followed without a word.

They were both shocked by what she had said; and Jane was so shocked that after tea she asked Ernest to take her to the pictures. And they went to the Blue Halls and saw a picture called 'One Night of Love'. And Jane thought about Mr Bryan.

20

POTTY

JANE, looking at 'One Night of Love' and lying awake afterwards, confessed to herself that she was mad about Mr Bryan – just potty. Not even Fay Meadows, not even the scene with Ernest, had cured her; and in the cold light of Sunday morning she was as potty as before. Last night she had seen on the screen, not Fairbanks, but Bryan. This morning she sang as she made Ernest's tea (to Ernest's annoyance), because within an hour she would be making tea for Bryan. She glanced at the *Sunday Gazette*, dropped through the hatch by Mr Peacock's boy, and the first name she saw was Bryan – not her Bryan, but still, a Bryan. She ran across the wharf, and the sea-gulls circling over the barge made a noise like 'Bryan! Bryan!' She pulled up the blinds, and looked over her shoulder with excitement to see if the beloved person was awake. She trembled as she took him his tea, and by accident his hand touched hers. She looked down at him, and admired his blue silk pyjamas, and said, 'What for breakfast, Mr Bryan?' and blushed.

The beloved gentleman said, 'Nothing, thank you,' and yawned wearily; for the beloved gentleman had a headache. Fay Meadows and her friends had dragged him to a party, mixed his drinks, and kept him up late. He was angry with himself and them.

'Jane,' he said, 'I'll never go to a party again.'

'Didn't you enjoy yourself, Mr Bryan?' she said.

'No,' he said emphatically; and 'One for you, Miss Meadows!' she thought. But he, too, thought of that lady, and added, 'Well, I did in a way,' and sipped his tea reflectively.

'Late hours do nobody no good,' she said, in what Lily called her 'bossing' voice.

'You're perfectly right, Jane,' he said meekly.

Something was worrying him. She longed to mother him, to sit on the bed and stroke his hair; but she said, 'What about lunch, Mr Bryan?'

'By the way,' he said, sitting up suddenly, 'you and your husband shouldn't have run away like that. My friends didn't frighten you, I hope?'

All the evening the thought had worried him that his less sensitive friends had behaved rudely and might have angered the difficult Ernest.

'Quite all right, Mr Bryan. It was ever so nice.'

He wished that she would not so often say 'ever so'; but he asked anxiously, 'Your husband didn't think they were rude?' He did not know how much they had heard from the wharf.

'What an idea, Mr Bryan!'

'That's good. I'm lunching in town.'

'Damn her eyes!' she thought.

But it had been warming to hear those anxious questions. Even Fay Meadows could not make him utterly forget her, it seemed, thought the potty Jane. All this fitted in with her plans.

Plans? Not exactly. But all night her mind had fluttered like a frenzied moth round Mr Bryan, exhausting and hurting itself; and from these mad gyrations some kind of purpose had emerged. She did not quite know what she hoped, or even what she wanted; she knew only that she worshipped the man, class or no class, and would like to be his companion and slave for ever. At half past eleven the visions were romantic: she was cabin-boy in the 'cabin-cruiser', and they sailed through the dark night down the river and out to sea; she wore white trousers and a yachting-cap like Mr Gandy of the Sailing Club. About midnight she was imagining a Night of Love – Oriental, on the lines of the film; the executioner was to chop off their heads at dawn, but till then she had Mr Bryan to herself, together with palms and fountains, roof-gardens and starry skies, plentiful attendants and goblets of wine. At half past twelve she was married to Mr Bryan – why not? – he would love her in the end, if she had half a chance. They lived in Park Lane (wherever that was), or else in a yacht. Had he not been disappointed not to see her on the canal? Had he not been quite, quite different at the tea-party, noticed her clothes, looked into her eyes, laughed at what she said, promised to take her for a sail in his boat? He did not like these classy girls, had refused to marry one; he did not like these smart parties where they kept late hours. It was simple girls, like Jane Higgins, he liked best. Perhaps, if the truth were told, he loved her already, but did not dare to say so, there were so many people in the way. '*Bryan, Man of Honour, Fights Back His Passion*' – that would explain a lot. There was this Fay Meadows, of course, always hanging about him. But she, Jane, would deal with Fay Meadows. Actress, was she? Well, her name was never in the *Sunday Gazette*. What was she, after all, but a little bit of fluff? ... At one o'clock Jane was still busy humbling and routing the insignificant Miss Meadows. At that luminous hour, in the absence of Miss Meadows, the road was clear and easy. '*A Girl of the People.*' At one-five the '*Smart Adventuress*' was humbled.

She had made an impression at the tea-party, and she must follow that up. The picture was the thing – make him get on with it, Ernest or no Ernest. If he got worked up about it, as he had been before, anything might happen. Might be the 'Picture of the Year' (whatever that was), and he would owe it all to her. Besides, sitting to him, she would be even with Fay Meadows and her fine clothes. She had no furs and white frocks, but she was as good as Fay in her birthday. She shouldn't wonder if Fay was fat round the middle – flabby, like Lily. At half past one the picture was finished. To-morrow she would ask him about sitting. Mornings. Next week Ernest was on the morning-shift, and this must be done quickly, before Ernest made more unpleasantness.

Ernest! She had almost forgotten Ernest. What was the use of making plans? What was the use of Mr Bryan loving her? Ernest would still be in the way, putting his oar in, making scenes. Would Ernest always be in the way? All her life? What was that awful thing she had said to him: 'I'll do for you!' So she would too if he lifted a finger to Mr Bryan. If only Ernest was out of the way, how simple everything would be! Lily could come back. See Fred again. Marry Mr Bryan the moment he spoke. But Ernest was there, snoring in the other cabin. Half-asleep, her head whirling, from half past one to two Jane eliminated Ernest. Shocking thoughts – mad thoughts – irresponsible thoughts of the night. There had been a good murder in the papers recently. Husband poisoned – wife and lover in the dock. The lover was to be hanged; they had let the woman off, though everyone agreed that she was the villain of the piece. Both of them were popular heroes; crowds collected at the prison-gates; tomorrow the *Sunday Gazette* was to publish the life-stories of the two of them. Nobody was to publish the life-story of the murdered man. By all accounts, Jane thought, he was rather like Ernest – a nagger, a nuisance, in the way. The other two had had a romantic passion, and this man had made trouble. Most people in the Black Swan thought he had got what he asked. She could never use poison – too slow; or explosives, or knives – too loud, too messy. Coo! whatever was she thinking? But the thoughts rambled on, impossible to stop. Here on the river it would be easy. Ernest could not swim. One push on a dark night, high tide, and a strong tide, and Ernest was out of the way. Christmas! what was she thinking? She jumped out of bed, sponged her face, and stared at herself in the cracked looking-glass, horrified. Was this the Jane Bell who had lectured Lily and tried to keep her straight?

Shocking thoughts – mad, uncontrollable, irresponsible thoughts of the night! She shook them out of her head. But in the morning there was left still a small, vague residue of purpose: she meant somehow to capture Mr Bryan, to what end, to what degree, to what extremity and risk she knew not. Somehow he must love her, and that was all. And it was no use to sit still and do nothing. There had been a piece in the paper about that, by that Mr Douglas, who knew all about Love. She had cut it out and put it in her bag:

'We should not wait for Love to come to us. We should go out and search for it, and let it work its miracle in our heart.

'Without Love the soul is a desert. If you keep Love alive in it, nothing can harm you. I am sure that Love is the quintessence of the soul. A little Love keeps the half-dead soul alive.'

That was it; her soul was half-dead without Mr Bryan. She would not wait for his love: she would go out and search for it.

So now she said meekly, 'I could sit for you tomorrow morning, Mr Bryan, if you like.'

Mr Bryan thought, 'Damn the girl! I don't want to paint her to-morrow – meant to finish those bollards.' But she seemed so set upon it – wanted the money perhaps; and he felt so kindly to-wards her, especially since yesterday, she was such an interesting, friendly little waif, that he thought, 'Oh, well . . .' It would be a change from bollards.

The next morning, therefore, when Ernest was safe in the bowels of Down Street, Jane sat on the couch again, and posed for 'The Blush'. She did not blush now, but she trembled and her heart raced as she held the cloak back. Nothing happened, on that or any other day. She did not faint; Mr Bryan did not come within ten feet of her, did not say anything to suggest that he was fighting back his passion; did not say anything much, except when she rested, and then he was kind, but formal. He did not even speak of her figure, as he had in the old days. She had expected something, she did not know what; but she was disappointed. Mr Bryan could have told her that to most artists the human body is only one kind of raw material, not much more exciting than the forms of flowers or the bodies of fishes. Like the doctors, they are spared the general illusions about the undraped female form. Indeed, Jane had almost learned that lesson herself from her other employers; none of whom had shown more interest in her than they would have found in a naked antelope or a very graceful daffodil. All this she had often, in vain, tried to explain to Ernest. But they were stodgy old blokes not like Mr Bryan; things being what they were, she thought, he might have been different, though she could not say how; but he was not.

Still, the main purpose was achieved, for he 'got worked-up' about the picture, and asked her to sit every morning that week; and she was content to sit there all the morning and look at him, giving the best that she possessed to his work. 'With my body I thee worship,' she thought on the first day – and how could any-one do that rather difficult thing better than she was doing it?

It was a dangerous game; for any evening in the alley Mr Bryan might drop some remark to Ernest which would give the show away. It was the week before Christmas; on Friday the Christmas Handicap Championship Cup was to be played for, and all the club were busily practising in the evenings. The Cup was now on the shelf of the *Blackbird*, for Ernest had won it the last two years, and, if he won it again, could keep it. All the week Ernest was restless and moody. He did not know where he was, what he suspected, and whether really he suspected anything. His pride told him that he should assert himself, do something; but Jane seemed to have lost all sense of discipline and obedience – had as little respect for his authority as he had for the authority of the capitalist laws – and if he went to Mr Bryan he might only make a fool of himself. Things got about so in this neighbourhood – he did not want to be the laughing-stock of the Black Swan. Still, something must be up, Jane was so bright and chirpy all of a sudden; and it was nothing to do with him – he was sure of that. She seemed to have a secret joy, was always singing, always singing that maddening song about her heart standing still, or else a song about 'My Big Man'.

On the Monday Ernest decided that the best thing to do was to make a clean break. That had succeeded in Fred Green's case. Fred had never been near the barge again. But then, could he be sure of that? How did he know what went on when he was on the night shift, safely shut up at Down Street? The barge was not like a house in a row where the neighbours saw who came and went and immediately reported it to everybody else. The gate in the fence could not be seen from a single window. Perhaps that Fred *had* been prowling about – perhaps all this singing was about him. 'Big Man', eh? On Tuesday afternoon Ernest strolled along to the creek and inquired if the Greens' boats had tied up there recently. No, said the wharfman, not been there for a month.

That evening, when he came back from the alley, Jane was washing stockings and crooning to herself 'My Heart Stood Still'.

'Can't you get another song?' asked Ernest irritably.

'That one's good enough for me, thanks,' said Jane cheerfully. 'How's the skittles?'

'Mustn't grumble. I hit three nines – just missed the "Roll of Fame".'

Jane did not congratulate or condole, but said, 'How's Mr Bryan doing?'

'Might be worse.'

'Got any chance of the Cup?'

'Him – or me?'

'Him, I meant. I know *you* have, silly.'

'Well, he's got a good handicap.'

Jane squeezed out a stocking and began 'My Big Man'. Ernest made his decision. 'See here, Jane,' he said, 'after this week you got to stop working for that bloke – see?'

Jane stood up and faced him. 'You've got a cheek! What next, I wonder?'

'I mean what I say. Better give him a week's notice tomorrow.'

'And what for, may I ask?'

'Never you mind. Them's my orders.'

Jane was pale with anger, and too angry to be cautious. She knew she was a fool to make a fuss; but that was the worst of being potty about the man – the moment his name was mentioned her heart flew into her mouth, and gave her away. 'And what's it got to do with you who I work for, Ernest Higgins?'

'I'm your husband.'

'That don't give you the right to boss me. I'm enancipated, aren't I?' (Jane had never got this word, one of Ernest's favourites, quite right – she had a vague notion that it celebrated the life-work of some big Socialist woman called Nancy.)

'You're my wife.'

'Well, I'm not going to be your bond-slave – see? You told me women had a right to earn their own living, same as men. If you think I'm going to be beholden to you for my daily bread –'

'You can go to the Ravens',' said Ernest, disdaining the economic argument.

'I'll go where I choose – see?'

'You'll do what I say,' said Ernest doggedly, though he had very little confidence in that prediction.

'Think I'm going back to that basement? Not me!'

'All right then,' said Ernest. 'I'll go to the bloke himself.'

'What d'you mean?' said Jane, wary at last.

'If you won't give the bloke his notice I'll tell him he's got to sack you – see?'

'Just you dare!' said Jane, advancing a step, white, quiet, her hands clenched, for this was a real menace. If Ernest asked for that Mr Bryan would certainly agree – he must; and that would be the end of everything – no more calling, no more morning tea, no more tidying and folding clothes; she would be back where she had been, a hundred miles away. 'You do that, Ernie, and you and me will part – see? I can earn my own living, thank you.'

'You're potty!' said Ernest, shaken by her rage.

'Potty or not potty,' said Jane, 'you leave me alone, or you can clear out off of this barge – see?'

Ernest was silent, though he hated to be reminded that his home did not belong to him. He was afraid of this furious, loud-speaking Jane who had sprung up since the night of the spanking, and now popped out on the smallest provocation. He had an uneasy feeling that she might be as bad as her word and leave him. Seemed to have no sense of duty or obedience. A damn sight too independent. Downright rebellion. It did not occur to Ernest that he had been busily implanting in his wife the spirit of independence and the mood of rebellion ever since he had first hugged her under the oak-tree and denounced the capitalist bosses. But there it was – and for three days he brooded over his threat and did nothing.

Jane thought that she had won. It was surprising; but it seemed that when it came to threats and violent words she could go one better than Ernest. He wanted her, and she didn't want him – that was the secret of it. She enjoyed the sensation of power; and that night in bed she saw herself as '*The Tigress at Bay*'.

But she thought with wonder, as she had thought before, of the change which had happened to Jane Bell. The gentle, 'pi-face' Jane, who had always thought of others – of her father, of Lily, of Mrs Higgins – who had been shocked by Lily's lying and goings-on – where was she now? Lying herself, scheming, shouting, flying into tempers, fighting for what she wanted, not caring what Ernest wanted, thinking only of herself. Ah, but it was not fair. If she had ever had Love's Bliss it would have been different. If Mr Bryan had loved her she would never have thought of herself, and even now she would do anything he asked, go to prison for him, throw herself off Hammersmith Bridge. Did she not, even now, almost like washing-up for him? And if she had married Fred she would have been a good wife to him; but Ernest had done the dirty, and he must pay for it. As for Mr Bryan, she was potty, and no mistake. Perhaps there was more of her father in her than she had thought. For all she knew Mr Bryan was engaged to be married – tomorrow he might leave Hammersmith and never come back – yet here she was, risking everything, deceiving her husband, lying to Mr Bryan, going all out for an outside chance – yes, that was like Dad.

Poor Dad! He and his betting had been the cause of all their troubles, in a way.

The next morning, in spite of these reflections, she asked Mr Bryan not to mention the picture to Ernest, because she wanted it to be a surprise. (When it was finished, she thought, she would tell him the truth, and then he would keep it dark until the Exhibition. Ernest would never see it at the Exhibition.)

Mr Bryan was thinking hard about his painting, and said shortly, 'Yes, of course'; and then, fearing that he had been rude, he said that he hoped Jane was coming to the Christmas Championship on Friday. And Jane sat there, holding back the cloak, a little cold but contented, a little stiff but at peace, because she could gaze at Mr Bryan with her eyes and serve and worship him with her body, and because he had expressed the hope that she would be in a certain place at a certain time. Nor did she once that morning regretfully say to herself, 'I've told another whopper.'

On Friday afternoon at about five o'clock, having washed and dressed after his afternoon nap, Ernest resolutely crossed the wharf and knocked at the studio door. He had decided at last for action; he must be the master at all costs.

Mr Bryan sat reading by the stove, a reading-lamp beside him; there was no other light in the studio. 'Come in, Ernest,' he said, and stood up.

Ernest, wound up for war though he was, could not suppress the disturbing thought that, after all, he rather liked the bloke. In the presence of this quiet and friendly *bourgeois* he had not, on the barge, been able to employ his customary tone and vocabulary, even upon general political matters; and now, most strangely, he found that his ruthless ultimatum was, by some hidden force, being watered down to a polite request. He could not say, 'Bryan, you're a dirty dog! Anyway, I mean to keep my wife out of your reach.' Strangest of all, he was compelled to say 'sir'.

He said, 'Mr Bryan, sir, if you'll excuse me, I want you to give my wife her notice.'

'Yes, Ernest? Anything the matter?'

'She's doing too much, Mr Bryan, not looking the thing. She won't give it up on her own, because she likes the work, you see. So I thought if it was to come from you, sir.... It don't matter about the money, I can look after her.' Here a faint note of the Ernest pride sounded.

'Of course, Ernest,' said Mr Bryan. 'She can leave whenever you like. I hope I've not overworked her. I'll be sorry to lose her – she's looked after me perfectly; but of course –'

'Much obliged, I'm sure, Mr Bryan, and sorry to put you out.' Ernest had a queer sensation that the interview was quite unnecessary, that he had been making mountains out of molehills. Thus men go to the doctor complaining of violent pains, and while the doctor examines them can feel no pain at all.

But there was a second chapter to the lesson he had prepared, and he stumbled on, like a poor speaker who has learned his speech by heart and cannot stop, though he knows that there is now no point in it.

'There's another thing, Mr Bryan, if you'll excuse the liberty.' He paused. But this was not at all the way he had rehearsed it; there was to have been a swift, sharp question – nothing else.

'Yes, Ernest?'

'When we was married, Mr Bryan, I told Jane she wasn't to sit no more for artists, not in the nude, you see.' He paused again. 'She hasn't been sitting for you, sir, has she?'

This, the grand inquiry, was to have been a challenge, a declaration of war; it was uttered almost in the tones of apology.

Mr Bryan had been thinking quickly. So the girl had lied to him, damn her! Deliberately – God knew why. He detested lies, but he could not let her down, that was clear. To him the notion that painting from the figure was a kind of vice, or the cause of vice, was ridiculous; but he knew that that was a common opinion, and in a young, possessive, and jealous husband it must be respected. He must take the man very seriously, and, liar or not, protect the girl.

He said gravely, 'No, Ernest. Of course, she sat to me a long time ago –'

'That's right, Mr Bryan; I know all about that. You'll excuse my speaking, only I thought perhaps you might think of giving her the job again. Well, I dare say it don't seem much to you, sir, but to a man in my position it don't seem very nice, you see.'

'Of course, Ernest! I quite understand.' Mr Bryan admired Ernest then, he was so simple and genuine. But he saw the other's eyes beginning to wander round the room, and he remembered that 'The Blush' was still sitting on the easel, shiny and wet with fresh paint. It was in the shadow against the wall, it was twenty feet away from Ernest – but there it was. What to do? Put a bold face on it and show him the thing? Say he had finished it without a model? Use Jane's own lie, and say it was intended for a 'surprise'? How much would he believe? Damn it! thought Mr Bryan, why do people tell lies? But here and now, he decided, he did not dare to tell the truth.

He said quickly, before Ernest's eyes had reached the fatal spot. 'See you tonight at the alley, Ernest?'

'You bet, sir. I want that Cup for keeps.' The wandering eyes returned, and Ernest held out his hand. 'Well, good-bye and thanks, Mr Bryan. You'll pardon me, sir, if it's all the same to you, but I'd sooner you didn't say anything to the wife in regards to this interview.' Ernest's vocabulary generally expanded with his confidence. 'I'd sooner it came from you, if you'll pardon the liberty. What I mean, perhaps you could say you was compelled to make a change, or something of that?'

'Good God, more lies!' thought Mr Bryan. But he said, 'Very well, Ernest. Good-bye. And all the best tonight!'

'Thanks! And the same to you, sir. Good-bye.' They shook hands, and respected each other. Ernest turned to go and Mr Bryan stepped politely before him to open the door. And as Ernest turned his eyes fell upon the dim and distant painting of his wife.

Mr Bryan's back was turned, and Ernest paused for a second. He could not be sure. It looked like the picture he had seen at the tea-party, but now there was so much more of it that he could not be sure. That sense of delicacy which even his politics had not been able to destroy forbade him to stand and stare. He gave the thing the benefit of the doubt and passed on.

Outside, he thought, 'Shiny, fresh paint, new work; but these artists have plenty of models.' And Mr Bryan had acted like a sport – straight as a die, that bloke. But if that was so, Ernest asked himself, what was he making the fuss about? Ernest, almost for the first time, confessed that he was in a muddle. Well, anyhow, he had put a spoke in Jane's wheel. If Bryan was above suspicion, she wasn't. He had made a clean break, that was the thing. Teach her a lesson, perhaps. Teach her not to throw herself at gentlemen's heads. It would be one in the eye for Jane. And he, Ernest, would know nothing about it. He would say, 'What did I tell you? Class is class.'

Mr Bryan stood in front of the perilous painting, thought it was good, and cursed it. It was not so simple making friends with the poor. A difficult, dangerous business. Why had the little devil lied to him? Even now her husband might drag the truth out of her; and then where would he, Mr Bryan, be? It was all so silly.

And tomorrow he had to give his little 'help' notice. That was a bore. He realized that he would miss her – not as a model, but as a 'help'. Not posing in the sensational nude, but messing about in an apron with a broom. But why had the little devil lied? What was the point?

He had half a mind to destroy the wretched picture. But he decided against this. It was all so silly.

21

THE CHRISTMAS CUP

'ALL that hard work, and then a tie-up!' said Mrs Pewter scornfully.

'Don't be carbolic, missis,' said her sunny husband. 'We didn't do it a-purpose, did we?'

'Who's tied, then?' Mrs Pewter wanted her bed.

'Young Ernie and Mr Bryan's tied. Playing off directly.'

Jane sat up – almost woke up. She was not quite asleep, but she was drowsy with tobacco-smoke and one glass of port wine; she was weary of skittles, and, like Mrs Pewter, wanted her bed. It was half past ten, and, like most of the wives, she had sat dutifully on the narrow bench since eight o'clock, dutifully admiring the men's play, and dutifully laughing at their jokes. As a spectacle the Championship was disappointing – for it was a handicap affair, all against all, as in medal-play at golf; the handicaps were secret, and no one knew how anyone was placed until the last man had played his seven 'frames' and the figures were worked out.

'Too much figuring for me,' said Mrs Pewter. She and Jane preferred the team matches between the clubs – eight straightforward single combats. Bert beat Bill, and Ernie beat Albert, and you knew where you were, and even a woman could add up the 'chalks' on the board and tell which was winning, the Black Swan or the Man-in-the-Moon.

But this was a monotonous business – and solemn. Sir William Briggs, the Member, who had presented the Cup, was present, and nearly all were on their best behaviour. Mr Fox, who had had too many old and milds, made funny remarks from the crowd by the door, but even he was always suppressed with an indignant 'Stroke, please!' 'Might be in church,' whispered Mrs Pewter once to Jane, and drew a stern, 'Stroke, please, ladies!' from her own husband. Man after man stepped forward 'into the arena', serious and determined. Time after time old Harry, the fat 'sticker-up', set up the fallen pins, and skilfully trundled the heavy cheese back to the player. There were thirty competitors for the Cup, and each of them played seven 'frames'; two hundred and ten times Jane had stared expectantly at the unbroken nine and thought that it looked easy to knock them all down. The ladies had to sit sideways with their legs tucked close against the bench, for the alley was narrow, and no waving ankle must distract the thrower's eyes. Jane was stiff, sleepy, and bored. The men, when they were bored, stepped outside and went to the bar; but the ladies were assumed to be thoroughly enjoying themselves until they stated the contrary.

Ernest had not played his best, and, Jane thought, could not have won the Cup. He had been nervous and uncertain, and at the interval for refreshments he muttered to her that he had played like a cow and had no chance. Jane was sorry for him, for he had set his heart, she knew, on winning the Cup 'for keeps'. Mr Bryan also had disappointed her, though he had not disgraced himself; several times his first throw had promised big things: he would knock down seven and leave an easy 'double', knock down only one of the inviting pair and go 'three' instead of 'two'. 'Bad luck,' murmured Jane every time; but nice Mr Rogers, the sewer-man, shook his head and whispered, 'Lost his acc'racy. Too much of a hurry.'

Mr Bryan was indeed in a hurry, having been stricken by 'nerves'. Nothing in his cricket career had been so alarming as this occasion. He had never seen the little building packed with people, had never played skittles before an audience – and this was an audience of experts. Most of the men there had been skittle players for fifteen or twenty years, and many of the ladies knew as much of the fine points of the game as he did. And there they were, only a few feet away – so close, so critical (he thought), judging every movement, eyeing his clothes, staring at the strange gentleman who thought he could step in and play a workingman's game as well as working men after a few months' practice. He felt himself an intruder, as conspicuous as a gold-fish in a simple bucket of water. Potts and Latimer, the artists, were somewhere in the crowd, and there was Sir William – but they were not trying to throw this uncontrollable cheese at those immovable pins. He was making a fool of himself; they were laughing at him by the door, and he had better get it over as quickly as possible. Thank Heaven – the one comfort – Fay Meadows and her friends had not turned up, as they had threatened.

Mr Bryan misjudged the audience, who were not laughing at him, and wished only to see him do well. When the ordeal was three-parts done he heard a veteran at the back say, 'Throws a beautiful ball, don't he?' and he finished with a better confidence. But his score, thought Jane, must be much lower than Ernest's, though, as a 'novice', he would receive a generous handicap. His final throw knocked down eight pins (next door to a 'floorer'), and she joined in the clapping, as pleased and proud as if she had been his mother.

Then Mr Pewter announced the interval. In came the jugs of tawny ale, the bread and cheese, the bowls of gherkins and onions, and, special treat, tongue sandwiches for the ladies. Mr Bryan, reassured by the kindly comments of everyone upon his play, handed round the onions, and presently found himself offering the onions to Jane. 'Topsy-turvy, Mr Bryan,' she said. 'Fancy you waiting on *me*!' and she took an onion, because he had offered it. Then he remembered his conversation with Ernest, and he thought, 'Oh, Lord, that's what's been worrying me!' She condoled with him on his 'bad luck'. He noticed what fine little teeth she had as she nibbled at her onion; and while they talked, he wondered whether he should warn her that he had lied to Ernest because she had lied to him, and now she must be ready to lie again. What a business! Would it be safe? He looked quickly round the chattering crowd and suddenly saw Ernest. Ernest was standing ten feet away, a plate of sandwiches in his hand, not offering sandwiches to the ladies, but staring intently at his wife, as if even above the noise he hoped to hear what she was saying.

And Ernest's expression shocked, chilled, and alarmed Mr Bryan. 'My God,' he thought, 'this is serious!' The face was unmistakable. It was the bitter face of a jealous man. 'But, my God!' thought Mr Bryan, 'is the fool jealous of *me*?' This was too much. 'Damn them both!' thought Mr Bryan, and without another word to Jane he stalked away and offered an onion to Sir William Briggs.

Jane was thinking how nice it was to be talking to him like this, on equal terms like, without any master and servant business; and at his sudden disappointing departure she looked about her in surprise, and she too saw the face of Ernest. And she scowled at Ernest, which did not improve matters.

Sir William Briggs, M.P., was speaking with enthusiasm of this kind of gathering; he said that the pub was one of the few places – perhaps the only place – where the classes could meet on equal terms, easy and natural, with no class nonsense. Mr Bryan took an onion and heartily agreed; but he was thinking, 'My God, is the fool jealous of *me*!' Was he, the Hon. George Gordon Bryan, really suspected of a common intrigue with a servant-girl? If so, much was explained – everything was explained. Ernest's extraordinary visit, the girl's ridiculous lying. But what a situation! Mr Bryan really did agree with Sir William Briggs. He believed in pubs generally, and in the Black Swan particularly. He liked and admired these simple straightforward, friendly, hard-working people. In this pub, in this alley he had felt himself, for the first time, genuinely, though distantly, in touch with the people of England. He had enjoyed their companionship with gratitude and a kind of humility. And now was it all to be spoiled by a foolish fellow ridiculously jealous about his comic little wife? Worse – a man who had looked at him like that was capable of making a scene, causing a scandal! Imagine Mr Pewter's face! Well, he would certainly give the girl the sack in the morning – willingly – good riddance! He thought, as Ernest had thought, probably she was the one to blame. And yet – she was a pathetic, interesting little thing. What a business! It was not so easy making friends with the poor.

Sir William Briggs said that if the upper classes were compelled by law to visit a pub twice a week there would be a lot less Bolshevism; and Mr Bryan heartily agreed.

After the interval Jane had had no more interest in the proceedings; but now, hearing that Ernest and Mr Bryan had tied for first place (after handicap adjustments) and were to play it off, she sat up and her heart beat strongly.

Drama and excitement at last enlivened the scene. The final was to be decided by match-play – seven 'chalks' up – chalk against chalk; but, by ingenious calculations, Mr Bryan, the 'novice', was to receive a handicap of two 'chalks'. Ernest, the expert, must win seven 'chalks' before Mr Bryan won five.

The Cup stood on the scorer's table; Sir William Briggs sat beside the table, beaming behind a long cigar. The bar had been closed at ten (or a little after), and Mrs Higgins, having seen to the washing-up, came in to see her son win the Cup, and was given a seat beside Sir William, who rose, bowed, and addressed her affably as 'Mrs Hancock'. All who could find a seat sat down. Mr Pewter weightily announced the conditions of the contest, and the names of the combatants, and begged that perfect silence would be maintained by one and all 'on the stroke'; Mr Fox, at the back, attempted a jocular remark, but was so sharply suppressed by his neighbours that he did not speak above a whisper until the match was over. A solemn hush descended as Ernest stepped into the 'run' and picked up his 'cheese'; and Jane, wedged tightly between Mr and Mrs Pewter, shivered with excitement, and felt quite ill. It was a knock-out, this, she thought; it had been bad enough watching Mr Bryan play before, but this was a fair knock-out. Her two men in the final! It only needed Fred to walk in, and that would finish her.

She did not know what she wanted. She wanted Ernest to have the Cup, which he wanted so badly; it would be nice to see the Cup sitting on the ornament-shelf of the *Blackbird* again. But she wanted Mr Bryan to win.

Very soon it appeared most improbable that Mr Bryan would win. In less than five minutes Ernest had won three 'chalks' to Mr Bryan's none; that is to say, the score stood at 3–2, Ernest leading; Mr Bryan's start had been wiped out, and, on level terms, against an experienced player, in good form, he had no real chance. 'A walk-over,' whispered Mr Fox to Mr Paddock, who answered automatically, 'Stroke, *please*!'

Ernest was in good form; he had thrown off his nervousness, the occasion stimulated him, and he rose, as they say, to the occasion. He played with grace and fire. In a breathless silence he fondled his twelve-pound cheese, and fitted it at last to his hand; he bent low, he crouched, he poised, he swung his arm forward and back – two steps, left, right – and as his long right leg crossed the line he sped the heavy ball swiftly at the magical angle to the magical spot on the right shoulder of the front pin. Biff! Wallop! A stranger to the game could not have told how it happened, but in less than a second the frame was clear – not one pin standing – a 'floorer'. Next time it was eight pins – two (it is generously assumed that the player can knock down a single pin with a single throw). Mr Bryan 'went three'; that is to say, he took three throws to knock down all the pins; another chalk to Ernest: 1–2–1– deadly figures. Mr Bryan's answer had been 2–3–2 – good figures, too, for a novice, but not good enough. Mr Bryan, also, was nervous no more; he had everything to gain and nothing to lose: Ernest, the coming Champion of London, was too good for him, and there was no disgrace in that. Mr Bryan was enjoying the game. Only, as he said, for the third time, 'Good shot, Ernest!' he thought, 'My God, is the man jealous of *me*?' After his 'floorer' Ernest smiled a sort of apology at Mr Bryan, sat down on the other side of the scorer's table, took a sip of his lemonade, and modestly looked at his feet.

Jane thought she would fall off the bench with excitement. It was no longer only a question of the Cup – the match was now entangled with her Destiny. If Mr Bryan won it would mean that, somehow or other, Fate intended her life to be mixed up with his; and if Ernest won Mr Bryan would 'fade out' and she would end her days with Ernest. Mr Pewter pinched her arm and whispered, 'It's not all over. Ernie's throwing too fast!'

A fast ball is effective, given unfailing accuracy; without accuracy it may be fatal. Therefore it is safer to play slow. But Ernest was not in the mood for safety; he had made a spectacular beginning, he had a novice against him, one chalk down, and already he saw himself making a spectacular finish. Two more 'floorers', perhaps 7 chalks to nothing – that would show 'em! Jane should see what he could do when he was roused.

Mr Bryan had 'gone three'. Ernest, full of triumph, flung his ball faster than before, playing for a 'floorer'. But his aim was not so accurate as before; the cheese dashed through, and left three pins standing: three pins in a horizontal line across the centre of the 'frame' – the dreaded 'London Bridge'. Rarely, very rarely, a man 'does London Bridge'. The cheese must be dropped almost vertically to touch the very edge of the outside pin, so that it rolls over slowly and hits the middle pin, which rolls over also and takes the third. The betting is about 500–1 against the shot. Ernest made one attempt for luck, knocked down one pin only, and said cheerfully, 'Stick 'em up.' Surrender. Two throws – two pins still standing – 4. Chalk to Mr Bryan. Score: 'Three all!'

A long roll of applause followed this announcement – the

normal tribute to the under-dog making a good game of it; but it nettled Ernest. 'Don't want me to win, don't they?' he thought savagely. 'I'll show 'em!' And, still full of confidence, he threw a ball like a torpedo. And again he was left with 'London Bridge'.

The company murmured, 'Bad luck, Ernie!' But Mr Pewter shook his head and muttered, 'Too fast, boy; too fast.' This time Ernest made two attempts at the dreadful shot, but the result was the same: another 4. Ernest said crossly, 'I'm a cow,' and walked to his seat in an excited silence.

Mr Bryan's first throw also left him three pins standing; but they were easy pins – the 'Novice's Three', which should be struck down by any man with a single blow. Mr Bryan, suddenly nervous again, did not do this. He knocked down the first pin, and left the 'Long Two' standing, one of the most delicately difficult shots on the frame. A murmur of disappointment ran round the room – the novice had thrown away a golden chance, and Ernest became confident again – never had he seen his pupil do the 'Long Two'; he could count on a tie.

The 'Long Two' cannot be fumbled; luck can do little; precision is everything. It is a prettier shot, more exciting even, than the 'floorer'. The ball must be dropped on the outer skin of the corner pin so that it rolls or slides along the edge of the 'frame' and knocks down the back pin, two feet away. To his huge astonishment Mr Bryan did this. Always before, though he hit the first pin fairly, it had slid off the frame on to the cokernut matting below. Now, as though inspired, it executed a neat somersault along the edge of the cliff, and as it rose to the perpendicular again caught the back pin square in the belly. And a shout was heard far more excited and joyous than Ernest's 'floorers' had provoked – 4–3, Mr Bryan leading. It was Mr Bryan's turn now to smile an apology. Ernest smiled back, and clapped with the rest, but he was thinking, 'No more of this!' Mr Fox, quite sober now, pushed through the crowd, and whispered to him, 'Not so *fast!*' and Ernest nodded knowingly. No more nonsense.

Jane did not applaud – she did not dare, for fear of Ernest's eyes, to say nothing of the neighbours. But now she had no doubt – she wanted Mr Bryan to win above everything; she clenched her small fists and willed him to win.

Mr Bryan, inspired by success, threw an easy, confident ball, and knocked down eight pins – 2. Ernest, careful enough now, should have tied in 2, but a 'dead' pin, lying on the frame, spoiled his second shot, and he missed the back pin by the thickness of a coat of varnish.

'Bad luck, Ernie – robbed by the dead!'

But, 'Bad luck butters no parsnips,' growled Mr Pewter. Figures are figures, and the figures were 5–3, Mr Bryan leading. Ernie, said everyone, must pull his socks up.

Ernest saw the Cup slipping out of his reach; and even Mr Bryan for the first time began to think it conceivable that he might, with luck, win this exciting match. He was enjoying it. He had forgotten Jane and her tiresome affairs – the game was the thing. Ernest was no longer a ridiculously jealous husband, but a man who had just 'set him a "floorer"'.

A swift change came over the game. Mr Bryan's reply to the 'floorer' was a good, true shot which left two pins standing. Both these two had been touched, both tottered tantalizingly upon their plates, and, urged on by the loud entreaties of the company, both seemed about to fall. But they stood – 5–4.

Mr Bryan had struck a bad patch. Ernest won another chalk easily – 5 all. Applause, loud and long; but Ernest thought that it was not loud enough. He had it in his head that the boys were against him, that everybody there was on Mr Bryan's side. Of course they liked to see a novice put up a sporting fight – anyone did – but there was reason in everything. Did they not realize that this match, to him, meant winning the Cup for keeps – setting up a record? 'Lot of snobs,' he thought. 'I'll show 'em!'

There followed a tie in three; and then another. 'Great match,' said Mr Pewter. He had to get up at four next morning, as usual, to harness the baker's horse, but he would rather stay up all night than miss a match like this. The room quivered with excitement. 'On the stroke' there was a silence like that of a regiment on parade; nothing could be heard but the howling of the wind. The women held their breath, the men let their pipes go out and hastily struck their matches after the stroke was made.

But as Ernest picked up his cheese for the next stroke, old Mrs Edwards, sitting close to the pins, opposite to Jane, decided that, what with the smoke and the excitement, she was going to faint. She rose, and tottered past Ernest to the door, followed by Mr Edwards and their daughter. Ernest put down his cheese and frowned. Interruptions always upset his play; everybody knew that. The slightest thing put Ernie off, especially, Mr Fox used to say, when Ernie was losing.

The men by the door squeezed back and made a passage for the Edwards family. Ernest looked round impatiently to be sure that they had gone, and picked up his cheese again; but Mr Fox called 'Hold on, Ernie!' There were steps on the stones outside, an indolent female voice, a high-pitched laugh, and Miss Fay Meadows appeared at the door. She opened her big blue eyes very wide, she peered into the smoke, smiled disarmingly, and inquired in angelic tones, 'Is Mr Bryan here?'

The question seemed funny to the spectators of that great match, and they laughed. But Mr Bryan swore silently. What a time to arrive!

'Come in, come in!' he said, as impatient now as Ernest.

'Hullo, Gordon! My dear, it's a *foul* night. Arctic!' She shivered charmingly. 'What a cosy place!'

Mr Pewter, impressed by the fur coats of the two ladies and the gentleman's white scarf, stood up and beckoned them towards the seats left by the Edwards. And Miss Meadows led her friends past the waiting Ernest as unhurried and easy as if she were the cause and centre of the whole proceedings. Her two friends looked self-conscious and felt intrusive. But Fay sat down, settled herself, wriggled, crossed her legs, smiled at Mr Bryan, and looked about her as much as to say, 'Well? The guest of honour has arrived. Now amuse me.'

Mr Bryan smiled back (one had to smile when Fay smiled, however naughty she was). He thought, 'What poise! What pluck! But how little tact!' And he made signs to her, which she did not see, to draw her legs in.

Ernest, now fuming (and no wonder), picked up his cheese for the third time. 'Ernie's upset,' whispered Mr Fox. Mr Pewter realized now that he had made a mistake, remembering Ernest's capacity for being upset in a match. But any friends of Mr Bryan's were welcome, and these had looked something out of the common.

Ernest fixed his eyes upon the magical spot upon the front pin, turned the cheese about in his hand till it was comfortable, stooped – and saw a small foot in a golden slipper bobbing gently above the left edge of the run. Distracting, impossible sight! Ernest, with a heavy sigh, laid the cheese upon the ground again and stood up; and there was a roar of good-humoured laughter.

'Stroke!' 'Feet, *please*!' 'Legs!' Mr Bryan stepped across the run, and explained to Fay that she must make the least of her legs. This was a very new and strange suggestion to Miss Fay Meadows, but she graciously complied; and, having done that, she recognized Jane and gave her a gracious nod.

'Stroke, *please*! We'll be here all night!'

Ernest was definitely upset; he was determined to be upset. How the devil could a man play skittles with a lot of West End 'tarts' throwing their legs about the alley? It was just like the fellow to bring a row of his friends in at the critical moment. Ernest was so set on being upset that he would have been almost annoyed if he had scored a 'floorer'. No one was surprised when he went 4, and no one was sorrier than Mr Bryan, who felt somehow responsible.

Mr Bryan was even more upset than Ernest by his friends' arrival. Apart from their effect upon Ernest he half expected Fay to burst into loud laughter at the sight of her friend in his shirt-sleeves earnestly trying to throw a heavy missile at a set of ninepins.

Fay did not laugh. But Mr Bryan went 5; and if the lawful maximum had not been 5, he might have gone 6. Chalk to Ernest – 6–5, Ernest leading.

Six–five. Ernest thought he had his man now and would polish him off. One 'floorer' and the Cup was his.

Jane too thought that Mr Bryan was done for, and she harshly attributed this to the presence of Fay Meadows. Blast her! swanking there with her furs and her pearls and her long silk legs! She was Mr Bryan's evil influence, and Jane detested her.

The rest of the company (Ernest excepted) took a much more generous view of Fay's presence; and Mr Bryan might have spared himself his sensitive alarms. The Black Swan delighted in the radiant creature; the men, between the strokes, gazed reverently at her legs (and, to a lesser degree, the legs of her companion, Miss Stella Marble); the women eyed her all over, not in envy but in admiration and the desire for knowledge. Mr Fox, at the back, made ribald remarks, but he felt towards 'Bryan's tart' as kindly as the others.

Mr Bryan, a little reassured on this point, prepared to make his final throw. He had no more hope of winning now; his one thought was that he would like to show Fay that he could do something better than 5 – was not a hopeless outsider at this queer game.

He dabbled his fingers in the club sponge, and tried to remember all the little tips that all his tutors had given him – swing the arm well forward and back, keep the arm straight, not too fast, a touch of rotary spin, keep that thumb well out, concentrate, concentrate on the front pin, and step out with the left foot straight ahead, don't step across. Skittles has much in common with golf.

Having thought of all these essential aids, and more also, Mr Bryan decided suddenly, 'Oh, well, what does it matter? Better throw the thing and chance it.' He threw an easy, deliberate ball, and he scored an impeccable 'floorer'.

Yells of delight. Protracted clapping. Grins all round. Bright smile from Fay, at last impressed. Tender glance from Jane, almost in tears. Wan smile from Ernest, apprehensive again.

Sir William Briggs was thinking that this was better than the House of Commons. Mrs Higgins was wondering whether she could persuade Sir William to intercede for her with the licensing justices about the proposed alterations of the Public Bar and the back lavatory. Fay Meadows, as Ernest stepped into the run, was heard to say, 'My dear, the *grace* of it! I'd *no* idea ...' Ernest, afterwards, said that that bitch had talked on the stroke; but this was unfair, for twenty throats cried, 'Stroke, please!' and Fay did not speak above a whisper again.

Ernest was quite capable of retorting to a 'floorer' with another 'floorer'; indeed, had often done it. But now he could do no better than six pins.

'Six all!' Anybody's game. Long round of applause; and then an electric silence. Jane felt as if her body had left her; she was a mere tangle of nerves, all throbbing, and icy cold.

'Six all – Mr Higgins setting,' called Mr Pewter, suddenly pontifical.

Ernest did all that an expert can do to propitiate the gods and command success. He used the sponge to moisten his fingers, and the towel to dry them. Before picking up his cheese he examined the pins with a hostile eye, and asked Harry, the 'sticker', to give a turn to the centre pin, which was leaning slightly. This done, he fumbled with his ball for so long that Jane thought she would scream and Fay began to look about the room again. At last he adopted the famous crouch, assumed an air of intense ferocity, and sprang. Only four pins fell. But those left standing were the combination known strangely as the 'Waterloo Five', which may in theory be demolished with a single blow.

' "Waterloo Five",' whispered Mr Pewter. 'All to come.'

' "Waterloo Five",' whispered the man next to Fay, a taxi-driver. She smiled divinely at him, and whispered, 'How sweet!'

But Ernest, with a lovely shot, laid low only four out of the five pins. The back pin quivered agonizingly, but remained erect. Groans. 'Bad luck, Ernie!' Now, Mr Bryan, only three to beat, and the Cup is yours. Jane could not look at him; she bit her lips and frowned at the fatal ninepins.

Mr Bryan had arrived at the conclusion, common among golfers of little skill, that the more thought one gave to this difficult business the less well one did. 'Take it easy' – that was the only golden rule. Natural and steady.

Mr Bryan took it easy and knocked down seven pins. There remained standing the back double – an easy 'double' – the back pin and its nearest neighbour on the right. An easy 2.

But Ernest had seen his pupil miss an 'easy double' many times, and still hoped for a tie.

And now it was Mr Bryan's turn to do some thinking. He hated the 'easy doubles', especially this one, which, in fact, was very difficult to do correctly. And that raised a quaint and charming point of skittles etiquette. There were two ways of attacking these two pins – one the pretty way of the expert, and the other the fumbling way of the novice. The expert threw his ball edge foremost, so that it delicately touched the outside edge of the outer pin and pushed it across to the other. The novice 'split the double' – that is to say, he flung his ball with a wide open face between the pins – easier, surer, uglier, but no less lawful. But for the expert this was 'not skittles' – not in the sense that certain things are 'not cricket', but as a matter of craftsmanship: a question not of morals but of art. Now Mr Bryan was technically a novice still, and no man could blame him for taking the safer course at this supreme crisis, when he had only to kill these two pins for the Cup. Indeed, he heard behind him an anxious whisper, 'Split 'em, sir!' But this pretty point of pride had always pleased him. Mr Rogers, the sewer-man, would not think of 'splitting' them, if the Championship of the World were at stake. And should he, a cricketer, fall short of the lofty tradition of a pub? Mr Bryan decided to try the bold thing, though probably he would miss the outer pin altogether, as he generally did.

It was a very near thing. The ball, thrown perfectly otherwise, only just touched the pin – another millimetre to the right and it would have sped vainly into the netting. But it touched, and the pin fell slowly over, reluctant, it seemed, to surrender for so slight a wound. It fell full but faintly against the back pin – so gently that for a tormenting second the two pins, like two drunkards, leaned lurching against each other. They trembled, they tottered, the people shouted, and they fell.

Mr Bryan had won the Cup. The company cheered as Ernest, with a good grace, gave a hand to the winner, according to custom. Then, 'One for the loser!' cried Mr Pewter, and Ernest received the customary tribute to the runner-up. 'All very well,' thought Ernest, as he put his coat on; 'they didn't *want* me to win.' Also, at the finish, he had caught sight of Jane, able to restrain herself no more, clapping, laughing, crying, her eyes on Mr Bryan.

'All right, my girl,' thought Ernest. 'You wait!'

Sir William Briggs then made a long speech.

22

POOR ERNEST!

THE skittle-alley was in a sheltered corner. Out on the river they found a wild easterly night, one of the noisy nights which Ernest detested. The ebb had just begun, and the east wind whipped the river into a stormy sea. Jane's dinghy bumped furiously against the side of the barge, had broken one of her mooring-lines, and was tugging hopefully at the other. Jane looked down from the *Blackbird*'s deck into the splashing darkness, and decided she must do something.

'That other rope'll give soon, if this goes on.'

'Who cares?' said Ernest, shivering, and went below.

'I'll get his tea first,' thought Jane, and followed him.

They had said at the Black Swan truly that Ernest took his defeat very well; but on board the *Blackbird* he took it very badly. Jane made tea for him, said he had had no luck, and was truly sorry for him. 'Poor Ernest!' she said, and kissed him.

But Ernest would have none of her sympathy. 'Fat lot you care,' he said. '*I* seen you cheering the bastard.'

'Anyone cheers the winner, don't they?'

'There's reason in everything.'

'Well, two can't win, can they? You played beautiful, Ernie, and no man can't help having bad luck. I wanted that Cup, same as you did.'

Ernest, sore and restless, prowled about the room like a tiger anxious to get at somebody. Outside the wind howled, the waves slapped the flanks of the *Blackbird*, the tide swished and gurgled against the wall. The dinghy charged the barge with a thump, and Jane feared for her precious boat.

'Blast this noise!' said Ernest. 'Can't hear oneself speak.'

'Kettle's nearly on the boil,' said Jane, comforting.

'Yes, and I'm on the morning-shift. Lot of sleep I'll get tonight.

'You taught Mr Bryan wonderful,' said Jane, still trying tact.

'Yes. And then he brings his "tarts" in! That's what upset me. Put me right off me stroke.'

'Well, how could *he* help it?'

'Did it a-purpose, I shouldn't wonder.'

'Don't talk silly!'

'Lot of West End bitches, chucking their legs about —'

'Here, not so much language, thank you!'

'Talking on the stroke. How could *anyone* play?'

'Well, *he* didn't do so bad,' said Jane, goaded into rashness.

'Oh, yes, you're on his side, of course. I know that. Bloody parasite!'

'Here, less of it!'

'Anyhow, my girl,' said Ernest, anger making him throw caution aside, 'I've put a spoke in *your* wheel. *You'll* not fetch and carry for *Mister* Bryan no more!'

'What d'you mean?' said Jane, setting down the kettle and facing him in alarm.

'What I say. You get the sack tomorrow, my girl.'

'*Ernie*! You *beast*! What've you been doing?'

'What I said I would, that's all. I been to Bryan and give him a piece of my mind. And after tomorrow you don't put foot in that studio — see? Never again!'

So he had done it — the little snake! — ruined everything, taken the one comfort of her life! Jane was too full of fury to choose her weapons or her words.

'Oh, don't I, then?' she snapped. 'And what about the picture, eh?'

'Picture? What picture?'

'*My* picture — going to be in the Exhibition! Can't do that without sittings, can he?'

Ernest took a step towards her, suddenly quiet, but breathing menace. 'You've been sitting for that bloke?' he said, low and intense. 'Since we was married?'

Ernest in this mood was really frightening, but she had gone too far to retreat.

'Well, what if I have? It's my profession, isn't it?'

'*Stripped?*' said Ernest, terribly, his face quite white.

'I've got a right to earn my own living, I tell you —'

'You —!' With a very rude oath, Ernest took her by the throat. 'I give you my orders, and you gone against them, that's all. Let's hear the rest now – out with it! You been his fancy-girl?' He shook her and she struggled, half-choking.

'No, Ernie, *no*! Let *go* of me, Ernie!'

'Likely tale! If he lies about one thing, why not another? By cripes!' – cried Ernest, his mind switching suddenly to the full enormity of Mr Bryan – 'that bloke was lying to me all the time, and I swallowed it all! By cripes, I'll show him!' Roughly he threw Jane towards a chair, from which she fell to the floor. He looked about for a weapon – anything would serve to bash the bastard – standing there as meek as you please, shaking hands, making a bloke respect him, say 'sir' to him, and all the time lying, lying, and laughing up his sleeve; and then coming down to the alley with his West End bitches and walking off with a Cup meant for honest working men! Cripes, it was too much! Sitting to him, eh? Every morning, while a bloke was away at work! A nice thing! Cripes! Ernest, as they say, 'saw red'. He also saw the wood-chopper. And having snatched up the wood-chopper, he ran to the ladder, shouting, and clambered on deck, bumping his head against the hatch, as usual.

Jane, lying terrified and panting where he had thrown her, found her voice when she saw his feet disappearing up the ladder; and, too late, she cried, 'It was a surprise, Ernie – a surprise for *you*. It's all right, Ernie! Ernie, I *swear*!' But he had gone. 'Oh, God, he'll kill him! He swore he would.' Ernest was going to kill Mr Bryan; and, bruised and breathless, she stumbled after him.

At the top of the ladder she halted for breath and listened. Nothing could be heard but the wind and the water; she could not see Ernest; there was no light showing through the skylight of the studio. Thank God, Mr Bryan had not come back – had gone off with his friends. Or was he in bed and asleep? Mr Bryan never locked his door, she knew. At that moment the light sprang up in the studio, and blazed across the wharf through the open door. God! She ran across the wharf, crying in her heart, 'Oh, God, save him!'

The east wind, sweeping in unchecked, was working havoc in the studio. The curtains bellied and tossed and swung; the two hand-lamps had fallen over, and sketches and papers flew heavily up and down, or fluttered across the floor like a host of injured butterflies. Jane saw that the bed was empty, and thanked the God to whom she had just prayed for the third time in her life.

Ernest was standing before 'The Blush' – stock-still, staring, his eyes wide open, his lips moving. He held the hatchet above his right shoulder, as if ready to strike, and he was muttering with awful malignance a string of meaningless blasphemies, which, by their variety, might equally have been addressed to the picture, the painter, or the original. Jane crept up behind him, and surveyed for the first time (for Mr Bryan had covered it up and forbidden her to peep) the almost completed picture of her naked charms. Even in her fear she found time to think proudly that it was ever so like, and ever so nice, and why ever didn't Ernest like it? Any man would if he really loved her. Just then Ernest stopped swearing for a second, and she had a wild hope that he might be cooling down, changing his mind. But Ernest was only collecting his forces. He raised the hatchet high above his head, and, with another gust of oaths, he dashed it into the belly of the painted Jane. Jane shrank back with the cry of a wounded thing, as if the weapon had entered her own tender flesh. Ernest dragged out the hatchet, gripping the canvas with his other hand, and he slashed again, this time at the face. Then canvas and easel crashed to the ground together.

So shocked was Jane by the spectacle that for a moment she forgot her fear. She cried, her mind flashing back to the wrecking of Fred's pictures, 'That's all you're good for – breaking up pictures! Make a habit of it, don't you? You're a beast!'

Ernest turned; she saw his wild eyes and a sort of foam upon his lips; she thought, 'He's mad!' and she backed to the door, where she drew a curtain across her body, as if that would protect her.

But Ernest paid no attention to her or her words. He was looking for Mr Bryan, and he stalked round the room shouting, 'Where is he? Where is he? Come out, you bastard!' The papers and sketches fluttered about him grotesquely. He slashed at the empty bed with his chopper and passed on to the little room at the back, which was still dark. Jane heard him routing about there, and hoped he was not destroying more pictures. He came back presently, and saw on a table the Christmas Cup. Mr Bryan had slipped across and deposited his trophy there before going off to see Fay Meadows home. And when Ernest saw it, he uttered a savage laugh, and with one savage blow of his hatchet swept it from the table to the floor.

'Brave boy!' thought Jane. If he had not been Ernest she would have said that he was drunk.

'Where *is* the Christmas champion?' he shouted, and, ranging the room again, he began to rave in the strange jargon of his political faith, 'Class is class. Where *is* the filthy parasite and exploiter? Christmas champion! Christmas parasite! Steal the wives of the workers, would you? Spawn of the bosses, come *out*, you bastard!'

It crossed Jane's mind, as she peeped from the curtain, that Ernest, his real rage cooling, might now be only showing off for her benefit; but she could not be sure, he looked so wild. Ernest, in truth, was beginning to fear that he might be making a fool of himself, though he still wanted very much to hit and hurt Mr Bryan. Meanwhile there was Jane; he would make her pay for all this. He turned on her suddenly and shouted, 'Where *is* he? Where *is* he? *You* ought to know – you —!' He dropped his hatchet and made for her; and Jane, not waiting to test her theory, fled out in terror on to the wharf.

By instinct she ran first towards the wharf gate, making for the open, where there were people and policemen. But before she reached the gate she thought, 'We'll meet Mr Bryan coming back, and Ernest will kill him.' She must draw him off from Mr Bryan – save Mr Bryan. So she doubled round to the right, between the pile of timber and old junk and the fence, and so back to the *Blackbird*. Ernest, close on her heels, tripped over an anchor, and fell so heavily that he did not even cry out. He hurt his hands and a knee; and long before he had picked himself up and stopped swearing Jane was safe on the *Blackbird's* deck. She would not go below – too dangerous; but she crouched down in the dark near the stern, where she had the after-hatch and the steering-wheel between her and the wharf. The wind was bitter, and she shivered with cold and fear. It was a Spring tide, and the deck of the *Blackbird* was still almost flush with the wharf. Peeping over the hatch she could see Ernest limping across the line of light from the studio door. Then she flattened herself to the deck.

Ernest hobbled on board, chastened by his fall, but cursing terribly. He knelt down, groaning, and shouted down the ladder 'Jane! Jane!' It was horrible to lie there and make no answer to her husband only a few feet away; but she was afraid.

'Jane!' he called again, but in a milder tone, 'come up, girl! I won't hurt you. But you and me have got to talk to this bloke – see?'

Jane wondered. He sounded more sensible. But was it a trap?

'Come up, Jane,' he said, reasonably. 'And bring my overcoat. I can't come down, because I've broke my bloody leg, you see.'

That, she knew, was a lie. So he was on the warpath still. She was so cold she could not lie there much longer. She thought angrily that she had a good mind to creep up behind him and pitch him down the ladder – break his silly neck!

'Jane?' he called, almost plaintively, 'why don't you answer, girl? We've got to talk to the bloke – see? Both of us. You and me.'

She braced herself, scrambled to her feet, and said, 'Here I am, Ernie.'

Ernest got up slowly and said, 'Oh, you're there, are you? Been listening all the time, have you?' And now his voice had that menacing ring again. He moved towards her, a stealthy shadow, and stood by the wheel.

'Stay where you are, Ernie! What d'you want?' cried Jane in terror. She had been a fool, she saw. Here in the stern she was cornered; she should have gone forward of the hatchway, where there was room to move. Her skirts flapped about her and pinned her legs; if she was not careful she would be blown overboard.

'I only want to talk to you, Jane,' said Ernest. 'You and me have got to talk – see? Don't be frightened. You've hurt my leg,' he added. His voice was mild and reasonable again. Poor Ernest! He was divided in his mind between two ideas – one, that he did not want to hurt Jane, and the other, that, having made an impression this time, he ought to keep it up.

But Jane could not tell what was in his mind. She said sharply, 'Well, stop where you are! I don't trust you, Ernie – not after the way you've been going on.' Behind him, along the Mall, she could see the lights of a motor-car coming towards the wharf: perhaps a taxi bringing Mr Bryan home. If she could hold Ernest off till he came . . .

'Trust me?' sneered Ernest. 'That's good.' And he moved a little nearer. Now he was only five feet away. What did he mean to do? After his violence this stealthy approach struck panic into her. She had seen him drop the hatchet – but suppose he had a knife? There was still a small space between him and the barge's side; she thought she might dodge past him and run forward. If his leg was really bad she might give him the slip. She made a dash, but the wind in her skirts held her back, and Ernest, leg or no leg, stepped swiftly across and barred the way. She retreated to her corner, one hand behind her, clinging to the post which supported the washing-line, pinned against it by the wind, and shivering.

'No, you don't,' he said quietly. 'Don't be frightened, Jane.' He stepped forward, and gently put out his hand, groping for her; his hand touched her shoulder. What was he after?

She screamed (but the wind tossed her tiny voice contemptuously into the west). The tigress rose in her, she sprang at Ernest, her small hands beating at him to keep him back. Ernest took a step back, astonished, put his foot on an oar, lost his balance, and went overboard backwards into the troubled waters.

'You *bitch*!' he yelled as he fell. There was a splash and he was gone.

Jane screamed again 'Help! Help!' and looked wildly to the shore. But instantly she began to grope about on the dark deck for the oars and rowlocks of the dinghy, always kept on the barge for fear of marauding boys.

Mr Bryan, coming through the gate on to the wharf, saw with surprise the light streaming from his studio, saw the dim figure on the barge, and heard, but faintly, her cry. He ran across the wharf. Jane was still searching for the rowlock, but she looked up at his step and shouted, 'Help me! Ernie's in the river. He can't swim, and I can't find the rowlock!'

'How long?' shouted Mr Bryan, jumping down to the deck.

'Just this minute!'

He stepped to the side and stared down at the black water, whipped off his coat at the same time, and squeezed off his rubber shoes with his heels.

'I'll go in!' he yelled. 'You bring the boat!'

'No!' she cried, jumping up, rowlock in hand. 'No! It's no *good*!' And she put out a hand to hold him back. But he had gone.

Mr Bryan, as he dived, thought, 'I am a damned fool. I shall be drowned myself. But here goes!'

The water was icy. He struck the muddy bottom with his hands, and turning down-stream, swam under water as far as he could, thinking that a non-swimmer in this cold would sink like a stone. But his open eyes saw nothing but blackness, and his groping hands touched nothing but mud and stones. After a few strokes he had to come up, gasping, exhausted, and already aching with the cold. He was no great swimmer, and he could not dive again without a rest. Treading water, he looked about him. The chopped waves slapped his face; he could see no sign of Ernest. But there was Jane with the dinghy, nearer the shore. The fierce tide was sweeping her down, the boat was heavy to row, and she was struggling with the oars and shouting over her shoulder, 'Get in! Get in!' Yes, he must get in, or he would sink himself. 'I've done more harm than good,' he thought to himself. He swam towards the boat; but to swim across a racing tide needs power, and there was little power left in him. Jane's right oar flew out of the row-lock, the boat rocked, and she missed the water with the blade. For twenty yards they were carried down on almost parallel courses. Jane was in a panic for Mr Bryan – if he was drowned too she would throw herself in. Now she had the boat moving well, and he was nearer – another three yards and he was safe. Then, for one dreadful second, she thought she saw, many yards down-stream, a small black shape, which might be a man's head. Ernest? She could not see – it had gone. Whatever it was, she must save Mr Bryan, floundering feebly a few feet away, his head scarcely out of the water. He made a desperate effort, and got his hand on the gunwale; his numbed fingers could hardly keep their hold. Jane left the oars and gripped his arm, he heaved one leg over the side, and panting, struggling, she somehow pulled him in.

He lay at the bottom of the boat, coughing out the muddy Thames, and Jane took the oars again.

They were under the Mall now, where the street-lamps threw a faint light on the river, but the shadows, dancing from wave to wave, made it even more difficult to see surely. Jane rested on her oars and peered about her. Foaming rollers and hissing crests, leaping yellow peaks of water, deep black valleys of water – nothing else to be seen. They drifted past the Stork and were approaching another belt of blackness. 'Hopeless,' she thought; and then she saw the lights of a police-boat plodding up against the tide. 'Police, ahoy!' she called, but had to hail them three times before they heard.

Mr Bryan sat up. Jane was very calm now, and as the black boat with the three caped figures came near she began to think of the story she would tell.

'This young lady's husband's in the river. Can't swim.'

The sergeant knew both of them by sight. He took them on board and the dinghy in tow. The constables wrapped their capes round them and sat them near the engines, which gave out a little warmth. Jane sat shivering, and thought things out. Whatever happened, Mr Bryan must be kept out of this.

'Know how it happened, sir?' said the sergeant in a low voice. Mr Bryan shook his head, but Jane had heard and she said:

'The dinghy broke loose and we was tying her up. Ernest slipped and fell over.' Thank God, that was done.

Presently a second police-boat appeared, and the two boats ranged up and down, backwards and forwards, like two black hounds.

'Pretty hopeless, I'm afraid, sir,' whispered the sergeant at last. 'I'll put you ashore before you catch your death. Then we'll get out the "drags".' (The second boat was using the drags already, but he did not like to produce that ugly instrument before Jane's eyes.)

He put them aboard the *Blackbird*, and then went off, promising to return.

What now? Jane thought quickly. Mr Bryan, trembling and blue, must have a hot bath; but the police must not go into the studio and see the chaos there. It would be better if they did not go to the studio at all; but they might – they would want to ask Mr Bryan questions. Still, if she were quick, she could clear up the mess and be back on the barge before they came.

'I'll do the bath, Mr Bryan,' she said, and darted ahead into the studio, where she turned on the geyser, and ran to the sideboard for brandy.

Mr Bryan stumbled after her; his legs would scarcely move, they were wrapped in ice-cold steel. But his eyes still obeyed him, and cold and wretched though he was, he stopped short in amazement at the sight of his disordered studio. The wrecked easel – the mutilated picture – the battered Cup! And the hatchet on the floor. This must be Ernest's work. 'My God,' he thought, 'I'm mixed up in all this!' Still staring, he began to fumble at his sodden clothes; but his fingers would not undo the buttons.

Jane ran at him with a tumbler of brandy. 'Don't stand there!' she said. 'Drink this!'

He took a gulp of the spirit, and chattered feebly, 'W-what's b-been h-happening?' his eyes on the easel.

'Don't worry!' she cried. 'I'll see to that.' And with her own cold fingers she began to tear at the stubborn buttons.

'Here, have some brandy yourself,' he protested, but 'Want to get pneumonia, do you?' she snapped. 'You do as you're told.' She seemed possessed by a demon of determination; she was like a mother with an only child. Mr Bryan should not die of pneumonia if she could help it. She sat him on a chair and tore off most of his clothes. She rubbed his legs and arms, and thrust him into the bathroom, already warm with steam. Then she put the Cup, the hatchet, the easel, and the remnants of the picture into the little room next to the bathroom, and picked up most of the sketches and papers. That done, she felt suddenly faint, and took a sip of the brandy. She opened the wharf door and listened. No sign of the police. She tapped on the bathroom door and called, 'Are you all right, Mr Bryan?' The taps were running, and she had to shout.

'Fine, thanks. What about you?'

'Quite all right, Mr Bryan. I'm going back to the barge now.'

'Right! I'll come over.'

'You ought to go to bed, Mr Bryan.'

'No, I'm all right.'

She dared not shout what she really wanted to say. So 'Turn off the tap, please, Mr Bryan,' she commanded.

He obeyed, wondering. She opened the door a few inches, and

whispered into a wall of steam, 'Don't say nothing about the mess, Mr Bryan. It was Ernie, you see. I've cleared up everything.'

'Right,' he said; but she had gone.

Mr Bryan lay in his bath, thawing but anxious, alarmed but admiring. 'Extraordinary girl,' he thought. 'Thinks of everything.' But what the devil was it all about?

Far down the river Jane could see the lights of the police-boats dodging about. She went below and threw some wood on the stove, still glowing, and huddled herself before it in the basket-chair. The wind blew stronger: Ernest's 'noises' were worse than ever. Ernest was out there in the river, and all this time she had not been thinking of Ernest – she had been thinking of Mr Bryan. Even now she was not thinking, 'Will they save Ernest?' but 'Will Mr Bryan get pneumonia and die?' Now she tried to make herself say, 'Oh, God, save Ernest!' but she could not do it. She was a wicked girl, she thought, and would come to a bad end.

So Mr Bryan found her, cold and exhausted. They assured each other that they were all right. He had brought the brandy, and made her take some.

She smiled at him gratefully, and said, 'Would you like some tea, Mr Bryan?'

'No,' he said, 'but I'll make some for you. Have you had a hot drink?' She shook her head. 'Good God!' he thought. 'Thinks of everything except herself.' He set to work, and she was too tired to protest.

The two teacups were ready on the table, the tea was ready in the pot – as she had left them when the row with Ernest had begun. Ages ago that seemed! 'Funny,' she thought, 'I was making tea for Ernest, and now Mr Bryan's making tea for me. Same tea. Funny.' And now Ernest was drowned. And she must think. Those policemen were coming back in a minute, and she must think.

'D'you think they'll find him, Mr Bryan?' she said.

He shook his head, and said gently, 'Not alive, I'm afraid.' He expected her to cry – but no. Why didn't she cry?

She said, 'I'd better tell you what happened before the police comes.'

'If you feel like it, perhaps you'd better.'

'I'm quite all right, Mr Bryan. Well, Ernie was wild, you see – and he said he was going to do for you –'

'But why on earth – ?' he put in resentfully, though he had an uncomfortable feeling that he knew the answer.

Jane thought, 'Well, it's no good covering things up no more.' She said slowly and humbly, 'Well, you see, Mr Bryan, he thought you was gone on me.' She hung her head. 'And he knew I was gone on you, you see.' There, it was out now, and she felt better.

In spite of his fears, in spite of his embarrassment, Mr Bryan was touched. He gently laid his hand on her head and said very kindly, 'My poor child.' But, he thought, 'What a mess! What have I done to deserve this? What a scandal it would make!' He said, 'But why *tonight*? What happened?'

'Well, you see, he was a bit wild about the skittles, and then we had words, and then he found out about me sitting for you, you see –'

'How?'

'Well, I s'pose I let it out, Mr Bryan.'

So that was it.

'My dear,' he said reproachfully – he could not be harsh with her just now – 'you told me he didn't mind. You lied to me, so I had to lie to Ernest – for your sake. Then he finds out – and no wonder he's upset. You shouldn't have done it. No, it's all right. I'm sorry.' For she had begun to cry.

She was crying, not because he reproached her, but because he was kind, and had called her 'my dear', and she felt humble and wicked.

He left her and looked for the milk, thinking it was just as well for her to cry, since the police were coming.

Later, when she was drinking her tea, she said suddenly, 'Do you think it's murder, Mr Bryan?'

'What do you mean, Jane?' 'My God,' he thought, 'what's coming next?'

'Well, you see, when Ernie ran across with the wood-chopper I ran after him, you see; and after he'd broke the place up, you not being there, you see, Mr Bryan, he turns on me. Well, I ran away, because I was ever so frightened, you see, only I didn't like to go out in the street, because I thought we'd run into you, perhaps, and then there'd be trouble, Ernie being so wild, you see; and then Ernie came after me, and he got me in a corner and I was frightened, so I give him a push to keep him off, you see, and all of a sudden he was gone. D'you think it's murder, Mr Bryan?'

'No, no. Self-defence. But I thought you said something about the dinghy breaking loose?'

She said gravely, 'I had to say something, Mr Bryan – otherwise they'd have dragged you into it, you see.'

It was his turn to feel humble. She might have drawn him into this mess with her folly, he thought, but she had certainly done everything she could to get him out of it. And she thought of everything. What a nerve!

Again he touched her little head, and he said, 'Don't worry, Jane. It's all right. You're a brave girl. Keep it up.'

'You're too kind to me,' she said.

He poured more tea into the pot. Jane closed her eyes, and lay back, drowsy. Whatever had happened, or might happen, there was Mr Bryan making tea for her in her own home, while she lay back like a lady. It must be a dream. It was nice. She ought, she knew, to be thinking about poor Ernest and no one else; but there it was, it was nice.

Then they heard the police-boat bumping against the *Blackbird*'s side. Mr Bryan met the sergeant on deck. They had found nothing – seen nothing. Tomorrow they would try with the drags again. The body would turn up somewhere – might be Putney, might be Blackfriars.

'Poor chap!' said Mr Bryan. Poor Ernest! He was sorry for Ernest. All those ambitions, those ideals, gone to nothing. There was a lot of good stuff in him. Poor Ernest! But Mr Bryan realized with a shock that he was quite content that the police had not brought back poor Ernest alive.

The sergeant was kind. Jane's story was as short and simple as Mr Bryan's, and she told it as easily. Mr Bryan, having heard the truth only a few minutes earlier, marvelled at the assurance with which she lied. And he, the respectable son of a peer, by standing there and saying nothing, was making himself an accessory or something. Well, he was too near the mess himself to trouble about that; she was keeping him out of it, and he must stand by her.'

'Poor little waif!' he thought, watching her pale, small face. Damn it! in any case he would have been on her side.

The sergeant made few comments. People were always falling into the river and drowning themselves, either on purpose or by accident; and those who could not swim were often the most careless. He was one of those who had often said that this living on barges would lead to no good, and now he was not surprised.

'No lifebuoy provided on the vessel?' he inquired.

'No, sir.'

He made a note, 'No lifebuoy', which he afterwards developed into a recommendation that there should be a 'tightening-up of the regulations'.

23

'INTERMISSION'

'Extraordinary girl!' The next morning, much earlier than the usual time, there she was, pulling up the blinds as usual, murmuring as usual, 'Your tea, Mr Bryan.' One could not help admiring the girl. No moral sense, perhaps, but one had to admire her. He wondered how Fay, with all her impudence and vitality, would have weathered such a night.

Jane had slept well, but she was tired still, and apprehensive of the future, with its police interviews and relatives and inquests and she didn't know what. She felt feeble, yet strangely at peace, as the body is feeble but at peace after a dangerous operation. Ernest, who for so long had been the foreign body, the poison in her life, had been removed; and the relief already was as great as the shock.

She did not admit this, even to herself; but she did know that she could not face going over to the Black Swan and telling Ernest's mother that her son had been drowned. There her nerve failed her. But somebody must do it – last night she had forgotten all about Mrs Higgins – and she had come early to the studio to ask Mr Bryan if he would do it for her.

'I'll go at once,' he said. 'I tried last night, but couldn't make anyone hear. You'd better go back to the barge, and I'll bring her over to you.'

'But your breakfast, Mr Bryan?'

'I can manage. She'll want to see you.'

Jane understood. Mrs Higgins must find her mourning for her husband, not cooking eggs for another man. Obediently she went.

Extraordinary, thought Mr Bryan, as he dressed. Already they had slipped into a kind of tacit conspirators' understanding. It was he and this quaint, uneducated waif against the world. How the devil had it all begun? And what the devil would be the end of it? Meanwhile, he must go through with it.

*

Mrs Higgins came on board weeping, and wept over Jane, but not for very long. Ernest had never been indispensably dear to her; indeed, poor Ernest, who had devoted so much of his life to the advancement of brotherhood, had not succeeded in inspiring the real affection of a single human being. He had helped his mother with the accounts, but he had despised her business and was generally rude to her. But Mrs Higgins was very fond of Jane, and, after the first shock, thought more about Jane than about her son or herself. She wanted Jane to go and live with her at the pub.

'You can't stay here moping by your lonesome, ducky. You'll go off your rocker – anyone would. I always said there was no luck about the place. Many a time I said it to Ernie. "Ernie," I said, "you'll have no luck living on the water; it isn't natural." We was never a family for the water. And now he's gone.' Mrs Higgins looked about her and shivered. Only once before had she visited the *Blackbird*, for she had a horror of the water, and would not even trust herself to a pleasure-steamer.

'It was my fault,' said Jane penitently. 'I made him.'

'Don't you fret, ducky. What's done's done. Nobody can't tell what's right till they've tried. But you come over to me, ducky. There's the two of us alone in the world now, and we ought to cling together. I'll put you to bed in the spare, and let nobody come near you.'

But Jane would not go. She was quieter on the barge, she said, and Lily perhaps would come and keep her company. Mrs Higgins's kindness made her feel mean and horrid. She was afraid that if Mrs Higgins went on being kind she would cry out suddenly, 'Don't be so kind to me! I was a bad wife to Ernie, and it was me pushed him overboard, if you want to know.'

But everybody was kind. Mr Bryan sent telegrams to Lily and her father, telephoned to the police, and ordered away the people who sidled on to the wharf and stared. Mrs Higgins sent over a hot dinner and some money in an envelope. Old Mrs Staples climbed painfully down the ladder and asked if there was anything she could do. All kind – too kind. What would they say, Jane thought, if they knew the sort of girl she really was?

Lily arrived in the afternoon, and it was nice to have Lily on the *Blackbird* again. But she was afraid to tell everything, even to Lily.

The odd thing about Lily was that living in sin seemed to have done her good. She was very happy, adored Mr Moss, and had the air of a settled matron; she had even become domestic, and now, on the barge, did readily the tasks which she had neglected or avoided in the old days. It was funny, Jane thought, that Lily, who had gone to the bad, should be all serene, while she, the respectably married woman, was all over the shop.

Lily was kind too, and asked no questions. She suspected that there was something more in all this than met the eye. Jane, she thought, had always had a bit of a 'crush' on this Mr Bryan, and he seemed to be properly mixed up in the doings. But it was no affair of hers, and she could not summon up a single sorrowful thought for Ernest. A good riddance.

Mr Bell arrived on Sunday, and that evening the body of Ernest was found, at Wandsworth, near the mouth of the Wandle. On Monday, Jane had to go with her father to a horrible place, and 'identify the remains'. That was a dreadful business. She gave one look, nodded, and turned away.

The inquest was on Wednesday – two days before Christmas. 'A nice Christmas-box for us all,' said Mrs Higgins.

Jane knew from the *Sunday Gazette* that inquests were nearly always 'dramatic'; witnesses 'broke down'; relatives made scenes at the back of the court, and jurymen put searching questions. She had not seen any of the neighbours since the fatal night, and did not know what they might be saying. Perhaps they were saying she had a guilty passion for Mr Bryan, and had pushed Ernest in.

Mr Bryan also was aware that things had a way of 'coming out' at inquests, that even more was heard about the lives of the living than about the death of the deceased on these occasions, and that the coroner sometimes made 'strong comments' on the conduct of 'a witness described as a gentleman'. And he approached the court with some disquiet. Mr Bryan was discovering that, although a man of independent mind, who went his own way and despised convention, he was increasingly reluctant to be involved in a public scandal.

It has been wisely observed that the human mind does not notice the coincidences which don't happen, and Jane and Mr Bryan had failed to consider the many thousands of unexciting inquests which are not recorded in the *Sunday Gazette*. Neighbours are not universally as suspicious as neighbours are in the newspapers, and Jane's neighbours had not been talking. There was nothing to make them talk. Ernest's pride had prevented him from mentioning his suspicions to anyone but the suspects. Real trouble between husband and wife was an exceptional event to the patrons of the Black Swan; divorces and separations were as rare as diamonds, and Jane and Ernest had only been married a couple of months or so. Jane was a favourite, and not a man or woman in the bar would have listened to a word against her. Ernest was not a favourite, but no one, without direct evidence, would have suspected him of beating or assaulting his bride so soon.

If some passing policeman had happened to put his eye to the fence while Ernest was rampaging in the studio, or chasing his bride across the wharf, there might have been awkward questions. But no man had seen anything, and because of the remoteness of the wharf and the noise of the storm no man had heard anything.

So the inquest, like most inquests, produced neither 'scene' nor 'sensation', and it discovered nothing except the identity of the deceased, and the fact that he had died by drowning through accidental causes. Jane was pale and pathetic in her black; Mr Bryan had a secret fear that she might break down and give things away; but she never faltered. The only comment the coroner made was:

'Eleven-thirty, you say. Late hours for a working man.'

But that was easily explained by the skittles championship and the storm.

One juryman made remarks about lifebuoys. The coroner commended Mr Bryan for his gallant act, and no one was to know that this well-intentioned endeavour had been in fact more hindrance than help.

Only Lily, looking pale, but not pathetic, in her black, wondered if they had heard the truth, the whole truth, etc.; but Lily, for once kept her mouth shut.

'Girl Bride Bereaved' was the heading of the local paper. Only one of the big papers noticed the affair, and that paper was attracted only by the midnight plunge of 'Peer's artist son'. Poor Ernest was not even named. The principal character in the drama was referred to shortly as 'a drowning man'.

It was odd, perhaps, that through all these trying days it never entered Jane's head that she had got her wish and was living like the pictures.

Much worse than the inquest was the funeral. Mrs Higgins cried all the way to the cemetry, and for a long way Jane could not cry at all. Then she thought of poor Ernest talking so seriously to the Sunday School, talking so bravely in Hyde Park, and she too cried.

Mr Bell announced that he had given up his Liverpool job and was going to stay on the barge and look after Jane. Lily said that she would stay over Christmas, as Mr Moss had to spend the Christmas holidays at his grandmother's in the country. And on Christmas morning Fred walked in. The *Prudence* and the *Adventure* were lying up at Brentford over the holidays, and Fred had heard the news from a passing waterman.

Lily tactfully took her father on deck.

Fred said for the second time, 'Hard lines, Jenny.'

And Jane said again, 'Poor Ernie.'

'Plucky job, that bloke going in after him.'

'You're right.'

Fred's eyes wandered to Ernest's Underground poster of 'Chestnut Sunday at Bushey Park', and she knew that he was wondering modestly why they had covered up his castle. She could not bear Fred to think that she was responsible. She said: 'I'm sorry, Fred. Ernie wasn't so gone on them.' She felt it was mean to give Ernest away; but then, that was the meanest thing that Ernest had ever done to her.

'It's all right, Jenny,' said Fred.

'S'pose you couldn't do some more, Fred – one day?'

' 'Course we could, Jenny. Anything you want – you've only got to say – you know that.'

Jane sighed. 'It's ever so nice, seeing you again, Fred.' There was a long pause.

Fred looked at the floor, at the roof, and at all the Underground posters; then he looked at the stove and said, 'Ruth's getting married – Syd Carter.'

'Go on?'

'Dad's retiring, Whitsun.'

'Go on?'

No more was said, but Jane knew that Fred had said, as delicately as possible, that he was still waiting, and, as soon as was decent, she might be queen of the *Prudence*.

Everybody was so kind. Was no one going to punish her for all her wickedness?

So those four spent Christmas together – the Bell family and Fred – very quietly, for had not three of them buried Ernest the day before? But it must be confessed that they were happy. The Bell family were glad to be together again on the old barge. Lily had got what she wanted, and Mr Bell had hopes. Fred had suffered through Ernest, and he too had hopes. And if the ghost of Ernest was walking the deck, looking for sympathy, he must have gone sadly away.

They tried to forget Ernest but remembered their black clothes. It was difficult, for Lily would say things which made them want to laugh, and they felt that a laugh would be shocking. Once Jane did laugh, to her shame; and Lily thought, '*You* won't be a wasting widow for long, my girl!'

In the evening Mr Bell went ashore to comfort Mrs Higgins. They took port wine in the back parlour, and Mr Bell inquired whether he could not be a help to her while he was looking for a job. Mrs Higgins said he could, for she had already discovered that Ernest had been more of a help than she had thought; and when it came to arguments with the brewers or filling up forms for the justices and the taxes she needed a man.

Mr Bryan went away for Christmas to a rather noisy country house-party. After his disturbing week at Hammersmith the change of scene and society was refreshing. But often his thoughts turned to the 'poor little waif', and he wondered what he could do for her.

He recognized gratefully that he had had a narrow escape, possibly from a violent death at the hands of Ernest, certainly from 'unpleasantness' and public scandal. If the police had walked into the studio and found the mutilated portrait of Ernest's wife, immediately after Ernest's death by drowning, the inquest on Ernest might have occupied a large space in the *Sunday Gazette*. It made him cold to think of it. And one clear, selfish course was to be warned in time and cut loose from the dangerous little female – give her money and the sack and let her fend for herself. Yes, she was dangerous, he really believed. She was 'gone on him'. Well, servant-girls and gallery-girls had these passions, far-away hero-worships, he knew – but this seemed different. It looked like an active, determined pursuit. He had the feeling now that she was after him – had always been after him, perhaps. Many little things came back to him now. And supposing that Ernest had come to the same conclusion, then Ernest's strange behaviour was accounted for.

And what a will the little creature had! He laughed as he remembered how she had bullied and snapped at him on the fatal night, torn off his icy trousers, thought of everything, managed everything. A pocket dynamo. Yes, he was at least a little afraid of her. He had a notion that she would stop at nothing. For all he knew she had deliberately pushed her tiresome husband overboard. No, he could not believe that. He liked the little thing – he liked her very much. And it would be a mean thing to desert her now, in her time of trouble. Although he deemed himself quite innocent in the affair, it was because of him that trouble had come to her. Also, he owed her something; she had saved him from the newspapers, perhaps from 'grievous bodily harm', and he must do what he could for her.

So, on the morning after his return, while he sipped his tea, he inquired what were her plans. One thing that she liked in him was that he woke up wide-awake (as a rule), instead of half-conscious, like Ernest or Mr Raven.

She said, 'Nothing special, Mr Bryan. Dad and me can manage together. I thought I'd do some more sitting, perhaps.' And she went on, humbly, 'But I'd like to stay on here, as long as you want me, Mr Bryan.'

'You wouldn't like to learn a trade, would you? I could have you taught typing, or fancy cooking or something. A girl like you – you ought to have a decent job.'

She shook her head and said gravely, 'I'd sooner look after you, Mr Bryan.'

Again her simple devotion touched him.

'Sit down,' he said, and she sat on the bed. This, today, seemed a natural and easy thing to do. They had shared such secrets and fears on what she thought of as 'the night' and since; he had made tea for her, and she had mothered him; they two, alone in the world, knew the truth about 'the night'. She felt more at ease with him than ever before.

'But look here, my dear' – he took her hand, because what he wanted to say was so difficult – 'you mustn't be "gone on me", you know.'

'I can't help it, Mr Bryan,' she whispered, and she fixed her sad brown eyes on his.

'Like a dog,' he thought. How could he hurt her? 'You mustn't,' he said vaguely.

'It was you began it, Mr Bryan,' she said softly. 'You didn't ought to have kissed me.'

'Kissed you? *When?*' Monstrous girl – what was she getting at now?

'Once on the stairs at Number 7, and another time here – the time I fainted.'

'Oh, *that!*' For the moment he had really forgotten. 'But, my dear, you know I didn't mean anything.'

'It meant a lot to me, Mr Bryan. I shouldn't have thought about you so much only for that.'

Good Heavens, he thought, if this comes of being kind to the poor, how careful a man should be! But he said kindly, none the less, 'Well, my dear, I'm sorry if it's my fault –'

'No, no, it isn't, Mr Bryan! I'm wicked.'

'No, you're not. But you mustn't think about me – like that. I'm not worth it.'

'You are,' she said stoutly. 'You're *good.*'

To this embarrassing tribute he did not know what to reply. She went on anxiously, 'But I won't be a fuss, Mr Bryan. Let me look after you, that's all I ask. You needn't speak to me, not if you don't want. Only don't send me away, or I'll do something desperate perhaps.'

Her voice was urgent and fearful. He said gently, 'Very well, my dear, we'll leave it at that.'

So Jane and her father lived quietly on the *Blackbird*. Mr Bell talked less and less about getting another job, but made himself more and more useful to Mrs Higgins. He had a number of suggestions for the improvement of the garden. How would it be if there was a covered shelter against the wall at the back, with tables and chairs, to which the mothers and children could retire on showery summer evenings? There might be fairy-lights – red and green. And how would it be to have open-air darts in the summer – get the boys out of the stuffy Public Bar? One strong electric lamp over the board would be enough. And what about doing something about the garden? The last two years the show of flowers had not been what it used to be in Mr Higgins's times. Mrs Higgins had never had the energy for improvements (it took her all her time, she said, to keep things going); and she told him to go ahead, if it didn't cost too much. Mr Bell replied wisely that money well spent never did any harm; and the next time the brewers called they were surprised by the new spirit of enterprise which animated Mrs Higgins.

One Saturday night, when Harold was laid up with a poisoned foot, Mr Bell nobly stepped into the breach and worked at the beer-engines behind the bar. At first he served a good many 'old ales' in mistake for 'bitters', and mixed up one or two customers' change; but the brain which had been exercised so long in the calculation of odds was soon equal to the complicated sums of the barman – such as the total price of two mild and bitters, one old and mild, two small ports, one lemonade for the old lady, and a drop of Scotch. And there were so many jokes about the 'new landlord' that Mrs Higgins blushed frequently. Mr Bell enjoyed himself, and the business was better than usual.

Mr Bell had brought home ninety-five pounds from Liverpool – saved from his earnings, or gloriously gained on the dogs. He went seldom to the London dogs (the wooing of Mrs Higgins took too much of his time); but he was betting quietly on the horses again, and was having quite a run of luck – that is to say, he won about three pounds a week, and lost only three pounds five. Jane said nothing, for she felt that she had no right to lecture people now. Besides, he so much enjoyed telling her in the morning what horse was going to win in the afternoon, and explaining in the evening the combination of forces which had prevented it – it was like old times.

She wrote to Mr Potts and Mr Latimer and her other old employers and posed for one of them most afternoons. But the morning was her happy time, when she swept out and scrubbed and polished and tidied, and pottered about the studio, stealing sly glances at Mr Bryan's back and sometimes inventing jobs which would keep her for a few minutes on the beloved premises.

'You've polished that floor twice this week,' said Mr Bryan testily one day.

'You make such a mess with your pipes,' said Jane.

He thought, 'Damn the girl! She talks to me like a wife.'

One day she dragged into the big room the remains of 'The Blush'. Mr Bryan looked up from his work and saw her piecing the jagged fragments of canvas together.

'What a *shame*!' she said; and he saw that there were tears in her eyes.

'Never mind,' he said, 'I'll do another of you.' She gave him an eager glance and he said quickly, 'Not like that!' (he was taking no more risks). 'I tell you what – I'll do you as you are now, in your apron, washing-up.'

'*Washing-up*, Mr Bryan?' Horrible idea! Washing-up, of all things. Nobody had ever proposed to paint her washing-up. In Potts's and Latimer's pictures she was generally a wood-nymph, Psyche, Diana, or Helen of Troy; in all her experience as a model she had never been less than a ballet-dancer. Washing-up! The thing she hated more than anything in the world, the only thing she did not really enjoy doing for Mr Bryan.

'Do you mind?' he said, surprised.

'No, Mr Bryan, it's quite all right.'

Whatever he wanted he could have – that was the only rule of her life now.

So, two weeks later, she stooped over the sink, her hair disordered (by request), her hands in the big metal basin, and about and above and behind her Mr Bryan arranged piles of plates, cutlery, teapots, and dishes, and hanging saucepans, in which he discovered some exciting geometrical patterns.

It was a tiring pose, and Jane found it depressing. Washing-up – that was all she meant to him – just a girl washing-up. And now, if she was in the Exhibition, she would not be a queen, a fairy, a ballet-dancer, or somebody standing in a pool with nothing on, one of those women with comical names such as Mr Latimer painted – but somebody washing-up; might just as well be Mrs Staples.

'I want you to look tired, my dear,' said Mr Bryan tactlessly, 'but not suicidal.'

And then the absurd girl began to cry.

'My God – women!' thought Mr Bryan, as he strode across to comfort her.

'I'm ever so sorry,' she whimpered at last. 'It's quite all right, Mr Bryan.'

'No, it isn't,' said he. 'Now, just sit down and tell us all about it. What's the trouble? Here.' He sat down and put his comforting arm round her, and somehow or other she was sitting on his knee.

'It's nothing, really, Mr Bryan, only the washing-up, you see, because I've always hated the washing-up, more than anything, you see; and when I left the Ravens' I thought I'd finished with washing-up – sort of improved my "stattus", you see. Of course, I don't mind doing anything for you, Mr Bryan – only then when you wanted to paint me washing-up, I thought –'

But she could not say exactly what she thought, and Mr Bryan could only dimly imagine.

'Well, my dear, I told you you ought to have a better job, didn't I? But you mustn't be ashamed of washing-up. Washing-up? It's the most important job in the world!' His tone was jocular and cheerful, but he thought the moment ripe for a little lecture. 'Nobody wants my pictures,' he said, truly. 'Nobody'd care two pins if I never painted another. But if all the girls stopped washing-up there'd be the devil to pay. It's one of the jobs that *matter* – washing-up and scrubbing and all that. Besides, it's one of the jobs where you've really got something to *show*. Half the world works hard all day and has nothing to show at the end of it – people in factories, clerks, politicians, nearly everybody. But look at your nice clean plates, look at your nice polished floor – you've really *done* something. Think of it that way, my dear.'

How kind he was! She wished he would kiss her. She knew she was a widow only a month gone; but she wished he would kiss her. But Mr Bryan was not going to be told again that he 'began it'.

'Yes, I know I talk silly,' she said; 'only I wanted to get on in the world, you see, Mr Bryan, and I don't seem to get no further.'

'Well, you've just taken a bad knock,' he said; 'but you're only a kid. You'll fall in love with some nice boy and get married again.'

'Fred wants to marry me.' She felt she could talk to him about anything now.

'Fred? Oh, that's the barge-chap?'

'Yes, Mr Bryan. He asked me once. Only I thought that –'

'Well, there you are,' said Mr Bryan, delighted, it seemed. 'You like the water. Couldn't have a better life.'

'I'd like to have a good time first,' said Jane sadly. 'I've never had a good time, you see, Mr Bryan – you know, nice clothes, and that. Lily has a good time. When Lily got off she went to a big hotel and had a private bath and everything. But when I got married we went to a rotten little hole, with no bath or nothing. Lily has nice clothes, too. I don't seem to have no luck. But don't think I'm grumbling, Mr Bryan,' she said, smiling an apology at him. 'I'm not a one to grumble, only I used to think I was born for better things, you see. Shall we go on with the picture now?'

'Do you go to the pictures much?' he said.

'I used to, Mr Bryan.'

'That's where you got these funny little ideas, I suppose. Everybody can't be a star, you know, can they?'

'I s'pose not, Mr Bryan.'

'And everybody can't have nice clothes, unfortunately. Do you ever read the Prayer Book?'

'No so often, Mr Bryan.'

'Well, do you remember the bit about "doing my duty in that state of life to which it shall please God to call me"? That's what none of us want to do these days. Everybody wants to do something else. And I'm just as bad as you. I broke away from my lot, and you want to break away from yours.'

Jane, a little fogged by this, said, 'Some people get on, don't they, Mr Bryan?'

'Do your job, my dear. That's the main thing. We all want something for nothing these days.' Mr Bryan was pleased with his little lecture, but felt that possibly he had overdone it. He went on, 'I tell you what – one day, later, when you're out of mourning,

I'll take you up to the West End and give you a good time. Would you like that?'

'Of course,' said Jane, blissful. 'Only I've got no clothes.'

'Well, we'll see about that.'

Jane then insisted on posing at the sink again. She was happy, as always, after her talk with Mr Bryan – even though he was so anxious for her to marry Fred. Mr Bryan thought again that he was absurdly fond of the poor little waif; and he wondered what she would be like with good clothes and a bath or two.

February was cold and bright, clear skies and north-easterly winds. The *Blackbird*'s stove ate up the wood greedily, but there was plenty of firewood in the water. Mr Bell, with a few pounds from his Liverpool hoard, had had the dinghy painted and refitted; the sail was dyed the faded blue of Jane's desire, there were nails or screws where before there was string, the floor-boards were varnished, and the fine new halyard and sheet were a joy to handle. Jane sailed proudly about under her blue sail in the wintry sunshine, gathering firewood, or stole round the island watching her herons and the duck. The water-fowl knew her, or her boat, she often thought, for the haughty heron would stand unmoved while she glided past, and the duck sat still among the osiers, sleeping on one leg, or cleaning themselves; but if any strange rowing-boat came near them, away sailed the heron on his slow, majestic wings, and fifty duck flew squawking and flapping towards the sky. Alone with her boat, she was contented always. She was queen of an island, mistress of her fate. The troubles of the shore seemed as far and faint as the sound of London's traffic; the set of the sail, the chuckle of the water at the bows, the pull of the tiller, were all that mattered. And then, on the stormy days which she loved, there was the warning ruffle of the water to windward, a gust, a squall, coming down a side-street as out of a valley, a sudden heel, and she must use all her small strength to keep the tiller up and the river out. Dusk falling, no other craft in sight, the blinds drawn in every window on the shore; the chance of an icy swim or a lonely death if she dared too much or was caught by a cruel squall. But Jane found her lonely sails as soothing as they were exciting; the small sailing-boat, almost alone of man's works, supplies at once the appetite for serenity and adventure.

The evenings, now, were her difficult times. Mr Bell, nearly always, was at the Black Swan; a mourning widow still, she could not go with him there, she thought, or go to the pictures with any-one else. And, alone in the long room, though she never thought of Ernest if she could help it, she could not help thinking of Ernest. When the wind was in the north the Aladdin lamp flickered in the draught from the little side-windows, and Ernest was among the dancing shadows, holding out his hand and saying, 'See here, my girl.' When the tide was up and the wind was high and Ernest's 'noises' were strong, she would hear Ernest growling through the partition that he could not sleep a wink; and she would expect to see him peep round the door in his shirt, saying, 'What about a bit of love, my girl?' And when she had these thoughts, she felt queerly guilty and fond of Ernest. She went over in her mind that scene on the deck, and wondered what he had meant to do, what would have happened if she had not sprung at him like that. Some-times she concluded that he had meant no harm, and she was just a common murderess. She had talked about 'doing for' him, had even thought about it. Sometimes, half awake, she saw herself going to the police, confessing all, and asking to be tried for murder; and this picture, strangely, made her feel noble and good. One objection to it was that Mr Bryan was always dragged into it as well; but, some nights, even that had its consolations. For the jury, after a thrilling trial, acquitted her; the surging crowds in the street were on her side; but Mr Bryan lost caste with his own friends, was turned down by Fay Meadows, and he and Jane went off into exile, hand in hand.

The return of Mr Bell, with his cheerful chatter about the day's losses and the news of the pub, dispelled these brooding fancies, as a rule; and in the daytime they troubled her not at all. If she thought of Ernest the thought was that the worry of Ernest was over. Good or bad, he had been a worry to her from the very first night she walked out with him and he had begun to 'paw' in the passage. It had always been, 'Shall I let him?' 'Do I like him?' 'Ought I?' 'Is it right?' 'Would he mind?' or 'Will he find out?' And now the worry was over. In the daytime Jane never thought of giving herself up for murder, never wished that Ernest was alive; she lived in a dim contentment, basking in the warmth of Mr

Bryan's acquaintance, and thinking very little about the future, or anything else. When her mourning was decently over something would happen – she did not know what.

One week-end she spent with Lily and Mr Moss. She envied Lily her cosy little flat, high up in a side-street in Soho, and she envied Lily's air of settled domestic bliss. But at night the noise of the streets was terrible; she could not sleep, and swore she must always sleep on the water. On Saturday evening they took her to the dogs; she soon tired of the dogs, and lost twelve shillings. And on Sunday afternoon she sneaked out by herself and went to church.

The *Sunday Gazette* had recently begun to make a feature of God. The argument about the Deposited Book had shown that God was saleable news, and, properly handled, might hold the public as long as a good murder. Therefore there were series of articles by well-known novelists and racing-men on such subjects as 'How I pray', 'What God Means to Me', and 'How Would God Vote?' Special reporters were sent to write up the services and sermons of fashionable divines, and readers were exhorted to go to selected churches guaranteed by the *Sunday Gazette*. Those other seductive features of the paper, which did as much as anything to keep its readers out of the churches, the life-stories of murderers, the gossip of Society, the accounts of past horse-races, and the reasoned forecasts of horse-races to come, remained as before.

But the *Sunday Gazette* did send Jane, for one, in curiosity to church. She went to St Sebastian's, Fish Street, the rector of which church was constantly in the papers – the Fairbanks, as it were, of Religion. It was about as difficult to get a seat as it was at the Royal Picture Palace; she had to stand in a queue, and this made her think there was something in it. But, as a show, the service disappointed her. She liked the organ's preliminary music, sliding about in the roof and booming about under her seat, but she thought the organ at the Royal was better, and at the Royal she could see the man playing – he ascended out of the floor, manuals and all, and played tuny music in full view of all, lit by two beams of heliotrope lime-light descending upon him from the roof. The parson pleased her at first. The Trinity, the Holy Ghost, Redemption, had no meaning for her – she had no idea what the man was talking about. But she liked his droning, musical voice; and there was much in the service which attracted and moved her. She liked the singing, the hymns, the unintelligible unanimous babble of the congregation when they knelt and prayed out loud together. She felt then as she felt at the skittles matches, when they called, 'Three cheers for the Man in the Moon!' – that they were all jolly good chaps, one and all. She liked the anthem, with a fine bass solo about all flesh being as grass, and all the glory thereof; and most of all she liked the hymn which preceded the sermon, 'The day Thou gavest, Lord, is ended.' The lovely tune touched her. She listened to the words about her brethren 'neath the Western sky which the man beside her was singing with passionate fervour, and her eyes grew wet. She thought of her father, and Lily, and Fred, and Mrs Higgins, and Mr Bryan, and even Ernest; and she decided once more that she was a wicked girl who had pushed her husband into the river, was potty about a gentleman, and would very soon be thrown into the eternal fire which had been mentioned somewhere earlier in the service. Still, at the end of the beautiful hymn she sat down feeling excited and good.

But the sermon spoiled everything. It was like an unconvincing third act of a promising play – though this comparison did not occur to Jane. The celebrated rector, when he talked, was as droning and as musical as before; but now, she thought, he was soapy and bossy, and talked rather like Ernest when he was laying down the law. His text was, 'Repent ye, for –', and Jane gathered that, whatever she had done, if she repented she would be all right – she would count as a sheep and not as a goat, and go to Heaven. She thought, mystified, that she would just as soon be a goat as a sheep – the goat was better, in a way, more lively and amusing. She remembered two or three goats she had seen tethered near the canal banks, each of them more interesting than the silly sheep she had seen by hundreds in the fields. But, what was much more serious, she found, when she thought about it, that she did not really repent. She tried hard. She realized that the preacher knew all about her, about Ernest and about Mr Bryan, and was talking specially to her and nobody else; but in spite of this alarming conviction she could not pretend she was really sorry about Ernest, or about loving Mr Bryan. Love was the greatest thing in life, the books said, and the pictures said, and even sometimes the *Sunday Gazette* said – so how could she be sorry about it? The only thing she repented was messing about with Ernest when she had not loved, not really loved him; and that, after all, was Ernest's fault. All she had done was to go out and search for Love, as Mr Douglas had told her to.

But she felt, from the sound of his voice and the look of his face, that the celebrated preacher would not understand all this, and, if he really knew all about her, would be against her. (This opinion was probably wrong, but the fault was perhaps the preacher's, who should have used in the pulpit the same natural and human tones which he used in private life.) But though she enjoyed the last hymn, 'Now thank we all our God,' she went away disappointed and chilled. When she returned to the flat Lily said, 'Been to church, have you! Whatever next?' as if she had done something rather disgraceful. But Jane, believing in the *Sunday Gazette*, thought that there must be more in God than she had discovered; and after that she went many times, by herself to the Chiswick Church in the little old village street beside the river. She came out always just before the sermon, and stuck her fingers in her ears while the parson prayed in that hot-potato praying voice; and, so long as she did this, she came away with a sensation of peace and goodness. For the next few days she would say over to herself often that bit of Mr Bryan's about 'doing your duty in that state of life', and when she had thoughts of a 'Night of Love' she said to herself, 'You're a bad girl,' and thought about something else.

In the last week of February the *Prudence* and the *Adventure* lay up in the creek for three days. On Saturday and Sunday Fred and Mr Green took down the Underground posters and painted hearts and castles and roses again. And Mr Green said that any time Jane felt like a trip up the 'Cut' she had only to say the word. But she could not go with them then, for Mr Bryan's 'Washing-Up' was not finished yet. On Sunday evening Mr Bryan was invited into the *Blackbird* to admire the castles and roses and meet the Greens again. He admired the castles and roses very warmly; they had the same grand disregard for formal exactitude as his own work. They were direct and lively and gay; and they had come down to the Greens through generations of English boatmen, like their knots and splices and the shape of their boats. Mr Green was so pleased by Mr Bryan's praise that he gave him a biscuit tin decorated with roses and the legend, in yellow, 'A Present from Mr Green', though this had been intended for Jane. Mr Bryan liked Fred, but thought that he was a little slow, perhaps, to be the husband of Jane.

'Washing-Up' took a long time, partly because Mr Bryan could not get it right, was in a muddle, and kept putting it away. Bollards were easier. He had the saucepans right, and the teacups and the plates, and the sink and the window behind it, through which one wan ray of sun came in. They made a capital pattern, though their shapes and colours were perhaps unusual. To fit smoothly into the general scheme of the composition Jane would have to be as unusual in shape and colour as the saucepans. He saw clearly how this could be done; if she had been one of his other models he could have done it swiftly, but, since she was Jane, for some odd reason he could not do it. He wanted Jane to be like Jane. But if she was like Jane the saucepans would be wrong, and the saucepans, he thought, were really fine.

Also, just now, there were good excuses for putting the thing aside. Most of his work for the 'Show' was ready, and, a quarter of a mile down the river at Mr Bale's yard, the 'cabin-cruiser' was building. She was to be called the *Water Gipsy*. The hull was complete; soon they would be stepping the mast; and the nearer she came to completion the more often must Mr Bryan visit the beauty, pass his hands fondly over her smooth, clean, timbers, admire her proud curves, and yarn with Mr Bale (quite needlessly) about halyards and cleats, sail area and head-room, anchors and chain, and all the rest of it. He was mad about her.

Day by day, while Jane stooped over the sink, Mr Bryan would report the progress of his ship; and always she said to herself, 'I'll be his cabin-boy.'

One morning she said, 'What made you call her the *Water Gipsy*, Mr Bryan?'

'Don't quite know,' he answered. 'I believe it was something *you* said, about the canal. You're a water gipsy, aren't you, Jane?'

'Cool' she thought, 'We *are* getting on!'

And in a day or two she had persuaded herself that the boat was named after her.

24

A GOOD TIME

March was mild and sunny. In the garden of the Black Swan some of Mrs Higgins's crocuses (packet of twelve) showed themselves; on the island they cut the withes for the basket-makers; there was talk about the Boat Race; the small boys shouted, 'Give us a ride, Cambridge!' at every passing eight. Spring was in sight.

By the end of March, Jane reckoned, she would be out of mourning. Three months was enough for any man, surely, and she was tired of her black. And one night in the third week Mr Bell came home and said, solemn and shy, with a good many coughs, 'Jane, my dear, I have a communication.' He coughed. 'At last, my child, you are going to have a mother.'

Jane, ignoring the strange form of this announcement, cried, delighted, 'Oh, Dad, not Mrs Higgins?'

'How did you guess?' said Mr Bell.

She sprang at him and hugged him. She was overjoyed. She did not think he would manage the pub very well, but he would be happy. And the next morning she left off her black, for she too was happy. There was a warm, soft breeze and a warm, soft sun, the Oxford crew were expected tomorrow, Mr Bryan was pleased with 'Washing-Up', and why should she not be happy?

Her father had got what he wanted, Lily had got what she wanted, and now, at last, why should not Jane get what she wanted, perhaps? Meanwhile, every day she saw Mr Bryan, and talked to Mr Bryan; every night she thought about Mr Bryan before she slept. Every day, now, she thought he liked her better, though of course he could not say anything yet; and one day he was going to take her into the West End and give her a good time. But every Sunday she was going to church; and up to Tuesday or Wednesday 'a good time in the West End' meant nothing more than a trip to the Zoo, or perhaps a 'tea-dancing'.

Then one morning he said casually, without a word of warning,

'You'll have to be looking for another job, Jane. I'm giving up the studio. Going away.'

Going away! Her world collapsed. She went white. It was the end of everything. She ran to him and clung to him and put her head on his breast, half-sobbing, and pouring out her heart without restraint or shame.

'You can't go away! You can't! You shan't! I shall die, Mr Bryan! I shall give myself up! I'll go and tell them I pushed Ernie overboard that night, and I'll say I did it for you, because I was gone on you –'

'Jane! Jane! What's the matter with you?'

'It's true, too, Mr Bryan – well, it is in a way, because I did use to think if Ernie was out of the way you might love me, perhaps; only of course I never meant anything that night; but if you don't love me, I don't care what happens, you see. Can't you love me a little, Mr Bryan, before you go, only a little – I don't ask no more?' Calmer now, she raised those pathetic, pleading, dog's eyes to him.

Mr Bryan, whose only real vice, perhaps, was a short-sighted kindness of heart, said seriously, 'I'm very fond of you, Jane.'

'Kiss me, then,' she commanded. 'You never kissed me – not properly.'

And being only flesh and blood he kissed her – 'properly', according to Jane's interpretation of the word. Pathetic, loving, desirable little thing.

She sighed, in ecstasy. 'Love's Bliss' at last – the long, heroic, clinging, close-up kiss of the pictures; there had been nothing in her life like this.

'You can't go away,' she sighed, 'not after that. Love me.'

'But, my dear, I don't love you. I never said that.' Goodness, the girl was never satisfied!

'Love me a little,' she persisted. 'I'll make you. If I have nice clothes and everything like your friends, I'd be ever so different.'

'I wonder,' he thought. 'Interesting experiment. Just what I used to say at Ascot. But was I right?'

He said curiously, 'What do you expect me to do, my dear – marry you, or what?'

'Give me a "Night of Love",' she whispered. 'Take me to one

of them big hotels with the bathrooms. I never been inside one. Then if you don't like me, I wouldn't worry you no more, you see?'

'And suppose I land you with a baby?'

'I'd *like* to have a baby of yours,' she said defiantly, 'if I never saw you again. You're a god!'

'My poor Jane,' he said gently. The girl was staggering. Nobody had loved him with this insane intensity before. He felt humble and foolish. Was it his fate to play Joseph all his life? And what the devil did he want? He had turned down the aristocratic Sybil, he had turned down the *bourgeois* Mrs Raven, he could never be quite sure whether he was in love with Fay, the charming Bohemian; and now he was turning up his nose at a working-girl. What sort of woman *did* he want? Perhaps none, for very long.

'Only one night,' she pleaded. 'Something to remember when you're gone, you see.'

Why not? She was a dear little thing. It would be fun to have her washed and dressed up, take her out and see what sort of figure she would cut. Plenty of the little models at studio-parties spoke not much better than she, and had not half her pluck and intelligence. But then he thought of Ernest: he would be doing the very thing that Ernest had suspected – the rich man exploiting the poor girl. And then there was this Fred fellow. Probably there would be more trouble; Fred would pursue him to the West End with a wood-chopper. And what would they think of him at the Black Swan?

'My dear,' he said, 'I'm not fond enough of you to marry you; but I'm too fond of you to do the other thing. I respect you too much.' Humbug, he thought. Yet it was not wholly humbug. He respected Jane, and he respected himself; and, more, he respected Fred and Mr Green and Mrs Higgins and the Pewters and all the Skittles Club, and their decent, respectable standards of behaviour. They had welcomed him, and trusted him, accepted him as one of themselves, though he belonged to a suspected class; indeed, since the attempted rescue of Ernest he had become a kind of hero. And now, to amuse himself with one of their girls and then throw her aside – what a come-down! Other artists might go about with their 'little bits' for a month or two, and then drop them, as one drops ballast from a balloon; but they were not living among the relatives and friends of the 'little bits'.

'Only one night,' she repeated softly.

And yet, in the face of a passion like Jane's, how churlish it seemed to stand there telling her that he respected her! Well, he would think about it.

Now he shook his head. 'Be sensible, Jane. I'm going along now to look at the boat.'

But she clung to him still. 'Where are you going when you go away?'

'Cruise round England. In the boat.'

'Who's going with you?' she demanded jealously.

'Nobody.'

'Not all by yourself? Out at sea?'

'Captain Slocum sailed round the world by himself. I'm going to sail round England.'

Jane did not know or care anything about Captain Slocum.

'Take me, Mr Bryan. I'll be ever so useful.'

'Be sensible, Jane,' he said. 'I'm very fond of you, Jane, but you must be sensible.'

'All right, Mr Bryan,' she whispered sadly. He kissed her and went out.

Extraordinary girl, he thought – extraordinary situation! Instead of the gentleman pursuing the servant-girl, it was the other way round. No moral sense, no shame, no fear, no restraint, no prudence, no education, no mother, too many films. But she had pluck, devotion, fidelity, intelligence, ability, industry – all the good qualities which are born, not made. If she belonged to his own class and had a bath every day, if she talked like *The Times* and not like Mr Green, if she knew more about pictures and less about films, if she wore furs instead of aprons – he believed he would be asking himself, 'Shall I marry her?' But, as Ernest had once said to him, 'Class is class – and you can't get away from it.' Quite right. But what a confession for Gordon Bryan!

The important thing, he thought, was to let the girl down gently, to leave a good taste in her mouth when he left her. He was not going to be the young squire of melodrama who ruined the village girl and ran away. The ghost of Ernest, addressing the

Communists of another place, should never be able to point at him and say, 'There's another of 'em! I told you so!' The difficulty was that this particular village-girl was most anxious to be ruined – or said she was. But that was probably hysteria, film-stuff. He could give her 'something to remember, you see' without going to those lengths. What she wanted was a little human attention. Mr Bryan decided on compromise, and approaching his beloved boat put the lady out of his mind.

The next afternoon, as a compromise, he nobly took her to the National Gallery; on Monday afternoon he took her to the Zoo; on Thursday afternoon he took her to the Tower of London; and on Saturday to the Houses of Parliament.

These blameless expeditions, the first of many, delighted Jane. They were exciting, though they were so innocent; for (to avoid talk) she had to meet Mr Bryan at some rendezvous in London, and she felt pleasantly guilty as she hurried along in her best, or peered this way and that at the meeting-place, wondering if he would turn up. When passing men stared at her (which was pleasantly alarming) she would give them a proud look, meaning to say, 'Less of it, my lad – I've got a better boy than you.' And then, what a thrill, to see him hurrying towards her through the crowd, smiling at her above the bowler hats! It was thrilling, too, the first time, to put a timid hand on his arm, crossing the dangerous roads; thrilling to sit at a table for two at the big Lyons' tea-shop after the Gallery. 'Quite a couple,' she thought, and smiled at him, and blushed.

It gave Mr Bryan, too, a queer excitement to see her pleasure; it was new to take a young woman about who enjoyed everything and was blasé about nothing. Jane made silly remarks at the National Gallery; but so, he remembered, had Fay. And Jane never pretended. She liked pictures for their subjects – landscapes, ships, boats, horses, handsome gentlemen; but Madonnas, Saint Sebastians, martyrdoms – no. Mr Bryan made no attempt to 'educate' her, but answered her questions and listened with interest to what she had to say. He felt that he was learning, not she – he was learning the mind of millions; and sometimes the mind was right. It was more often right at the Zoo than at the National Gallery. She loved the Aquarium – almost the best thing in London

– but hated the lion-house – perhaps the worst. 'Seem ever so happy, the fish, don't they? But those great lions, cooped up there – it seems a shame.'

She liked the Aquarium best of all the sights, and they went there a second time. 'Seems like fairyland, don't it?' said Jane, and she stood enthralled before every tank. 'Nothing to worry about, plenty of company, and regular meals. Better off than what they are in the sea, wouldn't you think, Mr Bryan? Oh, look at that flat one! There's a picture for you, Mr Bryan!' And she caught his arm excitedly as a big sole, like an aeroplane coming to land, descended gracefully to the sandy bottom, gave two quick wriggles and was hidden, but for one watchful eye protruding from the sea of sand.

Mr Bryan had been thinking that for his next Show he must specialize in fish instead of fishing-boats and bollards. And it was Jane's fresh enthusiasm that had opened his eyes to the fantastic beauty of captive fish, and set his artist's mind to work upon them. But how could any man hope to set down that beauty in paint – the unearthly light, the darting, dazzling, tiny, tropical creatures; the impossible sea-horse; the gallant, quarrelsome, common British stickleback; the peace and colour of those miniature worlds?

'Can't be done,' he sighed.

'Pardon?'

'Too difficult.'

'They say nothing's too difficult,' said Jane, 'if you set your mind to it, don't they?'

Jane had set her mind on 'improving' herself for Mr Bryan's benefit. She had bought some 'White Heather' scent at Woolworth's, and a new dictionary at Peacock's. She watched him carefully at the tea-places, the way he cut up his toast and used a fork for cakes. And she listened carefully to the waitresses' remarks, for they seemed to speak much more like Mr Bryan than she did. From them she had acquired the expressions 'Pardon?' and 'Granted', and she was proud of them. The trouble was that Mr Bryan did not help her – never told her anything, just treated her as if she was a perfect lady. That was nice, but it did not help a person.

Outside the Zoo Mr Bryan felt tired and stopped a taxi. Generally they had tea, and after tea separated. Today Mr Bryan, suddenly reckless, thought it was a mean and silly procedure, this slinking home one by one. He would take her home. What did it matter?

'Where we going, Mr Bryan?'

'I'll take you home,' said Mr Bryan. 'I'm rather tired.'

'All the way in a taxi? Fancy! Quite a treat!' She thought, 'Coo! he's forgotten about the neighbours – that means he likes me.' She slipped her arm under his, and sat silent and happy.

He thought, 'Restful little companion. Gives no trouble.' And it was 'quite a treat' to take a girl in a taxi to whom a taxi-ride was quite a treat.

At last, near Notting Hill, she said, 'You ought to pull me up more, Mr Bryan. I wish you would.'

'Pull you up?' said Mr Bryan, waking out of a dream about his boat.

'Well, I know I talk common, and that. Only you don't tell me what's right and what isn't, you see.'

'You be your natural self, my dear. That's the best.'

'Yes, but I don't talk like you do, do I?'

'A lot of people don't like the way I talk. The Americans don't. Very few English people do. If you talked as I do they'd say you were swanking.'

'Well, some's common and some's not, and I know I talk common.'

'You say what you mean, and that's the great thing.'

'Well, I want to do you credit, you see. Go on, tell me some things,' she pleaded, putting her face up to his. 'You might, Mr Bryan.'

Mr Bryan had decided that he would not try to 'educate' her. What was the use? His only aim was to give her a good time. And a few fragments of the Oxford accent and High Art would be of no great service to her as the wife of Fred. What was wrong with her speech was not its roughness but its refinements. Already, he had noticed, she had acquired some of the spurious elegancies of the tea-shop girl; and now, he thought, considering her eager little face, he might at least warn her against them.

'You'll talk better,' he said, 'if you don't try to talk so well.'

'Pardon?'

And he gave her a little lecture on 'Pardon?' and 'Granted', and

'Ever so', and 'You see', and 'Reelly', and other little things which had begun to be a weariness to him.

At the end she said sadly, 'Well, I never. Just what I thought was all right was all wrong it seems. Thanks ever so, Mr Bryan. I will try – really I will.'

He wanted to kiss the humble little thing drooping beside him. He thought, 'Damn it, no – only mean more trouble.' But he did kiss her. He thought, 'Damn it, this is all wrong – not a bit what I intended.' And he kissed her a second time. The 'White Heather' was powerful, but he thought, 'She's taken to washing. What a difference it makes!' And he drew her close and kissed her again.

'Damn you, Jane!' he muttered at last. 'You're making a fool of me.'

'Pardon?' she said, blissful.

*

It was dark when they reached the wharf. No one was about, and Mr Bryan boldly invited her to tea. 'I'm mad,' he thought, 'perfectly mad.' But the idea of a lonely tea in the studio had suddenly repelled him.

Jane went at once to the gas-ring, and then to the china-cupboard. But Mr Bryan, still mad, said with exaggerated courtesy, 'Please sit down, Mrs Higgins. I am the butler today.' And he took the tea-cups from her.

'You're tired, Mr Bryan,' she said.

'You have refreshed me, Mrs Higgins,' he said. 'Pray sit down. I am sorry the servants are out, but I will do what I can.'

Mad, perfectly mad! he thought. But rather fun. He would give her 'something to remember, you see'.

'Oh, certainly, milord,' said Jane, playing up nobly; and she walked to an arm-chair with the mincing step which Moira Myrtle had used in 'Only a Wife'.

'Will you take China, madam, or Ceylon?'

'A little of both, if you please,' she said.

Mr Bryan laughed, and solemnly began to make two pots of tea. He cut bread and butter, he laid the best cloth (kept for parties), and made some toast, and set the small table beside her. Jane lay back in her chair and watched him, wondering if all this was really happening. It was the nicest thing that he had ever done, she thought – the nicest thing that had ever happened to her; and one of her old captions came back to her: '*From Kitchen to Castle*.' Here it was, coming true. 'I've got him,' she thought. 'Surely I've got him now.'

'Isn't there something about a "Mad Tea-party"?' she said, recalling some old cartoon in the *Sunday Gazette*.

'There is,' he said, pouring out two cups of tea for her.

'Well, this is one, and no mistake.'

'That is the China, madam, and that the Ceylon.'

'Well, all the best,' she said, raising a cup in each hand. 'And you can take a month's notice.'

'Oh!' he said, as one deeply wounded. 'Don't you like the tea-party, milady?'

'It's ever so nice,' she whispered, and her heart shone from her eyes. She put out her hand. 'You won't really go away and leave me, will you, Mr Bryan?'

'Yes, my dear,' he said. 'The *Water Gipsy* sails on the fourteenth. Two days after the "Show". Then off you go and marry your Fred.'

The light went out of the 'mad tea-party', and he saw the light go out of her face.

'Well,' she said bravely, 'we must be thankful for small mercies, I suppose.' But she turned her head away from him, and her lip trembled.

He took her hand quickly, afraid of tears.

'You must be sensible, little Jane,' he said. 'I've got to leave you, and I'm trying to leave you as nicely as I can. Don't make it difficult.'

'All right, Mr Bryan,' she whispered. But why did he keep raising her hopes if he was only going to knock them down again?

'Listen,' he said. 'I've got a surprise for you.' And he related his comforting 'surprise' – which had only that moment entered his head. She was to come, of course, to the 'Show' and hear what the people said about her picture. That night some friends – the Murray Clares – were to give a big farewell party for him. She should go with him to the party – perhaps dine with him first. She shook her head sadly.

'I haven't got any clothes, Mr Bryan,' she said. 'Not fit for that.'

'Doesn't matter what you wear,' he said. 'It's only a studio-party. Lots of models and so on. Here!' – he took some notes from his case – 'go out with your sister tomorrow and buy what you like. Evening-dress, fancy-dress – anything. *Please*. I *want* you to come.'

'All right, Mr Bryan,' she said, faintly. Anything he wanted she would do.

'Could you arrange to stay with your sister that night?'

'Yes, Mr Bryan.'

'No!' Mr Bryan, intent on giving pleasure, had had another idea. He would take a room for her at one of the big hotels – four-poster bed, private bathroom, telephone, servants, and everything. For one night she should live like a princess. How would she like that?

'Ever so nice, Mr Bryan,' she said, with a little more spirit. But was she to go to a big hotel all by herself, she wondered? Funny man – he did not say. And now she was afraid to ask.

Mr Bryan was delighted with his plans. The little thing should have a glorious fling before she went off to her Fred: good food, gaiety, hot baths, fine linen – everything. Quite a romance, and all perfectly proper. He was surprised that she was not more excited.

Four days before Mr Bryan's 'Show', the Oxford and Cambridge Boat Race took place. Mr Bryan had a large party of guests to view the annual spectacle of two eight-oared boats proceeding upstream not very fast, in single file. So had Jane. But Jane abandoned her guests long before Oxford splashed past, and poured out teas and whiskies for Mr Bryan's friends.

Mr Bryan had, with delicate intention, not wished her to do this duty. 'I like having you to look after *me*,' he said, 'but I don't want to think of you as my servant otherwise, you see.'

' "You see",' she thought, smiling. He had caught that from her. Funny man – so nice and thoughtful in some ways, so blind in others. And the better she knew him the funnier he seemed.

Jane, in a spirit of jealous martyrdom, insisted on doing the job; she would not have any Mrs Staples butting into her studio. On the day, she regretted it. Fay Meadows was there, with many other dazzling and talkative young women. Jane handed them sand-wiches and teas and this and that, and they did not seem to see her.

She felt small. She said to herself fiercely. 'Yah! I know him better than all of you. We have a secret together. I undressed him when he was half-dead with cold. He took me to the Zoo – *twice*. I sat in that chair while he made tea for me – *and* hot buttered toast.' But it did not work. She still felt small.

Jane was mistaken. She was observed, but with perfect breeding, from a distance. At least two ladies pointed her out to their neighbours as the little model Mr Bryan was going about with. 'My dear, I'm *positive*! I *saw* them coming out of the Popular Café!' . . . 'Extraordinary.' . . . 'I *know* . . .' 'My dear, *quite* moribund from the neck upwards!'

Neither Jane nor Mr Bryan heard these remarks. Mr Bryan believed that none of his acquaintances had seen him wandering about the town with his model, and thought himself rather a cunning fellow on that account. These things were quite easy if they were done discreetly.

That was on Saturday. On Monday the *Water Gipsy* was launched, and had her trial trip, Mr Bale at the helm. She satisfied Mr Bale and enchanted Mr Bryan. On Tuesday afternoon he invited Jane to take a trip in the boat. Fay Meadows was to have been the *Water Gipsy's* first passenger; she had been invited three weeks earlier, and had accepted in lyrical terms, but at lunch-time she telephoned that she simply *had* to go to a dressmaker, but could come at four. Mr Bryan said that that would be too late for the tide, and Fay seemed to think that he was unreasonably refusing to alter the tide for her benefit.

He did not tell Jane this story, and the invitation delighted her. He gave her the tiller as soon as they were under way, and she sailed the boat in a rapture as far as Barnes Bridge. A southerly breeze, a soldier's wind, a good stiff boat, a mackerel sky, a dazzle of sun on the water, a green mist on the trees, the April air on her cheek, the tiller in her hand, Mr Bryan at her side – this was Heaven, surely. If only she could go with Mr Bryan in his boat – round England – round the world, anywhere!

She smiled up at him, and said, 'I'm coming with you, Mr Bryan.'

He shook his head and said, 'No, my dear.' But he thought, 'Why not?' She sailed the boat perfectly. And now, with that light in her eyes, that loving touch on the tiller, she was something more than a little animal who went to the pictures and said 'you see'. The spirit of the water, the poetry of sail, the blood of sailors, was in her glowing cheeks. Perfect companion for a difficult, perhaps dangerous, voyage. Why not?

Because the papers would say things; because Mr Pewter would say things; because her father would say things; because at every port he touched it would be 'Peer's Son and Servant-girl – Serious Allegations'. Unless he married her – and then it would be 'Romantic Union'. In either case the Baron would have fits; for he, Mr Bryan, might live to be the Baron.

He shook his head again; but he said, 'I wish you could, my dear.' And that was something.

25

MR BRYAN MAKES UP HIS MIND

WEDNESDAY was the great day – the day of the 'Show', the day of the party. She had bought her dress with Lily in Shaftesbury Avenue – a simple little length of green satin – and Mr Bryan had booked her room at the Grand Palace Hotel.

An alarming day, this last great day of Mr Bryan's planning. Jane left her bag at the hotel (as instructed), and was alarmed by the porters and the size of the hall. She reached the Exhibition just before three (as instructed), and that was more alarming still. The small room was full of people; all of them seemed to know each other, though, if one might judge from their excited talk, they had all been separated for a very long time. Jane could not see Mr Bryan anywhere, but she saw Fay Meadows, radiant as usual, with a white fur round her shoulders and a scrap of veil over her provoking eyes. Jane pressed slowly round the room, hot and shy, and peered between shoulders at the familiar pictures, looking for her own.

Before she found it, a friend of Mr Bryan's, a Mr Floy, officially 'opened' the Exhibition with a short speech. Jane did not understand a word of it, not knowing what was meant by 'correlation', 'objective phenomena', 'significant form', or 'plastic values'. But the speaker spoke warmly of No. 30, 'Washing-Up', which he described as a notable example of the artist's individual rhythm and instinct for pattern. Jane blushed both from pleasure and alarm; for she thought that everybody must be staring at her. No one, however, was even aware that she was there.

After the speech she worked her way to No. 30 and stood behind a knot of people who were discussing it. There was a small red blob in one of the corners, and from something somebody said she thought this must mean that it had been sold already. Mr Floy was one of the group and praised the picture highly, for he had bought it. Jane thought that she had better go, for somebody would be sure to recognize her now, standing there in front of her own picture. Mr Floy would say, 'Cool You're the very girl!' and

how alarming that would be! Mr Floy, however, was talking about
the rhythm of the saucepans and the tempo of the window-blind.
Neither he nor anyone else said anything about the girl or the
young woman in the picture, though Mr Floy did speak once of the
foreshortening of the figure, which Jane thought must mean herself. Soon she ceased to be alarmed, and became resentful. 'Lot of
toughs,' she thought. 'Wouldn't make no difference to them if it
was a giraffe washing-up.' She had never liked the washing-up idea;
she had known how it would be; if it had been that nude one, now,
it would have been another story. They would have talked about
her then. 'Ernest!' she thought. 'Blast Ernest and his silly
tempers!'

Then she looked up and found Mr Bryan smiling down at her.
'How do you like it now?' he said.

'Ever so nice,' she whispered.

'First one I sold,' he whispered back.

Oh, well, if he was pleased it was all right, she supposed; but it
seemed funny he didn't say to Mr Floy, 'Here, this is the girl in the
picture you spoke about!' Was he ashamed of her or what?

She opened her mouth to ask him about the red blob; but he
had turned away: two women on the other side of him were trying
to talk to him at once. One was Fay Meadows, the other was Mrs
Raven. Fay Meadows won. Mrs Raven drew back, and Jane
watched her, though to see her here was alarming too. The sad
eyes were fixed on Mr Bryan's back, and Jane thought suddenly,
'Coo! You're gone on him too, I do believe. Well, anyhow, I'm
one better off than you, my girl.'

Mrs Raven tried once more to snatch a word from Mr Bryan,
but someone else had claimed him, and she gave up. Her eyes,
drearily roaming the room, found Jane. She came to her and said
kindly, 'Well, Jane? Still washing-up, I see. How are you?'

Well, someone had recognized her – that was something.
'Mustn't grumble, Mrs Raven.'

'No, that's the spirit.' She stared at the girl, wondering whether
what she suspected (enviously) was true.

'Mr Bryan's kept busy,' said Jane, and looked across the room.
He was surrounded by talkers. No one was buying any pictures,
but everybody was praising some.

'Yes,' sighed Mrs Raven. She shook hands with Jane, and their eyes said to each other, 'Funny, but we're in the same boat, I believe.'

Jane slipped out and went to Lily's for tea. And at six o'clock she persuaded Lily to go with her to the alarming lounge of the Grand Palace, where she was to meet Mr Bryan. Nothing alarmed Lily. She stepped out of the revolving doors with the assurance of an admiral stepping on to his own quarter-deck.

Mr Bryan was sipping a cocktail, in low spirits. He had sold three pictures only, and the critics, he had heard, were sniffy. Fay Meadows had wanted him to dine with her and some others, and when he refused she had said shortly, 'Oh, don't apologize. I heard you'd collected a charmer.'

His charitable plans for the entertainment of Jane were beginning to seem fantastic and might prove tiresome; and the apparition of Jane's flashy sister disturbed him. He was sure she was the sort who talked; and she would misunderstand, he felt, his honourable intentions. While Jane signed the register and got her key the sour reception-clerk looked hard at the two girls with the common voices, he noticed, and curiously at himself. 'Snob!' he thought, and he asked them both to have a cocktail before Jane went to her room.

Jane had a sherry, and Lily asked for an 'Angel's Kiss'. Mr Bryan sat between them and hoped that nobody he knew would come in; but he thought again, 'Snob!'

Lily was quite at home; and she and the sherry cheered Jane up. This was Life! She had never seen so many beautiful page-boys, with such tight trousers behind, and so many buttons before, so much looking-glass and polished floor.

Lily said, 'Coo! I'd like to have seen your Ernie here. He wouldn't have half gone on. D'you know Mr Gus Antony, Mr Bryan?' she rattled on. 'Sitting under the mirror there, with the little bit in blue?'

'No,' said Mr Bryan, repelled by the appearance of the sallow Mr Antony.

'Thought you might. He's in the picture business. Father's a big frame-maker. Introduce you if you like. Friend of Bunny's. Dances a dream.'

Mr Antony and Lily exchanged smiles and bows. Mr Bryan looked elsewhere, and said to himself for the third time, 'Snob!'

Lily finished her cocktail and said, 'Have you got rooms at the back? I been here with Bunny once, and the noise is chronic over the street. I should ask, if I was you.'

'I dunno,' said Jane vaguely.

Mr Bryan felt hot. It was clear that Lily had misunderstood. Of course. She could not be expected to understand that he was giving her sister a night at a hotel for a treat, because the dream of her life was to have a bath in a luxurious bathroom. Lily was dreadful. And in another minute she would be introducing him to Mr Antony. He said, 'Would you like to go to your room now, Jane?' And, to make things quite plain, he added, 'Perhaps your sister would take you up?'

'Come and help me into me glad-rags, Lily?' said Jane, with an anxious appeal in her eyes.

Lily looked mystified and said, 'Oh, well, if it's only a minute or two. I mustn't be long, on account of Bunny, you see.'

And up in the alarming lift, with an alarming gentleman in uniform, they went.

'Room's all right,' said Lily, with condescension; but Jane thought it was wonderful. White panels, magenta curtains, a soft red carpet, bright white linen, a deep and many-coloured eiderdown; cupboards with looking-glass doors, looking-glass over the fireplace, the fire burning (thoughtful Mr Bryan), and a glass-topped dressing-table in a recess, with looking-glass all round it. Jane had never imagined such a room. When the chambermaid had left them she jumped joyfully on to the soft, sleek eiderdown and cried, 'Coo, Lily! What price the barge?'

But Lily had grown up. She had almost forgotten the first fine raptures of her first hotel. She said in astonishment, 'My dear, it's a *single* room! What's the idea?'

'What d'you mean?' said Jane, blushing.

'Oh, cheese it!' said Lily rudely. 'What's the *idea*? Isn't he gone on you?'

Jane abandoned pretence. 'It's only Platonic,' she said loftily. 'Just friends, and that.'

'Platonic!' sniffed Lily. 'I don't believe in them games. What did he bring you here for?'

'He's ever so kind,' said Jane feebly.

'Kind? No man's as kind as all that, my girl.'

'Well, if you want to know, I told him once about your having a good time at the hotel with Bunny – you know, when you went off the first time – and I said I'd never been to a hotel, you see, not with nice hot baths and that; so I suppose he thought he'd give me a treat, you see –'

Lily made her feel very uncomfortable; Lily was so old now.

Lily listened, bewildered. She said, 'Well, isn't he sleeping in the hotel himself?'

'I dunno,' said Jane. 'I believe he is.'

'Oh, well, then, don't you worry, my girl. It's all serene!' said Lily confidently. 'He's got his own ideas, I dare say. Didn't want to sign you in as his wife, I shouldn't wonder.'

Jane did not understand this remark; but she was pleased that Lily thought it was all serene. And Lily, assured that the programme was, after all, more or less normal, became helpful and gay. 'Take those clothes off,' she commanded. 'I'll get the bath ready.'

They inspected the bathroom.

'Coo!' said Jane, and stood in awe. 'Did you ever?'

Shiny green tiles, shiny white enamel, shiny silvery metal-work, the long, inviting bath, the thick, inviting towels, the looking-glass, the scented soap, the bowl of green bath-salts, the electric bell – it was the bathroom of her dreams, and more! And then the taps – the numerous exciting taps, with the mysterious names: 'Plunge', and 'Spray', and 'Shower', and 'Wave', and 'Flood'! 'Whatever's it all *for*?' she cried, turned on 'Shower' and 'Flood', and splashed her sister from head to foot. They tried every tap in turn, laughing like schoolgirls; they ladled the green crystals into the bath, and tore the paper wrappers off all the soaps; and Jane, really happy for the first time that day, said, 'Now, then, I'm going to wash my hair and stand under the shower.'

'I'll come in with you,' said Lily. 'I could do with a wash myself.'

'Is it better,' Jane asked anxiously, as they undressed, 'than the one you had with Bunny, Lily?'

'Best I ever saw,' said Lily generously. 'We was on the top floor. It costs a fortune, Bunny said, a room on this floor.'

Jane was delighted, not because it cost a fortune, but because her bath was better than Lily's. One ahead at last.

So they lay together in the vast bath and splashed like children and played with all the taps. And Jane thought gratefully of Mr Bryan. She was seeing life, and no mistake. Then they pranced into the warm bedroom, and dried before the fire.

'I'm ever so glad you came, Lily,' said Jane, bubbling with pleasure and affection. 'This is all right, isn't it?'

'You wait till tonight, my girl,' said the knowing Lily.

'Don't go on, dear. I tell you he's Platonic.'

'Platonic, my eye!' said Lily.

When Jane's hair was dry, Lily brushed and combed and arranged it, and supervised her dressing.

With her face a little flushed from her bath, her eyes bright with excitement, and her hair fluffed out and glossy, she looked rather sweet, Lily thought, but a little too simple for Lily's taste.

'What about the flower?' said Jane, holding against her shoulder a large green tinsel rose. 'Seems common, don't it?'

'You want something,' said Lily. 'The frock's plain, and a bit of ornament helps. Don't forget your pearls. And I should leave off that wedding-ring, if I was you.'

'Should you? It don't seem right.'

'You want a bit of fun, don't you, going to a party?'

'Not with anybody I don't know.' 'Not with anyone but Mr Bryan,' she thought. What an idea! Still, she took the ring off; there was no sense in reminding him of Ernest.

'Well, you never know. Powder your arms and shoulders. And you want some more colour – you look anaemic.'

Lily took from her own capacious bag a little box and began to paint her sister's lips a very bright red.

'Here, not too much of it!' Jane protested, with a scared look in the glass. 'It don't suit my style of beauty.'

Lily said firmly, 'The lights'll be bright where you're going.

You don't want to look like a dead moth.' And she continued her good work.

When she had done, poor Jane did not look so sweet. Surveying herself from every angle in the many mirrors she distrusted the green flower and she distrusted those bright and sticky-looking lips. But then Lily knew best about these things – Lily who lived in the West End; and Lily had been so kind, she did not like to take it all off.

'Now the scent,' said Lily, 'and then you're done.' And Jane dabbed some of her new 'Chypre' here and there.

'Behind your ears, dear,' said Lily, 'and a little down your front.'

Then the fine brocade cloak, with the ostrich feathers round the neck, which Lily had kindly lent her.

'Quite a picture,' said Lily, proud of her work. They kissed, carefully, because of the paint, and went down.

*

Mr Bryan also, as Jane came across the wide lounge towards him, thought that she looked rather sweet. He would not have recognized her if he had not expected her. She moved well, and held her head proudly, for she had thrown off her alarms; she wore a brave smile for him, her legs were as slim and silky as Fay's, and her shoes as gaily golden, though not so expensive; and, 'Damn it!' he thought, 'she might be anybody.'

Only at close quarters the little differences showed themselves. The simple little dress was inoffensive – but that dreadful flower! And the tapes, shoulder-straps (or whatever they were) of her undies were wandering untidily about her shoulders. And the skin of those shoulders, in spite of the powder, was not like the shoulders of Fay. And why, oh why, those scarlet lips? Still, she had made a brave show; she was really pretty tonight, he thought, and he was queerly proud of her.

He said, 'You look very nice, my dear. But why so much red on your lips? It's not necessary – you're pretty enough without it.' Blunt words; but this had been a constant cause of discussion between himself and Fay; and now, Fay said, she had a special make-up for him – her 'Gordon's Ghost' make-up. (But what a row he had had with Fay the first time he had said that!)

Jane stammered, penitent, 'Oh, Mr Bryan, I'm glad you said that. I'm ever so sorry – it was Lily, she made me. But I don't like it – really I don't; I never have before. I'll go and take it off at once –'

'No, no, my dear. After dinner will do. Anyhow, lots of girls – It's rather a fad of mine.'

'I'd rather go now, Mr Bryan, if you don't mind – really I would. I won't be happy now till I have.' And she ran back to the lift.

Good girl, he thought; amenable girl. Might easily be moulded. Pity he had not mentioned the flower. But better not, perhaps. It was probably a present from Lily.

They dined in the great grill-room – at one of the side-tables, in an alcove. Shaded electric candles. Oak panelling – like a pew. 'Coo!' said Jane, looking about her. 'Isn't it lovely?' The band, the soft carpet, the white tables, the evening-dresses, the trollies covered with tiny dishes, the cat-like waiters, the gracious, royal head-waiter – all were lovely.

'Wouldn't they laugh at the Black Swan to see me sitting here, Mr Bryan?' she bubbled.

'Wouldn't they?' he agreed. But he wondered, 'Would they?' Probably not. Disturbing thought.

But then Jane told him of the wonders of Room 22, of the fun they had got from the bath; and (there was so much fun in her voice and eyes) Mr Bryan told himself that by this alone his mad little plan had been justified. It was not every day that one could give so much innocent happiness to a fellow-creature; and it was not every man who would dare. Mildly, he patted himself on the back.

They had oysters and Chablis (Mr Bryan watching paternally to see that Jane did not have too much). The oysters alone would have been an adventure to Jane. She did not like them much and made pretty faces of alarm; but what fun it was to take a girl out who had never had an oyster on her plate before! She told him how she had asked for oysters on her honeymoon, and they had been refused; and how she had cried in the dismal bathroom at Brighton ('Poor kid! What a life!' he thought); and how she and Ernest had sat up in bed drinking champagne. And from that – set free by happiness and Chablis – she went on to the troubles of her marriage, to Ernest's strange ways – 'pawing about and dragging a girl down' – and Ernest's wooing, even Ernest at Richmond, the green boat, and her panic about the baby: all the most intimate secrets of her mind bubbled out on this most wonderful evening, with Mr Bryan's kind eyes drawing her on. He listened, enthralled and compassionate; and 'Poor kid!' he thought again. 'What a life!' And what a dirty dog was Ernest! Well, anyhow, he thought thankfully, he, Mr Bryan, had never 'pawed her about', or 'dragged her down, you see'. There were still as many 'ever so's' and 'you see's' as before. A pity. But she could tell a tale.

He said curiously, 'What's your young sister think about me? Does she think I'm "dragging you down"?'

'She's all right,' said Jane. 'I told her we was Platonic.' Fatal words! Immediately she regretted them. Goodness, she thought, wasn't he Platonic enough without one putting ideas in his head? 'Well, what I mean,' she went on, floundering, 'she knows you and me are different. I was never gone on Ernest, you see, not really.'

The waiter brought a 'mixed grill', Jane's own particular choice. Mr Bryan thought, 'Good! She's got that "Night of Love" business out of her head.' But also he thought, 'Damn it, am I really Platonic about her?' For Jane looked very young and pleasant in the green dress against the dark panelling (in spite of that abominable flower). He had seen her often with nothing on; but now, with her bright, clean, fluffy hair, and the little hollow of her bosom peeping out from the green satin, she was far more desirable. Platonic? It was rather insulting.

He talked about his boat, and about his cruise, and about Captain Slocum, who had sailed round the world by himself. And a cloud fell upon Jane. She was sick of this Slocum, with his stupid solitary ideas. She was jealous even of Mr Bryan's boat, which he loved so much better than her. But she shook herself and threw off the cloud – nothing should make her unhappy tonight – this last, lovely, unbelievable night. So she listened and nodded and smiled at him bravely while he talked of what he would do and where he would go – of sailing by moonlight and sailing in the dark, of 'making' this and 'opening' that, of the Pool of London, and the Foreland and the Needles and Portland Bill, of sailing into strange harbours and sailing out again – alone, always alone.

And at last she put her hand on his and said, 'Talk about something else, please, Mr Bryan. I can't bear it – really I can't.'

'I'm sorry,' he said. 'I'm a selfish fellow.'

'No, that you're *not*!' she said fiercely, and fiercely gripped his fingers.

He raised his glass to her, and they clinked their glasses solemnly and drank together – as Lily and Mr Moss had done, as Jane and Ernest had done. It was all coming true, she thought, what Lily had said – so far.

She thought, 'Funny man; if he likes me so much, why don't he like me more? Is it because I say "You see" and "Pardon"? But that's no reason. I don't say them no more – anyone can learn.'

And Mr Bryan thought, 'I'm in the deuce of a muddle about this girl.'

And Jane thought, 'Shall I tackle him again – ask him what he's really up to? No, I can't struggle no more; I'll let things slide to-night, have a good time, and see what happens.'

They had finished their delicious savoury – only something wrapped up in bacon on toast, but ever so tasty. Jane had a port wine with her coffee, and Mr Bryan his brandy and cigar. The room was so full that the management had decided it was a Gala Night; and the waiters were distributing paper streamers, balloons, dolls, squeakers and fans and funny hats. Mr Bryan received a squeaker, a funny red hat, and some paper streamers, and Jane a long-legged blue doll of indeterminate sex, in velvet. She loved the doll, which had dark eyes and a grave but knowing expression. She said it was like Mr Bryan. He blew his squeaker, and Jane delightedly threw the streamers far into the room, so that they twined themselves over the heads of elderly strangers, or hung like tropical creepers from the electric lights.

Already it was half past ten, and Mr Bryan said that they must go to the party. Jane turned suddenly cold. Here she was at home now; but the party was an unknown peril. Here she had him to herself; but there –

'*Must* we, Mr Bryan?' she pleaded.

He nodded. 'It's being given for me, and we're late already.'

But, surprisingly, he found that he was in no hurry to go to the farewell party which was being given in his honour. He would be very content to sit there and watch the poor little waif enjoying herself.

'Will there be a cabaret?' she said. At parties on the pictures there were always 'cabarets' – that is to say, young women with long silk legs did swift and fantastic dances on a highly polished floor before a crowd of men in evening-dress.

'There'll be a turn or two, I expect.'

'Well,' she said with a sigh, 'I suppose we must if we must. It's been ever so lovely, Mr Bryan. Something to remember.' She looked at him with sorrowful eyes, having a strange premonition that this was the end.

'I've loved it too,' he said, taking her hand. 'But don't look so sad, Jane. The party will be fun. You're going to see life.'

'Am I?' she said bravely. 'Come on, then, Mr Bryan.' And she tucked the blue doll under her arm.

In the taxi she nestled up to him, and he hugged her. 'Say when you're tired of the party,' he said, 'and I'll look after you.' He had nearly said, 'And I'll come back with you.' Why not? She was clean now, and did not smell; she was young and tender and loving, and he was fond of her. Why not?

Her eyes gazed up at him, wide and deep and adoring. 'Love me,' she whispered. He kissed her, and she said, 'I'm glad I took that horrid stuff off my lips. I knew it was wrong.'

The right instincts. And, given the right instincts, how much could be done with clothes and comforts and kindness – and soap! Already, tonight, she seemed twice the person.

'Platonic,' he thought, suddenly. 'Platonic, indeed!' And to himself he muttered, 'Damn!'

'Pardon?' she said, raising her head.

'You mustn't say "Pardon",' he said teasingly.

'I'm ever so sorry,' she said.

'Don't worry, my dear. It doesn't matter.' 'Poor kid!' he thought, 'it's hopeless!' And he kissed her again.

*

The Murray Clares lived in Bloomsbury, and had a flat (with studio) on the top floor. He painted vaguely, and she was vaguely 'on the stage'; but they had money definitely. They gave many parties, and their parties were famous, rather for duration than distinction. But they had many distinguished names tonight. The flat was full of ladies and gentlemen who, in the damning police court phrase, 'lived by their wits' – that is to say, of authors and artists, managers, musicians, actors and actresses, dramatic critics, film critics, essayists, newspaper-men, officials of the B.B.C., and a sprinkling of models and chorus-girls. The conversation and laughter of this elegant company surged down the four flights of stairs like the roar of a stage-crowd disagreeing with an orator.

It filled Jane with fear; she clung to Mr Bryan's arm and said: 'I'm frightened. Let me go back, dear.'

'There's nothing to frighten you, Jane. I'll look after you.'

'All right. Over the top, then.' And she mounted, trembling, towards the alarming din.

The other women in the small and crowded cloak-room did nothing to diminish her alarm. They all knew each other, it seemed; she thought the way they looked at her was unfriendly (though this, in truth, was only the frank stare of well-bred curiosity), and she noticed that most of them had very red lips, and were laboriously making them redder. She saw herself in the glass beside a young lady with a mouth like a letter-box, and she thought, 'Quite right, Lily, dear – I'm anaemic. A dead moth.'

Too late now; she would not borrow things from these stuck-up persons.

Mr Bryan had promised to wait for her in the hall, and there he was, talking to two beautiful women in rich clothes. She thought of bolting back into the cloak-room; but he had seen her. She stood fluttering before them.

'This is your hostess, Jane – Mrs Murray Clare. Mrs Higgins – Miss Beryl Anderson.'

'Mrs Higgins.' How awful it sounded!

'Pleased to meet you,' twittered Jane, and held out a hot little hand. She realized that she was still clutching the blue doll under her left arm. What a born fool!

'So glad you could come,' said Greta Clare, and kindly took her all in – the awful flower, the wandering shoulder-straps, the cheap frock, the nervous hands. Still, Greta was no snob; models were models, and could not afford to dress, and this one was a pretty little thing. But why so frightened? And why the doll?

'Didn't I see you at that *divine* "Show"?' said the other young woman, in languid tones.

'Pardon?' fluttered Jane.

'Poor kid!' thought Mr Bryan. 'Hopeless!' She had lost all the assurance of dinner-time; she was no longer twice the person, but had dwindled back to her own stature. Here, in the harsh light thrown by Greta and Beryl, the eye could not ignore the little differences which had not mattered in their happy chatter across the table. He had been a fool to bring her.

'My dear,' said Greta, 'Mrs Higgins is Gordon's *masterpiece*. "Washing-Up". The one Phil Floy bought.'

'Of course! How crass of me! But Gordon's portraits are *so* misleading.'

Mr Bryan came to the rescue.

'Come and dance, Jane. But you'd better leave your doll in the cloak-room.' And Jane fled gratefully.

'My *dear*,' said Greta, raising her pencilled eyebrows at Mr Bryan, 'democracy, as you know, is my passion – but *must* you?'

'She's worked hard,' said Mr Bryan, sheepish, 'and I wanted her to have some fun.'

But he thought, 'Snob!'

The studio was a mass of hot, heaving humanity. They were dancing – that is to say, they were fighting, in stationary couples, to the music of an inaudible gramophone. Jane enjoyed her dance with Mr Bryan. She was elbowed and buffeted and kicked from every side; they did not advance more than a yard a minute; but she was in his arms, nobody asked her difficult questions, and Mr Bryan looked down at her smiling, and said that she danced beautifully.

At the end of the dance he bowed politely and said, 'Thank you, my dear. It's hot. Let's find the drinks. Stick close to me.'

He took her hand and they pushed through the jabbering crowd towards the door. But immediately three or four people assailed him with loud farewells, congratulations, inquiries, and genial insults. In the crush by the door she had to let go of his hand; he was swept on ahead, and when she struggled through into the hall he was not to be seen. She was lost and alone.

More and more guests were arriving, more and more noisy, more and more variously dressed. White tie, black tie, stiff shirts, soft shirts, tweed suits, knickerbockers, velvet jackets, fancy dress; and Jane was astonished to see several young people in brightly coloured silk pyjamas. Many of the new arrivals were carrying bottles, for, though the Murray Clares were rich, they sometimes asked their guests to contribute refreshments, and this was a 'Bottle Party'.

A little fat man, carrying a bottle of whisky, rushed up to Jane; his upper half was dressed as a sailor in His Majesty's Navy and his lower half in evening-dress trousers. He shook her warmly by the hand and shouted, 'My dear, you're *exquisite*!'

'Pardon?' said Jane.

He peered at her, said 'Beg your pardon, my dear, thought you were in fancy dress!' and rushed away again.

Mad, thought Jane, and more and more alarming. The parties on the pictures had never been quite like this. The next thing, one of the pink-faced persons in pyjamas would speak to her, and she was not quite sure whether they were ladies or gentlemen. She must find Mr Bryan.

Timidly she peeped into one or two of the smaller rooms, looking for 'the drinks'. All the rooms might have answered to that address, for everywhere there were men and women with glasses; and there were glasses, empty or half-empty, on every shelf and table – glasses on the piano, and on the coal-scuttles, and a good many glasses, broken, on the floor. All the rooms were full of people, all talking; but she could not see Mr Bryan. It was very hot; the air was thick with cigarette smoke; she was lonely and alarmed; the more she saw of the people the less she liked them, and she did not dare to ask them.

'A proper Cinderella I am,' she thought. But Cinderella had had a good time at the Ball.

Crossing the hall she saw Fay Meadows sweep in through the front door, and rather than face her she darted into the little room in front of her, and surprised a lady and gentleman in a dim light embracing on a sofa.

'Oh, pardon,' she said feebly. 'Is Mr Bryan here?'

'Not yet,' replied the man in a high, calm voice. 'I dare say he will be.'

Jane stammered herself out. 'Beast!' she thought. 'What goings on! And what did he mean about Mr Bryan?'

Where *was* Mr Bryan? She went, or rather was swept, back into the studio in a flood of people, all chattering. They were all friends, all happy, but she.

The party was well under way, and the respectable managers and people with white ties were preparing to go home. There were gentlemen a little drunk, there were ladies sitting on gentlemen's knees; the floor of the studio was a litter of cigarette-ends, fragments of glasses, little pools of liquor (very different from the spotless floors of the parties on the pictures). A large negro pianist had arrived, and was sitting at the grand piano, surrounded by young ladies. She heard someone say something about an undressing-dance. A young man dressed as Dante stood in front of Jane and said cheerfully, 'Good morning, my dear. You're Mary Pickford!'

'Pardon?' said Jane. 'My name's Higgins.'

'No, it isn't. You're Mary Pickford. My name's Dante. Come and have a drink.'

He was quite a nice young man, though he had had too much punch; and Lily, she thought, would have fallen for him. But Jane wanted only Mr Bryan. This mad young man might help her.

'I'm looking for Mr Bryan,' she said. 'Please, where's the buffit? I believe he went there.'

'The buffit? Oh, the drinks? Yes, of course he did. I'll take you there.' He put a hand (sticky with vermouth) on her arm, and led her off to a second door, chattering still.

'Come along, Mary. Higgins? Impossible. Fantastic name! There *is* no such name. There's old Bryan. But first you must have a drink with Dante. Mary Pickford takes wine with Dante before anything else takes place. Most important. Rule of the house. What'll you have? Cocktail or punch?'

She wanted to run to Mr Bryan's side. She could see him standing by the buffet; but at his side was Fay Meadows, brilliant, talkative, and terrible, with Beryl Anderson and another man. She could not go near them.

She said, 'A lemonade, if you please. Fizzy lemonade.'

'Bizarre proposition!' said Dante firmly. 'Cocktail or punch – or possibly a thimble of fizz –'

'I'd sooner have some fizzy lemonade – really I would,' said Jane pathetically.

'Very well, my innocent,' said Dante, who was more sober than he seemed. 'Await me hither.' And he plunged into the battle round the bar.

This room, like all the others, was full of people and noise. Mad, all mad, thought Jane; and rather shocking. Funny, she had always wanted to see Life. This was 'Life', she supposed, and now she did not like it. It wasn't respectable. Lily would have liked it, but she was miserable. These, no doubt, were the 'idle rich' Ernest used to talk about – all drunk and kissing.

Mr Bryan was not drunk – she could see that; but he might be kissing before long. Perhaps, before long, he would be in that little room with Fay Meadows. It gave her a pain to think of it. She would just say good-bye to him, if that woman ever stopped talking, and then she would slip away. No one would care.

Yet Mr Bryan did not look happy, she thought. He looked worried and cross. He was. Fay was on the warpath. She was not wearing her 'Gordon's Ghost' make-up tonight; her lips were the hot sealing-wax lips which she knew he hated. And she was teasing him spitefully about the National Gallery, the Zoo, the Tower of London, and the Popular Café. It was all round the town, it seemed. Probably the town knew all about the Grand Palace Hotel. What a fool he had been! And yet – what pigs people were!

Turning his head away from Fay's accusing eyes for an instant, he caught sight of Jane, watching him afar off, like Ruth 'amid the alien corn'. With a smile and a lift of the brows he inquired if she was all right; and she, with a nod and a brave smile, replied that she was wildly enjoying herself. Fay followed his glance and saw her; and she said, 'Go on, boy. Don't let *me* keep you.'

Dante had come back, glass in hand. 'Sorry, my Pickford love, lemonade (still) is laid on, but lemonade (fizzy) – no. Can you bear it?'

'It's quite all right, thanks,' said Jane, and gratefully quenched her smoky thirst. Really, Mr Danty was not so bad, she thought; he was kind, and he seemed to understand that she was not quite at home. She listened with half an ear to his babbling, watching curiously two of the mysterious individuals in pyjamas, whose glossy heads were gracefully reposing against the wall.

'Mr Danty,' she said suddenly, pointing with her glass of lemonade, 'is that a boy or a girl?'

Dante's laugh was so loud and long that all but the most engrossed lovers looked towards them. The man behind him turned suddenly and jogged his elbow, so that half his punch was distributed over the front of Jane's green satin. Dante knelt, babbling apologies, and did what he could with a handkerchief. Jane bent her head in confusion; she did not care about the dress, she hated it, would never wear it again; but they were all looking at her.

And then, behind her, she heard the clear, slow, dying drawl of Beryl Anderson: 'That's Gordon's little bit. . . . He takes her *quite* everywhere, they say. . . . My dear, Fay's *livid.* . . . Says she wouldn't marry him now if he gave her free seats for Wimbledon. Well, *can* you blame her? *Look* at it! My dear, there are limits! . . .'

Jane covered her burning ears. To be not wanted, to be despised, was bad enough; but if, as well, she was doing Mr Bryan harm, dragging him down – then she was off out of it. Dante went to the buffet for salt and a cloth, she walked quickly to the second door and found a passage which led (mercifully) straight to the hall and the cloak-room. Down this she ran as fast as she could. She snatched Lily's cloak and the blue doll from the astonished old attendant, and ran out and down the stairs without a word, as if the place were full of devils.

Three flights down she halted to fasten the cloak and see what money was in her bag; and then she heard her name called and galloping steps above her.

Mr Bryan! Mr Bryan breathless, and his face full of distress.

'I saw you slip out,' he panted. 'What's the matter, Jane?'

She went up to him. 'I'm going, Mr Bryan. I can't stand it – really I can't. I hate them – they're *beasts* –'

'My dear, I'm so sorry,' he said. 'I was caught by people, and I thought you were having a good time.'

'So I was, Mr Bryan. It's not your fault – really it isn't. And I didn't mean they were beasts – not really. Some of them were ever so nice. Only I'd rather go home, you see. Just look at my dress.' Better, she thought heroically, that he should think it was the dress.

'Well, I'll take you back,' he said.

'No, no, Mr Bryan. I can manage. I've got the money for a taxi.'

And then down the staircase came a strong, querulous, commanding voice, 'Gordon! *Gordon?*'

Fay's voice.

'Hullo?' Mr Bryan called, scowling.

'What are you doing, dear? You can't go *now*. It's your *party*!'

'I'm not going. I'll come back in ten minutes.'

'My dear, you must come *now*. It's so *rude*. "Wiggs" is just going to play for you.'

Mr Bryan muttered something about 'that blasted nigger'.

But the voice went on, relentless, cool, 'And I *swear* I won't sing if you don't come at *once*!'

Mr Bryan swore softly. Then he called up, 'All right. I'll come. One minute exactly.'

'*Good* boy, darling,' cooed the triumphant voice.

Jane thought, 'I could shoot her.'

Mr Bryan said, 'I'll put you into a taxi. You're sure you can manage?'

'Yes, Mr Bryan.'

He called a taxi. He kissed her quickly and said, 'So sorry, my dear. I'll see you later, then,' and she was in the taxi and he had shut the door before she had time to say more than 'Thank you.' One wave of the hand and she was off.

Mr Bryan said, 'Blast all women!' and slowly climbed the stairs.

*

So Jane came back sadly to her beautiful cosy room, clutching her blue doll, a Cinderella who had not even enjoyed the Ball, had scarcely danced with the Prince, a bewildered, aching, miserable Cinderella.

She threw the blue doll on to the pillow. She went to the glass and stared at herself. She took off the green flower and stared at

374

herself again. Yes, she thought, the green flower was a mistake. Without the green flower all might have been well.

No, never. They were beasts. She did not belong to them, and never could. 'Class is class' – Ernest was right, and she was a born fool. And if that was 'seeing Life' she did not want to see it again.

She pulled the stained green satin over her head, and tried to tear it. It was too tough for her; but no matter – she would never wear it again, if it was ever so.

She put coal on the dying fire, and she went into the bathroom – her lovely bathroom. Someone had tidied it since she and Lily had splashed together; there were clean dry towels on the silver rail, there were fresh packets of the scented soap. She turned the hot tap, wondering if there would be hot water at this time of night in this sort of place – one never knew. The water was 'boiling'. Wonderful! She turned on all the taps and filled the bath; she threw in a handful of the green salts and tore the wrappers off the soaps – did everything that she and Lily had done, trying to re-capture the same excitement. But it was no use. Lily was not there – nobody was there.

She undressed and surveyed herself in the glass. She had never seen the whole of herself, and from all angles, like this before. It was quite a surprise. She thought she looked nice, but little and tired. A bath would refresh her. It was soothing to lie in the warm, deep water; and she lay in the bath a long time, thinking of Mr Bryan. Her mind was a muddle; she could not think clearly. Was it all over, even now, she wondered? What had he said, exactly? 'See you later, then.' What did that mean? And he had not even said 'Good night'. Surely he would have said 'Good night'. Surely he would come and say 'Good night' to her. She knew he was staying in the hotel, for she had asked him the question at dinner. Presently, if she did not go to sleep, she would hear him knock at the bedroom door. She got out of the bath and set the bathroom door ajar, so that she should hear his knock.

It wouldn't be yet, of course; he would have to see the party out; he would have to hear that little blonde beast sing. What was he doing now? Perhaps sitting in that little room she had blundered into – with Fay. No, she did not think that. He had been cross with Fay on the stairs – anyone could see that. He had to be polite to

Fay. But he would come and say 'Good night' to her in her lovely room.

Her lovely room! – and her lovely bath! She would never be able to thank him for this. And her lovely dinner! She could see his kind eyes smiling across the table. Only that horrid party had spoiled everything. But it was her own fault he had taken her there – all her talk about 'having a good time'! He had thought she meant that sort of thing. Perhaps she had. That was the fault of the pictures. A lot of lies. Well, she knew better than the pictures now. She would never believe the pictures again.

And she would not hear anything against Mr Bryan. Her lovely bath! Her legs looked so strange and white, floating about in the clear water over there. How tired she was! And how quiet and lonely it was! Ever so quiet, after the noise of the party. This must be a back room, from what Lily had said. Thick double windows. Hardly a sound from the streets – only the drip of the tap and the ripple of the water when she lifted her hands. Lucky Lily – she had not been alone in her lovely room. But Mr Bryan would come.

She was sleepy, sleepy, so sleepy. And presently she fell asleep in her lovely bath.

She woke with a start. Was that a knock? She jumped out, and ran, dripping, to the bedroom door and listened. Not a sound. Only the tap dripping in the bath. Her wrist-watch was on the dressing-table. One o'clock. But these parties went on till all hours, by all accounts. She went back to the bath and warmed it up, but turned off the taps soon, for fear she would miss Mr Bryan's knock, they made such a noise. Then she washed all over – there was nothing like getting your money's worth. She dried herself before the nice red fire, and looked at her watch. Half past one. Again she surveyed her pink body in the glass; but now she thought she looked nothing much. All the same, he had said she had a good figure once. Ages ago, that seemed. She had been a good girl then. And now she was waiting for a gentleman to come and say 'Good night' to her. Well, there was nothing in that. She was a good girl now, really. They would be Platonic. She only wanted to say 'Good night' – just one kiss – and thank him for the lovely bath.

She put on her new pink nightie, bought special for the hotel with Mr Bryan's money. She would not go to bed just yet, for fear of falling asleep; she would sit by the fire. And she thought of a joke. She put the blue velvet doll in her bed, with its head high on the white pillow. When Mr Bryan knocked she would open the door and hide behind it, and he would come in and see nothing but the doll. And how they would laugh!

She wrapped herself in the eiderdown (she had not dared to bring her old barge dressing-gown) and sat in the armchair before the fire. What was he doing now?

When she woke up the fire was low, the lights burned brightly, the tap still dripped in the bathroom. No other sound. Only the warm, bright stillness of her lovely room. She looked at her watch. Half past three.

He would not come now.

He would not come now; and tomorrow he was going away for ever. She would never see him again – not properly. This was the punishment for all her wickedness.

Slowly she went to the door and listened, slowly she turned out the lights, and slowly she climbed into bed.

Then she caught the blue velvet doll to her breast and sobbed: 'Oh, Bryan, Bryan, Bryan, how *could* you?'

*

It was about the same time that Mr Bryan, on his way to bed, came softly along the corridor and halted before Room 22; and looked up and down the corridor; and wondered whether the little waif was asleep, or awake and wanting comfort; and raised his hand and stood irresolute; and thought of Mr Pewter and Mr Bell and Ernest Higgins and Lily and Fred Green and Fay Meadows; and sighed, and softly passed on his way.

26

THE *WATER GIPSY*

THE *Water Gipsy* lay out in the fairway, her mainsail shivering in the westerly breeze, her green paint and varnish flashing in the sun.

Mr Bryan, looking strong and slim in his blue jersey, made fast the dinghy astern and went forward to haul in his anchor. The ebb had been running for two hours, and now he should be able to pass safely under the low span of Hammersmith Bridge. All was ready, and he had said his good-byes.

Two small clusters of people stood at the waterside on the muddy beach. In one was Fay Meadows (worried about her shoes), Beryl Anderson, the Murray Clares, Mrs Raven, and one or two more. In the other were Mr Bell, Mr Pewter, Mr Fox, the two Mrs Higgins, some of the skittles-players, one or two longshoremen, and many small boys. Between the two groups was a sharp division, a clear space; and that was occupied by a Press photographer (for a 'Gossip' writer present at the Clares' party had announced that morning the adventurous departure of the 'Peer's artist son').

Jane stood with her father, as far as possible from Fay and her friends. Mr Bryan had shaken hands with all of them, but last of all with Fay; and even when the two groups edged together to see the dinghy go off for the last time Jane would not press closer to get a special good-bye. She had had her good-bye in the studio that morning, and she was not going to cause any more talk. She was sensible now, and proud. She had been put in her place, and she knew her place; she had not been born for better things; she was going to do her duty in that state of life to which it pleased God to call her, and that. But it hurt.

He rowed away strongly across the sparkling water, his eyes quickly sweeping the line of faces.

'Good-bye, all! Good-bye, Mr Pewter! Good-bye, Mr Bell! Good-bye, Jane! Good-bye, Beryl! Good-bye, Clifford! Good-bye, Fay!'

And above all the other answers sounded Fay's chirping, possessive 'Good-bye, darling! Take care of yourself.'

Blast her!

Now he had the anchor off the bottom, and the *Water Gipsy* began to drop astern on the tide. And here, thought Jane sadly, was where she would have come in. She would have been standing by the halyards ready to whip the jib up while he was still hauling in the cable and getting the anchor on board. By now she would have had the sail up, and slipped to the helm. Oh, foolish, funny man – what a help she could have been!

But Mr Bryan was in no hurry. The anchor was secured, the jib fluttered up at last, the boat paid off, the sails filled, he put his helm over, the main-sheet rattled through the blocks, and away before the wind the *Water Gipsy* went.

They cheered, they waved their handkerchiefs, and Jane with wet eyes watched the white sails dwindle till they vanished through the bridge.

It was all over. She would be sensible. But if only he had let her go with him a little way – only as far as Greenwich, perhaps! He could have picked her up at the Chelsea pier, if he was so much afraid of his West End friends. And still her fond, insatiable heart said, 'I must see him again.'

She climbed on to the barge; she put on quickly her best clothes; she told her father she was going shopping; she hurried to the Underground, and took a ticket for the Monument station. The ticket-man said that that was the station for London Bridge.

London Bridge! He had talked so much about London Bridge the day they went to the Tower – London Bridge and Tower Bridge, the last bridges of all – the excitement of sailing under them, out into the Pool of London, where there were big ships and the sea began. She would see the *Water Gipsy* sail under those bridges into the Pool of London – the *Water Gipsy* which was named after her. She would give him his last good-bye all by herself. None of those Fays or Beryls were faithful enough, or fond enough, to think of following him to London Bridge. Perhaps even now – mad thought – he would take her on board for a little if he saw her on the bridge.

On the Underground she fretted because the train was so slow and stopped so often. She ran from the station down to the bridge, and, panting, peered up and down the river. Not in sight. She waited patiently, leaning on the parapet, among the out-of-works.

After half an hour she saw the sail far off in a patch of sunlight above Southwark Bridge. Slowly the *Water Gipsy* approached, small and incongruous among the cavernous arches of the bridges, drifting uncertainly among the eddies, the sails hanging limp. 'Coo!' muttered Jane. 'Don't half look tiny!' The tall sail of Hammersmith was no more than a napkin here. But, safe through the doldrums of the Cannon Street Bridge, the *Water Gipsy* caught the wind and came on proudly, the green paint shining, a swelling ruffle of foam at her stem. Jane's heart galloped. Would Mr Bryan see her, so high above him, so near, so far? A tug was swiftly overtaking him, and he was glancing anxiously astern, judging her speed and distance. 'He won't *see* me!' Jane cried tragically aloud, not caring who heard her. She ran across the road to the eastern parapet, narrowly escaping a horrid death under a motor-bus. Here were a long line of unemployed and passers-by, watching the ships unloading below the bridge, or gazing idly down the river, fascinated by the scene.

'Can I look, please?' said Jane, and squeezed herself into the tiny space between two burly men.

'Here y'are, miss,' one said kindly, and made way for her.

As she leaned over, breathless, the *Water Gipsy* came foaming through the bridge into the sunlight – immediately below her, but so far away. She could see the parting of his hair, the veins standing out on the hand which grasped the sheet. Two small boys on the bridge tried to spit on him. Jane called 'Mr Bryan! Good-bye, Mr Bryan!' But her tiny pipe was lost in the roar of the traffic, the hooting of tugs, and the thousand noises of the wharves. He did not look up.

'Mr Bryan! Mr Bryan! Good-bye, Mr Bryan!' she cried again, despairing; and the man at her side, taking his empty pipe from his mouth, supported her with a friendly 'Oy!'

Then Mr Bryan looked back. He looked up, dazzled by the afternoon sun. He saw a long line of faces, men and women, and he saw one young woman waving her hand. At every bridge somebody had shouted 'Oy!' and at nearly every bridge some young woman had waved her hand, so rare and pleasant a thing it is to see a sailing-boat travelling silently on the wind through the noisy heart of London. He waved his hand to the crowd, smiled cheerfully, and turned his back on her.

'Oh, dear,' Jane moaned. 'I don't seem to have no luck.' It had been so important that he should see her – that she, the Water Gipsy, should be the last to catch his eye.

'Friend of yours, miss?' asked the kindly man.

'Sort of,' she said.

Sort of – that was all.

The graceful boat sailed on beside the Tower, pitching and rolling in the wash of the tug. Then, a lonely patch of white, she passed below the Tower Bridge and was lost in the misty distance of the Pool.

'And that's that,' said Jane as she walked away. 'You're a born fool; you've no Destiny, and never had one.'

The wind was fresher in the wider spaces of the Pool, and Mr Bryan bowled happily along, lovingly handling his ship, free of women and their insatiable demands – free, as Fay had described it, to 'conduct a blameless liaison with a five-tonner'.

*

At Whitsun (on the Saturday) there was a double wedding at St Peter's Church. All the Black Swan faithfuls were there, and there was a great party afterwards in the alley. Mr and Mrs Albert Bell went off in a motor-coach for a week-end at Brighton, leaving a brother of Mrs Higgins (that was) to mind the pub. And Jane and Fred took Mr Ewer's taxi to Brentford, where the *Prudence* lay.

There were scores of the painted boats lying up for the holidays, tethered in neat pairs for a quarter of a mile along the bank. It was a floating camp, and no place for honeymooning. But Fred had thought of a plan. Nothing would move on the canal before Monday evening, and not far up the canal was a leafy corner fringed with great trees, which Fred had often thought was pretty and quite like the country, though Ealing and the Underground were not far away. There was a green meadow, with cows, on one side, and here till Monday they would be undisturbed, even by the walkers on the tow-path opposite. Arthur would look after the horse Beauty and bring him back to Brentford.

The boatmen gave them a noble good-bye. About half past seven, when the sun was low, the horse Beauty was brought out, gay with ribbons and rosettes and green leaves. Mr and Mrs Green kissed Jane for the fourth time; Arthur, in his blue serge, made one of the strange sounds which Beauty understood, and the *Prudence* moved slowly down the golden lane of water towards the sinking sun. The bride and bridegroom stood at the tiller, Fred with a red face and a rose in his buttonhole, Jane holding the posy of wild flowers which Mr Green had gathered for her. Jane steered close beside the street of boats, and, as they passed, the men on the boats leaned out and gave their hands to Fred, the women cried 'Good luck!' and waved their washing-cloths or shawls, the children stood on the cabin-tops and yelled and threw them faded flowers from the tow-path. Jane wanted to cry, they were all so kind. They seemed to have forgotten that she was a girl off the shore.

The horse Beauty moved on with dignity, wondering perhaps what it was all about. They passed the last boat, and slowly rounding the corner, saw the last shawl wave. 'Well, no one couldn't want a nicer wedding,' said Jane, and touched her eyes with a tiny handkerchief.

Beauty plodded on – clip-clop; and how much nicer were Beauty and the *Prudence* than that snorting motor-bicycle which had taken her to Brighton! Poor Ernest! But dear Fred – dear, faithful Fred! Of all the men who had crossed her path he was the only one a person knew where she was with. Always the same, gave no trouble, never wanted too much, easy to understand. And knew what he was about, too, though he couldn't read and write. Reading and writing didn't seem to matter so much, somehow.

She would be a good wife to Fred – steering the boat, working the locks, cooking the meals, polishing the brass, scrubbing the Turk's head, making herself useful, doing her duty in that state of life to which it had pleased God to call her, and that. It was a good life, too – travelling up and down, seeing the country, sleeping in the open almost: a better life, she thought, than going to parties with people like Mr Danty, that Beryl – and Fay. Not so good, perhaps, as sailing round England – But there, that was over and done with. Two months now since Mr Bryan sailed away, and not one word from him – not one. She thought perhaps he might have written – just a picture post card; but no. Oh, well!

Fred drew her to him and said, 'I'm not good enough for you, little Jenny. You know that.'

'Don't talk silly, Fred.'

'You'll have to learn me to read now, Jenny.'

' 'Course I will, dear.'

'I'd like to be able to read the newspapers.'

'Yes,' said Jane, kissing him, 'the *Sunday Gazette's* nice.'

*

The *Prudence* glided into the silent, shadowed reach at the end of which was Fred's corner. The sun still lingered in the tops of the high trees, but the water was like black marble. Fred cast off Beauty's line, the *Prudence* nestled gently into the reeds, Fred jumped into the meadow and made fast to the trees, and Arthur and Beauty clumped away into the twilight. Jane looked about her and thought that it was a lovely place for a honeymoon.

'This is all right, Fred,' she said.

'You're right,' Fred answered, busy with his ropes.

She went into the cabin to unpack her little bag. She lit the oil lamp and looked about her.

Here, in this tiny place, she would sleep with Fred and live with Fred till death them did part, have his babies and bring up his children, grow old at last like Mrs Green. Well, she was ready.

She took from the top of the bag a long-legged doll in blue velvet, and she stared at it, smoothing out the wrinkles of the velvet. She had nearly left it behind on the *Blackbird*, had nearly thrown it into the river. But, right or wrong, it was something to remember, that evening with Mr Bryan; and this long-legged doll was all that was left of it. She hung the blue doll near the door, beside the shiny brass knobs, and sighed.

Fred, that evening, said, 'What's that doll, Jenny?'

'I dunno. Somebody give it to me.'

'Pretty,' said Fred.

'Pretty, isn't it?'